SCATTERING THE ASHES

ISBN: 978-1-951122-11-9(trade paperback)
ISBN: 978-1-932926-78-1 (hardcover)
ISBN: 978-1-932926-79-8 (ebook)
Library of Congress Control Number: 2019936756

Artemesia Publishing, LLC
9 Mockingbird Hill Rd
Tijeras, New Mexico 87059
info@artemesiapublishing.com
www.apbooks.net

SCATTERING
THE
ASHES

a novel

by

Paul Russell Semendinger

Artemesia
Publishing

"No matter what a writer is writing about, if the writer is a man, he is writing about the search for his father."
William Faulkner

–PROLOGUE–

Sometimes the most beautiful scenes can't be captured in a photograph.

I realized this simple fact as I was paddling my Old Town canoe through Barnegat Bay in the early morning hours of June, feeling the rising sun warm my back. A picture might be worth any number of words, but no camera could capture the shimmering beauty of the sunlight reflected on the water. I took my paddle out of the water and rested it across my knees.

These quiet times alone on the bay give me room to pause. There are moments in one's life that can only be captured in the heart. This was one of them. But like the glistening diamonds of the dawn's rising sun on the bay, our emotions only matter if we take the time to actually process them. Emotions need time. Most often, we are too harried to give them the attention they deserve.

Alone in the quiet of the summer dawn, I allowed my emotions to get the better of me. The wetness in my eyes blurred the world of water around me, making the glints of light in my solitary scene shimmer like foil.

In that moment, in the early morning sun, alone, I wished that I had brought my camera. Though I know that light like this—moments like this—can never be captured, I still sometimes believe that if I take a picture at just the right angle, I can package a piece of the magic and take it home with me to hold forever.

If only...

But what the camera sees and what we see with our eyes are often two different things. I was focused on the raw natural

1

beauty brought about by the brightness of the sun, the gentle splash of the waves, and the salty smell of the Atlantic. But, a photograph would show others things as well. Things that were all too real: houses, telephone poles, wires, asphalt. A good zoom lens would even bring that floating water bottle into my tranquil scene. Until that precise moment, I had chosen to ignore these intruders on my solitary journey that morning on the bay.

A camera is impartial, neutral, cold. Sometimes it captures more than we wish to remember, more than we wish to see.

I thought about this as I dipped my paddle back into the water and drifted towards the quiet empty beach behind which our summer cottage rested. What is more real then? A moment as preserved forever in film or megapixels—or our memory of that moment? After all, a photograph can also tell lies. But either way, I realized, photographs don't change us the way memories do.

Sometimes our remembrances crystallize around a twinkling of time and forever lodge in our consciousness. These are what shape us and ultimately inform each decision we make.

The year my father died was like that. It was a year I'll always remember in ways more vivid and more profound than any picture or series of photographs could ever capture.

The year I lost my father was the turning point in my life.

–1–

For many people, it might be considered very late at night, but for me, it was the early morning. I glanced up from my pillow to check the glowing yellow numbers on the clock radio, and, like most days, I was a few minutes ahead of the alarm. It was slightly before 4:00 a.m. Each morning, it's me against the alarm clock. I like to see if my body will wake itself prior to the religiously set timepiece. On this day, I had won the match. It's good to wake up with a victory.

Most people wake up with a groan. Not me. On some mornings, I literally leap out of bed. This was one of those days. I pressed play on the iPod dock on my dresser, and "All My Loving" by the Beatles broke the pre-dawn silence. At this time of day, my humble house felt extra empty. I had thought that I would be married by now, that there would be more voices within these walls, but so far it was just me. Me and the Beatles. That was alright, I told myself. Without a spouse, I could do as I pleased. At least this was how I consoled myself as I listened to the Fab Four croon about love. Still, I looked forward to the promise that Saturday always affords.

The lightweight running shirt at the top of the pile in my dresser was one I had designed myself. It featured a picture of Rocky Balboa running in his iconic gray sweat suit with the words "There is no tomorrow" printed above the image. I smiled as I pulled my shirt from the drawer. I felt particularly energized this morning. I wondered if something as simple as a shirt could make me a better runner.

As I pulled the shirt over my head, however, a flash of the anxiety that had been building over the last few weeks interrupted my good mood. I was a middle school history teacher, and the academic year was coming to a close. The end-of-the-year meetings, celebrations, and paperwork left me with precious little free time. At work there was also a growing unease about the teacher contract negotiations, which seemed to be going nowhere. On top of all that, I wanted to make time for my friends, and hopefully their cute neighbors. I also had to make time for my dad, and I wanted to go for a run.

No, I *had* to go for a run.

Pushing the anxiety to the side, I laced on my Nike running shoes (bright yellow with blue swishes—I think I run faster in bright colors) and decided to take my long route to the Christian Health Care Center to see my father. It would be a solid six-miler with a few hills. The late-June weather was mild and the early mornings felt more like April than the dawning of summer. I appreciated the soft dew on the grass and the moisture in the air. I loved running in the spring; the summer not so much. The coolness would especially benefit me on this day. I didn't want to smell too much when I arrived. Then again, my dad wouldn't have cared anyway.

Recently, my running had been erratic. I was feeling more and more pain in my legs and feet. My right foot in particular ached each morning as I rose. Still, I always got myself out the door, and on most days, I pushed through the entire run—it takes forever to walk six miles. This I learned the hard way.

I rarely missed a Saturday morning run to visit my father and participate in our weekly ritual. We'd talk, or often times, I would. I liked to complain about how hard my life was. My dad often just listened. He knew I was exaggerating.

I might have lived alone, but I was mostly happy. I loved my job. I loved my dad. As my friend Ed would often say, "It's all good."

And this promised to be a good day. After spending the morning and having lunch with my father, I planned to see some friends. One of my buddies, Dan, was having a barbecue. He actually had a cute neighbor who I hoped would be there. I knew she liked me because she laughed a lot when I talked. I have a pretty good sense of humor, but I'm not *that* funny. I hoped that before I went to sleep that night, I'd enjoy a long, sweet kiss.

But first, I had a six-miler to cover and a few hours with Dad.

–2–

If you consider yourself a runner, the act of running often defines you. On days when you successfully cross that imaginary finish line, you feel like you can overcome anything. Other days, when you're not quite as successful—when your body, for instance, decides it would rather collapse in a heap on the sidewalk than take one more step—you sort of bring that perspective to everything. Those are not good days to start a new project. Or go on an adventure. Or really, do anything productive.

I call those days Failure Days:

"I failed to run ten miles."

"I failed to break an eight-minute-mile."

"I failed to hold my pace."

Whatever it was that I wanted to accomplish on my run, I

came up short. I missed. I failed. On these days, I begin to take that attitude into all other aspects of my life. I become less productive. I neglect to accomplish a simple task like paying a bill or cleaning my dishes. I find it hard to read for pleasure. Or write. I obsess over my failure.

But even with this, I am, at heart, an optimist. At least I tried, I eventually reason. There is satisfaction in that. While most people were sleeping, I laced up my running shoes.

It's the days when I don't even get out the door that are the worst. Failing to even try—there is no consolation in that. There really is no tomorrow. Every runner knows that the toughest battle is often that first step.

Running isn't always fun. In fact, most often it's not fun at all. It is hard. It hurts. There always seem to be hills. There is a time that comes in almost every run when I feel like quitting. Usually I don't.

A lot of life is simply overcoming the previous day's failure.

I should note that Failure Days are not to be confused with Injured Days. When you are injured and you can't run, it's far worse. Believe me.

The moment I notice a persistent twinge of pain, I start to think that I may never run again and that makes me want to run more than ever. I sometimes live in constant fear that my next run, or my current run, may be my last. Recently, those fears have been difficult to push away.

About a month ago, after having terrible pain in my right heel, I looked up that symptom in a book on running injuries and learned that I have a condition called plantar fasciitis. The first words I saw in the description were "most dreaded injury in running" and "your running days are over." After reading deeper and talking to friends (every single one said, "Oh, I had that"), I realized that through stretching (I hate stretching), other foot exercises, and sometimes medical treatment, runners can get by with plantar fasciitis.

About a week after this (self) diagnosis, I ran a great ten miles. I felt on top of the world. If running defines us, well, that run made me feel like a king.

The next day, and the day after, I limped around a lot. I didn't feel so royal.

This isn't a story about running though—or not primarily. It's a story about my dad.

My dad was also a runner. He took to jogging before the running boom made it popular. He knew, like we all do, that hard vigorous exercise is good for the body. When I was little, I couldn't wait to tag along on his runs. At first, I accompanied him on my bike, and then as I grew, I tried to run right alongside him.

I saw my dad run through pain like no other. Shin splints, side stitches, blisters, knee pain... he ran through it all. You couldn't stop him. I don't really think it's healthy, but he passed those traits on to me. "No quitting" was his motto, and those words ring in my head every time I run—because even on my best days, there are times when I want to quit. Dad taught me to push through and finish.

I always figured that one day we'd run at the same pace. I wanted my dad to be my running partner. It wasn't to be. As I got stronger, he became much slower. Never the twain did meet. I never expected to get so strong so fast, but that's what happens to a high school boy's body I guess.

I remember watching my dad struggle to keep up with me through an easy three-miler my senior year. I wasn't running that hard but I kept getting five or six strides ahead of him, even as we were trying to talk. It was the first time that I realized my dad was mortal. This came to me as a sudden shock. I didn't want to be stronger than my dad—not yet. He was a god. Who was I to eclipse him? My lean, young body felt strange to me suddenly, and somehow indecent. I wasn't ready to be a man.

I sped up with the hopes that the tears in my eyes would dry before my dad took notice, but eventually I allowed him to catch me. "What's wrong?" he huffed. I lied that I had pulled a muscle in my calf.

My dad gave me a quizzical look.

"Run through it," he said.

–3–

I never knew which dad would be waiting for me when I arrived at the Christian Health Care Center. There were times when my father was very talkative. Other times...not so much. It was my father's idea to come live at this place, but at times I think he resented it.

Because of the cool air, when I arrived at the top of the hill facing the apartment complex, I had barely broken a sweat. My father was waiting for me outside on the small patio with uncomfortable iron chairs and tables. He greeted me with a not entirely unkind, "You're late."

"No, Dad, I'm right on time."

"Weren't you coming at 9:00?"

"It's 8:56." (I checked my watch again just to make sure.)

"No, Sam, it's 11:15."

"Dad, that's Grandpa's old Hamilton watch you're wearing. It stopped working a while ago."

"I got it fixed."

"No, we talked about getting it fixed but we haven't done that yet."

"Oh. I could have sworn..." He waved his hand. "Whatever, here, sit down."

"Out here? Dad, if we walk to the other side of the building, there is that nice courtyard with the comfortable wooden benches. It's nicer than here."

"I kind of like these chairs..."

"Dad, let's go out back. As we walk through the building I can also get a drink of water."

In spite of this somewhat bumpy start, my dad eventually came around and was quite the talker. The slight chill in the air had pretty much faded as the sun rose. It was a beautiful day—especially because we were now overlooking freshly planted impatiens and violets rather than the asphalt leading up to his residence. My dad asked for an update on my brother Michael and my sister Melissa, but I hadn't talked, or even e-mailed, with them in a while. I had no news to share.

"We had more fun," my dad said quietly. His eyes followed a small butterfly fluttering between the colorful blooms.

"Who, Dad?"

"Us. You, Sam, with Mom and me. We had more fun."

"What do you mean?"

"The three of us, together, had more opportunities for fun than I did with your older siblings. They didn't have as much fun with me. Maybe that's why they don't call much."

I wasn't sure what to say to this. "I'm sure they had fun..." I said after a moment.

Dad shrugged. "When you were growing up, we—you and me—we played more. We traveled more. You liked having catches with me."

"Well, someone had to help you in your quest to make it to the Red Sox."

"This isn't the year, I'm afraid," Dad said with a laugh.

"I don't know. They just might come calling Dad," I teased. "They'll need to sign you out of the Old Man Retirement League."

"I can tell you this, Sam. Even at my age, if we had a ball team at this place, I'd be an All-Star."

"No doubt, Dad. No doubt."

Though I wasn't sure what to make of his comments about my siblings, on this day, I greatly enjoyed my visit with my father. He walked a fine line between grumpy and witty. He laughed. A lot. Me too.

Before I left, my dad brought me back to his room to take a look at his cable-TV. "The news comes in all fuzzy," he complained.

A moment after we entered his room, my dad rushed to his desk and flipped over a single sheet of lined paper. It looked like a letter he was writing, though I didn't get a good look.

"Now, let's get my TV fixed," he said.

−4−

A runner never feels as alive as when he or she returns from a great run. I was twenty-eight years old—energetic, strong, and, for the first time in my life had covered twelve miles in a single day—six miles to see dad, six miles home.

(I should note here that I was training for my first marathon. I had applied through the lottery system for the New York City Marathon and, to my great surprise, was selected. Most of my long runs were on Saturdays and I was beginning to map out and plan them around visits with Dad.)

After stretching for a few minutes on the front porch, I entered my modest home, opened the refrigerator, and poured myself a big glass of iced tea. Nothing could have tasted better. One good thing about living alone is that when you return home all hot and sweaty, it doesn't bother anyone. In the time I spent with my dad, the early morning chill had been replaced by some New Jersey humidity and the bright sun. I poured another glass, sat down at the table, and began glancing at the newspaper. I remember leaning forward and closing my eyes. A wooden kitchen chair isn't the best place to sleep, but I enjoyed a nice nap right there at the table.

I loved days like these. I had nothing to do. It wasn't quite summer break, but I already felt like I was on vacation. The flash of anxiety I experienced earlier that morning appeared to be overruled by the endorphins of my run and the fact that I had very few responsibilities that day. Any task—mowing the lawn, washing the car, painting, reading—could wait until later in the day. I looked forward to the coming summer. When you're a teacher on summer vacation, summer, at times, can seem endless—a series of tomorrows. Anything I needed to do on that particular day could wait until the next day. Or the day after that.

The tasks and responsibilities that became (or were) part of my job always kept me busy during the school year. I taught social studies, mostly ancient history, to eighth graders in Morningside, New Jersey. Grading papers, planning lessons, and taking part in school activities kept me very engaged. But since I had stayed late the previous day, not leaving my classroom until after 6:00 p.m., I had pretty much completed all of my most pressing work responsibilities.

I lived in my parents' old house in Midland Park, New Jersey—the small town where I grew up. It was a good house, small, but it fit my needs. Realtors call the house a Cape Cod. It was a one-story home with an unfinished attic and a full basement and a nice yard which held memories of snowball fights, adventures with friends, and some of the most majestic Wiffle Ball games in history.

Midland Park was a good place for a kid to grow-up—a nice, quiet, suburban town. The people of Midland Park weren't wealthy like in neighboring towns such as Wyckoff, Franklin Lakes, or Ridgewood. We were a typical working, middle-class family. We didn't have anything fancy or extravagant, but we also never went wanting and were never in need. It was a good balance.

I used to call Midland Park an "undershirt community." I was proud of thinking up that term. An undershirt community, by my definition, is a community where men feel comfortable going to the store, barber, gas station, or wherever, in their undershirts. In Midland Park, you saw a lot of men going about their daily business, especially on Saturdays, in their undershirts. My dad was one of them.

I never saw a man in Franklin Lakes walking around in his undershirt—not even in his own yard. I think those who did their own yard work in Franklin Lakes (and there weren't many) wore designer shirts, probably something from Ralph Lauren.

Since my parents had both been teachers, we traveled a lot in the summer time—each year going on a new adventure as a family—"family" meaning whoever was living at home at that time. We camped at the Grand Canyon, went to baseball games at stadiums across America, visited Disney World, and went to as many historical sites as my parents could find. I particularly loved the historical places such as Valley Forge or Gettysburg. Even as a young kid, I was awed by imagining famous people and events taking place on the very ground where I was standing. (I think it is no surprise that I became a history teacher.)

My brother Michael and sister Melissa are both a lot older than me. By the time I was old enough to form memories, most of these trips took place with only my mom and dad and me. My siblings had moved off to college in other states and were busy living their own lives.

In addition to the longer trips, we also visited New York City a lot. With no traffic we could get into the city in well under an hour. My dad loved New York. I think my dad liked all cities. We visited mosst of the big ones on the east coast—New York; Boston; Washington, DC; Baltimore. The only city I don't really remember visiting was Philadelphia. I always wanted to visit there, and we talked about it enough, but we never seemed to get to Philly. But of all these metropolises, New York was the one my dad enjoyed the most. He loved the fast pace, the grit, and the grime. He used to gaze at the New York skyline as we'd approach and state slowly, "The Greatest City in the World."

When we weren't traveling, we stayed at home where I loved to read, play, or watch baseball games. I would also watch the *Rocky* movies over and over, much to my father's chagrin. "You have those damn movies memorized," he'd say to me. "What more is there to see?"

"Dad," I'd respond, "it's *Rocky*. It's more than a movie."

I used to fall asleep dreaming of playing baseball for the New York Yankees (I was smart enough to know that I'd get my head bashed in if I tried to be a boxer like Rocky). I was certain I would eventually play in the Major Leagues, and I thought about it constantly. I watched every game that was televised. I read every baseball book that I could find in the library. I collected tons of baseball cards. And I was the best Wiffle Ball player I knew. I could hit the ball a country mile (or at least out of my back yard). I was certain that all of those attributes were the prerequisites for a long and storied career in the Major Leagues. When I was nine, I even wrote my Hall-of-Fame induction speech.

Life, though, moves on. We grow-up, we age, and our parents age as well. My mother who was nearly forty-five when she had me and was always much older than my friends' moms, passed away from complications with her kidneys the week after I graduated from college. Michael and Melissa both moved to Arizona. My dad and I shared the family house for a while, but eventually even he started to feel the effects of age so he moved to the Christian Health Care Center. His left knee, which had been gimpy ever since he slipped off the step ladder while hanging Christmas lights on the front bushes, gave out on him sometimes without warning. And he worried about being home alone all day while I was at work. In truth, I worried too. Dad explained that he never wanted to be a burden to anyone, especially me. He and my mom had frequently discussed moving to a place where they'd be properly cared for when they got old. "They'll take care of me, if I need it," my dad said. "You are too young to be burdened with having to care for and worry about an old man like me. What if I fall down the stairs? Worse, what if I get stuck and can't get out of the bath tub?" he grinned. "I don't want that for you or for me."

The truth is my dad had some problems with his heart. Two heart attacks and a few other close calls before the age of fifty made him worry a great deal about his "long-term prospects" (as he called them). "If my ticker goes, at least there are nurses around at the health care center," he said.

My dad gave these excuses, but I think that without his wife whom he loved so much, he was ready to leave the house where they created their lives together. I also think that as he saw me grow into an adult he wanted to give me the space to be me. What twenty-something guy wants to bring a girl home to the house he shares with his dear old dad? "Hey dad, please stay in your room while I entertain my new friend..." Of course, I didn't ever encounter that problem. The girl never materialized.

As such, I stayed in my childhood home as everyone else moved on—my mom to Heaven, my sister and brother out West, and my dad to the aforementioned Christian Health Care Center.

Ironically, as a kid, I had worked in the summers at the Christian Health Care Center. It was a clean and well-respected facility for the aged or aging located about three miles away from my home, and since I couldn't yet drive, I rode my bike there most days. Going there was tough—it was all uphill—but coming home... There was something poetic about flying down those hills with no more responsibilities after a day's work. And on Fridays, with a paycheck in my pocket, well, I felt like the world was mine for the taking.

My dad liked the Christian Health Care Center which made me feel better about having him move out and live there. It's located in the Township of Wyckoff—certainly not an undershirt community. But inside the building, among the elderly, the rules or expectations of the township didn't apply. My dad walked the halls as if he were back home, in a white t-shirt and jeans. The few other old men that lived there behaved in the same way. Maybe it came from growing up in the 1940s. I don't think they all originally lived in Midland Park.

During our visits, we would talk about many things, but most of all we'd discuss baseball. I know it broke my dad's heart that I was a Yankees fan since his favorite team was the Boston Red Sox. He loved the Red Sox—Ted Williams, Bobby Doerr, Mel Parnell—he knew them all, since the beginning of their history, and taught them to me. I might be the only Yankees fan who doesn't hate the Red Sox. (Although I still couldn't find it in me to be glad when the Red Sox won the World Series in 2004. I might not hate them, but that was too much, even for me, to handle.)

I woke up from my respite at the kitchen table feeling a bit stiff. One should never end a run by sitting down immediately, especially in a hard chair. But, I was new to this long running training and hadn't thought of that. I sometimes don't think of obvious things. I got up, realized I smelled miserable, thought about taking a shower, but instead, went off to clean the gutters. I'd shower later, before the barbeque.

−5−

The next morning, after I swung my legs out of bed, I realized I could barely stand. The plantar fasciitis in my foot screamed with pain every time I put even a tiny bit of weight on it. I had never felt such pain. Have you ever stuck hot needles into the bottom of your foot? I haven't either, but it sure felt like I had. In addition to this foot agony, everything else, especially the fronts of my thighs, ached. I wondered if I had pushed my body further than it was able to handle. Was twelve miles my limit? Maybe I wasn't built for a marathon. Dr. Alfonzo, my chiropractor (who is also a miracle healer), advised me to always stretch before a hard run and also to always ice this injury after the effort. Why didn't I listen to his advice?

I hobbled outside to get the Sunday morning paper. The sun was very low in the sky, and my house cast a long shadow over the lawn and our neighbor's driveway. The trees in the neighborhood, as well as the hills, blocked the daily sunrise which I felt a sudden longing for. Standing on one leg so as to lessen the pain, I thought of my canoe and the bay. I imagined that the cool early morning water would be an elixir on my throbbing foot. I gathered the paper with a sigh and limped inside to my kitchen table where I tied a bag of frozen peas and carrots around my throbbing foot. I turned to the sports section and began to read the scores before pouring myself any cereal. The Yankees had won the previous night. That pleased me. My days always begin better when the Yankees are victorious.

A small advertisement captured my eye. The Police Benevolent Association of Norwood, New Jersey, was hosting a "Trip Back in Time" for baseball fans that day. Former New York Yankee first baseman Ron Blomberg and former Boston Red Sox pitcher Luis Tiant were going to be in town hosting a clinic, meeting fans, and signing autographs.

I immediately called my dad.

"Heee-low." (My father has a unique way of answering the phone.)

"Hey, Dad, it's Sam. Want to go out for the day?"

"I don't know. To do what?"

"Hang out with Luis Tiant."

"Loooo-ie? How will you do that? You don't know him."

"He's going to be in Norwood, with Ron Blomberg too."

"Yeah? El Tiante and The Boomer?" (My dad knew all the nicknames) "OK. I would like that... a lot."

I was at the Christian Health Care Center within thirty minutes. My dad, wearing a weathered Red Sox jersey, was waiting outside the front door. Tucked under his left arm was his old Bob Feller baseball glove. In his right hand he held a baseball. He looked at me, smiled, and said, "You never know. Maybe they'd like to have a catch."

On the ride to Norwood, a good forty minutes away (residents of Northern New Jersey know that there is absolutely no easy way to get from Wyckoff to Norwood.), my father was very talkative. As we passed through the tree-lined streets and small business districts, we discussed topics ranging from baseball to politics. The conversation eventually came around to the teachers' contract in my district.

"Don't get wrapped up in all that," my father advised. "It's not worth the stress." He continued, "I have learned, and it took me a while, that it's just a game the two sides play. It's a serious game, and it upsets a lot of people, but, in the end, it's just a game. Rise above it, Son."

Much to my chagrin, we also discussed my lack of a love life.

"No girl yet? What ever happened to Carissa?"

"That was seventh grade, Dad."

"What about Bob Muller's daughter?"

"She's like half my age."

"How about that girl with the boy's name...Bobbie?"

"She's married."

"You know there is that nurse at my place, Mary. She's good looking."

My dad was right about this, but, "Dad, I am not dating a nurse at your place."

"Too bad."

The event wouldn't be starting until 1:30 p.m. so we stopped for lunch at Callahan's Hot Dogs along the way. Dad had a plain hot dog ("Just the meat and the bread"), mine came all-the-way. We shared an order of fries. Before I could stop him, my dad smothered the fries with salt and ketchup. Sitting on the plastic chairs at the plastic table, we were in a period I could call "any time." It was certainly today, but those tables and chairs looked like they could be the same ones from when this small joint opened in the 1950s.

"I like places like this," Dad said. "It reminds me of when I was a kid and getting a dog was always a big deal."

In spite of the distance, lack of a direct route and the lunch stop, we arrived in Norwood a good fifty minutes early. As I pulled my old Dodge into the gravel parking lot by Municipal Field, we saw two unmistakable figures talking alone. My dad opened the car door even before I came to a complete stop and nearly fell to the ground in his haste to get to the players. He rushed up to them as fast as his old legs could carry him.

"Lou-ie! Ronnie!"

The players turned to see this old man approaching, glove in hand, as if he were fifty or sixty years younger. Luis Tiant spoke first, "Hello, Mister. Thanks for coming to see us."

I couldn't believe what next came out of my father's mouth.

"Wanna have a catch?"

The love of something special, like baseball, can create magic. Both Ron Blomberg and Luis Tiant broke into huge smiles. They looked around and saw that we were the only ones there. Ron said, "Yes!"

For the next fifteen or twenty minutes I sat back and enjoyed watching two former Major League All-Stars playing catch with my father. I think I had as much fun as my dad, but maybe that wasn't possible. Luis Tiant nearly fell over laughing when my dad threw his signature knuckleball. In his Cuban accent, Tiant called out, "Old Man, you could peeetch in the Big Leagues." I am certain my father believed him.

The magic ended when other participants started arriving. Blomberg shook my dad's hand, and my dad embraced Tiant, the former Red Sox. As they broke their hug, he grabbed Tiant's hand, looked him squarely in the eyes and said, "We almost did it in 1975. I thought you guys were going to win it. Oh how my heart broke when you lost the World Series."

"Mine too," replied the All-Star pitcher.

As we drove back home, a used-book sale caught my attention. Inside, among the hordes of paperbacks and old hard covers, I found a book autographed by Carl Yastrzemski, another old Red Sox. The forty dollar price tag seemed too steep, but when I saw my dad holding the book in his hands and tracing the letters of the title "YAZ" with his finger, I was overcome with generosity. In addition to the autographed book, I found a collection of humorous essays by James Thurber, Dr. George Sheehan's "Running and Being," a beat-up Beatles LP ("Beatles for Sale"), and a book about the Marx Brothers. The sale was a home run.

My dad thanked me countless times as we drove back towards Wyckoff. He alternatively held the Yastrzemski book and pounded his hand into his baseball glove. I hadn't seen my father that jubilant in a long time.

Baseball often brings out the best in us.

–6–

The last two weeks of the school year passed uneventfully. I worked, I ran, I visited Dad.

I am usually pretty focused and task-oriented, but at certain times I procrastinate. One task I really don't enjoy is lawn-mowing, and I had been putting it off. I told myself it could wait until the school year ended. On this, my first official day of summer vacation, I noticed the result of my neglect. The grass was getting high. I reluctantly got out the old lawn mower. I rushed through the process, getting the clippings caught up in the mower blades too many times, and at the end found myself covered in grass that had stuck to my sweaty arms and legs.

It must have been while I was showering that the phone first rang. They didn't leave a message.

After leaving the shower, I went outside on my small wooden deck to look at some running books I had been meaning to read (it was a gorgeous day), and then ordered a pizza. Another one of the joys of living alone is eating whatever you want whenever you want. On some days, I'd have the privilege of having an entire pizza to myself. This was one of those days!

I knew the delivery kid from Brothers' Pizza because I taught him a few years before. We chatted for a few minutes outside when he arrived. I always gave him a good tip. I remembered that my mother always felt a dollar was sufficient. I didn't want a delivery person thinking I was cheap, so I always gave at least five dollars. What was it to me? (I also thought the pizza tasted a little better and arrived a little quicker when I ordered it rather than my mother.)

It must have been while I was outside that I missed the second phone call.

–7–

I did receive the third phone call. It came at about 8:15 p.m., I was sitting on the couch, just starting to relax as the Yankees were batting in the bottom of the second inning. The call came from Dr. Durant at Valley Hospital. My dad had been rushed in, his heart had stopped... they did everything they could.

"Your dad was a good man," he said.

My father passed away quickly and quietly at the Christian Health Care Center. A heart attack. He was dead before they even took him to the hospital. I guess all those nurses couldn't prevent any of this in the end.

"He was a good man." The doctor's words echoed in my mind.

I sat down at the kitchen table too stunned to speak or move. The crying came later.

I eventually stood and walked into the darkness of the cool summer night. It was now overcast and I could barely see the moon behind the thick clouds. I didn't know what to do and eventually found myself sitting on the cinderblock wall in front of my house. Our elderly neighbor from across the street, Roger Winkler, stood outside his front door and called to me as he started walking over, "Hey, Sammy, what's going on? Strange night to be sitting outside. How are ya? How's your pop?"

"Hi, Mr. Winkler. I'm just sitting here... thinking..."

"About what?" Mr. Winkler pulled his Levi's up by the sides and then tugged at his grey undershirt that had seen far too many wash cycles.

"Dad died. Just a little while ago."

"What? Died? Dead? Your father? Auggie? No. No. No, that can't be. Sam..."

"My dad died," I repeated.

"Sam, I'm sorry. I'm so sorry. He was a good man, your father."

Mr. Winkler sat down next to me, grabbed my hand, and began to cry. I never knew Mr. Winkler as a particularly affectionate man, but he wouldn't let go of my hand. "Everyone I know, they're all going..." he wept.

After about twenty minutes, I guess—I lost track of time, it may have been longer—I walked Mr. Winkler home. I told Mrs. Winkler the news and politely declined her offer for a cup of coffee, stating that I needed to get things in order and have some time to think. As I walked across the quiet street, void of cars, void of light, a gentle rain started to fall.

The days that followed passed in a blur, but certain scenes seemed to stand out as singular acts in a long and confusing play. The responsibilities for Dad's arrangements fell to me as I knew it would take my siblings a few days to get their families in order and fly to New Jersey. I didn't mind. The phone calls to Michael and Melissa were perfunctory. I was too distracted to be much of a conversationalist. I do remember Melissa stating, "Take care of yourself, Sam. We'll be out shortly." I recall hearing her husband in the background yelling at their kids before she hung up the phone.

The first thing I did the next day was rush to the Christian Health Care Center to get some of my father's prized possessions, including the baseball from that magical last game of catch. I had to have that ball. Next I made the arrangements at the funeral home for the viewing and funeral service. I tried to reach my friend Ed, an Episcopal priest, to see if he could conduct the funeral, but he was away with his family in South America touring, learning, and, I was certain, running. A distance runner, Ed always encouraged me to try the marathon. Without Reverend Ed, I had to settle for our church's new assistant pastor Reverend McNertney—a somewhat cold and distant woman. Dad was getting the bench player to conduct his final services.

Once home, I went into Melissa's old bedroom, long ago converted to an office. On a bookshelf between two windows was a row of family photo albums held up on either side by bricks that served as bookends. It had been a long time since I had looked at any of them, some I never even pulled from the shelf. The first album I came across had the words "FAVORITES AND MEMORIES OF MY LIFE – BY AUGUST P. HOLMES" printed neatly in my dad's handwriting across the top. My father usually printed in only capital letters. I had never known that he had taken the time to make an album such as this. Not entirely knowing what I'd find within (what were my dad's favorites?), I took a deep breath and slowly opened the brown leather-bound binder.

For the next few hours, I was a spectator to the significant events of my father's life. It was clear that my dad had put a great deal of time into this book. I was amazed that I had never seen it nor seen him working on it. The book covered everything—until he went off to live at the Christian Health Care Center.

The first few photos and relics were from my father's childhood. These consisted mostly of black and white photographs of backyard birthday parties, family trips, and all the cars my grandfather had owned over the years. As I turned each page, and watched my father grow up and grow old, I noticed a few items seemed to traverse the years with my father: a canoe, a tent, and lots of baseball. One picture had all three. It showed my dad in a baseball uniform standing next to his canoe at a campsite that I assume was on Saranac Lake in upstate New York. The smile on his face was similar to the one he wore, all these years later, when I'd visit him at the Christian Health Care Center.

It was a smile I'd no longer see.

My mother played a prominent role in the album of photographs, of course. There were a host of pictures of my mom posing at various places—hamburger stands, amusement park rides, and next to each of my father's cars. There were also plenty of pictures that showed my parents holding hands and even kissing. This was nothing new to me. My parents, even in their old age, always greeted each other with a kiss, which bothered me a lot when I was a teenager. I wondered now who had taken all those pictures. Probably a long lost friend, or maybe my grandparents. It wasn't like today where everyone has a phone camera at every moment.

As I traversed the years of my father's life, there were the expected wedding pictures and soon after pictures of my mother in various stages of pregnancy. After the babies, my older siblings, were born, though, there were fewer pictures than I might have thought. All the standards were there, baby photos, birthdays (again), sporting events, and a few modest vacations. My siblings took up plenty of pages, but I had expected more.

My father also had a series of photos of the men's clothing store where he worked evenings, weekends, and summers. My dad's main profession was as a school teacher, but he needed this other job to make ends meet.

I relished the pictures of Michael and Melissa playing with me. I am eight years younger than Melissa and eleven years younger than Michael. The difference in our ages was never that apparent to me until I looked back at these photos. We lived, in a real sense, different lives. I was struck the most by the pictures of Michael and Melissa, with cars full of belongings, in the moments before each moved away to live their lives away from the rest of us. One such picture showed me crying as a Ford Falcon drove off in the distance.

Neither of my siblings ever returned home for more than a quick visit.

As we came to the pages of my life, I flipped quicker. These photos were ones I was familiar with. Me and Robin Hood at Disney World, my dad and me at Yankee Stadium, my mom kissing me in front of a girl on prom night, and my graduation from King's College in Wilkes-Barre, Pennsylvania.

I flipped back to the photograph of Michael driving away to Arizona, put my head in my hands, and cried exactly as I did the day he left his little brother behind so many years ago.

-8-

Melissa was the first to arrive. My first reaction as she exited the rental car was that she was dressed more for an important meeting or a dinner party than a funeral. She was wearing a smart black business suit with a pearl necklace. The brightness of her red lipstick shocked me. Her hair was cut shorter than I remembered, but she looked good, especially after flying directly to New Jersey from Arizona. She hugged me for a long time in the parking lot of the Robert Spearing Funeral Home. As her three children tumbled out of the car and gathered around, she thanked me for taking care of everything. "You are a good brother and a better son," she said. My eyes filled with tears at this showing of affection from my sister. I hadn't expected that type of sincerity from her—or my reaction. She added, "Charles sends his regrets. He wanted to come, but was unable to break away from his responsibilities." I told her that I understood. I always try to understand.

As my sister and her retinue proceeded inside the funeral parlor, I retreated to my Dodge to try to regain some composure. I wanted to look stronger emotionally than I was. From the other side of the parking lot, some cousins appeared, and I watched them greet each other with smiles and hugs. My cousin Russ said something that made everyone laugh. I knew I should go out and greet them, but somehow I didn't have it in me.

I never know how to handle smiles or laughter at a wake.

Michael arrived shortly after. The lines around his eyes betrayed his otherwise youthful appearance. It was clear that my older brother was starting to approach middle-age, though he still looked good in his smart navy blue suit, Cole Haan oxfords, and designer tie. My brother was always one who dressed to impress. I envied his refinement.

Because it was summer and many people were away, I did not expect much of a showing. I hoped a few of my friends would come to offer sympathy and support. I was, therefore, surprised to see that the wake was well attended. Many of my colleagues arrived, some coming from quite a distance, and I was shocked that a fair number of my former students and their families also showed up.

Many of my father's friends and neighbors came to pay their respects. One man from our neighborhood, Bill Roebuck, just sat in an upholstered chair in the funeral home weeping. Mr. and Mrs. Winkler came, though they didn't stay long. It seemed apparent to me that this news took a great deal out of Mr. Winkler. He muttered a few words to me but did not seem to recognize either Michael or Melissa, although Mrs. Winkler did and gave each a sincere hug and a kiss. Another neighbor, Tom Nash, was at the funeral parlor from almost the moment we opened the doors. I was less happy to see him as I knew him mainly as the man who ridiculed my father for being a school teacher ("Can't get out of elementary school, heh?") and whose dog used my parent's property as a toilet bowl. But he turned out to be somber and subdued. He was the first person in line when the viewing began, and when he shook my hand he said, "A good man, your father. I'll miss him." I wondered if Mr. Nash's wake would be well attended.

I was soon trapped in the receiving line.

"Your dad was a good man."

"Are you ok?"

"Oh, Sam…"

"It's good your brother and sister came…"

"What can I do?"

This is what my day consisted of. Words. "Good man…" "Will be missed…" "Better than to suffer…" Interestingly, while some told me, "He went too soon," others remarked that, "It was his time." Had I a better presence of mind, I might have tried to keep track of which of those statements was more popular.

Funerals can be times of contradiction.

"Take care of yourself, Sam."

"Be strong."

"You'll be ok."

"It just takes time."

"If you need anything…"

If you need anything. What a saying. Why is that sentence never completed? People say it, they nod their head, they point at themselves, and they walk away. As I stood there among the hugs, I could not even begin to wonder what I might need.

I opted for an open casket and I was glad for it. Dad looked good. He was wearing a suit but no tie. It gave him a more casual look, my silent tribute to his favorite ballplayer, Ted Williams, who also didn't wear ties. My dad actually hated suits too, but I couldn't lay him out in his white undershirt. Why aren't people laid to rest in clothes they are comfortable with? I'd like to be in my pajamas. If it's the eternal sleep, what's more appropriate?

Many of my father's former students, now grown-ups themselves, came to offer their condolences. That was no surprise. My dad was a beloved teacher.

No one from the Red Sox came. As much as my dad gave them his unconditional love, they were unaware of his death and let the moment pass without any recognition.

It was a long afternoon that lasted into the evening. I remember many handshakes, hugs, and pats on the back. I don't remember many tears, except for those that came from Mr. Roebuck, who remained in an end chair in the back of room throughout the entire viewing. If he was crying, Mr. Winkler was expressing his sorrow at his own home.

I also remember being overwhelmed by the persistent smell from the flowers that we purchased and the ones that others sent. There wasn't an abundance of memorial bouquets, but their smell, while nice, became a little overwhelming at times. The flowery aroma of a funeral home is something I do not enjoy. Maybe it's the contrast between life and death—with death always winning eventually. Even the pretty flowers, now only kept alive in water, were slowing dying. In another few days, they too, would be gone

During the quieter times between the visitors, I looked around at the family members and friends who stood in little clusters around the room holding coffee in Styrofoam cups and eating the vanilla Oreos that had been laid out by the director of the funeral home. I felt some remorse for the times I neglected to call them or attend a family party. I reflected on how we don't seem to make ourselves free enough to visit with each other until someone passes. We are always too busy or not in the mood. I'm often not in the mood. Our priorities are backwards.

Mr. Donald M. Stevens III, the attorney with whom my dad wrote his final will and testament, also came. Mr. Stevens was a kind gentleman, seemingly from another era, which is probably why my father liked him. He was a tall man, immaculately dressed in a black suit and black tie with a black fedora pressed to his chest, and he entered the room with a certain majesty, silver head bowed and somber. While he walked with the straight-backed confidence of a person who knows, and is intimate with success, he also had an understated humility that drew people to him.

Mr. Stevens shook my hand and offered his condolences in a compassionate manner, but then he said, "You can't put your father's remains in a niche until we meet to review his will. He wished to be cremated, you know." This seemed like an abrupt statement for someone to make during the viewing of the recently departed, but I figured that Mr. Stevens was a busy man who had probably attended hundreds of viewings and needed to get his point across. I took no offense.

I knew that my dad wished cremation. I prefer that as well— when my time comes.

Since I had not expected a huge crowd, I planned for the wake and funeral service to take place on the same day, both at the funeral home.

My father was a good man, well liked and respected by all. His life was a good life. At the funeral service people shared many stories, and though you're not supposed to smile much at these gatherings, there was some laughter and good feelings. My dad was a man who made other people feel good about themselves. That spirit was reflected there that day.

At the conclusion of the long day, Melissa, her children, my brother Michael, and I had some time alone at the funeral home. They both had early flights the next day and neither had planned to come back to the house with me, so this was our only time together. I hadn't arranged for a repast anyway. They understood. We sat on the smooth pink couches in the lobby and shared some stories and more than enough awkward silences.

It wasn't that we weren't close, we were just not typical "best friends." Michael and Melissa, "the M & M kids," shared a childhood together; not me. They also knew a different dad than I did. And while it was all good, despite the longer hours that our parents worked then, it wasn't a surprise that they moved away and forged their lives someplace else. It wasn't a surprise, either, that I was the kid who stayed home.

It was about 8:30 p.m. when my sister and brother left for their hotels. They offered to take me out to Matthew's Diner for a meal together, but I told them it wasn't necessary. And, while they both suggested it—it also wasn't necessary to see them the next day before their flights. Life moves on.

I'm used to being alone.

As I sat, alone now with my father in the funeral home, the thing I most wanted to do was have a catch with him. I wanted us to throw a ball together. I wanted to watch him try to throw a few knuckleballs.

That was the thought I kept coming back to—I will never have another catch with my dad. I hoped that there was baseball in Heaven.

About an hour later, I closed up business with the funeral director. He was in his office doing a crossword puzzle. His terse replies gave me the feeling that I had overstayed my welcome.

That evening, in the quiet home of my youth and my present adulthood, I did not order pizza. Instead I poured a bowl of cereal and took out my old Strat-o-Matic playing cards. Strat-o-Matic is a baseball game played with cards and dice. Every Major League baseball player is represented on a unique card, and the cards are supposed to mimic how the real players performed. In honor of Dad, I took out his favorite Red Sox team set. We had made these sets years before, when I was a kid, and we often had long games and playoff series into the night.

I took off the rubber band and I flipped though the deck reading the players' names and positions: Jerry Remy, second base; Dwight Evans, right field; Jim Rice, designated hitter; Carl Yastrzemski, first base... For this team Dad replaced Carney Lansford at third base with a Rico Petrocelli card. For whatever reason, my dad had Rico Petrocelli play on every team he created. I smiled as I set his card down.

It may have been the day to remember Dad, but he wouldn't have wanted it any other way... I brought out my Yankees all-star squad to face his team. I didn't hate the Red Sox, but if I was going to play a game, I wasn't going to simply let the Sox win. No, Dad taught me well. When one plays, he gives his best. If his Red Sox were going to defeat my Yankees, they would have to work for the victory.

Nothing is supposed to come easy.

Thirteen innings later, an imaginary Sparky Lyle of the Yankees walked slowly off the pitcher's mound on my kitchen table after surrendering a homerun to Tony Conigliaro. The Red Sox had won. In my imagination, I saw their manager Ted Williams greeting Tony C. at home plate as the Fenway Park fans went crazy.

–9–

It was over a month before I finally met with Mr. Stevens at his firm on Kinderkamack Road in Hackensack, New Jersey. I had called right away for an appointment with Mr. Stevens but his schedule was booked solid. His kind secretary assured me that there was no rush in processing my father's will.

Maybe this was because I lived in Dad's old home. Maybe it was because I already had most of his possessions and because he was the type of person who always prepaid his monthly rent at the Christian Health Care Center. His health insurance took care of most of the costs from his quick, and unsuccessful, final visit to the hospital. What was left, I willingly paid. (It's not like I had lots of expenses or people to impress.)

Like many offices in this area, Mr. Stevens's may have once been in a modern building, but time, and style, changed the complexion of the area. This construction came before the malls and chain restaurants. Today the Riverside Square Mall dominates, and professional services—doctors, lawyers, accountants— have mostly made way for luxury retailers.

Mr. Stevens's set-up was still very nice, but it was dated and the steel and glass exterior of the tall, and somewhat out-of-place office building told of a different time.

The desk secretary escorted me through the heavy wood paneled doors into Mr. Stevens's office. I was offered a large leather chair across from his ornate mahogany desk. Mr. Stevens smiled at me as I took my seat. His blue eyes were kind, but he sat very straight in his chair, hands clasped in front of him on his desk.

"Hello Mr. Holmes—or Sam—if you don't mind. Your dad was a good man," he began.

"Yes, thank you, I know." I blinked my eyes rapidly at the sudden emotion I felt. "I miss him."

"We all do," Mr. Stevens responded. "We all do."

After offering me coffee, Mr. Stevens stated, "Let's get down to business."

I nodded.

"Your father was a good man, but he had a sense of adventure about him. I will cut to the chase and get right down to the details of his will. Since you live there, you get the house, and if it hasn't been paid off already, there is enough in your father's estate to pay off the second mortgage. The rest of the items, including the furniture in the home, will get divided evenly between you and your siblings. Your father, and mother, always wanted everything to be perfectly fair."

"I would have expected nothing else from them," I said. The truth was that my parents were decent and fair people. That was one reason why Melissa and Michael didn't come back out to New Jersey to examine the will. This all seemed like such a formality. We knew that the estate would be evenly divided between the three of us. I added, "And my brother and sister trust me to take care of things."

"Well, they should trust you," returned Mr. Stevens. "I know you're a good man too. Just like your dad. Your father spoke very highly of you."

"Yes, just like him." I looked up at the ceiling. The days were getting easier, but talking about my father could still overwhelm me with emotion.

"Let me continue..."

Mr. Stevens explained that he would not be able to turn the estate over into my name until I completed a few tasks.

"A few tasks?" I asked.

"Well, your father loved doing things with you—and your whole family of course—but he always felt that there was a special bond between himself and you. He had many great memories of places you traveled and the things you did. Tell me, what do you remember most about the places you visited together?"

I sat quietly for a moment. This meeting wasn't going anything like I imagined it would. After this pause I said, "My dad was happiest when we were together as a family. Well, at least with my mom and me. I don't remember too many vacations with my sister and brother. He didn't get angry often anyway, but I never remember him being upset on any trip. We always had a lot of fun. We went to the typical vacation spots of course—cities, museums, amusement parks, Disney World... But sometimes we would head miles out of the way in order to see something unique—a small fort or a tourist trap. We once went to Benton, Pennsylvania just to see if there were any signs or relics about something that was known as the Fishing Creek Confederacy."

"What was that?"

"The Fishing Creek Confederacy? It was..." I paused to reflect on this historical minutia. "I don't remember, but it has something to do with southern sympathizers who were resisting the draft during the Civil War. I think there was talk that they'd fight for General Lee and the rebel army if an invasion reached the area around Benton in Northern Pennsylvania."

"What did you find out there?"

"I don't remember if we found anything besides a few small,

mostly forgotten, historical markers and a covered bridge or two. I remember having lunch at a place called the Hoboken Hoagie Shop which was a strange name for a sandwich place in the middle of Pennsylvania."

Mr. Stevens's blue eyes exuded trust and understanding. As he listened to me, he nodded slowly. But when I mentioned the sandwich shop, he dropped our eye contact, and looked at a document on his desk.

If Mr. Stevens had a gift for allowing people to be comfortable enough to talk with him—he also had a manner that forced them to halt when he determined it was necessary. Once we lost eye contact, once he stopped nodding, and once he glanced at the document, it seemed my words were no longer welcome. I sat silently awaiting his next signal.

I continued to wait; longer than what would have been a normal comfortable pause. His response, once he looked up from the paper, made no sense.

"Well, I see nothing about Benton. In fact, I don't even see any mention of Pennsylvania, with the exception of Philadelphia."

"Mr. Stevens, sir, I am not quite sure I understand how Philadelphia and my dad are connected in any way."

Mr. Stevens looked at me with those kind, penetrating eyes. "Your father has passed, but he is not ready to go yet. He's not ready to turn everything over to you and your siblings. I've been settling estates for a long time, young man, and I have never written a last will with the stipulations your dad imposed. I knew when he and I wrote this that you and I would be having this conversation someday." He paused, smiled, and said, "Tell me more about your vacations."

"I'm not quite sure what my childhood vacations have to do with anything."

"Young man, just do as I ask. You will understand my curiosity very shortly. Tell me more... please."

I hesitated. "Well, Dad loved driving to places. I think half the fun for him was planning routes. My dad loved reading maps. He hated GPS. We didn't get lost very often either. When we'd get somewhere, even if we had never been there before, he would say, 'I knew exactly where it was.' He would say that even if we did get a little misplaced before arriving.

"We once spent half a day looking for a tiny park in New Hampshire, I believe, that claimed to have dinosaur tracks. We couldn't find the place. My dad didn't mind asking for directions if he had to, and in this case... he had to. When he asked a mailman, even he had never heard of the place."

"Did you find it?"

"Yes, eventually. And when we got there, Dad said, 'Yup, just where I suspected it would be.'"

"Were there any dinosaur tracks?"

"Well, I don't remember. Funny. I don't remember too many specifics today. I think I remember my mom showing me marks on some rocks behind a wall and saying 'There they are!' I pretended to see the tracks."

"She was a good lady, your mother."

"Yes."

"What else do you remember about the trips?"

Mr. Stevens and I spent the better part of the morning talking and reminiscing about my childhood and the various memories I had of my parents and the places we traveled to. I couldn't imagine why Mr. Stevens was so interested—we didn't do anything out of the ordinary. We were a regular family from an undershirt community, who took a yearly vacation. I am certain none of my stories were all that interesting. We never climbed a mountain. We never forded a raging river. We didn't hike to unknown destinations. We didn't stay in fancy hotels. We didn't meet any famous people. We did a lot of driving. Driving and camping. We visited a lot of historical sites. We spent many days in canoes and nights in tents.

At one point, we paused and Mr. Stevens ordered sandwiches for us. I was surprised that he was giving me this much time. He must have really liked my dad, I reasoned. Or maybe he did this with all his clients. Either way, it was nice. I hadn't realized how badly I had wanted to talk about my dad over the last month until Mr. Stevens started asking me questions.

It was while I was eating potato chips that I said, laughing,

"One funny thing about Dad was that he wanted to rush every-where, but he never wanted leave anywhere. It was funny. He always wanted to get to the next spot. He would say, 'Tomorrow we will visit such and such,' but when it came time to leave the place where we were, he seemed reluctant, sad. Once or twice I even saw tears in his eyes. He would often say, especially as we drove away, 'I can't wait to bring us all back here again.'"

"Young man," Mr. Stevens said gently, "you now understand why you are here today. Your father does not want his ashes to just be placed in a wall. Well, he wants some of them there, but let me be clear. Your dad wasn't ready to go. If he lived one-hun-dred more years, he still wouldn't have been ready to go because he would have then created even more memories. Your dad wants to visit a few places with you—one last time together. He wants you to leave a little part of him in all those places. You need to take him to those places."

"I have to what?" I asked, my voice rising.

"Before I can close out your father's estate, you need to take his remains and leave some of them in various areas—places you went together. I can't process any paperwork until you have fulfilled each of his last wishes."

"What am I supposed to do? How will I do this?"

"It is quite simple, son," said Mr. Stevens. "I will give you a card or a letter, written by your father. Do as it says, then return to me, and I will give you another letter. I have a few. Once you finish the tasks, I can close the estate, you can divide the belong-ings with your siblings, and life goes on."

"In other words, I have to travel all over the place before his estate is settled?"

"Yes."

"Well, I don't know if I can afford all this. Where will I find the time or the money? School is starting in a few weeks."

"The time, young man, I cannot help with, but your father was a good man. I have power of attorney," he chuckled, "sort of my job. I can release funds to support these adventures. You can itemize your expenses and submit them and you'll be reim-bursed. The money will be deducted from the estate. But you have to be reasonable. You told me yourself that your parents didn't stay in expensive hotels."

"We ate at Denny's a lot with my grandparents."

"Denny's is just about right."

I sat in a quiet stupor with, I must admit, a dizzying range of emotions—all in an instant. The thought of scattering his ashes all over the country was...absurd. I had responsibilities, things to do. The marathon was coming. School too. I loved my dad, but...this? This was unreasonable. One goes to a reading of the will to get his inheritance, not to be sent on a mission. I wanted to call my dad some names that I never considered calling him, at least not since I thought them as a teenager. Still, I was also overwhelmed by the thought and effort that must have gone into this whole process.

"What?" was all I could muster as a response. I began to rise out of my chair, but found some inner resolve that kept me planted in my spot. I noticed that I was clenching my left hand into a fist. I felt my eyebrows, which always give me away, bunched above my eyes.

The requirements seemed outlandish...far-fetched...unfair...unheard of.

I considered Mr. Stevens in silence. I'm not sure how long we sat there like this.

But, to be honest, I was also intrigued by what I had been told. As I sat there, fluctuating between bewilderment, anger, shock, and frustration, Mr. Stevens looked at me with those quiet eyes.

I think he understood.

–10–

Eventually, I asked Mr. Stevens for clarification. It was simple, he told me. He would hand me a letter and I would do as the letter said, which, in essence, meant bringing and leaving my father's ashes at a location he requested. I would then return home and, when I was ready, visit Mr. Stevens to receive another letter. Each letter, Mr. Stevens told me, was written by my father. Once I completed all the tasks, the estate would be settled.

"How will you even know if I do these things?" I asked. "Do I have to bring proof?"

"No. As I said, you can submit receipts, if you desire, to offset the costs. But, if you don't submit receipts, I will never know if you did as you were asked. It's not my business to doubt you."

"Well, I won't lie."

"I know you won't. And anyway, your dad won't be resting until you're done. He'll know."

Yes, I thought. He will know.

The hardest part, I then realized, was explaining all of this to Melissa and Michael. I expressed this worry aloud. Mr. Stevens told me, somewhat to my chagrin, that he had already explained everything to them. He had also provided them with an advance on their inheritances.

"They have some of the money already?" I asked incredulously.

"Actually, they have most of their shares already. Scattering the ashes is something your father wanted you to do. He actually wrote large checks for Michael and Melissa some time ago."

I rose from the chair, a little stunned. Mr. Stevens, stood, looked me in the eye, and handed me an envelope.

"I understand," I said, but I really didn't. I accepted the envelope with mixed emotions, including rage, and left the office.

I had spent the better part of the day with Mr. Stevens. I never thought that he might have had other responsibilities or other clients. Maybe he did. Or not.

As I walked across the parking lot, my first thoughts were petty, and I wasn't proud of them. I lingered on the idea of my sister, probably driving a new BMW courtesy of her inheritance while I was still driving an outdated Dodge. It didn't seem fair, or right. It then occurred to me that this old car would have to take me to various places on a new series of adventures that I neither wanted nor asked for.

It seemed my dad and I would be spending a lot of quality time together. My first task would be reading whatever was in the envelope. I sat in the driver's seat of my car and opened the letter written to me from my father.

–11–

Dear Sam,

Let me begin by saying what I tried to say to you a lot, but probably didn't say enough. I love you.

Let me also apologize. This idea I have is pretty selfish of me. I am asking a lot of you. I hope you will understand what I am asking. I never wanted any of our good times to end. I never wanted to leave any of the fun places we visited. I wished we could just stay at each forever. I am hoping that you'll help me stay at just a few of those places, in this way, forever. We will also get a few last trips together.

Hey, the good news is I'll pay our way. I'm sure Mr. Stevens told you that already. Just don't order anything over $5.00 on the menu.

Together we shared a love of baseball. I never minded that you became a Yankees fan. I delighted in the joy you had watching them win. I also know you have a soft spot in your heart for the Red Sox.

My first request (can you imagine that I am crying as I write this to you) is that we visit Cooperstown together. Let's go to the Baseball Hall-of-Fame. If you can, leave some of my ashes with ol' Teddy Ballgame.

Have a safe trip. Don't speed. We'll get there fast enough.

I love you.

Love,

Dad

My eyes welled with tears. How special it was to have this paper in my hand. A last note (but also knowing there would be more) from my father. These were his words to me from beyond the grave. He wrote the word "love" four times. I counted. As he got older, he said that word to me more often, but I realized that it almost can't be mentioned enough.

I was still parked in Mr. Stevens's lot. I leaned forward and pressed my head against the top of the steering wheel. I missed my dad in a way that was difficult to explain. I don't like finality; maybe I inherited that trait from him. I began then to miss my mother as well. Her constant smile, the way she always laughed at my jokes, and her penchant for pistachio ice cream. I even started missing my sister and brother. I longed for our times together as a family, pierced suddenly by the knowledge that those days were gone forever. In front of me, a never-ceasing jam of cars passed on Kinderkamack Road and Route 4. People rushing to places that only mattered to them, and that probably didn't matter much at all, and as I watched them, I felt completely alone.

After wiping my eyes and rubbing my forehead, I looked back to the office complex and Mr. Stevens's windows. I half expected him to be standing there nodding gently. But he was not. I turned the key, took a deep breath, and began to drive home.

Merging on to Route 4 West, I was nearly sideswiped by a new BMW racing up the slow lane to pass an old Toyota. I thought again of my sister driving her new BMW. How many miles of roads would I have to travel before I collected my inheritance? I wondered what kind of car I might purchase once everything was settled and then felt angry at myself for thinking of any benefit I might gain from my father's death.

This whole scheme my father thought up confused me... and again, it started to anger me. I wrestled with the idea that I should be excited about this adventure, but I couldn't get past the absurdity of it all. What was he thinking?

When I nearly hit a car entering the highway from Spring Valley Road, I knew I better focus on my driving. "Dad, I love you," I said aloud, "but this is crazy." Michael or Melissa could dump his ashes all over the country just as well as I could.

And then I felt guilty for those thoughts. "He chose you," I said to myself. "A father and his youngest son. A father and a son. A father...and...his son."

After arriving home (safely) from Mr. Stevens's office, I decided to go for a run. I had been sitting for most of the day, but all that sitting actually made me exhausted. I needed fresh air and some freedom from walls. I normally run with an iPod, enjoying upbeat music, but on this run, I figured it might be better if I simply ran "free." I was about to put my Road ID on my wrist when I realized that the phone number to call in case of an emergency was my father's.

No need for this, I thought.

I headed from my home into Wyckoff up the long hills, pushing my body but running at a controlled and even pace. Since I started training for this marathon, I had become more in tune with my body. This sense of "inner understanding" was unexpected, but it brought me confidence. As I got stronger, and more confident, I didn't worry so much about my physical ability to complete the runs. Instead the challenge became more of a mental thing. Did I have the focus to push myself as my runs required more and more effort? On good days, when I got in a rhythm, I felt almost as though the roads and I were becoming one, together, a single flow of man and muscle and earth.

There are times when The Run defines us.

Runners love to tell other people, especially other runners, about their latest runs. I don't think anyone really cares, but we do it anyway. Get two runners together and they'll both tell how great or terrible they are feeling based upon their most recent successes or failures. They might even be talking at the same time.

"I have an injury."

"I covered fifteen miles in the heat yesterday."

"I fell short on an easy two-miler."

"My back hurts."

"I have never felt stronger."

"My long running days may be over."

Sort of like two small children in a sandbox—parallel play. They go on and on, not even sure, or caring, if the other is listening.

Today, my run felt great. Maybe it was the lack of music.

Maybe it was the complete freedom from everything, except that exact moment, that a run can bring. Maybe it was the prospects of the adventure I was about to go on with my dad. I ran strong and hard and focused. I wasn't even thinking about the roads I was on (which is rare for me because I keep detailed records of every mile I run) until I reached the top of the hill by the Christian Health Care Center.

A few short weeks ago, I would have visited my dad here. Now another aging—and slowly dying person—was residing in his room. How long would this resident live there before his or her time was up?

I kept running, up Sicomac Avenue and then over Mountain Avenue well into North Haledon. At the Food Town, I stopped to purchase a Gatorade. At the store people shied away from me— keeping their distance as if I were a leper. To be fair, I probably looked pretty bad all sweaty and red-faced. Maybe Food Town should prohibit hot, sweaty runners from entering their store.

I continued my run and found solace a few miles up the road at the Audubon Society. This is a private nature center of sorts in Franklin Lakes consisting of a small museum, a handful of picnic tables, and some shaded walking paths. "Birders" come here to congregate and share stories about their latest sightings, but most people don't even know it exists. I sat down on the wooden bench of a table near a gravel path and let my mind wander. It was quiet in the preserve but for the chirp of birds and the distant hum of the road. In a nearby tree, I saw a goldfinch, New Jersey's state bird, which brought a smile to my face. The little guy took to the sky when an old Volkswagen Beetle loudly passed on the road behind. There were no other visitors and I enjoyed the solitude. After a while, I stood up, moved to the soft grass, and reclined with my hands behind my head. I may have even fallen asleep. I guess the Audubon Society was closed because no one came to chase me away or ask why I was sleeping by their tables.

It was here, while resting, that I decided to embark on the trip to Cooperstown the next day. Since it was August, I still had some time before the start of the school year. I usually like to go to my classroom in the summer to hang up new posters and prepare the room for the students. I still planned on doing this, but I figured the trip to Cooperstown could be accomplished with a quick over-nighter. Maybe it was the endorphins from my run or the peace of the preserve, but I no longer felt any resentment toward my father for setting up these adventures.

One of the worst things about stopping mid-run for a rest is trying to find the energy to begin again. Usually I can push through the discomfort to finish, but sometimes I just can't summon the strength, energy, or mental toughness to continue. When I was younger and this happened, I would call my parents for a ride. They would pick me up anywhere. Gladly.

On this run back home, I started to feel pain in my right heel. It distracted me so much that I began walking—a terrible admission of defeat. I was still four miles from home.

I had no one to call. A police car passed as I was walking and a quick thought flashed into my head to ask the officer to drive me home. I dismissed this out of hand. Police cars are not taxis for failed runners.

I should have brought my iPod, I thought.

I wished my dad or my mom was still alive.

I wished I had a wife. This thought struck me so fiercely that I almost wept.

It took me well over an hour to walk home, probably longer. I didn't have a watch. As I walked, I desperately wanted a candy bar, a Milky Way to be specific, but I had no more money on me.

As I walked, or when I gave into the heel pain and hobbled, I tortured myself by being all too aware of the lives around me.

A man, younger than me, jogged past (going uphill) with a pretty girl as his running partner matching him stride for stride.

Children playing in their yard—running, laughing, one eating ice cream.

A group of bikers flew past me. Some bikers ride with an air about them that seems to indicate that they own the road. Bikers, at least the ones I have talked to, tend to think they are better than runners. I don't know why they think this true. I wanted to yell, "Try covering a long distance without the wheels, then we'll see how tough you are."

About a mile from my home, I saw a moving van parked outside a house that had been vacant for some time. I am always happy when a new family brings a house back to life. Everything looks brighter and cleaner. It's the beauty of hope. I expected to see a lot of activity around the house—movers, furniture, boxes—but there was none of that. Instead I heard a soft, familiar, and wonderful sound—a father and his daughter playing catch.

In spite of myself, I stayed to watch and then surprised myself by approaching the man. "I'm Sam, Sam Holmes," I said, stepping onto the lawn and holding out my hand. "I live a ways away, in the next town actually, but I wanted to welcome you to the area."

"Ray... Ray Sheffield." The man smiled and shook my hand firmly. "That's my little girl, Gracie."

"Where are you from?"

"Oh, not far. We're coming here from Leonia. Years ago we lived in Brooklyn, but we've been in Jersey for a while." He nodded at his daughter. "Even before kids, we wanted to move up to this area to get a bigger yard, have a little more space, you know. I thought the traffic in this part of the county might be a little better, but it seems I was wrong about that."

"Yeah, we've got our fair share of cars."

"Hey Sam, you look beat-up. Can I get you a glass of water or something?"

I grinned. "A drink would be great."

Ray Sheffield handed me his glove and asked if I wanted to continue the catch with his daughter. Gracie must have been about nine or ten, but it was apparent she was an athlete. She could throw and catch at least as good as me (which might not have said much about my ball playing skills).

She and I didn't talk during our catch. We just threw. It felt great to toss a baseball.

Ray's wife, Rebecca, arrived with a tall glass of water with ice, which I tried not to drink too quickly. After a few minutes of small talk, I found out that Ray was an accountant and Rebecca, an attorney. Taking my leave, I thanked them for the cool water, the respite, and their kindness.

I attempted to run the last mile home. After a few strides, though, I couldn't maintain the pace.

Failure.

I had a lot of time for self pity and sorrow during that long walk home. I let the emotions flood me, enjoying the melancholy. I thought about the empty home I was returning to. I was angry and disappointed at myself for never making the effort to get serious with a girl so that I could have a family of my own. I had spent too much time focusing on my job, my father, and my running. And now, my dad's crazy wishes would distract me even further.

When I arrived home, I immediately began a hot shower. Full of defeat and disappointment, I wanted to be angry. I wanted to be angry at myself for failing—failing at everything. I wanted to be angry at my father for his ridiculous demands on me. I wanted to be angry at my siblings, enjoying, it seems for quite a while, the cash my dad sent to them, even before he died. I even wanted to be angry at Mr. Stevens, for his role in this stupid process that I would have to go through.

There was no Yankee game on that night. I wanted to be angry with them as well.

But I wasn't.

When I wanted most to be focused on self-loathing, hatred, and anger, instead I found myself smiling. I put all the distractions out of my head. It was the kindness of people like Ray and Rebecca, the innocence of childhood, and the joy that resounds in the simple passing of a ball tossed through the air, and into a leather mitt, that brought me peace.

–12–

I was up by 4:15 the next morning. I thought about going for an early run because I wanted to get the previous day's failure behind me but I decided it would be better to get on the road to Cooperstown as quickly as possible. I began the day, as I always did, with the Beatles and breakfast. Most runners strive to eat healthy foods. I do try, but I am most often not successful. I poured Lucky Charms into a plastic bowl as the music from *Abbey Road* filled the kitchen.

On a whim, I threw my old tent into the trunk of the car before packing some clothes and my toothbrush. Cooperstown, New York would be a good three to four hours away depending on traffic. I thought I should have some cash, just in case, so I opened up the safe in the basement. It was a small old safe, the color of gunmetal, that came from my great uncle's farm in Rhode Island and read J. Baum Safe and Lock Company (Cincinnati, O.) in yellow and red block print across the front. Like Mr. Stevens's office, it told of a different time. I always felt a sense of majesty when I opened the safe, as if it held special relics and riches. In truth, it didn't hold much: some cash that I was disciplined enough to store away, some broken jewelry, and other assorted items with value only to me like a set of keys from the first car I ever owned. I kept cash in the safe so I'd have it in case of an emergency. I don't have a lot of money there—I think the most I ever accumulated was about $1,600—but I usually have more than a few hundred dollars there, for any sudden need. I took out three hundred dollars and vowed to return the same amount when I received my first paycheck in September.

The difficult part came when it was time to pack up Dad. His ashes were in an urn on top of his old dresser where I had placed them a few days after his modest funeral. What would I do with the ashes? How much "ash" was there? What did it look like? Did it smell? How would I leave some with Ted Williams at the Hall-of-Fame? Should I open the urn and put some ashes in a plastic bag—or should I bring the whole urn? This was all new to me; I dare say it would be a new experience to almost anyone.

Eventually, I found a large, empty, photo-copy-paper box, filled it with bunched up newspaper and some throw pillows so that the urn fit snugly, and placed the box on the floor in the back of my car—right behind the driver's seat. I would deal with the actual ashes later. My first step was just getting to Cooperstown.

I stopped at the Hess station on the way out and filled the tank before heading north to the New York Thruway. I put the local sports talk channel, WFAN, on the radio and set my mind to the long ride. I figured I'd be in Cooperstown by the late morning—or early afternoon if I stopped for lunch.

North of Kingston, New York, I lost WFAN's signal and searched for a good music station. I didn't have much luck, and for the second time in as many days wished I brought my iPod. The best way to Cooperstown, I was told, took the driver up Route 145 through the Catskill Mountains. I remembered driving on these roads with my father heading to the same destination. Today, as I passed through East Durham, New York, I counted the shamrocks posted on the buildings, signs, and almost everywhere else. This was a tradition my dad began to help us pass the time. As a child I remembered telling my father that I saw "over a thousand shamrocks." That may or may not have been true, but my count on this day, while also keeping my eyes on the road, reached well over three-hundred. Those shamrocks were an excellent distraction.

As I began to get fidgety and need a break from driving, I saw signs for Howe's Caverns. We often passed Howe's Caverns on our journeys to Cooperstown, but this was one attraction we never made the time to visit. Howe's Caverns were never able to progress past "Next Time" status. I realized now that the next time never came.

I wondered how many things in my life I had assigned to Next Time status. How many of them were destined to never progress past that point?

I decided to take a respite to see what the caverns were all about. I parked my car in a huge parking lot, which, on this day and at this hour of the mid-morning, was mostly empty. I wondered if the lot ever filled up. Are there that many people who want to see the inside of a cave?

Before getting out of my Dodge I surprised myself by turning in my seat and saying aloud, "Well, Dad, I'm finally at the caverns. I don't know if this is a fun place or a tourist trap, but I'll soon find out. Take care, I'll see you later." I headed toward the entrance and souvenir shop not knowing if I was losing my mind.

The girl at the ticket booth was cute, and I imagined, for a minute, asking her out. She had red hair, brown eyes, and looked a little Irish. Maybe she lives in East Durham, I thought. We could spend our days counting shamrocks. But I decided that East Durham might be an overalls community. I didn't necessarily like undershirt communities, but figured I'd prefer them to overalls communities. I sure didn't have any ambition to be a farmer.

I paid the entrance fee and walked through the gift shop past the bins of special rocks, gimmicky bookends, and random ceramic statues. The first real shock came when I learned that we'd take an elevator to get into the cavern. An elevator? That sort of took the special rustic feel out of the whole endeavor. Why couldn't we just walk down? It felt strange to explore a cave in the same way that I might proceed to a parking garage or the maintenance area of a hotel.

Hey Dad, I thought, now I know why we kept skipping this place.

But, once inside I was surprised to find myself enjoying the caves. It was better than I imagined. My guided tour group consisted of nine people, and we began by walking for about a quarter of a mile underground. An elderly lady and her husband staggered along the path next to me. I was certain one of them would fall, but neither did. Whenever I glanced at them, the woman caught my eye and smiled. She probably wondered why I was alone.

As we walked through the dim tunnel, I felt a chill that wasn't only from the dampness or the cool air so far underground. I was struck by the beauty of the rock formations and their unique colorings. Every color of the rainbow seemed to be represented, but bright oranges, rich browns, and striking reds dominated the landscape. No two natural formations were the same. One tall and skinny column looked like a lumpy pretzel stick. Another reminded me of the top of a man's bald head. Some of the formations seemed to contain crystals. These sparkled in a way that reminded me of the early morning sun on the Barnegat Bay. I was embarrassed when the tour guide, a middle-aged and slightly heavy woman, caught me with a huge grin.

I really didn't want to like this place so much. But I did!

Eventually, we arrived at a subterranean stream and were placed in small boats. As we floated along, strategic lighting highlighted this strange and unique world. With some special effects from the Disney Imagineers, this place would have been a sensation!

The tour guide was actually quite funny. Her voice, while not overbearing or loud, carried throughout the tunnels and rooms. She laughed at her own jokes and she also taught us how to differentiate between stalactites and stalagmites. ("Stalactites hold on tightly to the ceiling," she stated.) She shared her impressions of the designs that had been formed underground—some, once she pointed them out, actually looked like common objects and famous people. Of course, younger audiences would probably not have known who Bob Hope was or that a specific rock resembled his signature profile. Still, I found myself laughing and having fun.

I was almost sad when the tour came to a close. I approached the guide and thanked her. She seemed surprised. I told her how I had passed the caverns many times and was glad I finally decided to stop and actually see them. I promised her I'd come back again. "It's great, it's really great," I said over and over. I imagine I was the most enthusiastic visitor she ever had.

Sitting back in the car before resuming my journey, I thought again of the red-haired girl. I almost generated enough courage to walk back to the ticket booth to talk to her. I began to imagine being out in the fields of New York State with her. I didn't even mind the thought of seeing her in overalls. In fact, I was imagining that she would look pretty good! Maybe I can work here, I thought. I could be a funny tour guide, and eventually she and I would fall in love.

Instead, I gave that idea Next Time status, turned on the engine, and proceeded out of the parking lot.

−13−

I am no world traveler, but of the places I have visited, Main Street in Cooperstown is one of my favorites. Driving down those few blocks, a visitor feels magically transported to a different era—a simpler time. There are no fast food restaurants, malls, or chain stores. Cooperstown consists of small stores (mostly selling baseball memorabilia), a traffic circle, a big public library, and the Baseball Hall-of-Fame and Museum. I smiled as I slowly drove into town and looked for a place to park.

I ended up on a quaint side street a few blocks from the Hall-of-Fame in a spot that overlooked Lake Ostego. I hadn't realized how close this large lake was to the center of town. Sitting in my car, I observed sail boats and power boats as well as swimmers and people fishing from the shore and from wooden docks. Children were laughing and all were enjoying the splendors of summer.

Lake Ostego wasn't a Next Time place in our lives; it was a "Never Was." I estimated that I had visited Cooperstown five times with my father, but not once did we ever venture those few blocks to see the lake. I never even knew it was there. I almost decided, right then and there, to rent a canoe to paddle out into this lake's splendor. I wondered if I could reach the opposite shore. The tranquility of the water beckoned me, especially on this hot August day. I felt a strong desire to experience all of Cooperstown, not only the baseball stuff.

And suddenly, I felt small. Cooperstown was a place I thought I knew, but I realized that I actually hadn't seen very much of it. I could tell people about the Hall-of-Fame, the Baseball Wax Museum (although I had never gone inside), Doubleday Field, the shops, and the Short Stop Diner where Dad and I always stopped for a milkshake and fries. But that was about it.

I was in no rush to get inside the baseball museum. First of all, I wasn't quite sure what I would do with the ashes. Secondly, it was almost evening. My visit to Howe's Caverns added time to my journey, and I had driven slowly. Unlike my father who never got lost, I missed the highway exit for Cooperstown, distracted by a daydream about a red-haired girl, a hill, tall grass, and... well, I won't comment on the status of those overalls. I walked past the formerly magnificent old library then stood in the shadows of the Hall-of-Fame. But rather than crossing the street to visit this hallowed ground, I headed toward the shops and restaurants. I wanted to experience the town. I wanted to find out what else I had missed on those previous visits. I would visit the baseball museum tomorrow.

I walked down the main street, meandering into stores and looking at the many items for sale. I had no desire to purchase anything. One store was advertising that baseball's all-time hit king, Pete Rose, was coming in a few days to sign autographs (for what seemed an exorbitant cost). Rose, of course, was permanently ineligible for the Hall-of-Fame, despite his many records and accomplishments, due to problems he had with gambling. I thought it was sad that Pete Rose felt compelled to come to the shadows of the museum he had been barred from, just to sell his signature.

I made my way down to Doubleday Field, a small stadium built on the spot where legend has it the first game of baseball was played. I know the story is pure fiction, but I revel in it anyway. Doubleday Field was originally erected in 1920 with a wooden grandstand, but that was replaced by a concrete and steel edifice in the late 1930s. From the outside, it is a simple orange brick structure with a red brick entrance and a green roof. Really, Doubleday is less a stadium and more a striking grandstand that provides shade for the only public parking lot in Cooperstown. I overheard some tourists reading out loud from a guide book that the ballpark could seat almost 10,000 spectators. I found this surprising. It didn't seem that big to me.

Most often the small stadium is open to the public, so I went inside and sat on some bleachers and looked at the empty field. There were a few other people doing exactly what I was doing—enjoying the view, the history, and the myths and fables of Cooperstown on a warm August night. "So this is where baseball was invented..."

I was enjoying the solitude as I pictured my dad's favorite players running out to the field.

"...at Third Base, Rico Petrocelli..."

"...in Left Field, Ted Williams..."

"...and now pitching, Luis Tiant."

A woman and a man entered the grandstand trailed by three elementary-school-aged boys all somewhat frazzled and disheveled. It was apparent that, after a day of exhibits and too many gift shops, the children were over-stimulated. They broke my tranquility by running through the ballpark stands—chasing, laughing, and screaming at each other. The father looked to me like a caricature of Jackie Gleason. I tried not to be bothered by his obnoxious children by thinking of the old *Honeymooners* television show that is still shown in reruns on our local cable TV channel.

My favorite *Honeymooners* episodes were the ones with Ralph Kramden, played by Jackie Gleason, getting himself into trouble for one reason or another. There was one episode where he was forced to fight a large man named Harvey. Another time, he tried to sell a junky kitchen appliance on live television. I laughed to myself as I thought of the lines from those episodes. I had seen so many reruns that I had memorized them. Mom used to love that show, which is how I got hooked on it too.

The episode I thought most about that evening, though, involved an old cornet that Ralph could no longer play. In that episode, Ralph talked about how he never hit the high note— with the small instrument or in his life. Thinking about this, he became determined to be successful. He began by taking stock of himself.

Sitting in Doubleday Field, I decided to take the advice of an out-of-date television character and consider my good points and my bad points similarly to what Ralph Kramden had done. I need not bore anyone with all the details. In short, I was proud I was a teacher. I was proud of my honesty and discipline. I was excited (and a bit frightened) to be preparing to run a marathon. I was able to list far too many flaws I saw in myself, but there was one I kept coming back to: as much as I did not want to admit it, I was lonely.

I realized that much of my life was spent alone. I had friends, of course, though few who I felt truly close to. I had companionship, but I didn't have a companion. I didn't even have a friend who would travel to Cooperstown with me. Not that I asked anyone, but still...

I put my hands together in what some might consider one of baseball's chapels, and prayed to God and Jesus...and my father.

"Dad, I miss you. I have been missing you for a long time, since I grew up, and you grew old. But having an old dad around, even if all we did was sit on a small porch in an assisted living facility, was better than having no dad around. I always enjoyed our Fathers' Day tradition of having a catch. In the beginning you had to support me, and in the end, I supported you. It's the circle of life, I guess. Dad... I don't know why I am here in Cooperstown. I don't know why I am doing this—or why you're asking me to do this— or why you ever thought this was a good idea. I am glad I can visit these places again, but it's not the same visiting a place when you have no one to share it with. Since I am doing this for you, so that you rest in peace in a variety of places (though I don't really know what else you have in mind after this), I am hoping you can do me a favor—help me find what I am looking for on these journeys. I'll help you rest in peace and you can help me live in peace."

I ended my prayer and slowly looked up. I'd like to say that the red-haired girl from Howe's Caverns was sitting beside me, but that would have been too easy. My dad didn't work like that, and I suspect, neither does God. I looked around and realized I was alone. The loud family had left. The other visitors to the ballpark had departed as well. By now it was night, and the sky had grown dark. I looked up to the bright stars (we don't have stars like that at home) and walked back to my car.

Though I had my tent in the trunk, I figured it was too late to find a campsite and I was not confident enough to set up my tent in the dark anyway. Instead, I drove out to a Best Western and paid what I felt was too much money for a small room. (*Dad, I'm definitely billing you for this.*) I brought up my bag, but left the urn in the car.

The Yankees were playing on ESPN that night. I put the game on, but I drifted in and out of sleep and don't recall much past the fourth inning. I believe that the Yankees were winning when I finally turned the television and the lights off.

–14–

And so I came to my crossroads. It was time to confront this first last request of my father's. Afraid of being seen, I parked on a side street a mile north of the Hall-of-Fame. If there is one good thing about being a runner, it's that no parking space is too far away. I could jog to the Hall-of-Fame, if I wanted to, in less than ten minutes, or I could walk and still be there rather quickly.

But, first I needed to be alone. This side street, about a mile from the museum, seemed like as good a place as any to deal with Dad.

After looking up and down the street for any people passing by, I climbed into the back seat with the urn and my father's ashes. I was fearful of opening the container. I had a sense of what the ashes would look like, but I was still worried that they would smell. I didn't know if I could handle an awful smell. I was also having trouble wrapping my head around the fact that the pile of dust in the container had once been Dad's body.

I needed to get the ashes into a plastic baggie so I could carry a small amount into the Baseball Hall-of-Fame. But I also needed to be careful so that I did not spill the ashes all over the inside of my car. I was certain that no part of my dad wanted to spend eternity in the upholstery of a cheap old Dodge.

As I prepared to open the urn, I had another crazy thought. I remembered the closing scene from *Raiders of the Lost Ark* when the Nazis opened the Ark of the Covenant and their faces melted off. I was prepared to fulfill the first of my dad's wishes, but I wasn't ready for my face to turn to jelly. This was a plain ceramic vase, not the holder of God or his commandments—but the thought still made me shudder. Buck up, Sam, I told myself. I couldn't take any ashes with me if I didn't look at them.

I slowly opened the urn, and, to my great relief, it wasn't a big deal. The ashes weren't much different, if at all, than those from a fireplace or camp fire. I held the urn in one hand and gently poured a small amount of these powdered remains into the baggie. I didn't know how much of my father to bring, but I figured I better be safe and take only a small amount. I started to imagine a never-ending series of "adventures" and panicked when I thought I might run out of ashes. I imagined someday meeting my father in Heaven and having him scold me, "You couldn't even bring me to the last few places because you poured out too much in Cooperstown? My last wishes... you couldn't help me out with my last wishes?"

An eternity is a long time. I didn't want to spend mine feeling guilty.

I placed the top back on the urn and put the urn back in the box in the back seat of my car. I carried a small part of my father's remains, in a bag, in my pocket, walking down the street to the Baseball Hall-of-Fame.

Back when I was a child, I was certain that I was going to be a Major League baseball player and I was just as confident that my career would end with my own induction into this esteemed and hallowed ground. I imagined feeling at home here strutting through the halls like this was my building. I smiled now as I realized that although many greats are pictured on the plaques on the wall, and many others are memorialized forever in the museum, no one to my knowledge is buried in the Hall-of-Fame itself. However abstract and strange this was, my father, or at least some part of him, was going to remain, forever, in this shrine to baseball. My dad would be the first and only person who rested for eternity in the Baseball Hall-of-Fame.

All I needed to do was figure out where to put him...

I walked through the glass doors of the large brick building and paid my admission at the counter. A guide gave me a detailed map of the museum. As a seasoned visitor, I didn't feel I needed the map, but I noticed that the interior had been remodeled since I had last been there. I saw that the historical displays were housed on the upper floors so I made my way up the stairs.

A docent, an elderly man who looked a lot like the former New York Met Ed Kranepool, approached me at the top and gently touched my shoulder.

"Hi ya, young man," he said. "Would you like to join the Hall-of-Fame as a contributing member?"

"No, thank you," I answered.

"It's a good deal," he persisted. "If you join today, you get a book that contains the statistics of every Hall-of-Famer and this nice print of Lou Gehrig delivering his farewell speech."

"It's nice, but I'm not interested today."

"Alrighty, thank you anyway. If you have any questions, I'm also here to help."

The only question I had was whether this old fellow really was Ed Kranepool. Maybe retired players come to the Hall-of-Fame to work, I reasoned, even though I knew that wasn't true.

The first room I entered had large display cases with items from the beginnings of baseball's history—old uniforms, baseballs, large bats, and tiny gloves. I particularly liked the little head coverings that were the first ever baseball caps. I continued along, following a chronological tour though baseball history, and soon I was in the 1920s surrounded by a plethora of items celebrating the great Babe Ruth. I lingered there for a while.

Since Ted Williams began playing in 1939, with a career that lasted until 1960, I knew I'd be seeing his artifacts soon, and as I turned a corner, there they were. Ted's locker from Fenway Park was on display, and his Red Sox uniform, number nine, was hanging on a hook in the locker behind a wall of glass. I saw the bat he used to hit over .400 and the glove that he wore in the outfield even if he wasn't remembered much for his fielding. I even came across a life-sized statue of Ted taking his legendary swing. My father never specified in the letter where he wanted his ashes, he only asked to have them with "ol' Teddy Ballgame." It was my job to figure out where to put them.

I glanced through my museum map and considered all of the locations and options that I had seen. I then wandered into the actual Hall-of-Fame Gallery, a long, high-ceilinged room with black marble pillars and panels of honey-colored wood. This is the most sacred ground in the building. It is where the baseball legends who are enshrined in the Hall-of-Fame have their bronze plaques hanging on display for all to see. Only the greatest in baseball history have plaques in the Hall-of-Fame Gallery. Dad and I used to playfully argue over some of the selections.

When I was a child, Dad would hold my hand and guide me around the sparkly white and black floor pointing out the plaques of famous players. "Here is Babe Ruth, the Sultan of Swat," he'd say quietly. "No one hit like the Babe." Or "Willie Mays, the Say Hey Kid." My father took pride in knowing each player's unique nickname as well as their legendary feats. I held my breath in reverence.

Once, when I was about fourteen years old, and thinking I knew as much about baseball as my dad, he made a friendly bet with me. He challenged me to find a player named "Ducky" in the Hall-of-Fame Gallery. I argued with him and said that his challenge was ridiculous. "There is no way there is a famous player named Ducky," I remember telling him. "Maybe in Disney World, but not here." When he insisted, the bet was on! I scoured the room, reading as much as I could, but I never found the player. "You tricked me," I said to Dad. "There is no Ducky in the Hall-of-Fame." With that, my father took my hand and walked me over to the plaque of Joe "Ducky" Medwick of the St. Louis Cardinals. Darn, I hated it when my dad was right.

Leaving my memories behind, I made my way to the wall that held Ted Williams's plaque. I had, of course, seen this before, but never quite in this manner. I looked the bronze bust of Ted Williams right in the eye and then read the highlights etched in raised block letters on the plaque itself:

THEODORE SAMUEL WILLIAMS
"TED"
BOSTON RED SOX
BATTED .406. 521 HOMERUNS.
MOST VALUABLE PLAYER 1946 & 1949.
PLAYER OF THE DECADE 1951-1960.

I touched the plaque. I looked around. I wasn't the only one doing this. Many people were touching plaques. I remembered visiting Abraham Lincoln's burial site on one of our family vacations and listening to the tour guide telling us that people would rub the nose on the bronze Abe Lincoln statue for good luck. Maybe it was the same here—people believing that good luck would rub off on them if they touch the plaques of baseball's immortal players. There is something inherently human about the need to touch things in order to develop closer relationships with them.

With so many people immersed in their own thoughts and private journeys, I figured that my task would not be so challenging. I reached into my pocket, pulled out the baggie, and covertly poured the ashes into my hand. I didn't take all of them. I looked around again. Each visitor was immersed in his or her own special world. There was a child nearby walking in circles, a middle-aged man and woman holding hands and reading the plaques one-by-one, and a man, probably about thirty-five, sitting at a small easel, painting a watercolor of the room. No one was watching me. Though I was surrounded by people, I was alone.

I said a silent prayer and wondered if, in the grace of Heaven and God's love, Ted Williams was right next to my dad watching me do this. I sprinkled the ashes on the thin ridge along the top of the plaque—a small pile, if it could be called that, or rather, a dusting, probably unnoticeable. With the residue on my hand, I touched the likeness of Ted Williams and carefully outlined his face with my fingers. I was certain a small, if microscopic, part of the ashes would find a final resting place somewhere in the plaque.

My father never played Major League Baseball. He never hit .406 or clubbed any home runs, but a part of him, maybe more than any ballplayer ever, now resided, forever, in baseball's Hall-of-Fame.

I stepped back and looked, one last time, at the Ted Williams plaque. I would never look at the Hall-of-Fame the same way again.

I still had a small handful of ashes in the baggie in my pocket, but I couldn't think of any other place to leave them. Then, as I walked behind the gallery, I saw a sort of statue garden through the large floor-to-ceiling windows. Standing sixty feet and six inches apart, the distance of a pitcher's mound to home plate, were statues of Johnny Podres, a pitcher, and Roy Campanella, his catcher. The pitcher's statue depicts Podres in delivery immediately after releasing an imaginary ball. This ball is traveling, for all eternity, toward the catcher.

Although these players had been Brooklyn Dodgers, I reasoned that my father wouldn't mind playing ball with them. My mom had been partial to the Dodgers. I headed outside with the intention to place some of my father's ashes in the batters' box, so that he could be part of this game forever.

I was disappointed to find that the home plate for this set-up is surrounded by ornamental bricks. I hadn't seen that at first. Sometimes I don't notice obvious things. But I didn't want to just toss these final Cooperstown ashes in an area where they'd blow away with the first gust of wind. Then I noticed, close behind Campanella, the catcher, a tree and a bench. If my dad couldn't be batting, he could certainly be on-deck or watching close by. I emptied the rest of my father's ashes from the baggie right into that garden area. Because they played in different leagues, I don't think Ted Williams ever came to bat against Johnny Podres. I guess my father wouldn't either.

My hands were now clean, as was my conscious. I had done a good thing. As I walked slowly away from the Hall-of-Fame, back to the main street, tears came to my eyes. I wondered when I would be back. I wondered if I would ever have a son to share this place with and tell him stories about Mickey Mantle, Joe DiMaggio, Ducky Medwick, Ted Williams, and of course, his grandfather.

I looked down the main street, toward the shops and children with their dripping ice cream cones. If they saw my tears, their parents would wonder what was wrong with me. I walked in the opposite direction, away from the town, and toward my car.

I didn't hate this task any longer. I wasn't angry any longer. I was, though, ready to head home.

I drove straight back from Cooperstown. The ride took forever and didn't take any time at all. I did not stop for gas, or food, or anything. I don't remember the highways, except going through the toll plaza in Central Valley, New York. I never turned my radio on. I didn't miss the sports talk. I didn't miss the music. I didn't even miss my iPod.

Once home, I took out an old Wiffle Ball bat and a bucket of Wiffle Balls. Standing in my backyard where home plate used to sit, I softly tossed ball after ball into the air, and batting left-handed as Ted Williams did, tried to hit as many as I could out of the yard and into the woods that rested on the edge of my property. These woods were the old right field porch. Many an imaginary fan cheered me from the grandstand out there.

I hit quite a few out. I kept swinging until it got dark.

And then, in the solitude of my back-yard, I quietly circled the bases in my homerun trot.

–15–

It soon became apparent that Mr. Stevens had more clients than just my dad. The day after returning home, I called his office to see if I could get an immediate appointment so he could provide me with the next letter from my father, but Mr. Stevens had no free time on his calendar to meet with me that quickly. Mr. Stevens's secretary scheduled an appointment for early the following week.

My favorite movies of all-time are the *Rocky* films. This is one passion that my father did not share with me. He didn't follow boxing; in fact, he hated it. Although I didn't fight, I always related on a personal level to the character Rocky Balboa. I think the first time I ever ran was after watching Rocky train in the first movie. Even as an adult, I continued to watch these movies for inspiration. The idea of pushing one's own boundaries always motivated me, but especially now as I prepared for the marathon. Just like Rocky, when he goes the full fifteen rounds, all I wanted to be able to do was go the distance.

Having a few days to kill, and not yet in the right frame of mind to head to my classroom (although the school year was inching ever so close), I took out my *Rocky III* DVD. I figured the movie might pump me up for a good long run.

One good thing about living alone is not having to live by anyone else's schedule or have anyone judge you for your choices. On this day, my movie watching turned into a double feature of *Rocky III* and *Rocky IV*. It was only after Rocky defeated the great Russian fighter Ivan Drago, that I went out for my run.

It takes a lot for a runner to forget a bad run like the day I stopped at the Audubon Society followed by my long and emotionally tortured walk home. I calculated the miles online and saw that it had been a good eight miles, but I wanted to run even further to be ready for the high miles I would have to cover in September and October. I wanted to have a successful long run without any walking as part of the experience.

I was battling plantar fasciitis, or as I liked to say, "The pain in my... foot." I then realized that throughout the entire trip to Cooperstown, my foot never ached. I had no pain. But of course now, as I prepared for what I hoped would be a good long run, my foot throbbed.

Is there more to pain, I wondered, than just the physical nature of it? Was some part of pain, at least on some level, not physical, but mental? Was I really injured, or was this only in my head? I knew there were times, after all, when I fought through a tired period and managed to run farther or faster than ever before. Ed, the running priest, would sometimes remind me that the pain we feel is a way we deal with stress, angst...and grief.

I did miss my dad.

To prepare for the run, I stretched and rolled my foot on a racquetball. The good thing about this injury was that as blood started flowing to the heel, the pain subsided. At least a little. It was only after the run that the pain set back in. Although sometimes, of course, the heel just hurt no matter what.

I began with a couple of loops around the neighborhood,

which included some hills, before heading out of my comfort zone. The toughest hill in the area is on Goffle Hill Road in the town of Hawthorne (a town more of an undershirt community even than Midland Park). I made my way there slowly, knowing that the ten-mile mark was waiting on the top of this two-mile incline. On this day, I had my iPod, and I kept skipping songs until I reached one that would keep my focus on the long climb. About a third of the way up, I found a song by Queen, *Don't Stop Me Now*. It was the perfect elixir. As the song neared its conclusion, the top of the incline was in sight. I imagined the drivers being amazed at seeing me cresting this leviathan. As I neared the top the hill, lungs heavy, thighs burning, I reached for the back arrow to play the same song again. Upon reaching the crest, I saw a side street, a continuation of this never-ending hill, called Cider Mill Road. I veered off course to conquer this new challenge. The road led to yet another hill, which led to another—a dead-end called North Highcrest Drive. Higher and higher I kept climbing past houses and driveways and cars, presumably parked with their emergency brakes on. A man stopped planting flowers to look at me. In spite of the fact that I could barely breathe, I smiled at him. This was impossible, but with Queen blaring in my ears, the song now on its third, or fourth, play, I pushed, dug deep, and made it to the top. I had defeated this paved mountain and regained the confidence I lost on my previous run.

Standing at the top, disappointed that there was no great view since I was surrounded by the houses and trees that make up suburban New Jersey, I patted my soaking shirt. Then I ran my damp hands through my hair and thrust my arms and fists into the air as a champion might. I wanted to capture and hold this moment forever. In spite of myself, I screamed "DRAGO!" at the top of my lungs.

If anyone heard me (I was too far away from the gardening man) they would have thought I was crazy.

But, if they had seen *Rocky IV*, they'd understand.

The run home went smoothly. Once I was on flat ground, my legs and breath fell into a steady rhythm, and my mind drifted pleasantly. If I felt this good on marathon day, maybe it wouldn't be so bad after all. I passed the Sheffield's house, I hoping to see my new friend Ray with the ball-throwing daughter, but he wasn't out, and I wasn't stopping.

–16–

As soon as Michael and Melissa, the M & M kids, graduated from high school, they left home and never looked back. It seemed as though they couldn't wait to get out of there. As a kid, only seven years old when Michael was eighteen, I felt abandoned. I didn't understand why anyone wouldn't want to live at home forever.

Sometimes Michael would have a catch with me or Melissa would indulge me in a game of War or Go Fish, but for the most part, they had their own lives. It seemed like they were always at friends' houses or school events, and it would only be me, Mom, and Dad at the dinner table. I thought that maybe as I grew up, the differences in age would become less obvious and we'd be better friends. It didn't happen. Now they live too far away. We never became particularly close. Still, I felt I should call my siblings to provide an update on my first adventure and the tasks my dad, our dad, set before me.

I wondered why they didn't call me, but I figured our relationships were like that. They probably each expected me to call them first, and when I didn't, they probably just shrugged it off.

I didn't know who to call first, so I dialed my brother.

"Lo?" (If my father had a way of drawing out his phone greetings, my brother's phone demeanor was abruptly different. It seemed he didn't even have time to fully say "Hello.")

"Hey Michael, it's Sam…your brother."

"Sam, I know you're my brother. Why do you always talk like that?"

"I don't know."

"Well, how are you? Is everything ok?"

"It's good. It is quiet out here without Dad."

"Yeah…I miss him too. I called him about once a week. The

other day I reached for the phone, but..."

"You know that Dad is sending me on a bunch of trips to scatter his ashes all over the place."

"Yeah. I know."

"It's kind of strange, isn't it?"

"Yeah. Dad, was, you know, unique. A true romantic, if you will. It's not really out of his character."

"But why me... or why just me?"

"Well Sam, you do live closer. Arizona isn't exactly next door. I can't fly out all the time to do stuff like that. You have a different job, it's easier. Teaching allows you more time. I have a lot of things to do during the summer."

"I have things to do too."

"Sure. But, I mean, it's different. Anyway, there's another reason why he picked you, and not me or Melissa."

"What do you mean?"

"The dad you knew and the dad I knew were two entirely different people. When I was born, and then Melissa, Mom and Dad were just staring out. They didn't have much. Mom worked, on and off, in a dry cleaner, and Dad was working three or four nights a week at Carnegie's Men's Fashions after teaching all day," Michael sighed.

"The Dad I knew, he was always tired. He wasn't always happy and he often felt humiliated. Do you remember the Mc-Gregors? They owned the real estate place in town. They had about fifty kids I think, something like that. I hated them all. Mr. McGregor was a stuck-up son of a bitch. Whenever he'd go into Carnegie's, he'd have Dad wait on him and say rude comments to him. He'd say, 'You play with my kids all day and then at night you get to serve me. You help me dress nice because in my job it matters to look good. You have to look nice to sell houses, unlike your job, if you can even call that work.' Stuff like that. It would burn Dad up."

"I never knew about that," I said.

"You knew a different dad than I did," Michael repeated. "The dad I knew had a heart but it was often obscured by the fact that he was tired and angry." He paused.

"I remember you wrote me a letter once. You must have been ten or twelve, I don't know. You told me that Dad had shown you a special grip to throw a better fastball. You told me that you and Dad played catch almost every night.

"Damn, Sam. I don't think I ever played catch with Dad. I never had a catch with Dad. A new special grip? I never knew any grip."

I bit my lip and looked outside the kitchen window to the backyard where Dad had taught me to play ball and felt the stab of guilt that I believe Michael intended to deliver.

"The dad you knew had achieved some level of satisfaction with life," Michael explained. "He had some financial security. When Grandma and Grandpa passed, he inherited a little money. That made a difference. He started to travel with you and Mom. You guys had fun. I never got to have that kind of fun. Disney World, come on. Not for me. I never got those memories. I was so damn jealous of you—my little brother."

"Look, Michael..." I began, but he wasn't finished yet.

"The dad you knew and the dad I knew was the same person Sam, but, in a way, they were really two different guys. He was a good dad. He worked hard for us. I miss Dad. I miss a lot about him. But I resent that I never knew *your* dad. I never knew that guy. It's okay that you are going on these adventures. I don't need to."

By now Michael's voice was high and tight. I didn't know what to say.

"Dad did it right. He sent Melissa and me the money we get. I can think of him when I'm in my new car. Did I tell you about my Lexus? Anyway. He still wants to play with you."

Those words echoed in my ears.

"He still wants to play with you."

–17–

I didn't call my sister.

–18–

My next meeting with Mr. Stevens a few days later was shorter than our initial get together. He listened intently as I shared my adventure, then apologized for his brevity, explaining that he had another client but had made the time to meet with me because he wanted to hear how my experience went, and more, give me the next letter.

Not wanting to repeat my previous performance in the parking lot, I waited until I arrived at home before reading the letter. This time I would do my crying in the privacy of my own home.

Dear Sam,

If you're reading this, I am going to have to assume that you returned from Cooperstown. I hope you found the Hall-of-Fame enjoyable. My favorite memory of our trips there was seeing you laugh as you watched Who's on First in the small theater in the basement of the museum. I still laugh when I think about that skit.

I must say it's strange writing these letters to you knowing that when you read them I'll be gone. I don't ever want to die—but I trust there is a Heaven and, God-willing, I'll be there watching you as you read this. I'll also be with your mother. I love you, son, but I miss her greatly.

I don't want to trouble you with too many places to visit, but I am hoping that you leave a little part of me at the Lincoln Memorial in Washington, D.C. I know you love history so this task shouldn't be too much trouble.

I hope for your sake—and the sake of our country—that America has another leader like Lincoln soon.

It would be an honor to spend part of my eternity with Honest Abe.

Be safe.

Love,

Dad

–19–

Washington, D.C. is about five hours south of Midland Park. I knew I could get there, do all needed, and be back in a day or two. Washington also has a thriving running community, so I figured that I would be able to meet one of Dad's last requests and still cover some miles in my Nikes. In fact, the thought of running around the monuments in Washington greatly enthused me. I didn't have a long run scheduled until the weekend, so I resolved to head to D.C. then. I even planned ahead and booked a hotel room. Since it was Labor Day weekend, it wasn't easy to find a room, but I finally found a vacancy at a Marriott in Foggy Bottom just north of George Washington University. It would be less than a mile from my hotel to the Lincoln Memorial.

The school year was fast approaching, and I knew I had been putting off setting up my classroom for too long already, so I told myself I would be productive before the trip. Some teachers seem to be able to walk in on the first day and hit the ground running, but I think they are the exception. I need a few days, at least, preparing at the school. I always enjoy redecorating my classroom. I take down some old posters and add a few new ones, ideally with themes that relate to popular culture (to get the students' attention) but that also tie into history. Movie posters with historical themes like *Gladiator* are always a big hit. I want the students to be excited when they enter my classroom. Every year I hope to be every student's favorite teacher.

It's a simple goal. I am motivated to be the best.

At the school I met a new teacher, a young woman, Beth, fresh out of college, who would be teaching in the sixth grade. She was quite pretty, with short brown hair and a blue floral shirt that matched her eyes. Wanting to be a good colleague, and make a new friend, I offered to help her hang the posters she was laying out on the desk tops. She looked down at the posters and smiled. "Oh, thank you," she said. "That's very kind, but I think I can handle it." I watched her climb on top of a small cabinet to hang a poster that read "You Are Responsible For You." She seemed to have it all under control.

After some small talk, as I turned to leave her classroom, she called, "My fiancé is coming later and I'd like you to meet him." I told her it would be a pleasure, but I felt a sudden emptiness in my gut. I sometimes have these crazy hopes that the next pretty girl I meet will actually have an interest in...me.

I was certain this fiancé was a hulking man who was also extremely wealthy but I didn't have a chance to meet him. After hanging a few posters in my own classroom (I also had a poster that read "You Are Responsible For You," but at this point, I did not feel like hanging it), I left the building and went out for lunch. I had every intention of returning, but didn't.

For lunch, I drove through McDonald's. I ordered a plain hamburger and was livid when I realized, after I drove away, that there was melted cheese all over the patty. I refused to eat it. My lunch thus consisted of soggy fries and a watered down Coke. To at least feel productive, I visited a teacher store and picked up a game about the Electoral College that I hoped would help make that topic interesting. I also bought a few hundred reward pencils and small erasers. The store even had a new selection of posters depicting Charlie Brown and his friends from *Peanuts* along with motivational messages. I bought almost every one— except the poster of Snoopy that began (in capital letters at the top) "YOU ARE RESPONSIBLE..."

As I was driving home, an old friend, Dan, called. He was going to be at TGI Friday's shortly to have a few snacks and drinks and he invited me to join him and some other people. I immediately agreed. I didn't ask, but I hoped his cute neighbor would also be meeting us there. I was at the restaurant within twenty-five minutes.

I'm not the best drinker. I don't always hold my alcohol well. Drinking tends to make me blubbery and vulnerable, especially when I am feeling lonely—which was definitely the case on this night. But, sometimes, you have to live life and see where it leads.

Before that night, I had never had a Manhattan. I always thought Manhattans were an old person's drink. Maybe they are. But, for whatever reason everyone in the group was having them—including some girls I sort of knew. I joined in on the fun. I figured that a drink or two wouldn't hurt. Besides I was running so much, and I was so strong, that I assumed I could tolerate whatever quantities of alcohol we were consuming.

We stayed at Friday's for hours. The empty glasses piled up. One girl, Jennie, stayed close to me and laughed whenever I said a joke. She was slightly taller than me, with dirty blonde hair, a smattering of freckles on her nose, and a trim figure. (I could tell because she was wearing a tight purple top.) Jennie's sapphire eyes seemed to follow me wherever I would go. When I came back from the rest room, she immediately made room in a booth for me to sit next to her and her right hand found its way to my left knee.

As members of our group began departing, it was obvious that I was in no condition to drive my car. I wasn't the only one. One of my smarter friends, John, a guy who didn't drink that night, offered to drive some of us home. Jennie invited me to stay at her place. She said her roommate was out (she shared an apartment in Little Falls) and there would be plenty of room. I believed that this might be just what I needed. I quietly laughed to myself as I thought of the new pretty teacher climbing on cabinets to hang posters. I didn't need her! All I was concerned with was whatever this young woman had in mind to do with me in her apartment.

We held hands in the back seat of the car as we were driven to her apartment. We laughed as she fumbled with her keys to the front door. Once inside, we sat closely on her couch and began to watch some television.

I knew it was my lucky night when she said that she was going to change into something more comfortable. As Jennie left, I saw her smile back at me over her shoulder.

I sat back a little more comfortably knowing I wouldn't have much longer to wait...

–20–

The next morning I awoke in my underwear, on the couch. I was lying under a pink comforter and my mouth felt as though it had been stuffed with cotton. I rattled my brain to remember where I was. I pictured the restaurant, the drinks, and the ride home. And there was a pretty blonde girl—what was her name? I sat with her, on this couch, watching TV. But what happened after that?

I got up and found my clothes folded neatly on a chair. I managed to pull on my pants moments before the girl came out of the bedroom in a bathrobe with her hair wet and bundled in a towel on top of her head. "Did you have fun last night?" she asked with wry smile.

"Yes," I replied. "Did you?"

"Sort of. I don't hold my drinks well. Last night I had too much."

"Me too. I'm sorry if..."

She cut me off. "Don't worry, nothing happened. After I got up to get into something more comfortable, you fell asleep. I brought out the comforter and tucked you in."

"My clothes were folded neatly on the chair."

"You must have done that."

"Are you sure?"

"Quite. You fell asleep. I went into my room, locked my door, and had a very restful night."

I sat back down on her couch, noticed the paisley design and sort of remembered contemplating all of the colors and intricate patterns the night before. I put my head in my hands and said, "I'm sorry."

"Don't be," she replied. "It's fine."

"You are coming out of the shower..."

"I'm dressed in sweats underneath this robe. I'm freezing.

I'm trying to make my stomach feel better. I don't do well the next day after drinking."

"So I had my chance and blew it?"

"I don't think you ever really had a chance," she said with a warm smile.

"But... you invited me up," I remembered her hand on my knee.

"Yes, you were drunk, and so was I, but I'm not like that."

"I'm sorry. I didn't mean to imply that." I stated.

"Well, if you like bagels, I have some. I don't feel much like eating, but I was going to force down a bagel and some coffee."

"Sure." I figured a good breakfast was better than nothing.

"How do you feel?" the girl asked.

"To be honest, pretty crappy."

"Well, it isn't what you were hoping for, but I wouldn't mind feeling lousy together with you today. We could sit together and watch TV."

She left the room and came back with a toothbrush, still in the package. I washed my face and brushed my teeth and then enjoyed (as best as I was able) a cheap, store-brand, toasted bagel.

Watching TV with a new friend wasn't what I had originally hoped for, but it turned out to be a nice way to spend the day. By early afternoon we felt well enough to order a pizza. After watching her soap opera and becoming extremely bored, not with her necessarily but definitely with the TV, I knew I was as sober as could be and determined that I should probably head home. I think she felt it was time for me to leave as well. I called a taxi to bring me back to the car I left the previous night.

As I sat in the back of the taxi, I suddenly remembered that I hadn't taken my dad's ashes out of my car when I returned from Cooperstown. It had been risky enough to leave the car overnight where it could have been towed or broken into, but how on earth could I live with myself if anything happened to the urn? The nausea I felt earlier that morning returned.

The taxi let me off at the entrance to Friday's, and I walked, with reluctant haste, to the parking lot behind the eatery. There was a ticket on my car because they don't allow overnight parking, but otherwise everything else seemed okay. The car wasn't touched. Dad's ashes were fine.

I can be a real idiot sometimes.

–21–

New Jersey is a great state. It really is, although so many people don't know it. Most people think of New Jersey the way it's presented on television: small, dirty, rude, obnoxious... To be fair, parts of New Jersey are like that, but not when you get off the highways and into the quiet neighborhoods.

New Jersey has great towns and villages and communities. The schools are terrific. (I had to say that—but it's true.) There is also always something to do. Within a few hours' drive, a person can take part in almost any activity: hiking in mountains, rafting, canoeing, visiting a city, enjoying an amusement park, or relaxing on a beach. We have boardwalks, arcades, and casinos.

New Jersey is also steeped in history—especially related to the Revolutionary War. The winters at Morristown were colder and harsher than the infamous one at Valley Forge. When George Washington crossed the Delaware, he came to New Jersey. We have an Ivy League college (Princeton) and a plethora of museums. Baseball was born in Hoboken. If you measure where she stands, the Statue of Liberty is also really in New Jersey. And we had Thomas Edison. His famous workshop was here. Just try to name a better inventor. (You can't.)

How many professional football teams play in New York City? The answer is zero. How many play in New Jersey? Two. It's true.

Frank Sinatra was from New Jersey. And Bruce Springsteen.

And New Jersey has some of the best food in the nation. There is nothing like a New Jersey bagel. Other places try to make bagels like we have in New Jersey, but they always fall short. Our pizza is also the best—even better than (most) places in New York. New Jersey sub sandwiches have no equal. We have great hamburgers and hot dogs. And, although they are now harder to find—I'd put some of our small ice cream parlors on par with any, anywhere.

Further, it's my humble opinion that there is no ice cream as good or better than Peppermint Stick (with chocolate sprinkles) from Van Dyk's Ice Cream in Ridgewood, New Jersey. Van Dyk's is a small ice cream parlor that consists of nothing more than a counter. There are no chairs or tables inside, so people buy their ice cream and sit outside the building on a stone wall or stand around, with ice cream dripping off their cones and over their fingers, next to their cars. Van Dyk's has been there for decades. Thank God. There's nothing quite like their ice cream—especially their Peppermint Stick ice cream.

During my childhood years we visited Van Dyk's often. On one occasion, I asked for Peppermint Stick, but to my deep shock, they were all out. I so had my heart set on Peppermint Stick. I refused to eat any other ice cream. They had Chocolate Chip, and Chocolate Chip Mint ("It's even green, like your favorite color," my mother said) and Cherry Vanilla. As much as I liked those other flavors, on that day, I only wanted Peppermint Stick. I refused every other flavor and sat, sad and angry, on the steps outside the ice cream parlor while the rest of my family enjoyed their own cones. I seem to remember Melissa eating her cone particularly slowly that night. I was proud of myself for standing on principle. Even though I didn't know that phrase, I did know what I was standing for:

"This Ice Cream Parlor Should Never Run Out of Peppermint Stick Ice Cream!"

I remember, on the way home, asking if we could stop at Baskin Robbins. (I had stood my ground, but now I wanted ice cream.) My parents refused. My mom gave me a cinnamon graham cracker when we got home. It was a small consolation.

Anyway, there is a lot to love about New Jersey.

But there is one thing I do not love about this state: the New Jersey Turnpike. And, in order to get to Washington D.C., you have no choice but to take the New Jersey Turnpike.

–22–

Car packed and Dad's urn tucked carefully into the box behind my seat, I headed out on my journey to Washington, D.C. The bulk of my travel would be on the dreaded Turnpike.

I love to travel, and I love to drive. But I hate the Turnpike. One reason: the road is boring. And endless. Eternal. When I am on the Turnpike, I never feel like I am making any progress. Plus, for reasons I do not understand, the exits on the Turnpike are confusingly numbered from 1 to 18E, which is different from every highway I know. On this trip, I would be picking up the Turnpike from the Garden State Parkway and would be traveling from Exit 10 to the end. Delaware seemed like an eternity away.

Most highways have their exits numbered at approximately the mile marker. Thus, on the Garden State Parkway, Exit 98 is about 98 miles north of Cape May, New Jersey. People from Cape May are proud to be at Exit 0. If I am traveling from Paramus (Exit 163) to South Orange (Exit 145), I know (traffic issues aside) it will take me approximately eighteen minutes to get there. The system makes sense and as I drive I can see the progress I am making. ("Hey, I'm now at Exit 151, six minutes to go.")

It's not like that on the Turnpike. Exit 7 is not one mile from Exit 8. I don't think anyone knows how far Exit 7 is from Exit 8. It's probably about seven or eight miles, maybe more. Some exits can be fifteen miles apart; others might only be a mile away. There does not seem to be any rhyme or reason for the exits or their numbers.

But that's not the worst of it. After the original construction of the highway, they have added exits. Not only is there Exit 7 and Exit 8, there are now Exits 7A and 8A. North of those exits they change the formula and have 15E, 16E, 17E, and even 18E and 18W. It is a confusing mess.

I always start to worry, "What if there is a 6A, and a 6B, and a 6C, and..." I start to think that they might never end. I think that I might never get to my destination, stuck as I would be with the endless Exit 6's.

The drivers on the Turnpike also seem to be a little more reckless. No matter how fast I am driving, people pass me going even faster. My mother used to say, "They drive like maniacs." It is disconcerting. Maybe they hate the road as much as me.

And then there are the rest stops. They are all named for famous people from New Jersey—although New Jersey's claim for some of these people's fame is tenuous at best.

When people hear the name Vince Lombardi, for example, they think of football. The Super Bowl trophy is named after Vince Lombardi because he became famous coaching a very successful professional football team—the Packers—in Green Bay, Wisconsin. Lombardi grew up in Brooklyn and later coached college football at Fordham University in the Bronx and at West Point, before working for the New York Giants. None of this has any relation to New Jersey. It is true that Vince Lombardi coached at a New Jersey high school for eight years. This is why he has a rest area named for him. Lombardi passed through New Jersey on his way to greatness.

New Jersey gets forgotten by travelers because it's a state that many people just pass though. Naming rest stops for a famous passer-by only perpetuates this image.

Alexander Hamilton also has a rest stop named after him. It can be argued the biggest role that New Jersey played in Hamilton's life was that he was shot and mortally wounded here in a duel with Aaron Burr. That is how most people associate Alexander Hamilton and New Jersey.

"Come to New Jersey where famous Americans, including the guy on the ten-dollar bill, are shot to death."

And then there is our old friend James Fenimore Cooper. Cooper was the famous author of such great works as *The Leatherstocking Tales* and *The Last of the Mohicans*. He was born in Burlington, New Jersey, where he spent exactly one year of his life. His family moved to New York State where his father, a United States Congressman, founded a town that he named after himself. That town, Cooperstown, eventually became the home of the Baseball Hall-of-Fame. But Cooper has a rest stop named after him in New Jersey.

Maybe if I become a famous author they'll name a place where people relieve themselves during a tedious drive after me. Is that really an honor? I think not.

My friends tell me I shouldn't worry about stupid things like this. They're probably correct, but thinking these thoughts helps make the time pass quicker on this endless road.

Delaware and Maryland only brighten my mood slightly. I dislike their rest stop names more than the New Jersey names. I think to myself, "They can't come up with better names than Delaware House, Chesapeake House, and Maryland House?"

Why don't they just call them Rest Areas?

I think to myself that this is one reason why I need a life companion. With no one to talk to on a long journey, I tend to get a bit ornery.

Finally, five hours after leaving my home, I pulled into the front of the Washington Marriott in Georgetown, just south of Dupont Circle. The valet asked for the keys, and for a second I panicked, wondering how I was going to get Dad out of the back seat without anyone noticing. I asked the valet to come back in a moment, secured the lid of the urn, and stuck it into my large duffle bag. Once I was safely in my room, I put the urn on top of a dresser and turned on the TV. I needed to decompress after the long ride.

After a few minutes, I felt like having a drink, although after the experience with the Manhattans, a few days ago the thought of something with alcohol still turned my stomach. I counted my change and went to purchase a can of Pepsi at the vending machine in the hall.

That bubbly caramel sweetness was just what I needed.

Sometimes it's the small things, like a Pepsi, that really brighten a person's spirits.

–23–

Washington, D.C. was one vacation spot my parents could afford while my siblings were still living at home, probably because it doesn't cost anything to walk around and look at the monuments and Smithsonian Museums. We visited numerous times. Judging by our recent phone call, though, Michael seemed to have forgotten about that.

Like most boys, my favorite Smithsonian was the Air and Space Museum. I gaped in awe at the airplanes and the rockets which seemed to be everywhere—even hanging from the rafters. Charles Lindbergh's actual plane, *The Spirit of St. Louis*, hung over the museum's entrance. I wished so much to climb into the plane and pretend to fly as I soared over the many visitors. Sometimes Mom and Dad would get frustrated with me because I spent too much time in the gift shop pouring over the model rockets and airplanes.

Once my parents finally dragged me away, we'd cross the mall to the Museum of Natural History, which was Melissa's favorite, or the American History museum, which Mom and Dad loved. Michael loved the Portrait Gallery best. I remember him showing me the paintings of the United States Presidents. Since Michael was so much older than me, I was certain that one day he would be the President. "When will your picture be here?" I asked him. "When I am President, kid," he said, "they'll build a whole museum just about me."

These were good memories, a special time for my family on the Mall—walking, exploring, learning, and eating soft ice cream. We had a tradition, no matter what age we were, that we would always ride the carousel. In the end, as my brother and sister stopped taking trips with us, it became only my parents and me on the mechanical horses. I wondered if my siblings missed those times as much as I did.

Most of our trips to Washington also included visiting the National Zoo—Melissa's request, I think. I wasn't really an animal lover and always wanted to rush through it. I felt there were more exciting places to visit, places with spaceships and airplanes. I did like the panda exhibit though. There was something about the pandas that brought me joy. Maybe it was the way they'd roll clumsily around on those big balls. I still can't look at a panda without smiling.

On one visit to Washington, when I was maybe nine years old, my parents were able to secure tickets for us to go to the top of the Washington Monument. We arrived there at the break of day—me still sleepy and foggy-eyed—so that we would not have to wait in a long line. My parents abhorred long lines (except, for some reason, at Disney World). Viewing our national's capital (and the Capitol Building) from the apex of the Washington Monument is a signature memory of my childhood. Up in the clouds, I felt like I was flying *The Spirit of St. Louis* above this little city, looking down at giant monuments now small enough to fit in my hands. I pretended to pick each one up and put them into my bag of toys so that I could play with them later. And then I became fascinated at how different, and yet the same, everything looked from the sky. I tried to locate places we had been and wondered if the tiny people I viewed knew that they were being looked at by me.

Dad looked out at the Lincoln Memorial and grinned. "I could stay right here forever."

We, of course, also visited each of the memorials and monuments countless times. Washington's obelisk, Jefferson's rotunda by the Tidal Basin, and the majesty of Abraham Lincoln sitting atop those steep marble stairs, they all were part of our shared experiences.

As a child I had a Kodak Instamatic camera; I think Melissa had it before me, but it may have originally been my mom's. The old thing was flat and resembled a small brick. I brought that camera on all our trips and vacations. Film may have already been a dying art, but this was my camera. Because of the cost of film and developing, I was very selective with the photographs I took, always trying to capture the perfect scene. Unlike my parents who took photographs of our family at the various vacation spots, I pointed my camera toward landscapes or buildings. My childhood photographs are a collection of structures, statues, waterfalls, and the like. My family members didn't make many appearances. In any case, the developed photographs that came from the Instamatic camera were always a disappointment. The subjects seemed distant and never matched the hopes that grew inside my mind as I pressed down the shutter. As a young teen, I longed for a high quality camera that would allow the pictures in my head to become tangible: printed glossy remembrances of the places and events of my life.

I never got that camera.

–24–

I understood exactly why my father wanted some of his ashes to be left in Washington, and I agreed with his thoughts. The nation's capital is a good place to spend an eternity.

I got up from the hotel bed where I had been laying on my back drifting in and out of sleep. I was not at all nervous about leaving Dad's ashes this time. Sprinkling a handful at the Lincoln Memorial seemed like it would be easy considering the crowds of people engrossed in their own picture-taking and memory-making. I figured that no one would notice a guy sprinkling a bit of dust on the ground.

It's strange how you can be surrounded by crowds of people and still feel lonely. Most people seem uninterested in the others with whom they are sharing time and space. People would see me at the Lincoln Memorial, but they wouldn't notice me. My cares weren't their cares. Each person at the memorial would be doing his or her own thing, living in their own worlds absent of mine.

I wondered why my dad hadn't considered Arlington Cemetery, located just across the river behind Lincoln. That would have been an even easier place to leave his ashes. First, of course, it was a cemetery! And it was so expansive. I would have been able to spread the ashes in total anonymity. If my mother had sent me on a mission like this, I bet she would have asked to have been scattered near the eternal flame that served as a tribute to John F. Kennedy at his final resting spot. She loved the Kennedys.

As I laced up my shoes, I determined that if I had the time, I would visit Arlington National Cemetery. To pay respects to my mother, I would visit the Kennedy site. I also wanted to witness the Changing of the Guard at the Tomb of the Unknown Soldier. Then I remembered that Joe Louis, the former Heavyweight Champion of the World in the 1940s, was also buried in Arlington. I wonder who or what else I might find there. After saying goodbye, again, to my father, I wouldn't mind getting out of the crowds and walking somewhere more peaceful; somewhere I could ponder life, and death, and in the quiet of eternity, hear myself think.

A short while later, ashes in a plastic bag in my pocket, I stood at the base of the Lincoln Memorial. Of the famous benchmarks in Washington, I am more partial to the Jefferson Memorial, but like my father, I always admired Abraham Lincoln. I looked up at Lincoln sitting high in his chair at the top of a long series of steps. Rocky should have trained in D.C.

Before heading up the stairs, I tried to imagine how my dad must have felt standing here with his wife and children. What lessons did he share about Lincoln or America as we visited? I know he, and my mom, were always teaching us, but on this particular day I did not remember any specific lesson or story. I wish I had.

I turned and looked at the reflecting pool and the Washington Monument off in the distance. My nephew Peter, one of Melissa's boys, once called the Washington Monument "the Big Pencil." I guess the pride I felt being part of this purely American location was lost on him. Masses of tourists crowded the pool and swarmed the steps around me. Many were in tour groups, led by someone carrying a bright umbrella or cloth flower. One tour guide waved a long stick adorned with a bowtie, high above the people's heads. Judging by the smile on that guide's face and the bounce in his step, I assumed this was a man who loved his work! Some people were rushing—others were much more reflective. Runners jogged by almost constantly, weaving in and out of the walkers. I wondered if they saw the majesty of these statues and buildings as they ran or if they were too focused on their own miles and physical struggles to notice.

Nearby, a father stood at the base of the steps with his three young sons. He was standing, but bent over with his hands on his knees so that he was about their height, and the boys seemed to be listening to him intently. Struck by his demeanor, I meandered a little closer.

"Guys, we can rush up those steps and then forever say, we saw Abraham Lincoln," the father was saying. "But, once we get there, we've reached the end of this journey. I'd rather not get there yet. I'd rather look at Lincoln from down here and create a picture that I can keep forever in my mind. Let's not rush. We will get to the top, but let's enjoy a view that most people don't take the time to ever appreciate."

I could tell that the children wanted to get to the top. They probably cared more about who could run up the stairs fastest than they did about a dead president from long ago. Maybe they wanted to get back to their hotel and the pool or the promise of an amusement park the next day. I was surprised when they resisted the urge to run and didn't talk back to their father. Instead they sat down next to him on a wall at the base of the stairs.

"When will we see the Vietnam Memorial?" asked the oldest son who looked to be about ten.

"In due time," said the father.

In my travels, with my family and alone, I always rushed each specific event—looking forward more to saying, "I did that" than appreciating what it was that I saw. I was the opposite of what this man was teaching his children.

I wanted to sit next to that dad and talk to him and tell him about my father and my journey and the ashes in my pocket. He noticed my glance and smiled at me. I smiled back. I wanted to tell him that he was an excellent father, but instead I looked down to the ground and started climbing the long stairs to the top of the Lincoln Memorial.

–25–

Of course, one can't help but be inspired—and feel mighty small—standing at the base of the statue of Abraham Lincoln at the top of that long series of stairs. I imagine that I might feel the same way, one day, standing before God. But I never pictured God being so big. Majestic, yes, but somehow I don't see God looming over me on a giant throne. I think I will feel just as small in the presence of God, but also, filled with his love and understanding, I'll feel a little more comfortable.

Not wanting to rush the moment, for me or for Dad, and maybe reflecting on that kind father at the bottom of the steps, I decided to read the inscriptions on the walls of the memorial before spreading my father's ashes. I know the Gettysburg Address by heart but forced myself to read each specific word chiseled into the wall. "Four score and seven years ago…" This took longer than I imagined. I was proud of myself for taking this time. Then I headed to the opposite wall to read the words from Lincoln's Second Inaugural Address.

As I walked to that wall, I glanced to see if the father was still talking with his children at the bottom of the stairs. He was! I was amazed at his resolve and wondered if maybe he was a little too reflective. If you loiter too long, pal, I thought, you'll never get anywhere.

I was still a little jealous of him.

As I approached the wall, I first noticed the words at the bottom right of the long inscription, the words that began the last paragraph of his address. It was the passage I was most familiar with.

WITH MALACE TOWARD NONE, WITH CHARITY FOR ALL…

I considered these words for a long moment. How many people, I wondered, did I hold resentments against? What type of malice, or spite, was in my heart? I thought of people close to me, my friends, my family members… My siblings, Melissa and Michael, were my only immediate family members who were still alive. While they had done little to reach out to me in recent years, I also hadn't done my part to build our relationships. I hadn't shared much of my life with them. I resolved to call each of them when I got back to my hotel. Maybe they would enjoy reminiscing about our D.C. trips.

I moved on to Lincoln's other words in that sentence and thought about charity and generosity. I considered ways in which I could be more giving of my time, my skills, and my money. I thought, "Can Lincoln's words, even today, help me be a better person?" I wondered if other people felt that all these inscribed words were talking to them. They were certainly resonating with me.

I continued to read the wall, scanning this engraved document for familiar words and realized that I was utterly unfamiliar with most of the rest of this speech. I searched for more familiar passages:

FIRMNESS IN THE RIGHT AS GOD GIVES US TO SEE THE RIGHT

BIND UP THE NATION'S WOUNDS

A JUST AND LASTING PEACE

I took a step back to see the wall more clearly, resolving to read Lincoln's Second Inaugural from the start, but as I tried to avoid a stroller close behind me to the left, I stumbled backwards into somebody by tripping over my own two feet. Two hands pressed on my shoulder blades and I lurched forward, trying to regain my balance as quickly as I could. My face reddening, I turned to see not a man, but a young woman with a smile on her face and her arms still outstretched.

"Excuse me," I said quickly, and in the same instant I noticed her eyes: big and brown and bright, and completely arresting.

"It's okay," the woman replied.

I blinked at her, heart suddenly hammering. She wore a kind smile and a loose Kelly green shirt. Just about my height, and I assumed my age as well, she was stunning in a way that I had never noticed or appreciated in a girl: trim but not skinny with wavy, shoulder-length brown hair that fell softly around her face. And those eyes!

I searched frantically for another line of conversation, but my brain seemed frozen. The best I could come out with was, "I apologize for tripping..."

"Really, it's okay," she assured me.

I grasped for something, anything, to keep the conversation going. "I've always been inspired by Lincoln." I blushed deeper.

"Me too," she said, turning toward the wall.

For a long moment we stood at that spot looking at that wall of words, though I could not focus my mind on a single one of them. It was as if I was looking at hieroglyphics.

"I always wanted to see this monument," she said after a while, "and I finally made it."

"And I almost knocked you right back down those steps," I returned.

After a moment, her eyes moved from the wall to mine. This woman had the kindest, most beautiful eyes I had ever seen. I didn't know what to say or do next.

"Lincoln was born on February 12," I said. She looked at me and a small smile appeared on her little lips. She glanced at the floor for the briefest of moments.

"The log cabin stuff is true. He was born in a log cabin..." words were falling from my mouth, but I wished I could stop them and just say, "You are beautiful" to this girl.

I swallowed, looked at her face, shrugged my shoulders, and just smiled at her.

Returning my smile, she said, "My name is Rachel."

No words came out of my mouth. In my head I said only one word, "Rachel."

It was the most beautiful name I ever heard.

–26–

Frantic to fill the silence, in spite of myself, I began rambling again, this time about the speech on the wall. "I like the words 'without malice' that Lincoln talked about. I helps me remember to try to be nice...you know, caring...and considerate." *Why do I sound so stupid?* I thought.

"How nice," Rachel answered. "This is my first time here. I wanted to see Washington, D.C. and just decided to come."

"Me too," I replied.

"You've never been to Washington before either?" Rachel asked.

"No, I've been here lots of times. I used to come with my dad. My whole family, in fact. But I only decided to come today."

"Alone? You're also by yourself?" Rachel inquired.

"Sort of. I didn't come to D.C. with anyone in particular. There are a few things I have to do while I'm here." I instinctively put my hand into the pocket that contained my father's ashes.

Then I noticed that Rachel was wearing running clothes— the Kelly green Reebok shirt and black spandex running shorts.

"Do you run?" I asked, already knowing the answer.

"Yes."

"Did you run today?"

"I was going to after reading about Lincoln up here. I've always wanted to run around the monuments. I bought this tour map. It seems I can run right down to the Capitol by staying on this road."

"It's very easy. You can't get lost if you stay here on the Mall."

"Do you run?" asked Rachel.

"Yeah. I run. Every single day, mostly."

I looked back up at the words on the wall. I didn't read them; I couldn't read them, but I needed a place to look. Rachel and I stood in silence for a good minute. Trying to be noble, probably truly intending to be noble, I said at last, "You know, it's always better to run with a partner..."

"Did you run today?" Rachel asked.

"No, not yet. You know, we could run together." I hoped I didn't sound like a thirteen-year-old asking a girl to a middle school dance.

Rachel smiled. "I'd enjoy that."

I had to catch my breath again.

81

Rather than just accepting my good fortune, and because I am often an idiot, I asked, "How do you know you can trust me?"

"I can see it in your face," Rachel said. "Besides, most bad guys don't spend their time reading the inscriptions at the Lincoln Memorial."

As we began to descend the stairs, I suddenly remembered my dad—his ashes in my pocket. I couldn't explain any of this to the beautiful woman walking with me. My mind racing, I thought about quickly tossing some ashes behind me, but I knew my dad deserved better. I wanted to make each of my visits special, like I had done with Dad and Ted Williams in Cooperstown.

I also didn't want to ask Rachel (I liked thinking about her name) to meet me at the bottom of the stairs. I didn't have the self-confidence to let her go away from me.

Dad, I reasoned, would have to wait. I hoped he would understand.

–27–

Deciding to postpone my private ceremony with Dad and God was an easy decision. Now I faced a harder one. I wasn't wearing my running clothes.

I began awkwardly as we descended the steps moving away from Mr. Lincoln and toward the reflecting pool. "I hope you don't mind," I said. "I swear I'm not up to anything, but my running clothes are back at my hotel. It's about a mile from here. Will you walk with me?"

I was surprised how quickly she agreed, and thought that maybe *she* was up to something. But I had a sense that wasn't the case.

As we walked, we enjoyed a pleasant "getting to know you" conversation. Rachel had a level of self-confidence and assuredness that impressed me. Before responding to any of my questions, she would pause and let a brief silence linger between us.

"So, where are you from? I'm just visiting. Do you live around here?" I asked

"Actually," began Rachel, "while I didn't grow up there, I currently live in New Jersey."

"New Jersey?" I responded.

"Yeah, it's nothing to be proud of."

"No. Wait... You won't believe this," I said. "I'm from Jersey. My whole life. I live in New Jersey."

"You do? Really?"

"Yeah. I live in a town called Midland Park. No one has heard of it. Where do you live?"

"I live in... Park Ridge."

"No way. That's like ten miles or so from me. We live ten miles away and we, umm, bumped into each other in D.C.?"

"Well," said Rachel, "you actually bumped into me."

Throughout the entire conversation, Rachel was friendly and agreeable but she also seemed to maintain control over the entire situation. She kept just enough space between us, although she didn't have to because I would never have had enough nerve to reach out to hold her hand or even brush shoulders. She set the pace; I had to walk faster than normal to keep up.

"Where did you grow up?" I asked.

"Just outside Chicago. I studied to be a teacher and after college my roommate's friend was able to help me get a job in New Jersey in Walnut Valley."

"You're a teacher?" I couldn't believe the coincidence and was afraid to mention that I was a teacher too. I didn't want her to think I was only saying things to make us seem similar.

"I was a teacher," she explained. "The district had a lot of budget problems and I wasn't rehired. I'm working as a receptionist in a small accounting office now."

"Why didn't you go back home?"

"I needed a job, and this opportunity presented itself to me." She shrugged. "They also pay pretty well."

"Doesn't your family miss you?"

Rachel shook her head. "I'm an only child, and both of my parents are deceased."

I thought of my own dead parents, but I didn't mention my crusade with Dad's ashes.

"It was easy to come to New Jersey when I was offered the chance to teach. I like it well enough. Our pizza at home is better though. Give me Chicago pizza any day over the thin stuff you serve in Jersey."

"Then you've not had the right pizza," I said teasingly. I had to defend our cultural heritage.

Rachel smiled.

I liked how our conversation centered on the smaller aspects of life. I was reminded of these types of conversations I had as a child. Because the topics were light, it was easy for me to talk freely. I also thought about skipping the run altogether and just going out for ice cream—Peppermint Stick in particular.

"So what do you do in your spare time?" she asked. "Besides running."

"I like to read and travel," I lifted my arms to take in the city around us. "I also watch baseball."

"I don't follow baseball," Rachel said. And after her signature pause she added, "But I have always wanted to."

I wondered if that was an invitation, but before I could make up my mind we soon found ourselves outside the Marriott.

This brought forth another awkward moment.

Even in my most secret thoughts or desires, I would never have the courage to invite a girl I just met to my hotel room. Some guys might be able to do that, but not me. On the other hand, I didn't want to leave my new friend alone outside the hotel or in the lobby. It would have been fine, but I was already being possessive and jealous of whomever might come and fall madly in love with her. One of my problems with girls might have been that I lived in a world of fantasies or fairy tales; in my own life, I kept waiting for magic to take place. If Prince Charming came by on a white steed, what chance would I have? And I was certain that there were a lot of Prince Charmings all around Washington ready to sweep Rachel off her feet.

"I'm a good guy, I promise," I began.

She looked at me with those soft and understanding eyes.

"You want to come up? I just got here, the room is clean. I can get my running clothes and change... in the bathroom. I'll change in the bathroom."

She said exactly what she stated earlier. "I trust you."

"Why?"

"I just know I can."

So there I was, taking a knockout of a girl up to my hotel room—with all good intentions. Still, I was taking a knockout of a girl, with a very pretty name, and other very pretty things, I imagined, up to my hotel room. I could count the number of times I had been in similar circumstances.

Zero.

We arrived at the door, and I put the room key card in the lock upside down three times (*That darn red light!*) before I finally turned the key over and we entered. I immediately moved the safety bar so the door didn't close fully. I then showed Rachel the desk chair. "Have a seat," I implored with awkward conviction.

I grabbed my duffle bag, walked as casually as I could to the bathroom, and locked the door. I didn't want to make any noise in there so I ran the water and yelled through the closed door, "Had a hotdog for lunch... just brushing my teeth." I wished that I had been smart enough to turn on the television.

I changed into my running clothes as quickly as I could. I chose my longest shorts and my loosest fitting shirt. I hoped to God that I would find Rachel waiting for me still sitting on the desk chair. I couldn't have handled it if she was on the bed.

To my great relief, she was at the desk reading a tourist magazine.

"See, it's all good," I said. "Let's go for a run."

I rushed out of the room. Rachel followed.

-28-

Over the years, I had, of course, trained with various running partners. It is a natural outgrowth of the sport. A colleague might say, "Hey want to go for a run after work?" Or I might meet a friend at the park. At times, other runners engage me during a jog and we stay together for parts of our runs. I've run many miles with other people, some of whom I never see again.

There are certain polite rules that occur when running with a partner. Pacing is the hardest. Usually one runner sets the pace and the other follows along. If the pace is too fast, or too slow, it can make the experience frustrating. There are also unwritten rules about bodily noises or needs. It is only polite to suppress any and all of these needs as best as one can.

Once, when I was training for a 10K race in Ramsey, New Jersey, another jogger came upon me and began running with me. He seemed like a decent guy. We were running on the exact course that the race would follow in a few weeks and since he had run the race before, he proved to be a good resource. "There is a steep hill around this corner," he'd say. Or, "Watch that you don't get boxed out here and pushed into those bushes." The advice he gave proved valuable, and I was enjoying our time—until he began to succumb to flatulence. The worst part was that he either ignored the problem or was oblivious to it. I couldn't wait for that run to end, and I hoped never to be caught running with that guy again.

My favorite running partner is my old friend Ed who has covered many miles with me. As a priest, Ed always brings a great spiritual aspect to our runs, which is something I cherish. He taught me my favorite Biblical passage on one particular run when I was in great pain and struggling to continue. "You'll like this Sam," he said. "*We rejoice in our sufferings, because we know that suffering produces perseverance; perseverance, character; character, hope; and hope does not disappoint us.*" He was correct; I cherish that passage. It often helps me through rough patches.

As an experienced marathoner, Ed had encouraged me to attempt to run a marathon of my own. His advice as I began my training was proving very valuable. But, like many things in my life, I never found enough time to run with him.

But as for my run with Rachel, I had already decided that I'd let her dictate the pace. The last thing I wanted was for her to think I was a show-off and run her into the ground. That wouldn't make a great first impression.

It turned out that Rachel was also training for a marathon. She had already run a few marathons, including New York City. Now, she was preparing for the Philadelphia Marathon which came a couple of weeks after mine.

"So you're a pro at this marathon stuff," I said as I stretched my calves outside the Marriott.

"Well, I enjoy it," Rachel shared. "But I'm slow. I usually run about 4:20 or so in my marathons."

"Yeah? That's not slow." I knew I would be thrilled if I broke five hours in my race. Although I had some speed, I had no idea how my stamina would hold up over all the miles of a marathon. Maybe I didn't have to worry about running Rachel into the ground after all; maybe she would try to run me into the ground. That was ok. Still, I was feeling strong and full of energy.

We began by running back to the Lincoln Memorial. This start, an easy mile or so, mostly downhill, allowed us to begin to establish a pace and a rhythm (awkward, at first) to our run. There were times when the sidewalk was crowded or there wasn't enough room for us to pass side-by-side. I always deferred to Rachel in these moments or sometimes drifted into the street to avoid stopping or bumping into people or other hazards. I've run into enough fire hydrants in my life. They are extremely unpleasant.

We planned to run out and around the entire Mall from the Lincoln Memorial to the Capitol and back, which would be about five miles. I was fortunate—the pain in my foot hadn't been bothering me at all.

To be honest, on this day, my lungs could have fallen out and I wouldn't have noticed.

Though I tried to keep my eyes straight ahead, I could not help glancing at the pretty form running beside me.

There were more street crossings than I expected on the Mall—17th Street, 14th Street, 9th Street, and sometimes we'd have to run in place while we waited for the traffic signal. Then our eyes would meet, and she'd smile at me.

I couldn't be in love—I just met the girl.

I was in pretty good shape, but Rachel was also a strong

runner and this was turning out to be anything but an easy training run for me. Rather than simply follow her pace, as I had planned, we alternately pushed one another. When we reached the opposite side of the mall near the Capitol Building, more than two miles into the run, we stopped at an ice cream truck and purchased Gatorade. Normally I wouldn't need a drink so early on, but it was hot—August in D.C. hot—and I was becoming a sweaty mess.

"Washington is a lot hotter than Jersey," I remarked.

"Or Chicago. At home, I enjoyed running by Lake Michigan. Especially in the fall—it's fantastic."

"I wish they had public swimming pools for runners to jump into."

"Well," said Rachel pointing off to the left of the Capitol building, "there is that fountain..."

I took off at a sprint toward this bubbler known as the Senate Fountain, a multi-tiered architectural marvel. Above the cascading levels was a geyser spraying clear water high into the sky. On the level below, there were numerous other little geysers each pumping the most inviting water into a picturesque spray. Rachel was just behind me. As she approached, she laughed at the little falls of water spraying through the mouths of limestone lions.

I put my hand in the basin. The cool water felt amazing. I am pretty reticent to take chances like this, but, on this day, anything seemed possible. I looked inquiringly at Rachel and raised my eyebrows as if to say, "What if?" But it was probably a good thing she just laughed, turned, and started running again. I am not a big fan of being arrested, especially in a city five hours from home.

After looping around the back of the Capitol building, we were now on Independence Avenue heading back towards the Lincoln Memorial. Off to my right I saw the top of the First Ladies Water Garden, another fountain that I longed to flop into. I was about to say that we should do something crazy, but I must have slowed down as I glanced at the fountain and Rachel got a few strides ahead of me.

"Hey! Wait up!"

As we passed the rear entrance to the Air and Space Museum, I suggested we take on the challenge of a few extra miles by running around the Tidal Basin. Rachel, strong as ever, agreed, and we jogged over the little bridge toward the Jefferson Memorial. I could have sworn when I looked at Thomas Jefferson in his rotunda that he smiled at me. I was sure glad Dad chose Abraham Lincoln's memorial, though, because had I gone to Jefferson's, I would have never met this girl.

The cherry trees we passed were well beyond their blooming season, but their reflections on the water added a soft touch and a nice contrast to all of the granite and limestone. So many memorials and monuments—Franklin Delano Roosevelt, Rev. Dr. Martin Luther King, World War II, Korea—we rushed by them all, and I didn't care. My only focus was Rachel, my heart—literally banging out of my chest—and my lungs struggling for air.

I backed off my pace for a brief moment. Rachel, seeing this, laughed and took off like a lightning bolt toward Abraham Lincoln. I resolved not to back down, partly because of pride—I needed to show what a strong runner I was—and partly preservation. I still feared that a Prince Charming might come along and take Rachel away from me in an instant.

I arrived at the stairs at the base of the Lincoln Memorial seconds after Rachel. She was breathing heavily and laughing in between small coughs.

"This is where we first met," I said. (I have a knack for saying stupid things.)

Rachel looked at her feet and probably tried to pretend that I hadn't said that.

Now what?

"I guess I'll walk you back to your hotel, or to a taxi or something," I said. "Where are you staying?"

"I didn't get a hotel yet," Rachel replied. "I drove down in these clothes."

"You are welcome to shower in my room," I said. "I'll sit in the hall and wait."

We walked to her car, a green Jeep Cherokee, a few years

past its prime, parked more than a few blocks away. Rachel took out two beach towels from the back to spread over our seats. We drove, mostly in silence, back to the Marriott where I was staying.

–29–

I'm a smart man, and I wasn't about to blow this chance at a special relationship.

Rachel took a shower in my hotel room.

I sat in the hall.

–30–

I didn't make Rachel wait in the hall while I showered. Still, I locked the door to the bathroom while I was in there. And, because I am me, I opened a new bar of soap. I had no right knowing that other bar of soap in any way.

Once I had rinsed off the sweat, toweled off (I hate hotel towels, they never get me dry), and gotten dressed in the steamy bathroom, I found Rachel sitting at the desk chair watching TV. I took a deep breath. "You want to go out to dinner?" I asked.

"Yes," replied Rachel. "I would like that."

I remembered a grand place called the Orleans House where my parents used to take us just over the river in Arlington. Its decorations were over-the-top: numerous staircases with ornate white and black wrought-iron railings leading in and out of the dining room; a life-sized tin man on the landing; hundreds of painted coats of arms in a multitude of colors; red velvet table cloths; and, the pièce de résistance, a salad bar in the shape of a large paddle wheel boat. The Orleans House was a site to see, and I laughed out loud as Rachel stood, mouth agape, at the entrance to the main room.

I told Rachel how we used to try to eat an entire Louis XIV, which was a huge cut of prime rib. I often couldn't eat the whole meal, but my dad was the "Louie Champion." He could polish off the entire cut along with the mashed potatoes, vegetables, and whatever else came forward. My dad seemed to be able to do things like this; he had a way of accomplishing unthinkable tasks. I don't know how he was able to eat that much because he wasn't a big man in any fashion.

I wondered how often men fall short when they compare themselves to their fathers. I doubted I would ever be the man Dad was.

At dinner, I told Rachel that this was one of the best days I had had in a long time and I wanted to get to know her better. I also suggested that she not leave Washington and drive home alone—especially since it was now evening. Any sensible girl would have considered me, at best, to be obnoxiously overeager, and, at worst, a conniving bastard.

But Rachel looked at me inquisitively. "I'm touched that you care so much about me," she said without any trace of sarcasm.

"I care...that's who I am," I responded. "But you can't stay in my room," I added quickly. "I don't think I could handle that." I could feel my face turning red again.

Rachel smiled. "That's fine. I don't like driving on highways at night and the thought of the trip home alone tonight was bothering me a bit."

"We can hang out in D.C. tomorrow. Maybe we can visit a museum. Then we can then caravan home together. I hate that drive up the Turnpike."

Rachel considered this for a moment. "That would be great," she said at last.

"Ok, then it is settled. When we get back to the hotel, we'll get you a room, and then we can meet in the morning. Do you like to eat breakfast?"

"Maybe we can get a bagel or something."

"I'd like that," I replied.

After dinner, it was still relatively early. I knew there were shops and boutiques at Union Station, so I suggested we take the Metro there. I figured we could walk the halls, look at merchandise, and just kill some time.

We enjoyed getting to know each other as we strolled the hallways of the old train station. We browsed in a book store and quickly found ourselves in the sports section grabbing, flipping through, and re-shelving books about running and marathoning. "I'd like to be a writer," I stated. It was the first time I had articulated this desire out loud to anyone, and I was surprised that I felt comfortable enough to do so.

After a moment, Rachel smiled and said, "The world is full of frustrated writers who never get published, but maybe you can do it." Her encouragement made me think that anything was possible.

At a card shop, Rachel purchased a Snoopy card. "It's my childhood friend Claire's birthday next week," she said. "I always try to remember her." I noticed that Rachel kept a picture of her parents in her wallet. I felt the desire to hold her, but I didn't have enough confidence to be so forward.

We perused a shop full of men's ties and marveled at the huge selection. There were even bow ties and tie sets with matching socks. The only similarity with all of the merchandise we looked at that evening was that it was priced above what I was willing to pay for any of it.

I knew Union Station had a long and storied history, but I didn't know much about this place specifically. I looked for signs or markers that helped to tell the story of Union Station, but I struck out on that. I usually love sharing historical facts, especially when I am with someone new, as these pieces of trivia always give me a topic to talk about. Trivia also helps keep discussions from getting too serious. Trivia can be trivial, and for me, that's a good thing. I wished I had some to share...

When the shops closed, we took the Metro back to Foggy Bottom and the hotel. The train was crowded and we had to squeeze in close together to make room. "Sorry," Rachel said, but I didn't mind.

And then, for the second time this Labor Day weekend, I was extremely fortunate. The Marriott had a vacancy due to a last minute cancellation, so we booked a room for Rachel in the same building where I was staying. I realized that I hadn't thought this out too well. What would she have done if we couldn't find her a room? And why hadn't I called earlier when she first decided to stay overnight?

I imagined myself sleeping in the hall.

We exchanged phone numbers, and I left the elevator for my room on the sixth floor. Rachel would be staying one floor above.

I tried to watch TV that night, but nothing held my interest. Sports one minute, news the next, even a rerun of the *Honeymooners*. I couldn't make myself care about any of it, not even baseball.

I wished that I brought a book to read, but even if I had, I doubt I would have been able to focus on it. I pictured Rachel, just a floor above me, flipping through the channels. I wondered if she was as distracted as I was. I didn't think she could be. I was the one who was desperate.

I had my iPod, but all my songs were tired. I wished I was.

It wasn't until 11:00, as I was banging my head into the pillow, that I remembered Dad. The ashes! "My God!" I exclaimed, jumping up. How had I forgotten? And how on Earth was I going to take care of my father's request?

I knew there was no way I could scatter the ashes the next day without explaining the whole thing to Rachel, and even though I really liked her, I wasn't sure I wanted to have that conversation yet. My only choice was to fulfill my father's wishes immediately. The only time I would have alone this weekend was now—in the middle of the night.

I got dressed and felt for the plastic bag with my father's ashes in the pocket of my pants. As much as I liked D.C., I wasn't exactly confident enough to walk a mile back to the Lincoln Memorial at that late hour in a city I didn't really know. I don't even like to walk around my own neighborhood late at night. So I went to the front desk and had them call me a cab.

As I waited for the taxi, I came up with an excuse for visiting the Lincoln Memorial this late at night. I figured I would tell the cab driver that I was a big fan of President Lincoln, that I had to leave early the next morning, and that I wanted to see the memorial before I flew back to California. Since this was, I would explain, my only chance to see the memorial, I would ask him to wait ("Sure, keep the meter running") while I ran up there. I was impressed with my own brilliance. In this way, the cab driver would be my bodyguard. If I got mugged at the Lincoln Memorial, he'd come looking for me...right?

It took about twenty-five minutes for the cab to arrive. I was thrilled when the driver agreed to wait for me. "The meter will run, pal," he said, "and if you don't come back, I ain't looking for ya." I hoped he was kidding about that.

The Lincoln Memorial looked majestic during the day, but with the white marble glowing against the black sky, it was even more spectacular late at night. I was surprised to find that I wasn't the only tourist visiting the memorial. There was nothing frightening about being there. My worries had been for nothing.

At the top of the stairs, illuminated by bright lights, Lincoln reminded me even more of God. I reconsidered my earlier thoughts and figured that God was at least this big and probably larger. I knelt down at the base of the giant statue, thought of Dad, and hoped Abraham Lincoln was now beside him, along with Jesus and God and maybe Ted Williams. I quietly prayed:

"Dad, oh, I'm sorry... Dear God, they say you work in mysterious ways. I want to thank you, and Jesus, for my blessings and my life and all that is good, and even for what is not good, because you understand the challenges we face...May I continue through my words and actions to glorify your name.

Dad, I am not sure if you planned all this, but today was the best day I can remember in a long time. I don't know when I have been this happy as an adult. If you had anything to do with today, I thank you—and even if you didn't, I thank you for putting me on this journey. I don't know what else you have in store for me, but this might be my last trip for you for quite some time. The school year begins next week.

As I place your ashes here at the foot of Abraham Lincoln, I pray, in your name and in God's Holy name, that a part of you remains, forever, here in Washington, D.C., where you can enjoy this city that celebrates what America is all about. I will always think of you when I visit here.

Amen."

I took the bag of ashes from my pocket and sprinkled them at Abe's feet. Maybe because I had been doing so much of it over the last few weeks, I didn't really realize I was crying. The cab driver did.

"Man, you must really like Lincoln. I never seen somebody come back to the car all crying after visiting him. Did he say something to you?"

"No," I replied. "But something did."

–31–

I woke up the next morning thinking not of Rachel, but of school. Work. My job. I felt an emotion probably common to all teachers: a sense deep in the stomach, an ache of sadness tinged with trepidation. Summer was almost over.

This isn't to say that I don't love my job. I do. It's just that the reality that summer is ending, or over, creates a feeling unlike those that I imagine are experienced in other professions. I think this is because teachers "start up" and "wind down" every year. It's like a sports season. A famed baseball writer once wrote the words, "Time begins on Opening Day." Laying in my bed and staring at the beige hotel ceiling, I realized that Opening Day was right around the corner.

Teachers switch from the calm laziness of summer to the frenetic pace of the school year seemingly overnight. Teaching, for me, and most good teachers, is a 24-7 job. I don't think many non-educators understand this. We're always planning, creating, thinking, and designing lessons. I even dream about lessons. Some mornings I get up for work after teaching a full schedule of classes in my sleep. I love my job, but during the school year it encompasses my very being.

I got up from the bed, flipped off that heavy hotel comforter, and realized that my room was freezing. I never do well regulating the air conditioner in a hotel room. I went to the box on the wall and turned off the fan. Outside the window, dawn was just arriving and the city was still dark. I knew Rachel would be asleep, but even if she wasn't, it was too early to call. 5:45 a.m. And I had slept in.

I was eager to begin my day, but knew I had to be patient. I wondered what time that father I saw at the Lincoln Memorial woke up each day. Was he like me, up and ready to move, or did he linger with a bowl of cereal and a coffee pondering the events of the day?

My thoughts drifted back to the realities of work. While I greatly enjoy the first days of school with the students, I have never relished the first "staff-only" days. I remembered the letter that had come in the mail a few days before I left for D.C. reminding teachers that the first day of school was coming. As if we didn't know. We get one every year, and it always says the same thing: "This is going to be a great year. Please join us for coffee and..." People have come to say it just like that: "Coffee and dot, dot, dot." For some reason, the whole thing annoys the heck out of me.

I hate "Coffee and..."

Labor Day is not really a holiday for me; rather, it is the last day of peace, sort of a signal that the fun is about to end, and real life and responsibility will begin anew.

I determined not to let the stress of school interfere with my day with Rachel. I hoped she was still in her room and hadn't run off without me. I looked at the clock. It was probably still too early. Would Rachel be up at this hour?

I put on *SportsCenter*, and watched two complete episodes, which are essentially repeats of one another, and eventually took a nice long warm shower. I forced myself to wait until 9:30 before calling Rachel's room.

She answered on the second ring, "Hello?"

I wish I could describe her voice. More, I wish I could describe the sensation I felt on hearing her on the other end of the telephone line. If the thought of the first day of school brought emptiness or dread, this sound brought the opposite. It was the sound of hope and warmth.

"Hi, Rachel... It's me, Sam."

"Hey," she said. "I know who you are, silly. How did you sleep?"

"Great. I slept great. I had a dream about Abraham Lincoln." *What was I saying?*

"Yeah?"

"Oh, I don't know, I'm just being silly. Ummm. How about we get started on our day?"

"Yes," Rachel replied. "I am already dressed."

I didn't know why that comment evoked another great feeling inside me, but, trying to act composed, I stated, "Me too. How about we meet in the lobby in ten minutes?"

"Sure."

I hung up the phone, grabbed my sneakers, and rushed to the lobby. I didn't even put my sneakers on until I was in the elevator.

It was a long ten minutes before the elevator doors opened and Rachel walked out. I thought of one of those trite sayings that are found on bumper stickers or in churches:

Today is the first day of the rest of my life.

-32-

Because I was most familiar with the Smithsonian's Air and Space Museum on the Mall, I took Rachel there. We wandered among the rockets and airplanes, and I felt a welcome relief from the pressure of continual conversation. Soon we were picking out our favorite airplanes in each room. As we stood on the second floor overlooking the entrance and gazing at Charles Lindbergh's *Spirit of St. Louis*, Rachel took my hand in hers. I turned and smiled at her and thought that life couldn't get any better.

I could have died of happiness at that moment. If I had, I would have wanted someone to leave all my ashes at that singular spot. No scattering required.

When I was a child, I spent a lot of time in the gift shop here looking at the various models of airplanes and rockets. I seriously considered purchasing one that day, but fortunately logic won. I may have certain skills, but the patience required to construct a scale model of an airplane is not one of them. I remembered a childhood full of fingers crusted over with model glue. Each unopened model box held the promise of a remarkable creation. In actuality, most of the models I tried to build eventually ended up in the garbage. This was one area where my father was also not much of a help.

Instead of a model, I purchased a zero-gravity pen. Supposedly this pen could write in any direction, even upside down, which was a lot better than the Bic pens I had that always gave me trouble. I figured it would also look great on my classroom desk. When Rachel left the shop to visit the restroom, I purchased a pair of rocket-shaped earrings for her.

I also bought "astronaut freeze-dried ice cream," like I had when I was a kid, and we laughed as we shared it outside on the steps of the museum.

We walked along some of the paths we had run on the previous day. It was still very hot and humid, but there was a bit of a breeze, and we weren't running, so we felt no need to jump into a fountain. I bought some hotdogs off a push cart, and we enjoyed a picnic lunch on the grass in front of the Washington Monument. We even strolled back to ride on the carousel.

As we wandered around the city and through the museums, Rachel told me more about her life. She attended The University of Illinois–Champaign, but during her sophomore year she needed to take a semester off to care for her mother who was sick with a rare form of bone cancer. Rachel's father had already passed from lung cancer brought about by his multiple pack-a-day habit of smoking unfiltered Camel cigarettes. When her mother died later that year, Rachel took her inheritance ("It wasn't much") and moved to an apartment off-campus to finish her degree. "Losing my parents forced me to grow up fast, so I never really experienced much of the college scene," Rachel explained.

When we were on the carousel, I asked Rachel if she traveled much with her family when she was young.

"About once a year we would go to Chicago to see a show or to look at the fancy stores on the Magnificent Mile," Rachel said. She looked up from the frozen mane of her pink pony. "My dad worked in a small factory, and my mom did odd jobs to make ends meet, so we didn't get out much. And they weren't well, health-wise. Once, we drove to Indianapolis to see the big car race there. That had been a dream of my father's. It was so loud... I hated it."

When she asked me the same question, I felt somewhat guilty sharing a short list of just some of the places I had visited throughout my childhood.

"You saw so much. You were lucky," Rachel said. "What was your favorite place?"

I laughed. "Was, and is. I have to admit that I can't get enough of Disney World. I guess I'm just a big kid."

"I never got there," Rachel said with a sigh. "I have never been to Disney. Maybe someday."

"Yeah, maybe someday. Adults go there all the time. You should go."

As the day began to wind down, we decided that we should tackle the highways before it got dark. I asked Rachel if she hated the New Jersey Turnpike as much as I did. She replied, "It's just a road. I don't have any feelings about it." That made me laugh. It also made me refrain from my long lecture about highway exits, toll plazas, and rest areas. Our budding relationship probably thanked me.

I didn't necessarily enjoy the ride home, but I did savor the little games we'd play in our cars, passing each other at various times on the highway and waving. Just outside of Camden, I caught Rachel's attention enough to signal that I was getting hungry. She followed me off the road at the next service area—the James Fenimore Cooper Rest Stop.

I can't say that I enjoyed the hamburgers and fries we ate at the Roy Rogers there, but I did appreciate the break from driving. It is interesting to me that I do not recall what we discussed, only that I felt completely at ease with her.

After our fast food dinner, we returned to our cars to once again speed up the eternal highway.

About an hour and a half later, we both pulled into the Commerce Bank parking lot right off Exit 160 of the Garden State Parkway.

I opened my car door and walked over to Rachel's car. She also got out and we stood uncomfortably for a moment before I said, "You know how to get home from here...right?"

Rachel smiled ruefully. "Yeah, I've been to Paramus once or twice."

I didn't try for a kiss, or even a hug. Instead I just smiled. I told Rachel that I'd like to see her again. She agreed that it would be nice to get together. I promised that I'd call her. Then she hugged me.

After our quick embrace, Rachel returned to her car. I stayed to watch her drive away.

My house seemed more empty when I arrived. I had forgotten to pick up my mail on Saturday, but the only letter in the mailbox was an advertisement from the Strat-o-Matic Game Company.

–33–

Morningside High School was the traditional location for "Coffee and...". The "dot, dot, dot" included the speeches from the administration and a host of announcements highlighting improvements to the buildings, curricular changes, and other information that, to be honest, wasn't relevant to me.

Before the speeches, the staff always had the opportunity to chat in the cafeteria over boxes of donuts, low-quality bagels, and Styrofoam cups of burnt coffee. Even though the district brought all the schools together for this yearly re-opening celebration, the teachers mainly stayed with the members from their respective schools. Over time, each school seemed to claim a different area of the cafeteria.

I grabbed a chocolate donut and stood among my fellow middle school teachers. A number of people offered me condolences on the loss of my father and expressed regret that they couldn't attend the wake. I think most of the sentiments were sincere. I have to admit, I spent most of that morning thinking about Rachel, and although I liked my colleagues, I wasn't ready to tell any of them about her yet.

"Hey!" someone called to me. "You look awful happy for the first day of work. Is today the day you get tenure?" It was George Patterson, a veteran high school teacher.

"No, I got tenure years ago," I replied.

"Well, you look abnormally cheerful."

"I just love teaching, I guess."

"Don't love it so much," Patterson said. "We don't even have a contract yet. This is an important year for all of us." He put his hand on my shoulder. "Don't be surprised if we have to put some pressure on the Board and the administration."

"I just do my job and give the kids my best."

"Well, that's fine, but don't be too gung-ho. You might be a fun teacher, and the kids might like you, but we need to really stick together and support one another this year. Having us begin the year without a contract sends a strong message that we're not appreciated."

"We'll get a contract," I said.

"Yeah? We'll see. The Board really wants to stick it to us this year. Listen, we only want to make a statement that we're not happy that the contract wasn't resolved last year or over the summer."

"But wasn't it *our* negotiating team that didn't want to meet in the summer?" I asked.

"That doesn't make any difference." He leaned in closer. "We have all decided that when the Board President finishes her speech, we will not clap. When Mary, our President finishes, though, we are all going to stand and applaud. Nothing over the top—just a little message for the people sitting up on the stage. They'll understand."

"This isn't exactly a motivational way to begin the new year."

"Just wipe that smile off your face when you go inside the auditorium. Oh, and no one is sitting in the front rows. We want to create distance—symbolic of the rift that exists between us and the administration."

"Whatever." I turned away.

I felt like a jerk following along and doing what everyone else did. The Board president actually gave a nice speech. She praised us and our efforts and pledged to resolve the contract as quickly as possible. She was still greeted with an awfully awkward silence.

Our association president then gave a long and meandering speech about salaries, work hours, lesson plans, homework, difficult working conditions, and declining benefits. She talked a lot about the state governor. She also kept using the word "respect." Not once did she mention kids. I thought the applause lasted longer than necessary when she concluded.

I was embarrassed for everyone, and even though I was an anonymous participant in the crowd, I felt humiliated. Later, as we were leaving the high school to head back to our own schools for the next round of meetings, I saw the Board President in the parking lot. I smiled at her and tried to say with my eyes and facial expression that we all didn't feel as our actions indicated.

The Board President got in her car. I was certain, as she turned to leave the parking lot and drove past me, that I saw her wipe a tear from her eye.

It was a depressing way to open the school year. I thought of Rachel. I wondered if being a receptionist in a small accountant's office was a better way to make a living.

Back at the middle school, we gathered in the student cafeteria. This was the only space large enough for the whole faculty to come together for our opening meeting with the principal. A lot of teaching is like that. We have formal meetings on small plastic chairs and benches in empty and cold cafeterias. When the new teacher I met the previous week, the girl with the fiancé, entered the room, I realized I had quite forgotten about her. Maybe it was the lighting, or her own emotions from that opening meeting, but she didn't look as happy—or as pretty.

–34–

Our first faculty meeting began with our principal, Dr. Alexander, who is a nice enough man, reading a quote attributed to Theodore Roosevelt:

"The credit belongs to those who are actually in the arena, who strive valiantly; who know the great enthusiasms, the great devotions, and spend themselves in a worthy cause; who at best know the triumph of high achievement; and who, at worst, if they fail, fail while daring greatly, so that their place shall never be with those cold and timid souls who know neither victory nor defeat."

Dr. Alexander does this every year. I happened to like the quote, but I knew that many people would laugh about it after the meeting. Dr. Alexander's statements were full of optimism and enthusiasm. He didn't mention anything about the teachers' contract.

After the Faculty Meeting, we are permitted to have an Association Meeting on "company time." This always leads to an uncomfortable pause when the principal leaves the room since he is not part of the teachers' union. Once we were left to ourselves, our building leaders applauded our actions from earlier in the day. While telling us that he could not discuss the actual negotiations, Charlie Rizzuto, a veteran teacher of over thirty years and a strong pro-union voice, stated that there was a significant gap at the bargaining table. "We have word," he said, "that the Board might be willing to come up another quarter of a percentage point for everyone, but we won't settle at that—and they haven't even offered that much yet. Rumor is that's the highest they'll go. If they are going to play hardball like that, we will have to as well."

One teacher asked what our negotiating team was willing to settle for. "Again we can't state anything as a certainty, but I would imagine that we won't settle for anything under what our colleagues in other districts got. Ridgefield Park recently settled for 2.9 percent and Fort Lee was able to get 3.1, for each of three years. We want at least that."

I hated this talk. I sat quietly as my colleagues discussed topics such as "respect." They talked a lot about wanting it. They didn't talk as much about giving it. Instead, plans and ideas were shared about how we, as an entire organization of teachers, would put pressure on the Board of Education to settle on our terms. Herb Hermanson, another long-time veteran teacher, crossed his arms and stated, "Let's go to the mattresses." In other words, no backing down. Doris Swap, the consumer sciences teacher (we used to call her class Home Economics, but the term was now passé) added, "When will someone tell Dr. Alexander that Theodore Roosevelt is dead?" and the room filled with laughter.

I resolved a few things while I was sitting there. First, I was never going to be part of a negotiation. Second, emotions were running high, so I was just going to do my job and stay quiet. Third, I reminded myself to never seek an administrative position. I didn't need this kind of grief and stress in my life. I secretly admired Dr. Alexander for his ability to stay above the fray.

As the meeting dragged on and on, I thought of all the time that was wasting when I could be in my classroom finishing preparations for the students' arrival the next day. I also thought about Rachel. The memories of our runs, the hand holding, and the hug, brought me some peace in that tension-filled room.

Finally, as the meeting concluded, we were told that we had to leave the building collectively at 3:40 p.m. exactly, the end of our contractual day. To show solidarity and strength, Rizzuto said, all the teachers would all leave together. I thought to myself, "We don't have a contract. How can we leave at the contractual time?" The logic of all this escaped me.

Nonetheless, even though I wasn't prepared for the next day, I left with my colleagues at exactly 3:40 p.m. I thought about sneaking back into the building, but after driving slowly around the block, I decided not to. I did not want to anger my colleagues. These were good people who truly cared about children and their profession. I had also heard that during the last difficult negotiation period Charlie Rizzuto had checked all the classrooms after hours to make sure no teachers were there. I did not want to risk being caught by Charlie Rizzuto.

There was, though, one risk I was willing to take. I drove to Park Ridge, bought a bouquet of flowers, found the building where Rachel lived (it was the only building on Park Avenue above a bagel store with apartments) climbed the stairs to the hallway and knocked on the door of what I hoped was Rachel's apartment. On the floor in front of one of the doors was a welcome mat with an abstract colorful design that made me recall the artist Sol LeWitt. I don't know why, but when I saw it, I was sure it belonged to Rachel.

–35–

I waited with eager anticipation for Rachel to answer the door. I hoped she wouldn't be taken aback by my unannounced visit. I also hoped to see that radiance in her eyes that had attracted me from the very first moment I saw her.

It was soon apparent that Rachel wasn't home, which, I reasoned, was probably for the better. We'd only recently met and now here I was on her doorstep. I decided to leave the flowers on her welcome mat, but I didn't know what to write on the card and was extremely thankful that whoever first thought of cards to go with flowers decided to make them so small. How should I tell a woman I hardly even knew that I was falling in love with her? I was certain that anything too serious would drive her away, so I simply drew a smile on the card and left there as quickly as I could.

As I climbed back into my car, I resolved that I should give the whole relationship a little time. I did not want Rachel to think I was coming on too fast. I'd call her the day after tomorrow, I promised myself. Besides, with the start of school I was going to be very busy anyway. Earlier in the day, when many teachers went out for a long lunch, I stayed behind and piled a multitude of teaching materials, including each child's textbook, in the trunk of my car. I still had a lot of work to do.

Sitting at my kitchen table, with the Yankees on the radio in the background, I completed some of the preparations I needed to begin the year. I dutifully wrote each child's name in the inside cover of each textbook and listed the book number next to their name on my student roster. I also completed my first week's lesson plans, which focused on the Stone Age and the birth of civilization (although I knew nobody, least of all the principal, ever read them). These tasks took all of the evening and continued well into the night. I was glad the Yankees game went into extra innings. Sometimes the players are considerate like that.

The first day with students is always a lot of fun for me. I love greeting a new class. My goal is to put them at ease, set the bar for high academic standards, establish the rules of the classroom (the most important rule being "Show Respect At All Times"), and make them laugh. I shouldn't admit this because people who don't understand me will take me less seriously as a teacher, but making the students laugh, to me, is the most important goal I set out to accomplish on that first day. I have to make them laugh, but I have to do it the right way.

I seek to make the students laugh through polite humor that brings us all up. I don't get involved in insults or making fun of others. Instead I try to find funny things in everyday life that children can relate to. I ask a lot of silly questions. Since I have been teaching for a while, I've quite perfected my polite "stand-up" routine. I call this approach "kind humor." As we practice respect, I, as the teacher, have to show the most respect. I always found that if you give respect in large doses, it comes back to you in larger doses. This was one of the important tenets my parents taught me. In order to get respect, you have to give it.

I was hoping it was the same with love. I wondered what Rachel thought of the flowers. She hadn't called me yet which made me somewhat nervous. Was it too early in our relationship to leave flowers? Was I asking too much? What was I even asking?

Eyes heavy, worn out from a whirlwind of emotions over the previous few days, I climbed into bed. I hoped I wouldn't be teaching the first day's classes over and over in my sleep.

–36–

The alarm rang and woke me up at 3:59 a.m. This pleased me. I hoped it indicated that I had slept well as I didn't wake-up prior to the noise.

Because of the pain in my heel, I had developed a routine of stretching my foot before getting out of bed so that it didn't hurt as much when I stood up and put pressure on it. A while back a friend suggested I also first step onto a pillow. That really worked. Last night, because my foot hurt before I went to sleep, I actually made a path of pillows (and sofa cushions) to walk across as I completed my early morning tasks. Not too many grown-ups wake up and play "Hot Lava," I thought. If anyone saw me, they'd think I lost my mind, but my heel appreciated the cushioning. Injuries make us do strange things.

I don't like to head outside to run when it is too dark, so I checked over my teaching materials one last time, went into my basement and lifted some old iron dumbbells, performed a few push-ups, and waited for the first sign of dawn. I was full of anxious energy. As I stepped outside, I felt the chilly air—a reminder that summer was not eternal and that autumn was coming. It always seems a little cooler in the morning on the first day of school. I went back inside and put on some light gloves and a baseball hat (I'm paranoid about being too cold and tend to over-dress)—and completed a nice easy five-mile run.

The first day of school—or as I like to call it, "Opening Day"—was successful. I began each class by seating the children in alphabetical order (this is one technique I use to get to know each child's name). Then I played the Olympic Theme on my classroom boom box, and, with an exaggerated wind-up, softly threw out a ceremonial first pitch to a student sitting in the front row. I didn't throw a baseball or anything like that, rather I threw a small squishy "stress ball" designed to look like a globe. Even if the kids missed the ball (and they never did), with the speed I threw and the softness of the ball it wouldn't hurt them. I always knew when I had an especially enjoyable class because in those sessions, the students would clap and cheer as the ball was thrown and caught. I would then go over, ask the student to stand, and we would pose for an imaginary photograph together. "This will be on the front page of the New York Times tomorrow," I'd always say.

Then I'd hold up the small globe to the class. "The world," I'd say. "The whole world, in my hand. So much has happened here. So much! There is nothing more exciting than learning about history. Some people say learning about history is boring. That's not true—and it's certainly not true in this classroom. Together we're going to explore this world. We're going to go back in time and learn about famous people and places and events. We're going to look at those events from the perspective of today's world. You think Julius Caesar doesn't matter any longer? You're wrong! He's nothing to be scared of either. What I know, you'll know, and by the end of the year you will all be historians. Just as important, we will also learn to think together. I don't have all the answers. Each of you will have some of the solutions. We might figure out ways to solve the big questions in the world of today as we learn the history and the lessons of the past." (One thing was certainly true; I had my Opening Day routine down to a science.)

I'd then toss the ball high in the air (and most often catch it), smile at the children, and make time for each of the students to tell me a little something about themselves. We'd begin the year by making personal connections. If they all seemed comfortable, and if they laughed, my day was a success.

I taught five sections of history. I went five-for-five in applauses and classroom laughs on that first day.

It was certainly not a failure day.

–37–

One of my fears in regard to my father's last wishes was that once the school year began, I wouldn't be able to give these tasks any priority. I was the type of teacher who becomes completely engrossed in his work. I spend hours planning my lessons. Every year I re-plan almost every lesson, keeping the best parts from the previous years, but always looking for new and better approaches. I want each lesson to be fresh, interesting, and exciting for the students. Because I thrive on positive reinforcement, I also want to be their favorite teacher. When the students are excited about class, I am even more energized!

I also give my fair share of written assignments because I want to get the children to think. I always try to hand back papers the day after I receive them. That's my goal, at least. It means a lot of late nights.

But this is the only way I know how to teach. I truly wondered how I'd fit my dad into this schedule. Something, I figured, would have to give.

In those first few days back at school, when I wasn't all-consumed with the process and art of teaching, my mind wandered to Rachel. She still hadn't called to mention the flowers and her silence was beginning to trouble me.

After teaching a day or two, I walked into my parents' room where I kept the urn with my father's ashes. I hadn't changed the room much since my dad had moved out. His personal effects were mostly gone, but the old furniture remained. I didn't particularly need or want these items, but since the room was unused, I didn't feel any need to redecorate. Now, for the first time, I looked around the room and wondered how else it might be used. Would I see a crib or a toddler bed in here someday?

In my solitary state, I sometimes talk to myself. I approached the urn and said aloud, hopefully to my father, "I hope you understand why I am asking you to wait."

−38−

The first few days of the school year went well. In spite of the union rhetoric, my colleagues all seemed upbeat and happy to be back with the students. That's how you can tell if your children are attending a good school—take a look at the teachers. If they are cheerful and enthusiastic, odds are they're good teachers, and they are motivating your children to learn. The staff I worked with was like this. Morningside Middle School was a great place for kids. (That's also what our slogan said— "Morningside, Morningside! A Great Place for Kids!")

To prepare for the New York City Marathon, I had mapped out a sixteen-week training program. I based this marathon program on online research and information from a few running books as well as tips from my friend, Ed. Each day's run was carefully planned in advance and each week slowly built on the progress of the week before. This detailed schedule was probably the only thing that kept me from panicking about the prospect of running 26.2 miles. Deadlines and schedules make a lot of sense to me. For example, if I am going to run 26.2 miles on the first Sunday in November, I better be able to run 20 miles the third Sunday in October. It's all about building strength, endurance, and confidence so that I will be able to complete the race.

It is interesting that most experts do not suggest ever running more than 18 to 20 miles in a marathon training program. This is especially true for first-time marathoners like me. They reason that a runner will be able to push through the last miles in the race once he gets that far. I understood the logic, but it made me nervous. I thought if I wanted to run 26.2 miles, I should run at least that, if not more, during a training run. But, the experts say that running too much can lead to injury. That's the main reason they want you to be careful not to exceed the 20 mile plateau. They want runners to be as healthy as possible when they reach the starting line. That way, if they get hurt during the race, well, at least they made it to the race, and at that point, I understood most runners can somehow finish. I hoped I was like most runners. I just wanted to finish.

I think most people who decide to run a marathon reason like I did. I was pretty sure that I'd do anything to finish. Part of the reason for this event, after all, was to see who I really was. I think runners are always asking who we really are. Maybe we use the marathon to answer questions about ourselves.

But one thing I was not excited about was "hitting the wall."

It had been described to me in various ways, and none of them sounded pleasant. In short, "the wall" is that point in a race when the runner feels like he cannot go any further. No, it's worse than that. They say it is when his whole perspective changes. The effort changes from challenging to impossible. It's the defining point in any endurance competition. Can the runner continue after exhausting every fiber of his body and going well past his emotional limit?

I hadn't hit the wall yet in training, at least not how they described it in the running books. I was concerned about how I would respond when it happened. This race would tell me, in the end, who I was.

One deadline I invented had nothing to do with running. It had to do with Rachel. Two days after I left the flowers, I still had not heard from her. I determined that I should probably wait at least another day before calling her. The waiting, I believed, was my way of indicating that I was not desperate. I also had this terrible feeling that the flowers annoyed her. Or worse, she thought I was creepy for figuring out where she lived.

If Rachel had a timetable, hers was a lot less rigorous than mine. Maybe our relationship, if you could even call it that, had already hit the wall.

What did it consist of so far? We talked at the Lincoln Memorial. We walked to my hotel and then went for a run. We took separate showers, and in trying not to "come on to her," I probably acted like an idiot. I took her out to dinner, we spent the night in separate rooms in a hotel, and then we spent the next day walking around Washington, D.C. Our time together ended with us chasing each other in our cars up the New Jersey Turnpike. After we said goodbye, I left flowers. I thought it was a start, but there wasn't much more there.

And I wasn't sure how to proceed.

–39–

The best way is often through. I decided to go right at the

real or imagined wall in our relationship. I walked outside into my backyard, sat under a maple tree on an old bench that I think had been made my grandfather, and called Rachel on my cell phone, breaking my self-imposed deadline.

I have a lot of bad traits, especially when I am nervous. One of those traits is that I talk far too much into telephone answering machines. I just don't know when to stop talking. I was frightened that Rachel would answer the phone, but I was more frightened that she wouldn't. I couldn't hang up once the machine came on; I'd have to leave a message.

I was a grown adult and once again thinking like a twelve-year-old.

After two rings, Rachel answered the phone. "Hello?"

I immediately felt the same sensation I experienced when Rachel answered the phone in her hotel room.

"Hey! Hi. It's Sam," I said. "How are you?"

After a pause, Rachel replied in a tone that sounded somewhat cold. "Fine. How are you?"

"Good. Did you get the flowers?" I was jumping much too quickly to the main point of the phone call, but I couldn't help myself.

"No."

"What? You didn't? I left flowers for you."

"I didn't get any flowers," she repeated.

"I left them at your apartment. Right outside your door. Do you have a colorful floor mat? I guessed that was your place."

"Yes, that's my mat. But no one left flowers for me."

"Rachel?"

"Yes."

I could feel my heart hammering against my chest. "I left a nice bouquet. Ummm... I didn't sign the card. It was on Tuesday... a few days ago."

"Sam, I didn't get any flowers." I sensed a smile on Rachel's face as she said this. My heart raced a little slower.

"Well, that's weird. I left you some... They were nice too. Ahhh, who cares? Anyway, want to have dinner?"

"Tonight? Ummmm... Ok," Rachel agreed. "I'm free."

"Is it ok if I pick you up in an hour or so?"

"Sure," she paused. "I am glad you called."

"Yes, me too."

–40–

After hanging up the phone, I put on some decent clothes. I don't know much about fashion, but I usually know how to dress in an acceptable manner. A golf shirt and khakis seemed to be just about right.

Since Rachel lived in Park Ridge, I thought we should go to a little Irish place called P.J. Finnegan's in Westwood, which wasn't too far away. It was a cozy place with a great deal of character—dim lighting, small wooden tables, a plethora of photos on the walls (including a picture of Lou Gehrig and Babe Ruth that I always found timeless), an engaging staff, and a good crowd, many of whom stayed at the over-sized bar at the entrance. They also had pretty good food. I had been there enough times that some of the employees seemed to recognize me. I hoped that familiarity would make me feel more comfortable.

When I met Rachel at her apartment, I handed her a new bouquet of flowers, picked up from the grocery store on the way over. They weren't as pretty as the first flowers I brought over, but they were better than no flowers at all. Rachel smiled, took the flowers, and brought them inside. I followed her in.

Rachel's place was unlike the apartments of most single people I knew. Though it was small—just a tiny kitchen and living area—it was very clean and orderly, and her furniture looked like it could be chosen from IKEA's latest catalogue of apartment living. A moss green couch and matching arm chair, a chevron-patterned navy rug, and a dining set of pale birch wood. Above the couch hung a black and white photograph of a wave crashing against a lighthouse. Off to the left was a small hallway that led, I presumed to her bedroom. I wondered how that was decorated, but I didn't dare ask.

While I was scanning the room, Rachel worked quickly at

the kitchen sink, trimming the flower stalks and putting the collection in a vase. "I love tulips and roses," she said. "You picked a great assortment of colors." She placed the flowers on the small coffee table in front of her sofa.

"You're a nice guy, Sam. Shall we go?"

I drove to the restaurant and found a parking spot about a block away. As we walked to the entrance, I reached for Rachel's hand. She smiled at me with those tender eyes.

I smiled back at the world.

I probably looked very stupid.

I didn't care.

Inside, as we made small talk at our little table, our knees almost touching, the waiter asked what we wanted to drink. I was somewhat relieved when Rachel asked for a Diet Coke. If she had ordered beer or wine or a "real" drink, I would feel like I had to also, but I'm not much of a drinker, and I was concerned about that. What guy doesn't like beer?

Following Rachel's lead, I ordered a regular Coke.

With my stomach thinking louder than my head, I requested French onion soup as an appetizer. Rachel ordered a salad.

Rachel shared that she had always wanted to be a teacher. "When I was a girl, I used to have a classroom with my stuffed animals as the students," she told me laughing. "But when I lost my job due to the budget cuts, I began to question my future. I had always been a teacher, and now I wasn't."

"I don't love my job in an office," she continued, "but I've learned a great deal about the business world. I don't know..." She took a sip of her drink and looked up at me before looking back down and fiddling with our basket of small bread sticks. "My boss is nice. He's a good guy. He sometimes makes me laugh. He employs three of us and has more than enough work to keep us all busy. One girl in the office even works evenings—filing papers, organizing reports, and answering the occasional telephone call. It's something, I guess..."

We were interrupted by a young kid who seemed to be about the age of the students in my school. "Water?" he asked.

Rachel unwrapped the small bread stick package and took

a small bite of one of them. Her eyes grew glossy. "Getting that pink slip hurt me more than I expected, I guess. I might try to get back to teaching. Well, I will, eventually, but right now I am just trying to find some stability and decide if I will even stay in New Jersey. Plus, this job pays pretty well. It beats what I was making as a teacher."

Before I could think of something to say (like beg her to stay in New Jersey), our food arrived. Rachel's salad and my French onion soup.

After the waiter set the bowl in front of me, I picked up the soup spoon and looked down at the marvelous creation. The thick cheese oozed over a huge bread crumb crowding the whole top of the crock. A bit of broth spilled over the lip onto the saucer underneath. It looked and smelled delicious, steam rising from the top. But I began to wonder how one attacks a monster like this. Pushing down on the cheese and bread would cause more soup to spill. The only way I could think to begin, which I had always done, was to start with the cheese. I realized, though, that this would mean, at least at some point, having cheese stretching from the bowl into my mouth—and would require me to pull at the cheese with my other hand. I don't think I have eaten French onion soup any other way. At some point, I always use my hands.

I was horrified as I thought of my eating habits. My mother kept talking in my head, "Don't touch your food with your hands," she said. "Don't slurp!"

I looked around and hoped to gain some expertise by watching someone with manners manage their own bowl of French onion soup. At first I didn't see anyone attempting the challenge I was about to undertake. I figured they were smarter than me. Here I was trying to impress a girl and I ordered the most awkward food ever. I finally saw a woman about our age slowly breaking the strand of cheese that stretched from her mouth to the bowl with her free hand. She was using her hands! She ate like me! That was no help; that method would not work tonight!

If I waited much longer before tasting the soup, Rachel would think something was wrong. What was I doing?

In retrospect, it probably wouldn't have been such a big

deal if I just pulled the cheese from my mouth. It would have been much preferable to spilling the soup on my lap.

Yes, almost anything would have been better than spilling the soup on my lap.

In my effort to act casually, I bumped the crock with my elbow and the soup, bowl and all, fell directly on me...

I spilled the entire crock of French onion soup in my lap!

The soup was piping hot. I yelled (only for an instant, I swear!) and several waiters rushed over with napkins and towels. I was not badly burned, thanks to my khakis, and the napkin in my lap, but I was a mess: wet, dirty, and humiliated. Through the commotion, I kept looking at Rachel for some affirmation or a sign that she didn't think I was a complete idiot, but I couldn't tell if her expression was one of shock, humiliation, or humor. I hoped for the latter.

Once the emergency restaurant rescue squad had returned to their regular duties, Rachel asked if we should leave. Putting my head down, I nodded in the affirmative. The waiter didn't even bring us a bill when I asked. I guess spilled French onion soup is free at P.J. Finnegan's. Sodas too. That's good to know.

I had an old blanket in the truck of my car. I placed that on my driver's seat and set off to drive Rachel home with one thought going through my head over and over.

"You are a failure."

–41–

This is not *that kind of story*. But, it would be wrong of me to not share at least the basics of what happened next. I want to handle this with tact.

In short, because of the French onion soup incident, I got into Rachel's pants.

As we drove home, Rachel, sensing my humiliation, reassured me. Any terse word, any rebuke from her would have crushed me at that moment. She didn't laugh at me, but she smiled—and she did chuckle, a little. She also said, "It's ok" about forty-five times. She said it enough that I started to believe her.

When we got back to Rachel's apartment, she told me that she wanted me to come up with her. Because I am a gentleman, I declined a number of times before she insisted. "You'll never get those stains out of your clothes," she said.

She brought me inside and insisted I take a warm shower. I locked myself in the bathroom and removed my soiled clothing, folding it up as best as I could (lest she think I was a slob) and leaving it neatly on the floor. She had a bottle of body wash called "Everlasting Sunshine." I thought that the body wash described Rachel exactly.

As I came out of the shower, I noticed a note slipped under the door. It read, *"It's ok. We can laugh about this. I left some clothes just outside the bathroom door."*

Laying neatly at the base of the door were a pair of pink sweatpants and an oversized University of Illinois t-shirt. I put on the clothes—yes, I got into Rachel's pink pants—and walked in to her small living room.

"Cute look," she said.

"Yeah. I'm sorry."

"Don't apologize. It was funny. Do you like my sweats? I call those my big clothes—good for flopping around in."

"I don't feel the most comfortable."

"Well, you look cute. Want to watch TV?"

And so we did. For the next few hours we watched HGTV, *American Idol*, and a few reruns of M*A*S*H (which my parents got me hooked on as I grew up) although I'm not sure either of us were paying much attention. We tried a second time for dinner, ordering Chinese delivery (no soup).

Rachel had taken my clothes and was soaking them in a plastic tub in her kitchen sink. At one point, she got up and scrubbed them with a brush. "I think I can save these," she said proudly.

I leaned back and put my arm over the top of the couch. I felt very comfortable with Rachel. We laughed, a lot. When it became time for me to go, I asked if I could try taking her out to dinner another time. She laughed and nodded.

"You should pick the restaurant, though. My choice obviously didn't work out."

"You choose," she said. "I trust you."

As I stood by her door, Rachel took my hand. I looked at her, trying to find the right words, and trying harder to breathe regularly.

"I like you," Rachel said. She squeezed my hand and gave me a soft kiss on my lips. I never felt so good and proud and wonderful in my life.

I smiled and turned away quickly lest I try for another kiss. I didn't know where that might lead me. "See you soon," I said as I opened the door and hurriedly walked out.

I had humiliated myself once that evening. I didn't want to do it twice. Real men don't wear oversized pink sweatpants. Real men also don't cry when they are kissed by a beautiful girl.

–42–

The next morning I was back at work, but my mind was far from my lessons on the Assyrians, the Babylonians, and the Ancient Persians. I was thunderstruck. I could not get the kiss out of my mind. I am prone to smiling a lot, which was a good thing in this instance because I had this stupid grin that I couldn't seem to wipe off my face.

Later in the day I looked at myself in the mirror in the men's room and had only one thought: "Pathetic." Many guys my age were married. Others were out in the dating scene, seemingly with a variety of women fawning all over them—or so they told me. Here I was, all giddy because of a kiss. A simple little kiss.

At the very end of the day, immediately after the students departed, Dr. Alexander, our principal, walked into my classroom. I was sitting at my desk preparing to read student papers and record some grades in my roster book. I always looked forward to the quiet of the "post-instructional" classroom. The contrast between the frenetic pace of the school day and the almost complete quiet after school always struck me. This was my favorite place and my favorite time to complete important work.

Because we all had to leave at a certain time, I especially wanted to make productive use of the little time I had here.

Dr. Alexander approached me and sat in a student's chair in front of my desk. The dynamic was strange. Here I was in a comfortable chair behind a desk, and there in front of me was my boss, sitting uncomfortably in a small plastic chair.

"How is it going, Mr. Holmes?" Dr. Alexander asked.

"Fine, real fine, Dr. Alexander," I replied.

"I know this contract stuff can be difficult," he began. "I want you to know that I notice all the hard work you're doing and I appreciate it."

"Thank you."

"I don't want people to get discouraged. I have been at this for a long time. These things always get settled. Sometimes it gets ugly first, but they always get settled...eventually."

"I know. To be honest, I am not all that concerned. I just want to teach."

"Well, you're one of the good ones," Alexander said. "I have seen contract talks negatively impact good people. They get angry. They get greedy. They stop doing their best."

"You don't have to worry about me, sir."

"I know. I'm simply making the rounds checking in on everyone letting them know I appreciate them and their hard work. Well, I'll get out of your hair. I'd like to see a few more teachers before they leave."

"Thanks, Dr. Alexander," I said. "Thanks for stopping in and seeing how we are doing."

−43−

I didn't get a chance to see Rachel that weekend. She had plans with her colleagues from work and tedious responsibilities like grocery shopping and paying the bills, as did I. Well, at least I said I did. (I didn't want it to sound like I had nothing to do.) But I knew things were ok with Rachel and me because she frequently texted. We shared a few e-mails and even short phone calls on Saturday afternoon and Sunday night. I began to savor the anticipation and then the delight in hearing her voice on the other end of the phone.

Something changes, though, when you receive a kiss. It's funny, when you have no opportunity to be kissed, you don't seem to miss it. But once that emotion is turned on, the absence of that tenderness can be almost devastating. All weekend I had this longing deep in my gut. I knew I needed to be with Rachel. I wanted another kiss... and another one after that!

Was I rushing it? Were my feelings truly for Rachel or was I just excited that a woman, any woman, enjoyed being with me?

I called my friend Ed. As an Episcopal priest, he had a great deal of experience counseling people in relationships. And besides, like many of my friends, even Ed, a man of the cloth, was married.

"Hey, Ed," I began when he picked up the phone. "There is this girl I really like..."

–44–

On Monday, I called Mr. Stevens's office during my lunch period to set up our next meeting. His secretary told me that there was a cancellation and he had some open time that very day at 4:15 p.m. Normally, I wouldn't make an appointment at that time because I often worked in my classroom until well past 4:30 or 5:00, but the teachers' union was still insisting that we leave at 3:40. So I was free.

I had to admit, I wasn't sure what we as teachers were trying to prove by leaving work at the earliest time permitted in our contract. Did our union think that this made us look more valuable? Did they believe the Board of Education would pay us more if we worked less? Even though many teachers brought their work home with them, including myself, I absolutely didn't like the scene we created by all walking out of the building at the same time.

I thought of all the workshops we attended on "bullying."

I wondered if we were acting like bullies—always standing together, walking out of the building as a mob. But I didn't share any of these feelings with my colleagues lest they think I was an idiot or unsupportive.

4:15 p.m. arrived and I was sitting in Mr. Stevens's office. I found I began to look forward to our chats together. He was nothing like my father—far more formal and composed—but something about Mr. Stevens still reminded me of him. Maybe it was the compassion in his wrinkled blue eyes. Or maybe it was simply a generational similarity. I liked the somewhat antiquated names Mr. Stevens called me: *young man*, *lad*, and *son*, among others. I was also struck by the way he carried himself with such confidence and authority, and yet every word he spoke was kind and considerate. I wondered if I would ever be able to command so much respect just by being present in a room.

Mr. Stevens leaned back in his leather chair and asked about my progress thus far. I told him about my trip to D.C., although I didn't mention Rachel. Before submitting my receipts, I reviewed them to make sure that I was only asking for payment for my own expenses, none of Rachel's. Mr. Stevens was a smart man; if he checked the receipts, I didn't want him to ask about the other person or think I was eating enough food for two at the Orleans House.

In our discussion, I asked Mr. Stevens how many more envelopes he had for me. I did not want to sound like I didn't want to continue this task, but, on the other hand, I wanted to know how much more was expected of me. Mr. Stevens paused and looked at me carefully.

I immediately felt that I had disappointed him somehow, and I was slightly terrified that he would scold me for asking.

Mr. Stevens got up slowly and crossed to the far side of the room where a heavy metal box sat on top of a chest of mahogany drawers. The padlock on the box seemed out of place, I thought. Were the items inside really so valuable that Mr. Stevens worried that they might be stolen? He selected a small key from a ring in his vest pocket, opened the lock, moved some papers around, and stood for a moment with his back to me. Breathing heavy,

Mr. Stevens then closed the box and returned to his seat.

"My dear boy," he said, "I know your father is asking a lot of you. And I know how it pained him to do so. There were numerous times where he told me to forget this entire idea." He paused and turned in his seat to look out the window. I followed his gaze. Once, years ago, the view from this spot may have been enjoyable. There used to be woods, and maybe the Hackensack River, off in the distance, would have been visible. Today, though, all we could see were concrete buildings, malls, cars, traffic lights, and miles and miles of asphalt.

Mr. Stevens turned to me and stated somewhat plainly, "I have six more envelopes."

I tried to imagine the places I would have to visit. "Do you know where I am being expected to travel?" I asked. I was thinking about the weekends away, the hotels, the hours alone in my car. But, still. I didn't know why I was pushing this with Mr. Stevens. I *was* grateful for Dad's thoughtfulness.

"I might, but even if I did, I couldn't tell you. Your father wanted you to find out each in its own due time."

What I said next surprised me. "Did he ever think that I might reject this plan?"

Mr. Stevens looked deep into my eyes. "No. He did not. He knew he was asking a lot of you, but he also figured you would see the joy in all of this. And he knew you would do each task. Do you know what he said? He said, 'I can trust him.' But..." Mr. Stevens stopped and turned again to the window. "There is one other envelope, the last one—I can give it to you if you decide to end this. Legally, I cannot require you to go on these quests. I can get that last envelope for you."

"No!" I replied almost immediately. "I didn't mean to say I wouldn't do it. I just was wondering..."

"I understand. He is asking a lot of you. I was afraid you might bail on this. The temptation to cash in is real. This is a most unusual situation. I am not your father; I'm only his former attorney. But don't bail," he said softly. He repeated in a whisper, "Don't bail."

I felt alone, like I drove this good and decent man away from me by showing my selfishness. Why couldn't I just let it be? I ran my hand through my hair and pinched the bridge of my nose. After a deep breath, I asked, "May I have the next envelope please?"

"Absolutely."

–45–

Dear Son,

Well, it's time for our third trip together. Thank you for being so understanding. Please know that if I was alive, I would be treasuring these moments together, just as I always did. I never wanted our good times to end. I never wanted to grow old. I don't want to die, but I guess it's too late for that.

Thank you for reliving some of our memories of baseball and our nation's capital. We had a lot of fun together. I am so proud that you became a teacher. I hope when you teach about things I taught you that you remember me. Keep me in your thoughts.

When you were little, your mom and I used to take your sister and you up to Newport, Rhode Island. I loved the shops and the salty air. I loved the mansions. Most of all, I loved the Cliff Walk. It was on the Cliff Walk that your mom and I first fell in love. It's a very special place for me.

I would love to spend part of my eternity forever looking at Easton Bay from the Cliff Walk. I hope this isn't too much to ask.

I can't imagine how much I will be missing you—all of you: Melissa, Michael...your mom. Your dear mother was the joy of my life. I know there is a Heaven—and I take comfort knowing that as you read this, I will be watching you and giving you strength. I'm sure Mom is there too, holding my hand, and watching over all of you.

With My Love,
Dad

I put the letter down on the kitchen table and sighed. It must have been so hard for my dad to write these letters. How many times had he wanted to tell me about this crazy request he had for me. I admired his strength for keeping the secret. If he had mentioned any of this when he was alive, I might have said something like, "That's crazy." Probably those words would have prevented him from ever sharing the sentiments he wrote in these letters—words from beyond the grave that he wanted me to see and I now treasured so deeply.

I wondered how much comfort it gave my father to know that I would be able to hear from him, even after he passed— that he would be able to say things to me one last time and that we would travel together, in a sense, and that I would relive old memories.

I loved the idea of going to Newport. This was another trip I could accomplish in a weekend. I was appreciating the fact that my dad had kept these destinations reasonably close to home, and I no longer felt the same hesitation I expressed in Mr. Stevens's office.

I also had someone I wanted to spend that weekend with.

It was tough for me to find free time during the week—it was turning out to be an especially busy one at school, and I needed to go to bed early in order to have the strength for my early morning runs, which were getting longer and harder. Because of this, I had arranged for Rachel and me to go out on Friday night. I decided to take a few gambles this time. I even took the letter from my dad, now neatly folded and back in the envelope, and put it in the pocket inside my sport coat that I placed, with some other dressy clothes, in the back seat of my car.

But first, I had to be a little silly.

I knocked on Rachel's door wearing her pink sweatpants and the University of Illinois t-shirt. This made her laugh. Then I went inside and changed into the "real" clothes I had brought.

Next, I brought Rachel right back to P.J. Finnegan's.

When we entered, the waiter from the previous weekend greeted us with a big smile and began clapping his hands. "I am so glad to see you! I am so glad to see you!" he repeated. He sat us immediately, bringing us to a table ahead of people who had been waiting; some, I gathered by the looks they gave me, for quite some time.

Before we had a chance to order, the waiter brought us each a glass of white wine. I was shocked when the chef came out from the back and began walking toward me carrying a large tray with a French onion soup crock placed squarely in the center.

"Don't look now," I said to Rachel.

The waiter started laughing when the chef placed the crock in front of me, and I saw that it was empty. "There is nothing here to spill," he said. "I will bring you anything you wish, sir, for you and your beautiful lady. And tonight it is all on the house."

In one of my greatest accomplishments to date, I ate the entire meal, including an order of French onion soup (I used my hands a few times to break the cheese), without making a complete mess. Rachel and I laughed a lot. At other times we sat holding hands on top of the table. I identified some of the people in the photographs and portraits around the room and quizzed Rachel to see if she could name them.

"I'll give you a nickel if you can name that guy," I said.

"Sam, you're a big time spender."

Rachel impressed me, and earned a tidy 60 cents or so, by identifying John F. Kennedy, James Joyce, Babe Ruth, Mel Gibson, Van Morrison, Jackie Kennedy Onassis, and Zooey Deschanel, among others.

The food was great. We were stuffed—and there was no bill. I left a big tip anyway.

Some people might have felt humiliated by all this. Not me.

After leaving the restaurant, Rachel and I walked down the main street in Westwood. We stopped for ice cream at Conrad's. I bought Rachel a chocolate heart as well. We held hands. At one point Rachel kissed me. Her kiss was soft, tender... and cold. I enjoyed the sensation of the cold kiss that came from the ice cream. I knew I could never get enough kisses from Rachel.

"I like you," she said.

I wanted to scream out loud, "I LOVE YOU!" but I instead, I just smiled and said, "Me too."

Across Broadway in Westwood there is a gazebo. We sat there and talked. We talked about everything, and we talked about nothing. The stars were shining; there was a soft chill in the air.

I decided to take my third gamble of the night—and planned my fourth. I asked Rachel if she would like to go to Newport with me. I even offered to get separate rooms if it made her more comfortable.

She agreed to go. When I asked if next weekend was too soon, Rachel smiled and said, "No, it's not too soon. It sounds fun. I've never been to Newport."

I had just broken out in a huge grin when Rachel added, "Can I ask you something? I saw something strange in your hotel room in Washington."

–46–

My heart nearly stopped and the grin fell from my face.

"I hope you're not angry at me for asking..." Rachel said hesitantly.

"I'll answer whatever you ask."

"You had an urn on your hotel dresser."

The fourth gamble I was ready to take was telling Rachel about my dad and his unique last requests. She beat me to it.

"It seemed," continued Rachel, "a little weird."

I had been prepared to discuss this, eventually, but now I wasn't sure where to start and Rachel, who always seems to take her time before talking was asking questions and making statements before my mind could process each.

"It looked like the one that held my mom's ashes, which was why I noticed it. At first I thought it was a strange hotel decoration but there wasn't one in my room. Where did you get it? And why did you bring it with you to D.C.?"

"To explain this, I might actually need a drink," I said.

As we were talking, the weather had turned much cooler, so Rachel suggested we continue the conversation back at her apartment.

As we walked to the car, Rachel mentioned that she didn't have wine or "anything like that," at her apartment. So on the way, we stopped at a liquor store and purchased a bottle of pinot grigio.

After we each had a glass of wine—ok, after we each had two glasses—I began.

"My Dad, in some ways, I think, he never wanted to grow up or especially grow old. In some ways, he was still a little kid, or, at least he had a kid's heart, right up to... until the day he died. A short time before he passed, I took him to meet some former Major League baseball players. He basically jumped out of the car before I even put it into park. He just wanted to play. Always."

"That's funny. I can't believe he could still throw a ball," Rachel stated.

"Oh, he could throw. He lived for playing catch. Anyway, while I know that he truly believed in Heaven and all of that, he also didn't want to leave this world. He never wanted to leave anywhere. My dad wanted to make each moment last forever and at the same time he wanted to rush on to the next adventure."

"He must have been a fun dad," said Rachel and enveloped my hand in hers.

"He was. Anyway, my dad was also an original. A true original. When he died, he left a request, a crazy request, with his lawyer. Basically, I am not able to inherit my portion of the estate until I take his ashes and leave them at various places that were special to him. I have to scatter his ashes..."

"What about your siblings, are they doing the same?"

"No, they got their portions of Dad's estate. Dad left this task only to me."

"That sounds unfair."

"Well, I have felt that way at times too, I'll admit, but this is something that he wanted me to do for him... with him. I was the last person he had at home. I get it. I don't always like it, I guess, but... I get it."

"So what did he do, leave you a long list? How many places do you have to go to?"

"Well, that's the thing. He...he didn't leave a list. I have no idea how many places I have to go to. He left a bunch of letters with Mr. Stevens, his estate attorney. Mr. Stevens gives me a letter, I leave some of my dad's ashes where he requested in the letter, and then I go back and get another letter. I assume one of the letters will tell me that I'm done."

"Who wrote the letters? The lawyer?"

"No, that's the thing," I said as my shoulders sagged and my head fell into my chest. "My dad wrote them, from the home where he lived. He wrote them to me. They don't just say 'Go to Newport,' or wherever. The letters are filled with his thoughts and memories, and, even... this sounds crazy... advice."

"Advice?"

"Yeah, let me show you." With that, I reached into my jacket and took out the last letter from my dad. I handed the envelope to Rachel who took it with some trepidation. "It's okay," I said. "I'd like you to read it."

"I don't..."

"It's okay."

With trembling hands, Rachel took out the letter and carefully opened it. I could see her reading the words, slowly, as tears welled in her eyes.

"Oh my," she exclaimed. "I can't believe he wrote like this to you. *'I'll be watching and giving you strength...'* That is, just, it's... beautiful."

I took her into my arms with tears running down both of our faces. "It's beautiful," Rachel repeated.

"If you come to Newport with me," I explained, "I'll have to bring my dad to the Cliff Walk and leave some of his ashes there. Besides that task, the rest of the time would be ours."

"Are you sure he would want me to come with you?" Rachel asked. "This seems like something he would want you to do alone."

"There is nothing I am more sure of," I stated. "My dad would have loved you. He will be glad you are joining me."

And so it was set. I would pick Rachel up at 5:00 a.m. the next Saturday morning. We would spend the day, and the night, in Newport, Rhode Island.

As we made plans, we finished the wine, I felt my head growing heavy and my thoughts fuzzy. Rachel suggested I spend the night on her couch, and I didn't argue. I was glad I brought Rachel's sweatpants back because I found I was wearing them again. Girl's pants might be cut differently, but these were much more comfortable to sleep in than khakis.

The next morning, after a small breakfast of eggs and toast, we went to the Ridgewood Duck Pond to run on the bike path for a solid twelve miles. It turned out that Rachel was as attached to running schedules as I was! The morning was cool and clear and I felt fortunate that the wine from the previous night held no lingering effects on my head or stomach. I couldn't imagine running, especially that far, with a hangover.

The Gatorade we purchased off an ice cream truck in Saddle Brook never tasted better. "I am treating you to all kinds of drinks," I said.

"Yes," said Rachel. "But, I like this better than the wine."

"Me too."

Then Rachel kissed me, holding on a little longer than ever before. When she broke away, she smiled. "Let's go, we have a lot more miles to cover."

I led the way, but we ran side by side.

-47-

After our run in the park, I dropped Rachel off at her apartment and returned home. I had to shower, of course, but I also had to clean the house. On the run, I had invited Rachel over for dinner (we'd order out), and to my great surprise and relief, she said, "Yes."

The day passed quicker than I could have hoped, although,

on the other hand, I wasn't quite ready. I didn't get the house spotless, but it was, at least, tidy. Or as tidy as it could be. In contrast to Rachel's organized and cute apartment, my décor was merely a collection of unwanted items. The sofa had been my grandmother's. Our easy chairs came from the neighbor when he remodeled. The book shelves once resided at my great-aunt's studio apartment in New York City. The books, too, were mostly hers, although I had a few. The paintings on my walls were created by family members or picked up at Sears or garage sales over the years.

As I looked at the house, I realized how cluttered it was, even after I dusted and vacuumed. I was really just residing in my parents' old house among their furniture, their collections, and their memories. I suddenly felt like a twelve-year-old secretly inviting a friend over while my parents were away at work.

I put on a false bravado and greeted Rachel at the door when she arrived. I gave her a quick kiss that she seemed glad to return.

"Nice place," she said. "It's much more space than I have."

"It's a simple little Cape. I'll get around to adding my own touch one of these days."

"Well, I like it. Do I get a tour?"

"Sure."

I gave Rachel the "Five-Dollar Tour" of my home. Five Dollar Tours were what my father considered first-class affairs. Rachel noticed a lot of things—a photo of my grandparents, the family Bible, a (dusty) collection of spoons from various tourist attractions—that went unnoticed by me in my daily routines.

"I like this picture," Rachel noted as she examined a framed photograph in the main hallway. "Is that you, out on the lake in the canoe? It's a beautiful shot. I love the coloring."

"That's actually my older brother Michael. We all love getting out on the water. I'm pretty sure that picture was taken in the Catskills somewhere."

Rachel took notice of my Strat-o-Matic baseball cards. (Why didn't I put them away in a drawer?) "Is this a game you play?"

"Umm. Yes. I don't really play. I was looking for something. A special card from... when I was a kid."

Rachel picked up the deck of Red Sox players and started reading the cards. "Is there a card for every player? Some of these guys have funny names—Yastrzemski, Conigliaro, Pesky... That's funny, Pesky. Oil Can Boyd? Was there really a player named Rico Petrocelli?"

"He was one of my dad's favorites."

"Maybe you can teach me how to play. I like board games."

"Sure. It's somewhat complicated. I played it a lot as a kid. No longer though. I would have to try to remember all the rules."

Rachel was so interested in my home that she even asked to see the basement when we passed the stairs. "This is fun. You have an interesting house, full of fun stuff and funny items." And then she said, laughing, "Rico Petrocelli."

In the basement Rachel took special interest in my father's old train layout. ("These are not mine. I don't play with trains. Really.") Over the years I had destroyed a few train villages with wayward rubber bouncy balls thrown against the basement walls, but this latest layout was intact. It was my father's last effort at creating a model train community of his own. There was a small village, an industrial center, a trestle bridge, two tunnels, and a castle.

"It's cute," Rachel said. "I like it. Although I have to say, the castle doesn't seem to fit with the whole design."

Now it was my turn to laugh. "That's my dad for you. That is Cinderella's Castle. It's supposed to represent Disney World. My dad had a collection of Disney-themed box cars too. He liked to drive them to and from The Magic Kingdom.

"Your dad must have been fun. Hey, is that your baseball glove?"

"No, that was my sister's. Mine is upstairs." I paused. "This sounds dumb, but—wanna have a catch?"

"Sure, I'll use this glove." She picked it up and turned it over. "This also has a funny name in it. Joe Rudi. I played a lot of softball when I was little, you know."

Moments later, Rachel and I were on the back lawn tossing a baseball back and forth. In my life, I had had many catches on this lawn—my imaginary baseball stadium. I enjoyed many hours of play over these blades of grass, with more people than I could count, including my dad, of course, but never had I had a catch with someone so beautiful.

–48–

Dr. Alexander was back in my classroom—this time as an invited guest to assist in the culmination activity for our lessons on the separation of powers as outlined in the United States Constitution. Our principal was serving as the President of the United States. The students, who served as the legislators, senators, and congress-people, presented bills to him that he would hopefully sign into law.

The students had been working on this project for weeks. They researched our government's structure and the legislative process and tried to get their classmates to sponsor or sign onto a bill they wrote. This powerful series of lessons was one of my trademarks—a Mr. Holmes special—and Dr. Alexander loved taking part.

A kindly older man, Dr. Alexander reminded me of how President Eisenhower might have looked had he been sitting in my classroom. He asked pointed questions that made the students think, but if they became too nervous, he released the tension with a hearty laugh. Dr. Alexander had command of the room in much the same manner as Mr. Stevens had command of his office.

The students had done well this year; most of their bills were signed into law by the "President." He especially liked the law that allowed schools to get extra funding if they met certain benchmarks that were not all related to test scores. "Now there's a group of congress-people that speak to my heart," said the principal.

As per tradition, we ended our congressional session with a lemonade party in the cafeteria. The students' parents met us there and delighted in listening to the presentations the children gave for both the new laws and the failed bills. Even the students whose bills failed (one suggested bill called for one water fountain in every school to serve soft drinks) gave enthusiastic presentations with decked-out Power Point slides.

Many parents approached me to offer their sincere thanks. "You are an amazing teacher," one parent told me. "I wish I had had a teacher like you when I was a kid."

As I passed by his office on the way to the parking lot, Dr. Alexander called out, "The President of the United States thanks you again. You always make my day with that lesson. Keep up the great work, All-Star!"

I would be heading to Newport, Rhode Island the next day sitting, in almost every way, on the top of the world.

–49–

"An awful what?

"Awful Awful."

We were standing in line at the Newport Creamery. This was the type of place where I liked to buy the drinks. Milkshakes, to be specific. And the Newport Creamery had some of the best that I knew of. They call them Awful Awfuls. They are Awfully Big and Awfully Good. I had a strawberry milkshake; Rachel had chocolate. It took her almost thirty minutes to drink hers.

"That was amazing," Rachel said.

"The best. If I lived here, I'd gain hundreds of pounds."

"No you wouldn't. I wouldn't let you. We'd run here before having each milkshake."

I laughed. "Great idea, Rachel. Now let's explore the town. After an Awful Awful, the exercise will do us well."

The Newport, Rhode Island streets and piers were humming with activity. Boutiques with ornate window displays lined the sidewalks—glassware, shirts, jewelry, and accessories galore. I tried to convince Rachel to buy a new handbag she liked, but she felt they were too pricy. The small eateries were also bountiful. As were the pubs. A few small stores sold local wines and offered taste testing. We held hands and breathed in the sea air deeply. One pier crammed with shops seemed to be still made from the original planks of wood, maybe a hundred years old. Some of the streets were cobblestone, and at one point, Rachel tripped on the uneven brick. I caught her as she fell and scooped her up, for the first time holding her entire being in my arms. I think she stayed there a moment or two longer than necessary, but I would have held her like that forever.

While we meandered in and out of the shops in the harbor area, I bought Rachel a pair of earrings made from tiny seashells from a local artisan and later, she bought me a "Life is Good" t-shirt. For dinner, we walked out of the main tourist strip to a little place I remembered, The Mudville Pub. This small alehouse had seating that overlooked the field of a semi-professional baseball stadium just off the center of town.

Holding hands on the top of the table at a restaurant was becoming one of my favorite activities. I also made it through dinner without spilling any of my food. I was getting good at this.

The October air turned chilly when the sun set, so after we left the restaurant we each bought sweatshirts. The streetlights turned on and the store windows glowed. Laughter spilled from the bars and alehouses we passed, and we looked in on residents and visitors alike sharing drinks and smiles. I felt as though I had an orb of light in my chest, warming me to the tips of my fingers, despite the cold night. I couldn't remember the last time I had been this happy. We decided to leave the Cliff Walk, and all that entailed, for the next day.

Once, when I was a kid, I found all my presents in the weeks before Christmas. My parents had tried to hide them, but I knew where to look. Some of the presents were even wrapped, but I gently peeled back the tape and discovered what was inside. When Christmas finally came, it was one of the biggest disappointments of my life. The surprise and magic of Christmas was gone. From that point on, I resolved never to rush things. Often I am unsuccessful, but that lesson was forefront in my mind as the evening advanced.

As, one by one, the shops began to close, Rachel ran ahead

of me toward a bench that overlooked the bay. I sat down next to her, and we held hands as we gazed at the dark water that shimmered with lights from the marina. A very strong part of me wanted to rush to the next step of our relationship—after all, separate rooms, or not, our hotel was just down the street. Yet much to my surprise, I was also content—content to simply allow the moment to envelope me, and us. As the moon slowly rose and glistened on the bay, I was reminded of the tranquility I find when I'm alone on the water in my canoe.

The dream that I held close inside my heart was that this special thing with Rachel might last forever. If it was to be so, I didn't necessarily want to open all my presents tonight. Although I didn't ask, and I'm certainly no prized gift, I believe Rachel felt the same way.

Maybe it's the discipline of being a runner, self-sacrifice and all that, but that night I resisted the temptation to sneak off to her hotel room, and I was happy when I finally felt myself drifting off to sleep. Somehow, even though there was an empty space next to me in the bed, I didn't feel so alone.

The next morning, Rachel and I put on our new sweatshirts and walked to the Cliff Walk. This was going to be different from the first two times I scattered my dad's ashes. For one, his instructions were less specific; it was up to me to find the perfect spot. But, more importantly, this time I had someone with me. Dad and I weren't making the journey alone.

It was about a mile's walk from our hotel to the Cliff Walk, and we held hands the whole way. If growing up means you can't feel giddy holding a pretty girl's hand, I thought, well, then I don't want to grow up. Ever. These were the moments I wanted to savor. The breeze smelled salty, and we passed beautiful houses and well-manicured lawns along the way. I don't know if Rachel would have minded if I had joined her in her bed the previous night. But this, just this, was pretty great.

We did not rush. The Cliff Walk is exactly what it sounds like, yet, at the same time, it isn't at all. One might imagine that it is a treacherous venue for adventurous travelers to explore. It's not. Yet, it's more than just a walking path. The Cliff Walk is a beautiful paved trail that runs atop the cliffs of Newport's rocky coast. In days long gone, America's wealthiest built their summer cottages here, overlooking the bay, although these were no ordinary cottages. The mansions built by the Vanderbilts and the Astors, among others, are still glorious today. Taking in the scene harkens one back to America's Gilded Age.

On this day, puffy clouds hung softly in a bright blue sky that seemed to go on forever, and the water below glistened in the early light. We passed along Salve Regina University and imagined what it would be like to go to college in a place as picturesque as the Cliff Walk in Newport. Maybe, someday, we would have children that attended this university, I thought, but I didn't say this out loud.

Rachel might have been thinking what I was thinking because she gripped my hand a little tighter and stopped walking. I looked at her, getting lost again in those eyes.

"A place like this is pretty magical," she said smiling.

I looked down at the asphalt littered with tiny pebbles and said, "You're pretty special."

"You are too Sam. I don't know any guy who takes a girl away like this, just to be nice."

"I have never met a girl a like you. This means a lot to me."

"Me too, Sam."

We meandered, sat, gazed at the horizon, and wasted away much of the day. As we passed by the magnificent cottages, we tried to pick our favorites.

"I don't know if I'd like to be that rich," Rachel stated. She sat down on the crest of a large rock overlooking the water and I crawled up next to her.

"Really? But think about how neat it would be. One of the mansions, as I recall, is called The Marble Palace. Everything is made out of marble."

"Marble can be cold. It wouldn't be comfortable watching TV sitting on a marble floor—especially in the winter."

"They didn't have TV back then..."

"Sam, I know. You don't always have to be a teacher." She looked over at me. "I'm just saying, I enjoy things that are more cozy. I don't need a mansion."

I felt a little chastised. "If I had that kind of money," I said, "I'd buy you whatever you wanted, Rachel. I'd take out the marble and install blankets and couches and pillows."

"That's sweet, but I don't need all of that. I think what we're doing, what we have here, is simpler—and nicer—than all that wealth."

Rachel had a point, but my mind wasn't on wealth or mansions, or even pillows and beds. Well, as I held Rachel's soft hand in mine, part of me was thinking about beds.

Eventually we reached a spot known as The Forty Steps, a set of concrete stairs that lead down to a small overlook above the sound. Normally the place is pretty busy, but today, amazingly, we were the only ones around. The look-out is far enough away from the most congested stretch of the Cliff Walk to be one of Newport's most tranquil spots.

"This is the place," I said to Rachel.

When we reached the bottom, Rachel took my hand. I didn't want to pull away, but I relaxed my grip and explained that I planned to say a prayer while I released the ashes. Rachel reached around her neck and removed a pendant—a cross that she wore on a chain. She placed it in my hand.

I took the ashes out of my pocket. As I poured them slowly over the ledge, into the wind and the water of the Atlantic, I looked to the heavens and said aloud,

"Dear God, Heavenly Father, and Jesus, I spread these ashes in memory of my dear departed father. May these parts of him stay here forever, enjoying the beautiful view and may these always bring my father, in Heaven, close to my mother..."

I am sure that what happened next was not planned, because if it was, I would not have had the courage, but with the cross still in my other hand, I reached for Rachel's fingers and continued,

"Dad, you brought me on this journey, I know not why, really. I do not think you could have ever imagined what I would find. I love sharing our memories—and I have found something new and wonderful. Dad, I wish you were here so I could tell you in person.

Dad...I think I am in love. I have found the most wonderful girl in the world. She's here with me, you can see her. I think she is beautiful. Thank you, Dad, for making this happen.

Thank you God for all my blessings. Amen."

I have friends who, once they mutter the L-word, immediately see their relationships deteriorate. A sane woman may have jumped at the word "love" and said, "Not so fast!" Not Rachel. She didn't say anything, but when I finished the prayer and opened my eyes, I could see that she was softly crying. I was as well, but I was used to that.

We climbed the stairs in silence, still holding hands, the cross radiating warmth between our palms. "Your father was very special, wasn't he?" Rachel said. I nodded.

We made our way to a bench not far from where we stood. We sat and talked. People say that love crowds the mind—it cleared mine.

"How many more times do you have to do this?"

"I'm not one-hundred percent sure," I said, "but I believe I have four more stops."

We looked at the sound, and the ocean off in the distance, and for a long time neither of us spoke. "I think we should probably head back," Rachel said at last. "It's starting to get later than we planned."

"Yes, we should. It's a long drive home. I feel bad, we didn't get our long run in yesterday or today."

"We could run together tomorrow."

"We could, I guess, after work. I'm not great running in the evening though. I prefer my long runs in the morning."

"Why don't we run in the morning?"

"I don't mind walking up at 4:00 a.m., but will you? And where will we meet?"

Rachel looked deep into my eyes, and a huge smile appeared on her face. She stood up and with her grin growing larger said, "This might be crazy, but how about here?"

"Here? Newport? But how?"

"We can stay one more night."

"I would have to call in sick. I have never done that before, when I wasn't sick."

"Then do it!" Rachel encouraged.

"I think you can convince me of anything," I said.

"Maybe, but for now, we better eat some carbs before our long run tomorrow."

After dinner at the same pub we ate at the night before, I sat next to Rachel at the edge of my hotel bed and called the substitute service. I was sure the quaver in my voice gave me away, but the person on the other end of the line didn't say anything. I could hardly believe that I was doing such a crazy thing. I'd be playing hooky. I was beating the system.

After I put the receiver down, Rachel moved away from me and sat at the desk chair. She started tapping her finger on the blotter.

"What's wrong, Rachel?"

"Sam, I like you a lot. A lot. I appreciate how patient you've been. But, most guys take girls away to hotels to get them into bed. That's what guys do... right?"

"Yeah. Some guys."

"Not you?"

"Not yet... I mean, ummm, no, not me."

"You've been patient with me. I like you a lot, but I've been burned a few times over the years. I'm not saying you're like those other guys, but I'm not ready for our relationship to get that serious yet. Part of me wants to, but I can't. Not yet."

"Rachel," I explained, "I'd be crazy not to want you, but I want you to respect me more than I want anything else. Besides, I think there was an article in *Runners' World* that said people shouldn't fool around before a long run."

She grinned. "I'll let you know when I'm ready. Ok?"

"It's okay, Rachel. I've never met a girl quite like you. I can wait. I didn't bring you up here for sex."

"I know."

Rachel and I both rose—me from the bed, her from the chair—and Rachel closed the distance and hugged me. After enjoying the beautiful scent of fresh air and salty water in Rachel's hair, I backed away, and, holding her with my hands on her hips,

I said, "It's time to get some rest. We have seventeen miles to cover tomorrow. I'll see you in the morning."

Following a much too brief kiss, Rachel departed to her room.

Why, I wondered, did being noble make me feel so lonely that night?

–50–

Although I don't keep the cleanest house, I do have some obsessive compulsive tendencies. I always keep important items in the same place in my desk drawers, for example, and my grade book is immaculate. I almost always return papers to the students the day after they hand them in. I submit all reports a day ahead of schedule. I keep lists of the books I read. And I record my runs meticulously in a journal. When I set a schedule for myself, I never miss a run—especially not a long run.

Sometimes this backfires on me, though, because when I know I have difficult mileage ahead of me, I can spend days worrying about it. I especially think about the weekly long run. I obsess over it. I plan the route I will take. I think about how I might feel at certain points. I calculate the distances between my water stops, and I locate places where I can buy food or drink.

I often live in fear of the long run. The night before it comes, I often go to sleep with a knot of dread in my stomach. What if I can't finish, I wonder. What if I run out of energy? What if...I'm a failure?

But, when it's all over, when I am back at my house with a glass of water, or better yet, iced tea, with many new miles under my belt, I bask in my accomplishment. I feel indestructible—even as I hobble on tired legs or an injured heel. Then I reach for my running log and immediately begin to fear the next long run.

That night in Newport, as I lay wide awake in the middle of the night, I was somewhat angry with myself for putting off my run. I knew the run had to be my first priority each weekend. If I skipped it I'd never make it through the marathon.

I told myself that I had to focus.

But, as I thought about Rachel in the room next door, probably quietly sleeping, I realized that I had.

–51–

As we stood on America's Cup Avenue and prepared for the challenge of a seventeen-mile run, I stretched my foot and worried about the temperature. This was not a typical October day in New England. It was humid and warmer than usual. Not to mention, I had never run this far before—ever.

I glanced at Rachel who was standing on one foot stretching her quad. She wore black half-tights and a bright blue shirt. Her hair was held back with a thin purple headband. I imagined that many guys would be jealous of me running stride for stride with Rachel.

There is something special about sharing a long run, as my friend Ed would confirm. When you have a running partner, you somehow become more close. I usually find that over the miles I share things that I normally wouldn't open up about. When your body is vulnerable, other walls break down as well.

When you suffer, you reveal who you truly are.

As we began our run, heading back towards the Cliff Walk and the mansions, I listened to Rachel breathing next to me. And I hoped, almost prayed (but God doesn't wish to be bothered with such nonsense), that I would not find myself mired in the hell that can accompany a long run. I didn't want Rachel to see the side of me that runners hope to never share. At the start of the run, at least, I didn't have to worry about this. I was still giddy after calling in sick to work—today was a bonus—a special holiday just for me. And I was running, far away from home—in Rhode Island no less—with the woman of my dreams.

We were about five miles into our run, at Fort Adams State Park, when we slowed our pace enough to squeeze some GU, which I had stored in my arm band, into our mouths. GU is an energy substance, a gel, with a consistency somewhat like the inside of a chocolate truffle, and during a run it tastes ok, but any other time it makes me gag.

As I handed a Mint Chocolate gel to Rachel, she said, "I love you."

"Well, thank you," I replied. "Lots of people say they love me when I give them good food on a long run. You'll love me even more when I buy you a Gatorade later."

"That's not what I mean..."

"Well," I continued, "It's, ummm, early in the run, but I'm also glad to slow the pace and get this energy too."

"Of course. But I don't care about the gel." She grabbed my arm to make sure I looked at her and said it again, only slower.

"I. Love. You. I really think I love you."

A true long run in preparation for a marathon has minimal stops. The goal is to push yourself as far as you can go. That rule went out the window.

Right there and then, overlooking Brenton Cove, I stopped, took her into my arms, and initiated the most wonderful, salty kiss I ever had in my entire life. There we were—two runners, dripping with sweat, embracing, sharing love and happiness.

"Hey," Rachel said. "We have a long way to go."

She took off at a pace I found hard to sustain, and I struggled to keep up with her. As we ran, I'd look at her and she'd look at me. I loved her eyes. I loved her smiles. I loved her form.

I was running well.

I was with a beautiful girl.

I was running when I should have been at work.

Soon I would be in the New York City Marathon.

I was with Rachel.

And she said she was in love with me!

–52–

A loud noise, probably a freight train passing on the tracks near my home, woke me from my deep sleep. I was alone in bed, and as I rubbed my eyes I was filled with the realization that everything in my life was going so well. It was early, too early, and my legs ached with the most wonderful soreness. The thoughts and memories from a most special weekend flooded my mind. I basked in the memories, not wanting the day to ever begin.

Why can't we hold special moments like these, full of reflection and hope, forever?

It wasn't until later in the day, much later, when Charlie Rizzuto strolled into my classroom breaking my special after-hours solitude that my good mood deflated. He said he wanted to provide me with an update on the lack of progress in the teacher contract talks.

As the longest-serving veteran teacher on staff and the former head of the Teachers' Association, Charlie was a powerful force in our building. His tenure dated back to the days when teachers were not paid well—at all—and had to fight at the negotiating table for every penny of compensation and every ounce of respect. It was leaders like Charlie Rizzuto in school districts across the state who had made teaching the respectable profession it had become. It wasn't easy, but Charlie was a fighter. Plus, he had credibility because he was also an outstanding teacher.

Children loved Charlie. He was the only person I knew who could quiet an auditorium of students just by walking to the front of the room. Even Dr. Alexander didn't have that kind of presence.

"We missed you yesterday at the Teachers' Association Meeting," Charlie said.

"Yeah, I was out sick," I said.

"Well, good for you. You're never absent. Those days are your right to take."

He began to tell me about the next steps our association would take to put pressure on the community, the administration, and most of all the Board of Education, to settle the contract. He explained that the association had decided that people needed to be more aware of the extra responsibilities in which teachers took part outside of contractual hours.

This was a fair point. We all worked well beyond the hours of our contractual language. We did this in various capacities:

curriculum writing, serving on committees, volunteering our time at school events, and so much more. This was all on top of the expected assignment of preparing each day's lessons and reviewing student work. I thought the union's new approach made perfect sense.

"Great, Charlie," I said. "No more leaving at 3:40. The public will see the long hours we work. They'll see us tutoring and coaching, writing curriculum and taking classes. This is what I thought we should do all along."

"No." Charlie replied. "You are confused."

"I am?"

"We are now in what I like to call Minimal Mode."

"What does that mean?"

"We will do nothing after 3:40 for the public or in the public's eye."

I tried to work through this. "Well, we are already leaving at 3:40. What does this mean?"

"Once 3:40 comes, you're done for the day—with everything. We won't respond to e-mails or phone calls. Don't hand back any papers you can't mark in school during your work day..."

"That's impossible," I stammered.

Charlie continued, "No volunteering."

"Wait, I assume you mean no more signing up for things in the future. What about the charity volleyball game next month?"

"No, we're out."

"But if we are out, who will play in support of the fund raiser?" I asked.

"Sam, that's not our problem."

"Well, it kind of is," I argued. "I don't know about you, but I gave my word I was playing. I love to play."

"Yeah, I know. You're a real jock."

"It's fun."

"That's not the point," Charlie said emphatically. "Fun or not, no one can make us do things after our contractual hours."

"No one is making me. I want to play. I like playing. I like volunteering."

"If you play, you'll be the only one." I could see the tension in Rizzuto's face as he continued. "You'll look like a fool. Plus, your colleagues will know that you don't support us. If you play, you are being selfish."

"If we don't play, aren't we being selfish?"

"No. Open your eyes, kid." Charlie threw his hands in the air. "They are messing with our livelihood. We are working without a contract. What don't you understand?"

"There's a lot I don't understand," I sighed.

"Well, you are part of an association. When you are part of an association, the association takes care of you. They are looking out for your rights, your benefits, and your salary. You weren't here before we had an association. It was rough then. We had to bargain for everything we have. We earned all our rights and benefits. The teachers that came before you paved the way by taking a stand. Now it's your responsibility to do the same."

I didn't know what to say. On many levels, he was right. "So what do we do?" I asked.

Charlie Rizzuto reached across the desk and patted me on the shoulder, "First, you need to tell Principal Alexander that you have to back out of the volleyball game."

–53–

Leaving work at 3:40 p.m. did have its advantages. I now had about four and a half weeks until my marathon, and I had decided to push hard for the first two of those weeks before tapering down. I wanted these two weeks to give me more strength and endurance and therefore resolved to incorporate "two-a-days" into my routine. That is, I would run twice each day—once in the morning and once in the evening. This wasn't part of any training plan I had read online or in a book, but I figured more miles would mean more endurance. And I was going to need every ounce of endurance I could muster. Already compulsive about my running, I was about to become maniacal.

Between the intense running schedule and the stalled contract situation at work, I no longer felt quite so lighthearted as I had in Newport with Rachel. I laid awake at night fretting about all the schoolwork piling up on my desk—that I wasn't allowed to do—and imagining nightmare scenarios regarding the marathon. I daydreamed about sweeping Rachel off her feet and marrying her, but I knew that wouldn't solve any of my problems, and anyway, it was too soon for that. A proposal might really scare her away.

When I was with Rachel, I tried to not talk about the issues at work. I did not want her to consider me a complainer or a bore, and maybe, too, I was afraid she would think me complacent for going along with every decision the union made. Backing off on my grading and after-school activities was saving me a lot of time—I couldn't deny that—and a part of me wondered if I was just giving myself an excuse to be lazy.

But not talking to Rachel about this meant I had no one with whom to share my struggles or confusion. I felt a familiar refrain in my empty heart. I wished my father were still alive. Of all people, he would know what I should do.

I hoped these "two-a-days" would help me with these tensions. It is said that running after work is a great way to eliminate some of the strain from life. "We leave our stress on the roads," someone once opined. I hoped they were right.

On the Thursday of that week, I enjoyed my first ever twenty-mile day. I woke up especially early that morning and ran twelve miles before heading off to work. Then, later that evening, I logged eight more miles. Those eight were slow and difficult, but as I pushed through, I repeated the same words over and over again: "Every step means a great deal. Every step means a great deal." It helped. When I arrived home, I collapsed with a sense of pride (and astonishment in myself) on my front lawn. A neighbor driving by stopped his car. "Are you alright?" he asked.

"Yes!" I responded. "Never better!"

-54-

As I headed into the last month of my training, I felt like a true marathoner. Rachel, the experienced one, provided me with plenty of encouragement. She was often at my side both figuratively and literally. Park Ridge was too far away for us to meet for an early morning run before work, so we enjoyed long weekend runs together instead. When we weren't physically together, Rachel sent encouraging words though texts and e-mails. Occasionally, I'd get a card in the mail from Rachel. One such card even contained the Theodore Roosevelt quote Dr. Alexander always began the year with. I was certain she was thinking of me as much as I was thinking of her.

Throughout these high mileage weeks my plantar fasciitis did not bother me any more than it had during my short runs before I started this intensive training. If we are defined by our runs, and if I was beginning to define myself as a marathoner, I was starting to consider myself a superhero. This was a period where I felt like I could move mountains. While I used to be fearful of the "failure day," I now had the expectation that each run would be a success.

I am not making light of serious running injuries, but I have found that with the right care and perseverance, a runner can overcome some of the pain. I have noticed, at times, that good feelings (like running with Rachel) made me forget that I was even battling an injury.

Still, I wanted to be careful so I was giving my foot a lot of attention. Each day I rolled it numerous times on a cold metal water bottle (stored in the refrigerator) or a small dumbbell. I also rolled tennis balls and golf balls under my feet. Each morning I would massage my foot with my thumbs before getting out of bed. And my morning game of "Hot Lava" on the pillows gave my feet a soft introduction to each day. I also visited my chiropractor, Dr. Alfonzo, who specializes in sports injury. He used a plethora of stretches, manipulations, and technology, such as laser treatment, to keep me moving. I finally listened to his advice about icing the injury and the importance of stretching.

The pain on mornings when I would forget to rub my foot, stretch, or step on a pillow was terrible. On some of those mornings I was barely able to stand, let alone walk, but the pain eventually passed with some stretching and rolling and ice. It was rare that I allowed myself to miss a scheduled run. I have an indoor exercise bike, just in case I need to get in some aerobic activity and can't run due to time, weather, darkness, or injury. But I hate the bike and rarely use it.

The evening of my successful twenty-mile day, Rachel came over for dinner and arrived as I was pulling it out of the oven— English muffin pizzas. This has always been one of my favorite meals. I usually can't be bothered making an elaborate dinner. English muffin pizzas are simple... and delicious.

As we dined on this non-delicacy, Rachel asked when my next trip to spread my father's ashes would be.

"I should be visiting Mr. Stevens soon," I replied. "I just keep forgetting to schedule my appointment. Once I know what is he asking of me, I will be able to figure it out. I can't predict what the next trip will be or what my dad will ask."

"Do you ever try to guess the location before you get the letter?" Rachel asked.

"Well, no, not really. The first request was a shock—well, the whole idea, of course. But, if I thought about it, I could have guessed that he would have liked his ashes to be left in Cooperstown. Dad loved baseball. But I had no idea what to expect for the second trip. Even the last one. We always liked Newport, but I didn't think that my father would want to spend eternity there."

"Maybe your dad will send you to Disney World!" she said.

I grinned at that. "No, I don't think so. While we loved Disney, that doesn't seem to be the type of place he wants to send me to. There is too much happening there with characters and rides. And gift shops. I get the sense that my father wanted to send me to places where I would be forced to be a bit more reflective." I paused. "Wherever it is that I have to go, I hope you can come with me. But I just don't know, and I just can't predict what he'll ask."

Rachel looked at me kindly. Those big brown eyes still made me feel weak. "I know," she said. "I hope I can come too, but I understand if you need to be alone when you do this."

"Thanks," I said. I explained that I didn't want to set any expectations for the journeys. On one hand, I hoped that my father had an exotic secret to share with me—that he spent a year in Paris or Rome or that he worked at a resort in Singapore and needed me to go there to leave his ashes. But I also didn't want to be let down when the request came for me to travel to a small campsite in the Adirondacks. As autumn was upon us, I also hoped that I wouldn't have to do any paddling on a cold lake in an aluminum canoe.

I didn't want my father, now passed, to be in a position to disappoint me, I explained to Rachel. And I did not want to disappoint him by seeming greedy for some remarkable trip. It was much easier to simply accept whatever the letter said and to try to relish the experience in answering that call.

"A big part of this isn't where I will go, but what I do when I get there," I said.

Rachel nodded and squeezed my hand. "I get that." She smiled. "I am glad we found each other."

"Me too," I offered. "I wonder if my dad knew that you would be at the Lincoln Memorial."

"If so, it would have been nice if he told you to not walk into me," Rachel said with a laugh.

"Are you kidding? Unless I did that, I would have never had the guts to talk to you."

Rachel laughed again. "I love you."

No matter how many times Rachel said this, I never tired of hearing it. In fact, each time she said it, I still felt surprised.

"Me too," I stammered.

I could have spent the rest of the night staring into those beautiful eyes.

–55–

A few evenings after our nice English muffin dinner, I was faced with miserable weather—torrents of rain and strong winds. As dedicated as I am to my running, I'm not stupid. This was not a good night to go out.

I was burning with energy though. The thought of the up-coming race filled me with nervous excitement. I needed the physical release that running provides.

Resolving to do something, I fiddled with the wires behind the TV and DVD player and hooked up the audio to my old stereo. Many people, it seems, have smaller and smaller speakers that produce louder and much richer sounds. I didn't have anything like that. I still used the big floor-bound cabinet speakers.

Next, I carried my exercise bike up from the basement and placed it in front of the TV. With the technology and equipment ready, I put a *Rocky* movie in the DVD player and turned up the sound as loud as the speakers would permit before becoming too distorted, and mounted the bike.

The weather may have wanted me to succumb, but this was certainly not a Failure Day. I pedaled hard for well over an hour, sweat pouring from my body. When the credits began to roll—legs feeling weak and my back sore—I toweled off and enjoyed a refreshing shower before heading off to sleep.

–56–

The heavy rains continued the next day, and the day after that. An exercise bike can only do so much. I needed to run.

Since I don't have a treadmill of my own, I dug through the coupons that come in the mail and immediately find their way into my recycling bin. I scanned each ad amid the days-old news-papers, flattened empty cereal boxes, and other paper stuff. I eventually found gold—a coupon for a free trial membership to our local New York Sports Club. I literally jumped for joy and ran to my room to change into my running shorts singing, *"Baby, I was born to run!"*

At the front desk of the exercise facility, I quickly completed the requisite forms and signed my name about ten times to various documents. "This is a trial membership, Mr. Holmes," the man at the counter said. I found out later that he was actually the manager. "We already like you, I hope you like us."

"I do already," I replied. "I just want to run!"

The treadmill area was packed with people. Everyone had been forced inside by the horrendous rains. I had to wait for over forty-five minutes for a machine.

When I finally got on a treadmill, my heart was racing. I was full of energy. I wondered if this excitement and anticipation was what a marathon was like. A place busy with fit people. Energy and focus permeating the air. Would I be this enthused, I wondered, on Marathon Sunday? I put on a playlist of songs about New York City that I had created for my iPod, covered my ears with my old style headphones, and started running...hard. I began the session at 7.0 miles per hour but was soon increasing my speed every quarter mile. 7.1, 7.2...7.5, 7.6...

I was flying!

As song after song about New York City blared in my ears, I discovered a whole new dimension to my favorite sport. I loved this treadmill running. I was in my own world—breathing heavily, pushing the pace, probably grunting, although I couldn't hear myself over the music.

By mile four, I was mouthing the words to the songs as I ran. I was euphoric. I was at 8.2 miles per hour when Frank Sinatra began singing *"New York, New York"* in my ears. I felt compelled to join him. I started changing the lyrics of the song to fit the marathon as I belted out the words, "I WANT TO *RUN THROUGH* A CITY THAT NEVER SLEEPS..."

I turned to my left, half expecting all the people in the facility to be amazed by my strength and form, but instead I saw an angry face. It was the manager, the man who processed my membership papers. He was holding out his flat palms toward me. I was confused. "What? Where?"

Coming to my senses, I searched frantically for the STOP button as my legs kept flying over the running belt. I was caught in two worlds. I finally found the button and the machine slowly came to a stop. Sinatra was still blasting my ears. The manager motioned for me to remove my headphones.

"We don't sing here," he said.

"What?"

"You are pissing everyone off. Can you please stop?"

"I'm training for the New York City Marathon," I stated with conviction, figuring everyone would be impressed with me and my upcoming accomplishment.

"I don't care if you are the flipping champion. I don't even care if you're Meb Keflezighi. You are bothering every single person here."

"Yeah?" I was honestly confused.

"Yeah. Your time on the machine is up. So is your trial membership. Over. Done."

"That quickly? I thought you already liked me."

"I was wrong. Go home."

And with that, the shortest gym membership in history ended.

Still full of energy, in spite of the public flogging, I left the building and ran five more miles outside in the deluge, which, thankfully, after a short while turned into a mist.

Sinatra was with me the whole time.

–57–

Endorphins are biological neurotransmitters that are released during exercise. They produce good feelings and optimism. Some call the effect from the endorphins the "runner's high." It is nature's special gift to an athlete. I had sure experienced this at the New York Sports Club—much to everyone else's annoyance.

Coming off the powerful exercise experience of the previous night, flooded with endorphins and confidence, I expected to bask in the self-glory of personal athletic achievement. I felt that my very presence radiated athleticism, power, and goodness. I was feeling great about myself and the upcoming marathon. I felt I could conqueror anything—that the world was mine for the taking. I believed that nothing could go wrong.

Since my conversation with Charlie Rizzuto, I found myself avoiding Dr. Alexander. I didn't know how I was going to explain to him that I would not be participating in the volleyball game. He served as the coach and always seemed proud that his teachers gave of their time to help the community through this fund-raiser. This year the money would be used to revitalize the library at our middle school with new furniture and large collection of e-readers and digital books.

But that day, while I was on recess duty, some eighth graders rushed over to me after running laps around the soccer field. "We are ready to defeat you in the volleyball game," they joked.

"Oh, I'm not playing this year," I said as casually as I could. I hoped it wouldn't be up to me to explain to them that actually none of the teachers would be playing.

The students laughed. "I don't believe you," one said. "You always play."

"And we always win," added another student.

"It's the highlight of eighth grade!"

"Remember last year when Mr. McCartney went for a spike and missed the ball?"

"Our team this year has matching t-shirts..."

"Morningside Champions."

"That's us!"

I wasn't quite sure what to say to all of this. An awkward silence hung in the air.

"Mr. Holmes, you seriously aren't playing?" asked Jonathan McNeill, one of the better athletes in the class.

"No, I'm serious." I said. I tried to stand up a little taller because I realized I had started to slouch as the students were talking to me. "No teachers are playing this year. I don't even know if the game is on."

The kids looked at me. One girl, Hayley, said, "But this year was our chance to play. You're not going to play when it is our year?"

"It's...difficult." I felt my face turning red and my eye brows becoming lower on my forehead. "Sometimes kids don't understand the things adults go through. Some of us want to play, I think. We can't. There are issues. Grown-up stuff. You'll understand when you're older."

After that explanation, the students slowly walked away.

Later I saw these same students talking to Dr. Alexander on the other side of the blacktop. Oh dear, I thought.

My schedule that year had me teaching three class sections after lunch and that day each class period began with a student raising his or her hand and asking if I was playing in the charity volleyball game. I told each class the truth. One student, Jordan Maine, raised his hand and said something I couldn't shake.

"You always say you are here for the kids, for us," he began.

"I am here for the kids, for all of you. You know that. I have always played before. This year is different."

"But you always told us, do what is right... follow your conscience, don't cave to peer pressure..."

"Yes, I know." I responded. "But sometimes you have to do things you don't want to do when you are part of a larger group. In an organization there can be times that you have to follow the majority."

I tried to turn the discussion into a civics lesson. We talked about the Industrial Revolution, Progressives, Muckrakers, the rise of unions, and more. I tried to make the students understand that there are some issues that are bigger than each of us. To be honest, it was one of the best lessons I ever developed on the spot. That being said, my lesson was delivered to a less-than-receptive audience.

As the final class period was closing, one of my most enthusiastic students, Amanda, asked, "I understand all you're saying, but schools are about the kids... right?"

I replied that she was, for the most part, correct.

"It's about the kids... except when it's not, Mr. Holmes," she stated. Then the bell rang, and the students stood up.

I had no response.

I did not wait until "contractual time" to leave at the end of the day. After the students left my classroom, I picked up my empty briefcase and was on my way to march out of the school when Frederick Roberts, one of my most able students, walked meekly in.

"Freddie Roberts," I said. "What's up?"

"Mr. Holmes," he began, "you're a good teacher. I understand about unions. My dad works in a factory in Edgewater. I hear about this stuff all the time. My dad says sometimes you just have to do the right thing. Maybe you can't play. Maybe no one can. But maybe you can do *something*. Maybe people will change their minds." He turned to leave. "I have to catch my bus," he said.

"Wait," I called out. "I'll see what I can do. I promise."

–58–

I walked directly out of the school building. I did not sign out at the office.

In regard to my promise to the student, with the prospect of facing Charlie Rizzuto and my colleagues, some of whom were just as determined as he that we never give an inch, I did nothing.

And, in regard to work, that's what I was becoming—a nothing.

–59–

Once home, I needed to run. These two-a-day workouts were becoming necessary for my sanity.

I had planned an easy six-miler for my post-work run. I had run this route for years, long before I ever began to consider running a marathon. This route was as familiar as any aspect of my adult life. I had run these roads for over a decade. Previous to my running days, when I was still a kid, I rode my bike on them, enjoying my first tastes of freedom.

Throughout my run, I perseverated on the same questions over and over. How fair is it, I thought, that I am expected to play in the volleyball game every year? Aren't I allowed to have a life? Does my life revolve around a silly game? The kids shouldn't be angry at me if I decided not to play, regardless of a contractual situation. I'm allowed not to play.

At what point, I wondered, do kindness and generosity become not appreciated, but an expectation?

–60–

The next day, a Thursday, I decided on a whim and without an appointment to stop at Mr. Stevens's office after work. I needed someone to talk to and I greatly looked forward to receiving my next letter, especially after Rachel's own interest in my dad's crazy request.

My timing was off. Mr. Stevens was with a client, his secretary told me, and would be with other clients for the remainder of his work day. Not wanting to waste a trip, I asked her if she would be able to provide me with the next letter. I wanted to talk, but the letter would have to suffice. She instructed me to wait in the reception area, outside the office. I hoped I didn't have to wait too long.

A short while later, an elderly women left Mr. Stevens's office with another younger, but certainly not young, woman. The older woman said aloud, "That was the hardest thing I have ever done, writing that... How does one prepare for death? How do I say goodbye?" I diverted my eyes to give them as much "privacy" as I could.

During my wait, another couple, not quite as old, came in carrying piles of papers and holding hands. I assumed they were meeting with Mr. Stevens to conduct their own estate planning and write their Last Will and Testament. The whole process struck me as sad. They sat with me in the reception area. None of us talked.

About ten minutes later, the secretary came out of Mr.

Stevens's office and handed me an envelope. "Mr. Stevens is disappointed that he did not have the opportunity to speak with you," she said. "But here you go."

I took the envelope, feeling that I had somehow let Mr. Stevens down. I began to wonder if he looked forward to our visits as much as I did. Hearing about my adventures, I reasoned, was much preferable to determining next of kin, power of attorney, or how much from the estate to give to the church.

Eager for some positivity, I tore open the envelope and read my father's letter while sitting in the driver's seat of my car.

Dear Sam,

I am enjoying writing these letters to you. They bring me close to you when you're not here visiting. Since you are, for the most part, my only visitor, these letters help me pass the time by allowing me to reflect on my life and the places we traveled.

Sometimes in our travels, we would head away from the main attractions to find a monument or a little-known place. I loved that sense of discovery. I still recall how delighted you were when we found Fort Knox in Maine. We were the only people there. You had so much fun exploring that abandoned fort.

I don't have many regrets, but I always wished that I had attended an Ivy League college. I am hoping you will bring me to Princeton University. It's not too far. I think it would be a good place for me...

I hear they spread Albert Einstein's remains across the university grounds. Maybe some of his brilliance will rub off on me. I wouldn't mind being one of the smartest people in Heaven.

While you are there, try to find something out of the ordinary to remember me by. Maybe you can find a monument or a plaque that tells an interesting story that you can share with your students. Maybe you can head to the battlefield. George Washington fought

157

there. Do you remember all of your somersaults?

Have a good trip.

Thank you for doing this for me.

Please know that I miss you terribly.

Love Always,

Dad

–61–

I had told Rachel that I planned for her to be part of my travels to remember my dad and fulfill his last wishes, but for reasons I didn't completely understand, I wanted to do this one alone. I called Rachel to tell her that I planned to head to Princeton immediately after work the next day, and told her I was sorry if I misled her. I needed her support and understanding. True to her nature, she gave me both.

The PTA had arranged a special assembly on nutrition to end the next school day. I didn't feel the need to spend an hour watching dancing carrots or hearing about Omega-3 fatty acids, so I asked a colleague, Mike McCartney, if he would cover my class so I could leave early. We did this sometimes—covered for each other. The proper thing would have been for me to ask Dr. Alexander for special permission to leave early, but since that day on the playground I had been avoiding him. I was not proud of being such a coward.

I was on the road to Princeton by 1:45 p.m. As I drove, I reflected on my father's latest letter to me. He was correct; we loved finding hidden sites off the main roads. The discovery of the little-known Fort Knox in Maine was a highlight of my childhood. I remembered running up and down the dirt mounds and hiding within the walls of the fort, fighting an imaginary war. As I recall, my sister sat in the car reading while my mother and father held hands looking out at the bay. My brother Michael had already moved out and was far away from my life. That must have been one of the rare days we weren't rushing to a new location. Each of us was able to find joy in our own unique way at Fort Knox.

I also vaguely remembered a visit to the Princeton Battlefield. I don't think we went to the university. But I was only four or five then, so maybe what I remember are just the photographs and the story that my dad loved to tell. In short, we had visited a monument of some sort, a good distance from the road. As we turned to leave, I asked my father if, instead of walking, I could somersault across the large grassy field back to the car. He allowed me, but cautioned, "You'll never make it." I must have been a very determined little boy. I tumbled and tumbled. Family legend has it that I made it to the car. I don't really recall, but hearing of my supposed epic feat made me believe, even as a child, that I could overcome any challenge.

I arrived in Princeton, New Jersey about an hour and a half later, and parked on the street across from the University's main entrance—the FitzRandolph Gate, an ornamental iron structure that looks like it dates back to the early days of the college. I took out an AAA Tour Book of New Jersey that I kept in my glove compartment and read about the university. The entrance across the street was named for Nathaniel FitzRandolph, a Quaker who was responsible for raising much of the money for the original College of New Jersey—the name of Princeton when it first opened. The graduating class always walks through the gate as part of their processional. It is also a tradition that Princetonian students avoid the gate until graduation. It is said to be bad luck to pass through the gate before one finishes one's degree. Knowing that I would never be a student at Princeton, I threw caution to the wind and entered through the gates that keep Princeton open to the community.

It was a beautiful fall day, and many of the trees still held their vibrant red, orange, and yellow leaves. As I entered the campus, I immediately felt as though I was walking upon dignified ground. I looked in awe at the majestic buildings that reflected the ideals of the most learned. Green ivy grew up the walls of Nassau Hall, a gorgeous structure built in the 1700s. Ivy League indeed!

I made my way to Clio Hall, a Greek-revival structure that served as the admissions building. As I arrived, a campus tour was just getting under way. I figured that joining the tour would provide me with some history of the campus and allow me to find the perfect place to conduct my father's unique ritual.

The campus tour took me past a number of places that seemed perfect for one of my father's final resting spots. I considered a regal archway known as Blair Arch. The campus tour guide explained that a cappella groups frequently sing there because of the wonderful acoustics. My father would have loved that. He loved classical music. A special composition by Bach came to my mind—his Second Brandenburg Concerto. My father absolutely loved that piece. He would say, in reference to these epic works by Bach, "They are all good, but if you had to pick one, you'd pick Two." He often sat quietly in the living room listening to the clarinets and violas as the music played on his stereo turntable. My dad was a traditionalist. Even with better technology, he stayed loyal to his old vinyl records. Sometimes, when she heard the music, my mother would come into the room and sit down next to my father. Even in their later years, they would quietly hold hands while they listened.

I also considered Prospect Garden, a beautifully manicured little park with brick walkways, flower beds, and, in the warm months at least, a bubbling fountain. The garden would offer my father peace and serenity, although perhaps it wouldn't be fitting because Dad never had been much for gardening. I tried to recall if I ever saw him planting bulbs or weeding a flower bed, but couldn't. Whether he had or hadn't mattered little now. The memories were lost with time.

I wondered how many other memories were now lost forever.

As the tour progressed, I realized that I was the only person on this excursion without a vested interest in Princeton's acceptance rates, average SAT scores, dormitory arrangements, or financial aid packages. I found it interesting to watch the prospective students and their parents as they listened to the guide describing campus life. Some parents kept prodding their children to ask questions or even asked questions themselves. I laughed when one mother, much to her son's chagrin, asked if the dorm bathrooms were cleaned on a daily basis. These people were making decisions for their futures, I, on the other hand, was looking to my father's past.

I could see tension and hope in the various faces of the young adults who were beginning to imagine what their lives might be like if they were fortunate enough to attend this prestigious institution. Some of the prospective students on the tour even took notes. One child tagging along with us was a younger sibling. He kept asking his mother when the tour would end. I had never before seen a parent use so many different facial expressions and silent gestures to indicate for a child to be quiet.

My parents had taken me on a few college tours when I was in high school. I remember not being all that impressed with any of the universities. They all seemed the same to me. I knew I'd have to go to college, but I didn't really care where I'd go.

From the tour I learned that my father may not have been correct in his assumption that Einstein had his ashes scattered across the campus. Apparently, the real location where Einstein's ashes were spread was never disclosed to the public. One rumor is that they were scattered across an area that is now an interstate highway. I liked the Princeton story better. I much prefer to imagine that Einstein was left on a campus rather than on Route 95 South.

By the time the tour came to end, I still didn't feel like I had found the perfect place for my dad, so I continued to wander the large campus. First, for inspiration, I went into University Chapel. This edifice's name is a misnomer. To me a chapel is a small structure; Princeton's University Chapel is a magnificent limestone cathedral—one of the largest in the world. The ceiling inside is almost eighty feet high. When I slipped through the heavy wooden door, I was immediately awed into silence. The many stained-glass panels glowed with the light of the setting sun and cast colorful patches on the limestone walls. Intricate Doric columns lined the main aisle on either side, soaring up to the ceiling like so many tree trunks before arching overhead. A few other people dotted the pews, but for the most part, this vast sanctuary was empty and remarkably quiet. I walked slowly toward the altar, and eventually sat in one of the many pews. This truly was a holy place, I thought—the perfect location for quiet prayer and reflection. I bowed my head and began to pray.

"Dear God,

Thank you for my blessings. Thank you for all the joys of love and beauty that you have brought into my life. Please know that I am working hard to live a good and clean life. Please forgive my sins...

Dad?... Dad, I hope you hear me. I never knew it would be this hard. I've always valued your guidance. I could use some now. I am not sure what to do at work. I'm confused. I'm conflicted. I understand what I need to do, but I also feel I'm not giving my job my best efforts. Am I cheating the profession and the students? Am I doing the right thing? On the other hand, are we being cheated because we don't have a contract?

These trips, I feel, are bringing me closer to you. But you've never seemed so far away.

Please give me the courage and the strength to make the right choices going forward. Always.

Amen."

As I got up to leave, I noticed a small pamphlet on the floor under the pew in front of me. I picked it up to throw away, but the title—"Unique Spots on the Princeton Campus"—grabbed my attention. I opened the leaflet and started reading.

I learned that on the university campus there is one location that would have absolutely delighted my father, a location called Cannon Green. One might picture Cannon Green as a special place that pays tribute to Princeton's role in the Revolutionary War. In a sense, that is a correct assumption. There is a cannon there, but it is displayed in a very unconventional way. The pamphlet described an historic rivalry between Rutgers University and Princeton, New Jersey's two oldest colleges. In the early days of the schools, the cannon became a symbol of success, and, as such, was a prized object that was alternatively stolen from each campus. At one point, Princeton won the cannon back, and to prevent Rutgers students from ever taking it again, they buried most of it. Today the only visible part of the cannon is the back end protruding from the ground. My father would have loved that tale.

It was at this spot that I decided to lay my father's ashes to rest. It was out of the ordinary in a way my father would have loved: historic, unique, and peculiar. And, because of its educational roots, it seemed a fitting place for a man who had dedicated himself to teaching young minds.

Before leaving the Township of Princeton, I visited the Princeton Record Exchange and bought a CD that contained some of Bach's works, including the Brandenburg Concertos. I wanted that special music to be the soundtrack for my drive home.

I knew that it was also time to take a break from the emotional toll of these trips, at least for a little while. While they brought me closer to Dad and helped me feel more at peace about his death, I now needed to mentally prepare for only one thing: My appointment with the New York City Marathon.

–62–

The next morning brought with it two things I loved: Saturday and sunshine.

This day—three weeks and one day from the first Sunday in November—would be the last long run of my training. The training book that I relied on the most (I had about seven books about marathon training that I kept in a stack next to my bed) called for an 18-mile run at this point. I hoped to get that far, and possibly push my run to twenty miles, before stopping. It would be the furthest I had ever run in one shot.

I was glad that the weather was bright and cool with puffy clouds because I had spent a restless night after returning from Princeton. I was relieved for accomplishing another of my father's requests, but once I got in bed, I thought only of the long run I had to face the next day. It is a singular sensation knowing that the next morning you will push yourself to, and possibly beyond, the breaking point of your endurance.

Since I would be running the marathon "alone" (with 45,000 or so other runners—also running alone), I felt I needed to accomplish this run by myself. Rachel and I were in the habit of doing our long runs together, and once again I was again changing the deal we had made. I called her early that morning at my first opportunity.

"Hey, Rachel, it's me, Sam."

"Hey, will you ever stop saying who you are? I half expect to hear you calling yourself Mr. Holmes."

"I don't want you to forget who I am," I said lamely. "Listen, I hate to do this, but today is my last long run..."

"I sometimes hate long runs too."

"No, I mean, I know we were thinking about running together, but maybe I should try this one alone, like in the marathon... when I'll be alone."

There was a long pause on the other end of the line. "Ok. But I was planning on doing my long run with you today, too, you know. I turned down a brunch invitation from my friend Kelly."

"I'm sorry. I really am. Is it too late call your friend back? I just—I don't know. I think I need to do this run alone."

"I get it Sam, and you're probably right. I'm just a little disappointed, I guess. Running alone is hard." There was a second long pause. "You cancelled our date last night too so that you could go to Princeton. Is everything ok, Sam?"

I hadn't put either of these things together. I began pacing the room searching for the words. The best I came up with was, "Yeah, of course, trust me."

"I do. I thought I could." I heard a slight sniffle.

"Rachel! No, I'm being stupid. Come on over, let's run together."

"It's ok Sam. I'll see you later."

The beep that ended the call came much too quickly. I stared at my cell phone for a moment, but all I could do was shake it off, lace up my Nikes, and begin stretching. I had eighteen miles to cover.

–63–

My long run was, at once, encouraging and depressing. My emotions vacillated with each mile, or so it seemed. At times I felt confident that come marathon day I would be ready. But then the fatigue would catch up to me and I'd notice the ache in my legs, the labor of my lungs, and the heaviness in my gut.

I was not overly familiar with the New York City Marathon course, but I had memorized some landmarks from my research on the race. I imagined how I might feel at those points as I covered those miles on this run:

"I feel good, mile five, that'll be in Brooklyn; I'll be great."

"I don't remember being this tired this early in a run."

"I will be strong at the Pulaski Bridge."

"I might die in Queens."

"I don't think I can do this."

"I can, I can."

As I ran, I also felt pangs of remorse and regret for treating Rachel so unfairly. She also needed to have a long run and had nobody but me to share the miles with. Why had I insisted on doing this alone? Why was I putting up walls?

I was proud and a little shocked when I pushed past the seventeen-mile mark and seemed to have more energy in me. Rather than pushing my luck, though, I determined to take the advice of the experts and conclude with a solid eighteen miles. I ran as hard as I could for that last mile, pushing towards my house—although, to be honest, I was probably moving at no faster than a slow jog.

As I approached my home, I saw a beautiful sight. Rachel was sitting on the front step. "I got here a long time ago," she said with a half-smile when I finally stopped and stood gasping, hunched over my trembling knees, in the driveway. "If you run New York at that pace, it will take you ten hours to finish."

I smiled and collapsed into Rachel's toned arms.

A short while later, after a refreshing shower, I sat with Rachel on the sofa in the living room and told her for the first time about some of my troubles at work—specifically the volleyball game. I also told her about my afternoon at Princeton.

Rachel said something that shocked me. "I envy you."

"Me? Why?"

"I never experienced a family like you did," Rachel explained. "My childhood memories are of friends from the neighborhood or school...some people whose names I don't even recall. My parents loved me, but we never had experiences like you did with your family. You're so fortunate to have had that."

I didn't know what to say. I never thought of myself as especially fortunate for having parents who cared about me, who played with me, encouraged me, and supported me. I knew our trips created great memories, but I never thought of any of my childhood destinations as places that I was particularly fortunate to go to.

"You probably think of those letters from your father as a burden or a task you must complete..."

"No," I interrupted. "At first I thought that, but now I...I look forward to them...and I am a little fearful of finishing too quickly. Part of me doesn't ever want to get to the last letter."

"I wish I had a letter," Rachel said and her body began to shake with sobs. I held her in my arms. I'm not sure how long we sat there like that, holding each other, but by the time I guided her head to a pillow on the sofa, the sun had set and the living room was dark.

I got up to eat a small snack, and when I returned, she had closed her eyes. I tucked her in with an afghan knit by my grandmother. As I watched her sleep, I longed for the day when we would spend a real night together.

–64–

Though I had handled the eighteen miles well enough the previous day, I woke up sore, and, for reasons I could not explain, full of doubt about my ability to complete the marathon. My legs were so stiff, I could barely limp to the bathroom. And once again the pain in my heel was excruciating. This put me in a sour mood.

I walked into the living room and found Rachel sitting on the edge of the sofa, flipping through an old *Good Housekeeping* magazine that must have been my mother's from years ago. The afghan and small pillows were strewn on the floor. Rachel looked tired, and her hair was a mess. The dark makeup smudged under her eyes didn't help. I noticed that many tissues filled the small plastic waste can at her feet.

"Thanks for leaving me something to change into," she said tersely.

I was startled by the tone in her voice. "You were asleep. I didn't want to wake you."

"You couldn't leave anything in the room or on the floor? Some sweats? A nicer blanket or comforter? Would pillows wake me up?"

"I didn't... I didn't really think of it."

"I guess you didn't."

"I wasn't thinking."

"Maybe you were."

"What?"

"You were thinking... only about yourself. That's you lately. Your miles are too important. Your dad's missions always come first. And, oh, you're the most stressed out teacher in the whole world."

"Rachel, stop." We'd never fought before. I sat down next to her, but she did not come near me or reach for my hand.

"What about me, Sam? I was a teacher too you know." Rachel gripped her hands together in her lap. "If you really wanted to, you could play in that game. Do you know what I'd give to get back into a classroom? I'd play volleyball every day if I had to."

"Well, I can't."

"No, you won't."

"No, I can't." I stood up, facing her.

"Sam, a man with convictions would do the right thing."

"I can't believe I am hearing all this. Rachel? What happened?"

"You always want it your way. You wanted to be alone at Princeton. You wanted to be alone on your run. Well, what about me? Me, you forget and leave on an old sofa with an itchy wool afghan from 1926 while you rested in a comfortable bed."

"You could have joined me."

"SAM!"

"Well, you could have. You know... waiting is hard."

"It's a two-way street, Mr. Holmes." Rachel picked up the one small pillow that sat next to her lap, tossed it into the easy chair across the room, grabbed a handful of Kleenex, and walked out the front door.

"Rachel... Rachel... Come on. Rachel. Rachel!"

–65–

There are times, at least for me, when none of my interests are interesting. I didn't want to run. I didn't want to ride my dreaded exercise bike. TV held no interest. I had no movies I wanted to see. Not even Rocky.

The thought of music, even the Beatles—or Bach—held no appeal.

And it was too damn cold to go out in a canoe.

I spent the day, instead, reliving the morning experience with Rachel.

I suffered and stressed all day. The only productive thing I did was write two lousy poems.

SELF –ISH

Am I selfish?
A man wondered, to himself.
Do I put my cares for others
on the back shelf?
Do I do what I want
when I please?

Do I blame others
when I'm down on my knees?

MARATHON

26.2 miles
Miles and miles and miles
to run.
Miles and miles and miles
to run.
26.2 of them.
I don't know if I can.
I don't need aggravation.
It's not going to help.
I have to run
miles and miles and miles.

–66–

Monday came without any word from Rachel.

I went through my day in a haze. I gave an assignment to the students rather than teaching. The kids must have sensed it was better to do the busy work than engage with me.

At one point I looked at myself in the mirror in the men's room and searched for a smile. I had none to give.

The school day ended, the kids left, and as always, we were left to our own until the mass exodus at 3:40 p.m. I sat at my desk, not doing anything, just waiting to leave, following all the rules. In fact, I was staring at the clock when, to my surprise, at 3:22 (exactly), Charlie Rizzuto walked in.

"If you have plans for next Friday night, cancel them. We need you to play volleyball."

"You settled the contact?" I asked, though with less enthusiasm than I would have expected. I didn't even rise from my chair.

"No," came the reply, and then Rizzuto began explaining.

Charlie Rizzuto, the grizzled old union-first teacher, had caved. A parent had seen him at a social event over the weekend. This woman asked how sitting out a charity event was going to help our cause. When Charlie answered, "It won't," he knew the gig was up.

Rizzuto called a special meeting of the negotiating team on a Sunday, of all things, an act that only he could pull off. While I sat at home stewing and trying my best to be E. E. Cummings, the power brokers of our association debated the merits of stepping up for the kids and showing an act of good faith.

While I was mired in unkind thoughts and pitiful self-loathing, goodness prevailed among the teachers' union.

In a turn of events that could only have happened through the power of a force like Charlie Rizzuto, the "Annual Volleyball Contest of Morningside (To Support the PTA)" was back on.

–67–

I was not quite sure of the status of the rest of the job actions we were taking, so for the next few days I kept to myself. I still did not do work at home, or otherwise, after 3:40 as we were originally instructed. I was distracted, and had been for a long time. I may also have been using the contract situation as an excuse to not give my best at work for the first time in my professional life. As a result of all this, I missed some things to which I otherwise would have been attentive. One of these things was reporting the mid-marking period grades of students who were not performing well. Interestingly, I seemed to have more students like this than in any previous year.

When I checked my school mailbox at lunch the next day, I saw there was a note from Dr. Alexander. The note contained two words, "See Me."

The meeting wasn't all sunshine.

Dr. Alexander shared that he had received more complaints about me during the last few weeks than he had received in the sum total of my career to that point. He said that it had recently come to his attention that I had not been completing reports. He also heard that I had not handed back completed assignments, or even tests, to the students.

"You are slipping," he bluntly told me. "We build our reputations by the work we do each day. That is how we will be remembered. I understand all this union stuff, but if you become focused on what you can't, or won't do, you will hurt only yourself. You are not hurting the Board of Education, or me, or even the parents. I could argue that you are hurting kids, but I won't even go there."

Dr. Alexander turned from me and looked out the window of his office before continuing. "When I hired you, there were more qualified people for the position. You know your material well enough, but you are not an expert on history. I know how hard you have worked to learn as much about your subject as you can. And you have done a great job in that regard. But that's not the point. When I hired you…"

Dr. Alexander looked at me squarely in the eyes. "When I hired you," he repeated, "I did so because you had character. No salary, no amount of money, is more important than character. You're not hurting anyone right now," he said, "except for yourself—and your reputation. The parents of the students in your class don't care what you did with other students last year—or the year before—they care about what you are doing for your students today. They care what you're doing for this group of children. This is the group of kids, their kids, that matters to them. And these kids should matter to you. To be honest, this isn't about your union either. Ever since that great lesson I saw, what you personally are doing is not a whole hell of a lot. Look around, your colleagues still get things done. I'm not getting complaints about them."

I was dumbfounded. I thought of offering a response, but I didn't have one to give. I looked down at the floor, and then I looked up at my principal, the man who hired me, evaluated me… and, to that point, had always supported me.

"I expect more from you—because of who you are," he said.

"I know your father died over the summer, and I'm willing to grant you some grace because of that, but I'll be blunt, I think you have found a nice excuse in this union stuff to do as little as possible. Your work has slipped and it's a bad look."

The silence that followed this lecture told me clearly that the meeting was over. I muttered, "Thank you," and left the room.

–68–

I thought I would love the taper, the period when a runner winds down and runs fewer miles in the last weeks before the marathon. The prospect of more time to myself, fewer miles, and a chance to relax before the marathon seemed like a true gift... prior to its arrival. In reality, I hated it. I had an unbelievable desire to go out and run—and run far. I could not sit down for long periods at a time, and when I did, I found myself jiggling my feet and legs. I did not sleep well.

I had not seen Rachel since our argument. I still called her each night, but we didn't talk all that much. I was trying to find the right words to immediately make it all better, but everything I said fell flat. I sensed that there was something more going on in Rachel's heart that she wasn't telling me; it was as though a wall had been constructed between the two of us overnight. In addition, she had been assigned to work evenings. That was not a cheap excuse; we knew this was coming. Rachel had to fill in for an employee who was taking a planned medical leave, but that didn't make it any easier. Tonight, though, was my chance to fix things. Rachel was coming over for the first time since our fight and I desperately wanted to patch things up with her.

After the meeting with Dr. Alexander though, I left the school feeling humiliated. That humiliation turned to anger as I drove home. I had hoped that this night was going to be special night, but now I felt that my mood had been ruined before the evening even began.

I planned to make something of quality—a better dinner than English muffin pizzas. Something Italian? I swung by the grocery store to pick up ingredients and, on a whim, decided to buy a bottle—no two bottles—of red wine. Maybe it would help me relax. And maybe it would help Rachel as well. We would drink some wine, eat a delicious dinner, and everything would go back to normal. We'd forget about that awful morning and the things we said. And then I could invite Rachel to spend the night again, but this time in my bed. Yes, I thought. It was about time.

I'd like to say the meal went off without a hitch, but I burned the garlic bread that was supposed to accompany our linguine with white clam sauce. I had to bite my lip to keep from swearing when I saw the blackened crust. As we ate the food that I didn't destroy, I spilled my thoughts about the Board of Education, our unsettled contract, volleyball games, unfair expectations of our personal time, my colleagues, and Dr. Alexander. We had, of course, talked about many of these things before, but this time I could feel my throat getting tight. *Change the subject*, part of me said, but I couldn't stop myself. Rachel became more and more quiet; she didn't even touch the wine I poured.

"If the Board cared about us," I said, "they would settle and give us what we deserve. Then everyone will leave me alone. Dr. Alexander had no right to humiliate me. I care about the kids. I do. I'm a good teacher!" I set my glass of wine down harder than I meant to, and a bit sloshed over the rim onto the tablecloth.

Rachel looked at me and frowned. She reached for my hands and held them in hers. I looked down at them, my heart still racing. I thought about the way she had left me so suddenly a few days ago, leaving me to guess at her ruffled feelings.

"You know how I feel about you," she began, "but your principal is right. You are better than that. This is what I was saying the other day."

I sat up quickly, released her hand, and leaned back in my chair. "You were quite grumpy the other day."

She paused. "You're right," she said at last. "I overreacted. And I'm sorry about that. I was really tired, and I'm never in a good mood when I don't sleep enough. But—that doesn't mean there wasn't any truth to what I was saying."

"You were acting ridiculous."

"Hey. That's not fair."

I shrugged.

"Look, Sam, I really like you. But I like you because of who you are. And now, the way you're acting—it's not you. It's selfish. I'm not saying I'm perfect either, but..."

"No. Stop. This is all too much. It's not me, it's them. All of them. The Board of Education... the principal... Charlie Rizzuto." I shook my head. "They're all killing me! This isn't my fault, it's them. All of them."

"Open your eyes," she said softly.

I missed the nuance in her voice and the tenderness in her eyes. I was beside myself with grief, or rage, or frustration; I didn't know which. I stood up aggressively, walked toward the window, and stared into the blackness that had become the back yard. I could barely make out the branches of the old maple tree against the night sky. Rachel went into the living room, but I didn't turn around to look at her. I heard her flipping through some running magazines as she sat on the sofa.

I stayed in the kitchen and stood by the window shaking my head. "Damn," I said. Deep in my heart I knew Dr. Alexander was right. Rachel saw this clearly. But I didn't want honesty from her or anyone at this point. I wanted Rachel to see my pain, the great burden I was under, and to provide me with a special night to ease the strain.

At that moment, I was tired of soft kisses and gentle hand holding. I wanted more. I felt I deserved more, and I thought the "more" would bridge the chasm that had suddenly opened up between us. I noticed that the small effects of the wine I had consumed had dissipated and left me feeling empty and cold. How long had I stared into the black night?

I walked to the living room, looked at Rachel, and stated, as unemotionally as I could, "I'm tired." I hoped she'd get the hint.

"Yeah," she said. "Me too."

But rather than coming towards me or accompanying me to my bedroom, she put her coat on to leave.

"You're going?" I asked.

"Yeah. It's better this way tonight."

"But…"

"Sam, you need some time. I get it. Tonight's definitely not the night." She touched my arm and kissed me softly on my cheek. "I do care about you," she said as she walked away and out of the house.

Again.

–69–

After Rachel left, I returned to the kitchen and, seeing her full glass, decided to drink her wine. Then I finished off the rest of the bottle and started the next one.

I went into my basement, put on my old baseball glove, and found an old pink rubber ball. As a child, when I wasn't watching the Yankees, playing Wiffle Ball, or facing off against imaginary foes in Strat-o-Matic, I would throw rubber balls against the wall in our basement for hours on end.

The true mark of my parents' love for me is that they accepted the constant "thump" on the wall when I played, especially in the winter. They never asked me to stop, even after I destroyed an intricate train set of my father's with my errant throws.

That evening I threw the ball against the wall until my arm ached. A sweaty mess and somewhat drunk, I sat down on the cold concrete that was our basement floor. I removed my old glove and I traced the autograph of Graig Nettles embossed on the pocket over and over again. Then I buried my head into the glove's soft leather pocket and fell asleep sitting up on the hard, damp floor.

–70–

Because of my taper, my long run that weekend was only eight miles.

I left the house without my iPod because I knew I wouldn't have the crutch of music during the marathon. I wanted to prepare my mind in addition to my body.

But, less than two miles in, as much as I hated myself for doing it, I needed to walk up a sharp incline on Erie Avenue. The pain in my heel had bothered me all morning. I had hoped the plantar fasciitis would subside as blood flowed into that area during the run. It didn't. And I was beginning to feel occasional sharp pains in my left knee and hip as well.

Had all the training caught up with me? Maybe the two-a-days had been a bad idea.

I walked, rather than ran, much of the remaining mileage. My heel was killing me and my mind was foggy and slow. Every time I told myself I was going to keep running no matter what, that I wasn't going to walk anymore, pain, exhaustion, and doubt engulfed me. Rather than building me up, all this did was create more doubt in my mind.

What if this happened on race day while I was in Brooklyn or Queens? How could I possibly complete the marathon?

–71–

Later, in the early evening, as I was watching a college football game, and drinking (I can't say enjoying) a rare beer, the phone rang.

"Hey," said a female voice.

"Hi," I responded.

"I'm bored," came the voice.

"Who is this?"

"Jennie."

"Jennie...?"

"You remember, from TGI Friday's a while ago. We kind of spent the night together."

"Oh, I remember. We drank too much and I fell asleep." Of course I had remembered.

"That was too bad." She paused. "I've been thinking about you. You are one of the nice guys. A bunch of us are at Friday's again. They want you to come down."

"I'm not sure. I'm actually tired."

Jennie urged, "Come on, it'll be fun. Everybody is here. What are you doing now?"

"Just watching football."

"So, come down."

I stared at the TV. The game was winding down, and the prospect of an evening alone with nothing to do weighed on me. "Why not?" I said.

I put on my best shirt, the one that I thought made my biceps look big, and left for what I hoped would be some much-needed laughs. I sure hadn't been having any fun with anyone else.

–72–

Jennie was at the bar when I arrived, drinking a margarita. She stood up and hugged me. "I am so glad you are here."

"Where are the others?" I asked.

"They left. My friends Bob and Marie might come later, but right now it's just us."

In retrospect, this should have been a red flag. But I was lonely and hungry, and I was tired of being the noble good guy. Anyway, I told myself, it wasn't a big deal; Jennie was just a friend. I suggested we get away from the bar and find a table or a booth. I was in the mood for some wings and probably a hefty burger.

When we sat, Jennie said, "I'm not really hungry. Let's get some appetizers and order drinks."

"Hey, one of us is going to have to drive," I said.

"They do have things called cabs, you know."

I ordered wings and a basket of chips and salsa. While I nursed a light beer, Jennie consumed at least two martinis. She was getting giggly and kept reaching across the table to touch my arm. I found myself struggling to keep my eyes on Jennie's face. The lace underneath her low-cut teal shirt was noticeable...

I tried to stare at the picture of Elvis Presley behind her. "You said your friends were coming..."

"Oh," said Jennie. "I'm not sure. They said maybe."

I took another gulp of my beer. I knew I had put myself in a bad situation, but I couldn't bring myself to leave either.

If humans have a singular need to touch things in order to develop a relationship with them, I was understanding that desire extremely well.

I contrasted this immediate desire to experience Jennie with the plodding manner in which my physical relationship with Rachel was progressing. I was trying so hard to be respectful of Rachel that I hadn't really pushed the envelope. I was trying to do it the right way, I thought. But I didn't want to wait forever, and the one night I had resolved to act on my urges, I drove her from my house.

We hadn't talked since our second disagreement.

"I'll bet you have girls calling you all the time," Jennie said. She flipped her blonde hair over her shoulder.

More wings and another drink arrived.

Later, after Jennie excused herself to visit the restroom, I sat alone at the table and considered what was happening. A few months previously, the best I could do was imagine a relationship with the girl at Howe's Caverns and getting into her overalls. Now I had a girlfriend and was sitting with a different girl who was making very clear what her intentions were. If I went home with Jennie, I'd be getting a lot more than the bagel she offered the last time.

When Jennie came back to the table, she smiled at me and slowly adjusted her top before sitting down. I half expected her to take her small blouse off right there and I wouldn't have minded—at all. Why was this happening now? When I was single, it didn't seem like any girls were interested in me.

"I'm getting tired of being here," Jennie said.

I looked into her eyes. They were big and blue, almost like sapphires, but...

"Jennie... you really are cute," I said.

"Aww, you're sweet," she replied, in way that made it clear she already knew it. This was the same look she gave me when first I arrived at the bar. "Want to get out of here?"

"Umm, yeah," I said.

"We could go back to my place. I have plenty to drink at home."

"Yeah." I took a deep breath. "But, Jennie, I can't."

Jennie's face fell. "You…can't? I thought we were having fun."

"No, not like that…I could. I can. Believe me, I can. But no, not now. I can't."

"We were having fun." Jennie wobbled a bit in the booth.

"Yes, we were. And I could really like you. Believe me…I could. I can. I did. You're very pretty. But… I started a relationship with someone else."

She blinked. "Someone else?"

"Yeah. I have a girlfriend."

"You have a girlfriend?"

"Yeah."

"You've been sitting here leading me on all night and you have a girlfriend?" She sounded angry now.

I swallowed. It suddenly dawned on me what a jerk I had been. "Yeah. Oh, geez, I'm sorry. Let me get you a cab. I could even ride back to your place with you so you get home."

"I thought you were a nice guy. I thought you were different. I guess I was wrong. You're just a jerk like all the others."

I cringed. "I'm sorry, Jennie."

I called a cab, and we waited together in awkward silence. Eventually, the beat-up yellow cab pulled up. We both got in. I never trust myself driving after having a few drinks, and on this night, I had more than a few. We drove in silence to her apartment. Jennie didn't even look at me. I didn't offer to walk her to her door, and she left without a word.

For the second time my car would spend the night in the parking lot behind TGI Friday's.

I spent another night in an empty bed.

–73–

Toward the end of the next week, just ten days before the

New York City Marathon, I sought out Charlie Rizzuto in his classroom. "Charlie," I began, sitting down in a student chair, "I am having the worst year of my career..."

He looked up from his desk. "You are young, pal...just wait," he said gruffly.

"Seriously, Charlie. I have kids down on me. I have parents down on me. The principal reprimanded me..."

Charlie raised his eyebrows. "If Alexander reprimanded you over union stuff, I'll have it out with him. What did he say?"

"No, nothing like that," I lied. "I'm not as prompt with my paperwork, I guess. Some parents were complaining."

"He has no right interfering with our negotiations."

"No," I said. "I can't keep up with the work. The shorter hours are killing me. And I don't feel like myself."

Charlie stood up and leaned against his lecture table at the front of the room. I felt like a middle school student again. "Listen kid, you're young. I know what you're feeling. We enter this profession to change the world—one kid at a time—and, over time, we see that it isn't what we thought. Administrators are often fools. They are out of touch with the classroom, even Alexander. He's a good enough guy, but he hasn't taught kids in what, twenty years? Listen, except for a few, the kids don't care, the parents don't care, and we get paid less and less, while more and more is expected of us."

"That's not true. The kids care. They love you."

"Me?" Rizzuto said, surprised.

"Yeah. You have them in sixth grade. I get them in eighth. You know what all the kids say? They call you the best teacher they ever had. They say that Mr. Rizzuto is the best. Parents too. In conferences, even when they praise me, they say the other great teacher at this school is you."

"I don't believe it. I don't listen to that stuff. You're just now realizing that the job isn't what you thought it was? You are not saving the world. No, you are just a guy whose job it is to meet regulations, and if you teach a kid something or make a connection or two along the way, well, consider yourself fortunate."

"No. I love my job." I paused. "Or did, until this year."

Charlie moved from the table and put his hand on my shoulder. "It's a good job, don't get me wrong. But it's often thankless. We played in that volleyball game, right? Did we make any progress in the negotiations after that? No. We actually had a bad meeting, and then the meeting a few days later was postponed. That's the thanks we get."

"This isn't the profession they talk about at college or in the few graduate classes I took."

"You are only now realizing this now, in what, your eighth year?"

"Sixth."

"Sixth. Really? Seems like you've been around longer. You are realizing in your sixth year that it isn't all fun, that we're not always appreciated, and that we're only numbers to others. You say that hurts you. Reality sucks, kid."

"But it sucks because I'm making it suck."

"I don't know what you mean."

"It's lousy because I'm not doing things for the kids. I'm not into it."

"Every year can't be your best year. Hey, in nineteen more years maybe you can retire." Charlie laughed.

"But it's not me. That's not what I do."

"I know. We all know. You are full of fire and energy and positivity. Some of the other teachers talk about you, you know— the ones who have been around and have seen it all. They say you don't understand where we've been and what we've been through. And, frankly, you don't. I knew, one day, I was going to have this talk with you."

"What?"

"You don't stop, Sam. You can't sustain that level of energy— not over a twenty- or thirty-year career. You are setting yourself up to burn out. No one goes 100% all the time. Just wait until you have real responsibilities besides being the favorite teacher and running everywhere. I used to run a lot. Maybe I'd do a marathon too if I didn't have a family and kids to put through college. You know, each of us here, we were also young once. It isn't all about you, kid."

I was dumbfounded. I thought, *Again?* Everybody seemed fed up with me.

"Look, kid," Rizzuto said. "I said all that, but I like you. Always have. You're an honest kid and a good kid. And you teach well. And you're fun to be with. I told everyone that you'd come around. I said that I'd look after you. I'd get you to see the right way. I have protected you... for a long time now."

"Protected me?"

"Yeah. You sometimes make the rest of us look bad. We're not paid to do all that extra stuff. When you do it—others expect the same from us. Teaching is a job. It's how we make our living. No one is going to say, at the end, that they wished they worked harder at their jobs. No, they just want their savings and their pension and their Social Security—God willing it'll be there for you—so they can retire in peace."

Trying to get the discussion back to my original purposes I said, "But I can't get the work done in the school day."

"Well then the Board should pay us more. If they expect us to work at night, they should pay us to work at night—"

"My father never talked like this," I interrupted.

"Yes he did," Charlie said tartly. "We knew your father. He might have worked in a different district, but he was part of our union. He went to county meetings. Your dad was a tough negotiator. He was ready to take his teachers and strike in the 1970s. We walked in support of his association. Years ago. That's how it was. We even had buttons made. And in the end, we won. We. Won."

"My dad?"

"Yes, your dad. Tough as nails at the table. We know—we heard stories. Hell, he told some of them himself. That's another reason why the others left you alone and trusted me. They knew your dad would kick some sense into your head eventually. He was the generation just before us. Back then, we looked up to those who came before us."

My head was spinning. I was arguing for the union when I was angry with Dr. Alexander. Now I was arguing for the other side. "No, I'm here for kids," I maintained. "That's where I get my satisfaction—not from a paycheck."

"Listen to yourself."

"But it's true. That's why I love my job."

"You're not supposed to love your job. You love your wife. You love your children. You can even love your frickin' car. Love anything, but not your job."

"But you're loved by the kids. Even Dr. Alexander tells me what a great teacher you are."

"What did Alexander say?"

"He told me on my first day, that if I wanted to learn how to really teach that I should watch you. He said that you are the best teacher he's ever seen."

"I don't believe that."

"Why would I make it up?"

"You are an original one, Sam Holmes."

"Charlie, listen, I can't work this way. I have to do that extra stuff."

"Then you're a fool."

By this time, our contractual day had long passed. Charlie Rizzuto looked at the clock. "It's ok, you were with me."

"Charlie, I really don't know what to say."

"I'm sorry your dad passed. He sheltered you. He allowed you to be a kid for a long time—right up to this very moment. I wish he were alive, though, so you could talk to him." Charlie's face softened. "Look, you can love your job, but you cannot be part of an association and act like you are better than the other members. We're all a team. You're a good teacher and a good kid. You're just confused."

"So what should I do?"

"Listen, we all still have to get work completed at home sometimes. You have to do your job. Do it. Just don't make it apparent that you're up to all hours grading papers or whatever. But the reports, the stuff you have to hand in, you have to do them. We can't ignore our responsibilities."

"I feel like I've been letting everyone down."

"No, it's ok. I'll talk to Alexander. I will straighten things up with you and him. Come on. We have to go home."

With that he stood up. I followed Charlie out of the building. I never had a chance to go to my classroom and get any papers—or even my lunch bag and briefcase. I didn't erase the board, take up the chairs, or even clean my desk.

–74–

One good thing about living alone (I kept trying to convince myself) is that when you are angry you can come home and scream and yell to the empty air. And no one would ever know.

I thrust open the side door of my house and marched in. Instead of grabbing any food—though my stomach was growling—I made my way into the living room. I found an old RUSH album, *Moving Pictures*, placed it on my turntable, and turned up the volume as loud as I could. As "Tom Sawyer" wailed loud and distorted in the air, I began cursing my bad luck.

I started to wonder if I even knew my dad. We never talked about his role in the negotiations all those years ago. At that moment, in spite of the compassion he showed me as we departed the school, I distrusted my colleagues, most of all Charlie Rizzuto. I hated my profession.

The Board of Education and the Teachers' Association... They were both making me miserable. I only wanted to teach. All I wanted to do was be a teacher doing all I could for kids. That is why I entered this profession—for kids. I screamed out, over the wailing music, "Just let me teach!"

I wanted to call my father and ask him all about this. I couldn't. He was dead.

There are times when even an adult needs his mom. She too was gone.

I needed to call Rachel, but knew I couldn't. She was working that late shift and calls to her at work weren't all that well received. Anyway, she made it clear that she didn't appreciate the rage I felt toward this situation. I certainly couldn't afford another bad appearance.

As I was preparing for the biggest physical test of my life—

the marathon, a time when I most needed simplicity, calmness, and a clear head—my entire world was seemingly falling apart all around me.

–75–

A few days later, the Thursday before the marathon, I finally had another chance to see Rachel. She was able to take the day off from work to go with me to the New York City Marathon Expo. I rushed out of work to pick up Rachel and head into the city. The first words I said to her when I picked her up were, "I'm sorry."

She nodded and squeezed my hand. I wondered if that meant I was forgiven.

Rachel and I took the ferry from Weehawken to the Jacob Javitz Convention Center in Manhattan. On the ferry ride over, we had a chance to sit alone outside in the crisp November air. We didn't talk about our fight, and I was somewhat relieved because a knot of dread was forming in my stomach as I contemplated the task that was now a mere three days away. Rachel seemed to understand all of this because she did most of the talking.

"First off, know this: you're ready physically. You've prepared well, much better than I did for my first marathon. The miles are in your legs. Now, over the next few days, all you need to do is relax. All the stuff from work, your dad—don't think about it. You're going to be running the New York City Marathon. You're ready. You can do it. You will do it. I'm proud of you."

I looked out across the Hudson River and took a deep breath. I found the words more than encouraging. I needed that support.

After the ferry docked, we started walking. We crossed the West Side Highway at the traffic light and gazed upon the bright glass exterior of the Javitz Building. Enormous marathon banners hung above the entrance reading, "RUN NEW YORK CITY" and "This is THE Marathon." Across the street were enormous billboards for Asics and Gatorade. An ad for Power Bar ("Just a few seconds per mile is the difference between finishing with the Kenyans and some guy named Ken") made me laugh out loud.

Inside the convention center, motivation was everywhere. Runners and their guests walked down a long aisle beneath colorful, motivational banners. Everywhere I looked, I saw signs with the words *Glory*, *Hero*, and *Champion* on them. The number 26.2 was all over the place. "I am doing this thing," I said aloud as we waited in line to enter the main hall. "I'm doing this!"

As we finally reached the entrance to the expo, a volunteer, a tremendously fit man, approached me. "You look ready. First time? You'll get your number back there," he pointed back and to the right. "Your t-shirts and race packet you get after you pick up your number. Good luck!"

Rachel and I were pushed along by the sea of humanity toward the various long lines where racers picked up their race bibs. I was clenching the registration card that had come in the mail as I searched for the line for race numbers 29,500–29,999. There were so many booths. I saw the line forming for racers with numbers in the 40,000's. This was a bigger endeavor than I ever could have imagined. I looked to the ceiling of the Javitz Center which was so I high I imagined I was in the largest gathering place in the world.

After making it through the t-shirt area, I stood with Rachel among the thousands of runners, volunteers, and lookers-on. I clutched the shirt and a cool breeze made my shoulders shiver.

"Put it on," Rachel implored.

"Now?"

"You earned it, Sam. Put it on."

I dropped my bag, race number, and jacket, and there, in the middle of the room, took off the grey sweatshirt I was wearing and put on the blue shirt that featured an outline of the New York skyline with the words, "Love It" written on the sleeves.

"My champion," Rachel said.

"I haven't done it yet," I said with wide eyes, trying to take in the whole scene. I laughed when I saw two other men disrobing and putting on their race shirts exactly as I had.

"You will."

"What do we do now?"

"We check out the vendors."

The vendor area of the expo has a flea market–type environment, but instead of selling junk, all the vendors peddle things like running shoes, gloves, shirts, shorts, Power Bars and gels, or they showcase innovative running products. I wanted to buy all of it. To my delight, as I walked through the wares, my spirits were buoyed tremendously. I was caught up in a wave of possibility, motivation, and enthusiasm, and for the first time in what felt like a month, or more, I was genuinely happy.

It seemed everyone there was excited and pumped up for the race. Runners were literally bouncing in the aisles. I wanted to see everything. I wanted to run the race. I began to wonder how I would get through waiting the three days until Sunday.

The best part of the day was that Rachel did not seem to hold any resentment against me. She held my hand and even kissed my cheeks, and said, "You're my runner!" She seemed as excited as I was for the event. We even met some authors of running books, Bart Yasso, for one. And Dean Karnazes. I bought a book that Liz Robbins wrote about the NYC Marathon, and she signed it for me inscribing, "The first time is always a Personal Record. Enjoy the day!"

I bought a racing shirt and had my name ironed to the front. "Now they will call your name when you pass by," Rachel said. "Ignore the pretty girls who call out to you. Remember, I'll be in Central Park!"

Every person at the expo seemed to be in a great mood. They shared their excitement and anticipation for the race with me:

"Your first marathon? Go get 'em!"

"You look great."

"You're going to love it."

"It's better than sex… at least when you finish."

"Just push through the Bronx."

"Dress warmly."

"Go out slow."

"You're gonna love it."

"The first of many."

"You look great!" (I heard that a lot!)

The expo helped to get me focused on the race. I am certain it is designed to do just that!

I hadn't even completed one marathon, but I left the expo with bags of items including brochures for at least ten other races: Walt Disney World, Marine Corps, the Boston Marathon, Big Sur, Berlin, The Great Wall of China, and other races. The day itself was a marathon. My arms ached from the many plastic bags I was holding. I was relieved to set them down on the ferry when we headed home across the Hudson River back to Jersey.

–76–

"There is something I have to tell you, Rachel," I said as my Dodge climbed the ramp and merged onto Route 3 West.

"What is it?"

My palms were sweaty on the steering wheel, but Rachel and I had spent such a good afternoon together that I knew I couldn't miss this opportunity to speak. I had to do this. "The other night, I sort of went out with a girl."

"You what?" I could feel Rachel's eyes penetrating me. I quickly glanced to my right and saw that tears had already sprung to her eyes.

"It wasn't like that. And it was a misunderstanding, but I need to tell you about it."

"Ok," she said stiffly. "Tell me."

"I was confused. I thought there were a bunch of people going to watch a football game at a bar, but it ended up being just a girl."

"So... did you do anything?"

"No. I stayed for a while, but then realized how stupid it was, and how much I care about you, and I told her I had a girlfriend."

"Well, I sure hope so."

"Yeah. I was a jerk for going. I was a jerk for staying. And she thinks I'm a jerk for all of it. Which I am."

"What's her name?"

"Jennie, but who cares? Rachel, I'm sorry. Nothing happened; I was only there a short while. I really expected other people to be there, but the guilt has been killing me."

"I'm glad you told me. You didn't have to, I guess."

"Yeah, I did."

-77-

That next day, the Friday before the race, was one of the longest of my life. I went through the motions of teaching, five periods, five lessons. In front of the kids, I still brought energy to my lectures, but I knew I wasn't giving my all. I couldn't wait for the weekend to start.

Charlie Rizzuto and Herm Hermanson stopped by my room right after dismissal and said, "Good luck on Sunday." Charlie gave me a thumbs-up.

A colleague I hardly ever talk to, Marge Carlton, followed them and gave me a Power Bar. "I ran one once, in the late 80's," she said. "They didn't have these back then, but it'll help you."

On my way out, Dr. Alexander stopped me. "I don't know why you'd want to run 26.2 miles, but have a good race. I hope you're well enough to make it in on Monday. I want to hear all about it."

At 3:40 p.m., as I was opening the door to my car, my cell phone rang.

"Sam..."

"Rachel?"

"I'm looking forward to the big pasta dinner tomorrow."

"Me too," I said. "It's all about the carbs, right?"

"Listen, Sam," Rachel said. "I want to thank you for being honest with me."

I sat down inside my car and closed the door lest anyone could hear me. "I do stupid things sometimes, but I never want to hurt you."

"I know. I also want to say that I'm sorry if I haven't been so wonderful either. You've got a lot on your mind. I was thinking back to the time before my first marathon. I think I cried every day. And I know you're still sad about your dad. It must be hard that you can't put that behind you—that there is always another letter."

I was now crying and very glad that the teacher's parking lot was empty.

"Sam?"

"Rachel, I can't wait until tomorrow night to see you."

"Me too. Go home, rest up. Watch TV or read a book. Lay down early, a runner needs his sleep. Trust me."

"See you tomorrow."

"Yes."

–78–

On that cold and damp Sunday November morning, I sat hunched on a sidewalk with nothing but a thin slab of cardboard as my cushion, wrapped in a much-too-thin garbage bag. Around me, forty-six thousand people were all doing similar things. I am certain we all had the same thoughts on our minds...a sense of foreboding, excitement, fear, and anticipation, all mixed together. The runners all seemed to be in their own little worlds gazing distantly at nothing in particular—alone in a sea of people.

The New York City Marathon begins at Fort Wadsworth on Staten Island where tens of thousands of runners must cram onto its lawns and sidewalks. The runners arrive hours before their start times, many on buses from Manhattan and New Jersey, like me, and seek ways to keep warm and pass the time. I was too young for Woodstock (and would have been too much of a square to go even if I had been a sixties' kid), but the scene reminded me of that type of atmosphere. People were all over the large lawns and streets, walking, sitting, talking, and sleeping. There was constant movement and noise. Even the people resting seemed to be on edge.

The previous night I had promised Rachel dinner at the Tavern on the Green, possibly the most famous restaurant in New

York City. The Tavern on the Green happens to be located in Central Park, steps away from the marathon finish line. I was excited for the special pasta dinner there hosted by the New York Road Runners Club.

After standing in a long line outside for almost two hours (not the thing to do the night before a long race), we arrived at the pasta party. But it seemed, in my haste to secure an extra ticket for the event (for Rachel—the runners are already invited to this "gala."), I didn't read the details closely enough—being enamored by the words "Tavern" and "Green." This pasta party was actually in a large canvas tent *adjacent to* the Tavern on the Green. We never even got inside the restaurant. Instead we sat on folding chairs in front of long plastic tables crammed end to end. People rushed to the seats holding their flimsy disposable plastic plates full of pasta and salad. The food itself was mediocre at best. The buffet line that we waited so anxiously for boasted nothing but cold noodles of various varieties: cold tortellini with a greenish sauce, cold ziti with marinara, and cold spaghetti with meat sauce. If any of it was once warm, it wasn't any longer. After the long line outside, the tent offered no solace to the cool November night. I wanted to find a seat by the tall outdoor heaters that insufficiently provided warmth, but people were stacked up in those areas. In the end, with so many cold and anxious runners, many of whom were irritable, the whole dinner and event was not as inspiring as I would have hoped. I think everyone just wanted the next day to arrive.

And now it had!

There I was, in Fort Wadsworth, in the areas outside the starting corrals of the greatest marathon in the world. After sitting on a curb for almost an hour, I was getting stiff, so I decided to walk around. This, actually, was a big decision. Thousands and thousands of runners had arrived after me, and now these spots on the curb were a luxury. The grassy lawns had quickly become slick with mud under so many feet.

As I walked, I stopped at the ecumenical religious service just as they were serving the Eucharist, and I decided to participate in this communion. My friend Ed was officiating the service, as he did every year, and as he handed me the host, he smiled and whispered, "Good luck." I realized that as I focused on my own training and my budding relationship with Rachel, I had neglected my friendship with Ed.

The time came, not nearly soon enough, for the runners to head to their starting corrals. I was starting to realize that it was a marathon of an undertaking just to get to the start of this enormous race. The starts were color-coded and there were metal barriers and barricades all over the place. Progressing from one area to the next was a confusing nightmare. Runners were shedding clothing and leaving them in heaps on the ground—sweatshirts, jackets, hats, gloves, and even, remarkably, sneakers. Who changes their shoes at a race? I thought. Officials and cops were everywhere, asking to see the runners' numbers before allowing them into certain areas. More than once I was accidently elbowed. Orderly confusion seemed to rule the day.

In order to get to the actual start location, everyone had to squeeze through a fence to get to the road that looped around through the toll booths. Everyone was on edge. Men were relieving themselves wherever they could—some on the wheels of the many buses that lined the road and served as additional barricades. We just kept walking forward.

And then we were there. We stood at the start of the greatest race in the whole world. We were about to run the New York City Marathon.

I looked around at the swarms of people on all sides of me—hopping nervously, rubbing their legs to stay warm, stretching. I felt close to them—and yet distant. We were each deep in our own thoughts when the gun went off and signaled the start of the race. Listening to the chords of Frank Sinatra's "New York, New York" blaring over the speakers filled me with excitement as I shuffled across the start line (boxed in on all sides by thousands of runners) and headed to the Verrazzano Bridge. It occurred to me that, although they say the race is run in all five of New York's boroughs, Staten Island gets the least mileage. Staten Island is a staging ground and the location for the start, but that's all. Brooklyn lay ahead!

The first two miles of the marathon were basically on the Verrazzano Bridge. One mile up. One mile down. All I could see, though, were the backs of thousands of runners as they began their epic journey. I heard heavy breathing, nervous talk and laughter, and the thud of a thousand footsteps. Some runners darted around me, but I did my best to settle into a pace (however slow in this moving wall of humanity) as I climbed the ascent of the bridge (it is higher than you might think) and came down the other side. I was not prepared for the wall of sound that hit me as I came off the Verrazzano Bridge. Upon arriving in Brooklyn, we were greeted by cheering fans, noise makers, bands, and total euphoria.

Now I knew why I decided to run this race!

I was caught up, immediately, in the love fest. People saw my name on my shirt and called to me. "YOU ROCK!" and "GO, SAM!" rang out time and again. Some women told me they loved me. I yelled back, "I love you too!" Kids reached out for high fives. I happily obliged them. On and on the crowds went. It was an amazing spectacle. I raised my arms in the air and yelled, "BROOKLYN!" The crowd loved it. I was fueled by their passion and exuberance.

The borough of Brooklyn is made up of a vast confluence of neighborhoods—each with their own distinct character and feel. I had never before been to Brooklyn, so I was experiencing the city, on foot, in ways I never had before. Many of the miles were filled with loud cheers and raucous crowds, but some neighborhoods were remarkably quiet. Along the way there were bands, curious on-lookers, and occasionally even people trying to cross the streets in, out, and around the runners.

At times I felt great pride. At other times, as I saw spectators holding signs cheering on their friends and loved ones, I felt a pang of loneliness. These signs were all motivational. Some were funny. The sign "Beer in 24 miles" made me laugh. The signs stating "I love you," and "Go, Daddy" twisted my heart. Rachel said that she would meet me near the finish, but I knew it would be a long 26.2 miles before I reached that point, with no one holding a sign for me.

I was glad I had my name on my shirt so that people could call out to me. That was a lot more personal than "You look great 29760!" I learned that these cheers and words of encouragement actually helped a great deal.

At around mile six, near 20th street in Brooklyn (I remember this because my mind was playing mental tricks, "20th Street, plus Mile 6 equals 26") about an hour into the race, I saw a former student and her family. They cheered me by name. That little encouragement carried me for a while.

Before the race, people told me that the marathon is fun because of the crowds and also because of the other runners. I was told that I would find many people to talk to and commiserate with. At one point, I looked to the runner on my left and said, "How you doing?" He looked at me with a curious expression and said, "French," meaning, I guess, that he was from France and that he didn't speak English. There went that idea.

The first half of the race, at least thirteen miles of it, is run through Brooklyn. Ahead lay three other boroughs. As I approached the Pulaski Bridge into Queens, the enormity of the task really began to weigh on me. I felt like I had been running forever, but I was almost two hours into the race and had at least that much more to run.

I could write a novel just about the marathon, I thought.

It was then, as the exuberance of Brooklyn faded, that I began to struggle. Rather than my legs, my shoulders started aching. It was too early in the race to start feeling such pain. But I knew that if I focused on my physical discomfort, it would ruin me. I tried to distract myself with a mantra, "I love Rachel...I love Rachel." I ran in rhythm to those lines. It made me smile and helped push me as I forged my way over the Pulaski Bridge and into Queens.

Queens had enthusiastic crowds, smiling police officers, and loud music, but it wasn't Brooklyn. I don't know why. To my eyes, it looked the same—city streets lines with stores, lots of asphalt, crowds, signs, bands—but the enthusiasm of Brooklyn was missing. I still gave hand slaps, I still yelled to the crowd, I was still fired up, but my shouts of "QUEENS!"—admittedly a little weaker now—did not garner the same reaction as my enthusiastic yells in Brooklyn. If Brooklyn felt like the inside of a major league baseball stadium, Queens was more like a summer concert at a small beach resort. There was energy, it just wasn't the same.

Close to mile fifteen, as I approached the Queensboro Bridge, the plantar fasciitis began to throb. "Don't forget about me," my foot yelled. I knew, in order to be a marathoner, I'd have to push through this additional pain.

I did not realize the vast array of emotions that would envelope me during the marathon. I felt alternately on top of the world and miserable within seconds. There were moments when I felt like crying—and probably did. And there were moments when I found synergy and a strong form and felt like I could run forever. The way these emotions came and went so schizophrenically was new. I didn't particularly like it.

The worst part was that the great feelings never lasted long enough.

The Queensboro Bridge is also known as the 59th Street Bridge. It was made famous by a Simon and Garfunkel song of the same name, but as I trudged up it, all I could think about was the crazy incline. I never imagined it would be so tough. And I didn't think I was tough enough. When I began the descent, I was feeling anything but "groovy." But I trudged on.

And then it came—maybe the greatest moment of my life. A moment that may never be replicated: Manhattan.

Manhattan!

When I came around the big curve that is the exit ramp from the bridge, I descended from into the very heart of the city. On First Avenue, I was met with the most amazing wall of sound. The street was lined with tens of thousands of screaming spectators waving signs and flags, jumping and gesturing.

Despite the pain, despite my exhaustion, I was euphoric.

Manhattan!

It was here, on First Avenue, that my spirits were buoyed. As a child I wondered what it would be like to be cheered at Yankee Stadium. I now knew. I felt like a professional athlete.

Although the throngs were not cheering specifically for me—they were, at least in part. When I turned to the spectators and called out, "MANHATTAN!" and "NEW YORK CITY!!!" they yelled even louder.

They loved me—and I loved them.

This cheering crowd carried me for well over a mile. Spectators yelled, "Keep smiling!" "You look great!" "You are awesome." One guy just yelled, "SAAAMMMMM!!!"

I was great. I did look good. And I was absolutely awesome.

A girl darted out of the crowd and kissed my cheek. I had heard rumors of things like this happening: women hugging or kissing runners. At that point, I would have believed anything. In the split second after the girl kissed me I was flabbergasted, but I also reasoned to myself, "I can see why she loves me." I felt so good and so strong. I figured that I was the model of masculinity.

Then I realized the girl was Rachel. "I love you," she said. I replied, "I love you too."

Then she said, "RUN!"

I resumed my pace and was delighted to see that she ran alongside me.

"I thought you'd be in Central Park... I have more than eight miles to go."

"I couldn't wait," she replied.

Talking was hard. "Are you allowed to run with me?" I panted.

"No, you can say I'm a bandit."

"Will you run the rest of the way with me?" I pleaded.

"No, I'm going to head to the finish in a second. You have to do it alone."

"A few more steps?"

"Yes, but then I have to get to the park," she said. "Enjoy the Bronx!"

"I hear it's lonely up there," I replied with tears forming in my eyes.

"I'll be waiting for you in Central Park."

"That will make me run faster."

"Bye." And with that, Rachel turned off into the crowd.

I turned and yelled, "Will you marry me?" But there was no response; Rachel had already disappeared. I was surprised those words came out of my mouth. A marathon can do strange things to a person.

While Rachel's surprise kiss and encouragement helped to bolster my spirits as I left Manhattan, the effects were short-lived. And it seemed the further I went, the more this was true. I couldn't sustain any good feelings. Every stride, every step, brought more suffering.

What was that Bible passage that Ed shared with me about suffering and hope?

I headed into the Bronx barely able to hold any thought in my head for more than a few seconds—besides the pain and knowledge that I had a long way yet to go. Every inch of my body ached. This was inhumane. It was torture. What was I doing? Six more miles? It's impossible, I thought.

Somewhere in the Bronx, I realized that I had now run farther than I ever had before. I surpassed the distance of any of my long runs. I was entering a world I had previously never known. These last miles were going to define my race—and more significantly, define me.

There is nothing I can think of to describe miles nineteen through twenty-three. Maybe if I run more marathons, my feelings will change about them, but, in short, the only word I can think of is—hell. Although *hell* doesn't quite capture it either because even though I was in the worst pain in my life, even though I thought about quitting more times than I care to admit, even though I felt like the finish would never come—despite all that—there was joy and anticipation in those miles. I knew the glory of finishing was coming. And I assume there is nothing like that feeling in Hell.

Nonetheless, it was torture and hard and discouraging and upsetting. At times I hated the race and everything about it. I couldn't quit, but the thought of pushing myself forward for another hour—or more (my pace had slowed so much)—overwhelmed me. Still, I kept moving forward.

I was surprised again that it wasn't only my legs and foot

that hurt. My neck hurt. My arms ached. I was chafing on my inner thighs. The marathon, I realized, taxes one's entire body. There were times I had to walk, but I always found it in me to try running again. Try.

"Come on 29760," a man yelled.

"I'm getting there," I responded.

"I didn't come to watch you walk."

He was right. I began running slowly and deliberately once again. Shuffling forward.

I looked at the runners on either side of me. Some were limping, others stopping. At the water stops we looked at one another in exasperation. Others just seemed numb, unable to focus on anything at all. I saw some runners actually sitting on the curb. I wanted to yell at them, "Get up, you are almost there. You can't quit here—not now!"

One runner kept grunting as he ran. Another kept running her hands through her hair. At this point in the race, no one had any shame. Our inner-most beings were exposed. Our personal idiosyncrasies demonstrated themselves in full bloom. No one seemed to care. We were trying to get through in any way possible. I was amazed that some runners, including a man who had to be in his sixties, still pressed forward at a steady pace—focused and seemingly not at all impacted by the distance we had covered.

Mile twenty-three brings with it Central Park. The joy of Central Park! Here, as in Brooklyn and on First Avenue, the crowds were deep and loud and full of encouragement. If those other miles were hell, this was glory. Maybe not "glory" like Heaven, because I was exhausted and in great pain, but it was euphoric. The joy of the crowds screaming, cheering, ringing bells, banging on small drums, and calling my name, MY NAME, along with the anticipation of finishing, was intoxicating. Still, schizophrenia ruled my feelings. Joy. Pain. Discouragement. Anticipation. Hopelessness. Reward.

Those final miles were more than difficult, but with the end so close...they were wonderful. I kept scanning the crowd, searching for Rachel. I didn't see her, but I saw extreme joy in all the faces. I was part of something spectacular.

Never had I wanted something to end so desperately. But, at the same time, I wanted to savor these moments in case I would never achieve this feat again. I continued to push. I watched the others runners who struggled alongside me. I looked for Rachel. My ears filled with the roar of the crowds. It was a remarkable and wonderful and horrible and torturous final push.

Toward the very end of the race, the course exited Central Park's east side and began to transverse west on 59th Street immediately outside the park's urban oasis. It was a half mile of city street running again, as most of race had been, but the crowds here were even more exuberant. "Go, go go!" they yelled. Eventually we re-entered the park at Columbus Circle. The end was nearing.

I had heard before the race that the final two-tenths of a mile are the most difficult. I disagree, by that point—it was all jubilation. Once I saw the marker reading "Mile 26," it was all good and great and wonderful glory. The end was in sight. One hundred more meters, fifty meters, ten—

I crossed the bright blue finish line and looked up at the sky in astonishment.

I had done it! In four hours, twenty-four minutes, and sixteen seconds. I completed the New York City Marathon.

I completed the New York City Marathon!

I WAS A MARATHONER!

The finish was as busy and frenetic as the race itself. A pretty girl put a medal around my neck. Some guy handed me a heat blanket. There were hundreds of volunteers smiling and encouraging and congratulating me as I walked through the masses. I was given a goody bag with treats. All around me finishers were panting and gasping and struggling to walk. Some fell to the ground, and one person near me threw up, but the sea of humanity pushed me along. Shoulders bumped, people stumbled. We were done, but were still being forced to push forward. I knew somewhere up ahead was a UPS truck with clothes I had sent from the start to meet me at the finish. Where were those trucks?

And where was a porta-john?

How much further would I have to walk?

People were crowded all around. In all my discussions about the marathon, no one had mentioned this part of the experience. This was horrible. Exhausted people crowded onto narrow pathways all jostling to get out of the park. The kindness that I found on the course was replaced by hostility as runners and spectators alike (how did they get in here?) pushed, elbowed, and forced their way through the rabble.

I had no idea how I would ever find Rachel. There were family reunion areas, but it seemed I would now have to walk twenty six miles just to get out of Central Park.

Eventually, I found the UPS truck, gathered my bag of warm clothes (although even after putting on another shirt I was still very cold and wet), and headed out into the streets of New York. I felt dazed. What had I done? Did I just do the marathon? I was shivering, with legs like iron rods that didn't bend so well, and was hungry, and still needed a bathroom. Where was Rachel? Would I ever find her? But still, I was flooded with endorphins and, as I looked down at the medal hanging around my neck, it hit me that I just now completed something monumental.

I thought of the phrase, "Pain is temporary, pride is forever." Finishing the marathon was something I would have forever.

Lost in my thoughts, I was nearly tackled by Rachel. "You did it! You did it! You did it!" she screamed.

–79–

I don't know if Rachel heard my yelled proposal of marriage. Even more, I wasn't quite sure if I meant those words that came out of my mouth. At our post-marathon reunion, she didn't bring it up… and neither did I.

As we walked along the streets of New York City, I was congratulated by many people and I offered accolades to many others. It was easy to spot the finishers. It wasn't only the silver heat blankets wrapped around their shoulders. There was something in the expression on their faces that made them seem tall and confident, even as they limped along on wounded legs. I was no exception. Even though there were thousands and thousands of finishers in that area, I felt like I had won the race and was the true champion. I guess I was!

I had never before seen so many people of one mind—runners and non-runners alike. Manhattan itself seemed to be happy. I had never before thought of the city as a place that could radiate such joy.

It was a long walk to the garage where Rachel had parked, but I didn't mind all of the extra steps even though I covered them in a hobble. On the way, we stopped at a pizza joint. They had extremely large slices and fountain soda. I always felt that cola tasted better from the fountain, and after running the marathon, I figured I deserved to eat whatever I liked. As I approached the counter, the man stated, "Hey, congratulations, Champ."

I ordered three large slices of the pizza, the tallest soda they offered, and a few garlic knots and drifted to a table to relax and to sit down for the first time since the race started, all those hours ago.

Rachel sat down next to me and looked at my shaking body. "You look so cold," she said.

"I am."

"You have dry sweats in that bag you've been carrying," she said as she pulled a sweatshirt out of her oversized purse. "And I got this for you." Rachel handed me a dark blue sweatshirt. It must have come from the New York Road Runners themselves, and it boasted the words MARATHON FINISHER in large capital letters across the front.

"You think I can change in the men's room?"

"Sure, go for it."

I hobbled off. The bathroom was small, and I was more sore than I had ever been, but I found a way to find the relief I had been aching for and then, somehow, change into the dry clothes. I never thought cotton boxers would feel so wonderful against my skin.

Soon I was back at the table.

"I am so proud of you," Rachel said. "You did it faster than I thought you would." She held my hands tight and smiled. That look I first saw in Washington, D.C. had returned to her eyes. The pizza came to the table, and I leaned back in the small wooden chair, which had now become uncomfortable. We were blocks away from the immediate vicinity of the race, and, as I looked around, I realized that I was the only runner in this joint.

A small boy, about five or six years old, and his mother passed our table. The boy stopped and looked at me hesitantly. Rachel said, "My boyfriend just finished the marathon." The child asked for a high five. I obliged him with tears in my eyes.

Moments later, a guy about my age came over. Rachel pointed at me and said, "That's my champion."

"How the heck did you do it, man?" The guy asked. "Every year I think I'll try, but I never get around to it. I can't run even five miles. Twenty five, that's nuts."

"Twenty-six," corrected Rachel.

"Point two," I added.

Rachel was not envious of the recognition I craved and received. In fact she encouraged it. I saw that she was able to delight in me and my success. This reminded me of a passage from the Bible, I believe in the book of Corinthians. In my current unfocused state I couldn't bring up the exact words, but it was something about how love delights in others and is never jealous. On this day, I saw that Rachel was the embodiment of that ideal.

By the time we left the pizza parlor, the sun had set behind the skyscrapers and I realized that this momentous day was ending. The marathon was more than a four-hour race; it was a complete experience that consumed the entire day, and it was now part of me. I looked up at the dark sky and the silhouetted skyline, patted my full belly, and realized that I was exhausted.

This day, November 2, would be a day I always remembered, but now tomorrow was before me. The marathon, the singular event that I had built up to, planned for, and worked hard to achieve, was—already—becoming part of my past.

I wasn't ready to let it go.

After a relaxing ride home with Rachel (as she drove, I nodded off a few times), I was alone in my living room. I kept flipping the channels on my television and scanning the Internet craving any coverage the networks had on the marathon.

Before heading to sleep, I searched for a Bible. The only one I could find was one that had been presented to me when I was eight years old. It was called the *Young Readers' Bible*. I had always kept this on my shelf, but I had never really read it. I promised myself that I would find the passage I had thought about earlier. I didn't quite know where to look for Corinthians, but I eventually stumbled across what I was looking for.

I read the following words from 1 Corinthians. The phrases seemed to jump from the page as I read:

"Love is patient and kind; love is not jealous or boastful."

"Love bears all things, believes all things, hopes all things, endures all things."

"Love never ends."

"...the greatest of these, is love."

I placed the Bible on my nightstand and closed my eyes. As I drifted off the sleep, I realized that the phrases I had found described Rachel exactly.

–80–

The New York City Marathon is always held on the first Sunday in November, and when I awoke the next morning, I was DETERMINED to go to work. I moved slowly and stiffly around the house as I prepared to head to school. Putting on my pants was a lot harder than usual. Even harder was getting my socks on—it was almost torture to have to reach down to my feet.

Once at work, I was surprised to find my classroom decorated with balloons and signs made by my colleagues and I believe a few students. As I perused the room I imagined that I was being welcomed as a hero. I had slain a dragon. I had won a war. I was a champion.

People took great interest in me that day.

"How was it, Sam?" they asked.

Herb said, "I could never do it."

Doris brought me homemade chocolate chip cookies. "You can enjoy some sweets now."

The young teacher who I had met on the first day, Sandra, said, "I told my fiancé about your race. You're the first person I've ever known who ran the New York City Marathon. Now he's said he's going to run it next year."

I filled the day recounting stories of my epic struggles and success. I don't think I exaggerated at all; I just told the truth which happened to be as good as fiction, maybe better. I told everyone that they should run the race as well.

"There is nothing like it!"

In my classes, although it didn't fit into the curriculum I had to teach, we focused on important battles in history: Agincourt, Hastings, Waterloo, Gettysburg, Salamis, and, of course, the Battle of Marathon—from which the race takes its name.

When I got home from work, still feeling the utter exuberance of my feat, I laced up my running shoes and headed out for an easy two to three mile run. I wanted to find those great feelings I had experienced the previous day when people cheered me across the five boroughs of New York City. I needed to capture those feelings again.

But on this day, as I ran through my neighborhood, no one seemed to notice me and no one seemed to care that I was running. "Look at me," I wanted to yell. "I just ran the New York Marathon!" The people I did pass were raking leaves, coming home from work, and putting out their garbage for Tuesday's pick-up.

The world took no notice.

No one cared about the runner with the gimpy foot hobbling along. In fact, if anyone saw me running that day they would have thought I was an elderly and feeble man.

Eventually, with no crowd support, I stopped running, well short of my two-mile goal. Where had all the cheering gone?

If I was a hero to many yesterday, as I thought I was, it was a fleeting moment. That moment was now over—maybe never to return.

I walked home, filled the tub with hot water, as I hot as I could stand, and sat down to a nice bath. I couldn't remember the last time I had taken a bath, but the water felt great on my sore muscles. When I was a child, my mother used to say, "Don't fall asleep in the bathtub." She was afraid I might drown.

I did fall asleep. I didn't drown, but I woke up shivering in the now tepid water.

–81–

If a high-backed leather chair ever felt like "home," this one surely did. I always delighted in its well-worn comfort.

"I was going to put off my father's last journeys for a while," I said. "But I needed to see you, and I am eager to read the next letter."

Mr. Stevens smiled at me from across his desk. "You really are something," he said.

"What do you mean?"

"Your father had this idea a long time ago. He asked me if people were allowed to put stipulations in their wills. As he formulated his plan, I advised him that his sons or his daughter might not wish to continue this game after a time. I'll never forget what your father said, I can hear him, even today, 'Sam will do it,' he said. 'I could give him a hundred places to visit and he'd do it.'"

A tear formed in my right eye and made its way slowly down my cheek.

Mr. Stevens's eyes, as always, radiated warmth. "Before I knew you, I had my doubts that any son would do what your father asked. The fact that you are following so willingly and enthusiastically, well, you impress the heck out of me, kid."

I shrugged. I didn't feel like I deserved all this credit. "My father meant a lot to me. I have found that these trips bring me closer to him."

"Well, it sure is a unique way to bring a father and son together. I am glad you embraced this."

"Mr. Stevens," I began, "I can't thank you enough either. I have talked to your secretary many times, and you have a thriving practice. It can be difficult to find an appointment, yet she always finds a time for me. And you, too, you are always so willing to talk. I want my father's next letter of course, but I also just wanted to talk with you... and to thank you."

Mr. Stevens nodded. "I'm touched by your words, son," he said. "But, please, don't thank me. I admired your dad. He was an amazing teacher. You probably don't know this, but one of my sons is a teacher because of your dad. I first met your dad when my son Donnie was in his class. In Donnie's whole life he never had a teacher as enthusiastic as your dad. You might think this is silly, but it was me who first reached out to your dad. I wanted to be his friend. These visits of yours help me to remember him as well. You help me get closer to a departed friend. I enjoy your visits. Anyway..." he said laughing, "your dad did pay me to do this. I am, or was, his attorney."

"It's funny," I said. "Funny and sad...like any occupation, right now my job is giving me a great deal of anxiety. The other day I needed advice. I picked up the phone and called my dad. It was only after I listened to a ring or two that I realized he wouldn't pick up the phone."

Mr. Stevens came around from his desk and sat in the leather chair beside me. "I remember when I lost my dad," he said. "I was about your age. I was overseas serving in the military. For a time I thought that I might want to be a career soldier. I was on a training mission and by the time word reached me that my father had passed, he was already buried. I missed the funeral. They moved my leave up to accommodate me coming home, but it didn't matter at that point. Unlike you, I never had a chance to say goodbye to my father."

"Well, I know I'm lucky. My dad and I have a special bond."

"You do," Mr. Stevens said. "That is why you just said 'have' rather than 'had.' He is still with you."

"Thanks, Mr. Stevens. I never knew my father taught your son. Thanks for sharing that."

"Good teachers matter, kid. They really do. Now before I give you the next letter, tell me about the New York City Marathon. I have never heard what that whole experience is like."

And so I began, "Well, it wasn't quite what I expected... it was better, and worse... mostly better. It was the most amazing day..."

-82-

Dear Son,

These letters are becoming harder to write because I now realize that time has passed in your life with each letter. How long has it been? I imagine you have been at this for months. I know this was pretty selfish of me. I hope you are having a chance to live your life too. Please always -

(You actually walked into my room here as I was just writing. I threw this note under some cards on my desk.)

I actually don't mind living here, although it is hard to come to grips with the fact that this is where I'll spend the rest of my life. Well, let's hope so. I hope I didn't die in a nursing ward or strapped to a machine in a hospital.

I love your visits. They get me through the long days. I am proud of you for so many reasons.

I hope you only remember me with happiness. And love. And your mom too. Your mother loved you so much.

When you were growing up, whenever I would suggest we take a trip, you would always say, "Are we going to Disney World?" We took you there a lot—I'll bet you went there more than most kids. But there were also times when I'd say, "No. I have other plans this year." I always saw the sadness in your eyes—even as you tried to hide it.

I figured since I was being selfish with these requests, I might as well also give you a gift. I'd love a part of me to spend my eternity in Disney World. Go—have fun—bring part of me along to leave there. Even though you are now a grown man, know that it is always a father's wish that his children be happy. Don't ever be too big to be little.

Tell Mickey Mouse that I say "Hello."

I love you, Sam,

Dad

–83–

I met Rachel at a coffee shop in River Edge. I don't remember the name of the place, but it was near Continental Avenue. I really don't like or drink much coffee so I ordered a hot chocolate instead and told Rachel of my next adventure with my dad.

"Am I in your plans?" she asked.

"Yes, absolutely. I hope you like Mickey Mouse."

She took a sip of her coffee and looked at me over the rim of her mug. "How about after the trip?"

"I wish I could spend every day with you," I answered.

Rachel replied, "I am really starting to feel that way as well."

–84–

The next day, during my class right before lunch, I gave my students time to work on their research projects, and I noticed one student, Luke, becoming more and more frustrated and upset. He did not seem to know what to do with the index cards, photo-copies, and Internet sites he had bookmarked. He stood up rapidly and all his papers fluttered to the floor.

I saw Luke starting to panic, so I approached him and said, "Stay after class. I don't have lunch duty today. We'll spend lunch together in the library organizing your material so you can make sense of it and begin to write the paper."

After class was dismissed, the student and I sat down in the library and began working on his research paper.

Not five minutes later, the door opened loudly and Charlie Rizzuto burst in. "Hey," he beckoned to me. "We have to talk."

I had a feeling I knew what he was going to say. "Not now," I replied. "I have to help this student."

Charlie grabbed my arm, "No," he said. "We have to talk now."

What followed was a heated discussion in the librarian's office. Charlie reminded me, time and again, how we are entitled to a duty free lunch—and that we are expected to make sure that it is duty free. He told me how I was hurting the cause for every teacher by working through my lunch helping this student.

"You don't pay attention, kid," he said. "We let teachers play in that stupid volleyball game. We figured it was an act of good faith. Weren't you at the meeting after that? What did playing get us? Do we have a contract? No. You knew that game was a one-shot deal on our part. You know the rules, kid. You know the expectations. Why are you weakening our position?"

I replied that our job was to help students—lunch or not—and that I was not going to back down. The kid needed my help. "We're entitled to a duty free lunch," I said. "But we don't have to take it. I don't want my lunch today. I want to help this kid."

Charlie glared at me. "The weak link breaks the chain," he said plainly. "And that weak link is you."

"I have more important things to worry about than the contract," I said, looking Charlie in the eye. "I have students to teach." I turned to leave.

Charlie grabbed my arm again. "Your father would roll over in his grave if he saw the way you treat this job action."

I took a step away and then turned back; I looked at Rizzuto with a pounding heart and said nothing. He glared at me. I walked back to the student who had remained frozen at the library table.

"Now listen, Luke, writing a research paper isn't all that difficult. We just have to take it one step at a time..."

−85−

The story of my argument with Charlie Rizzuto spread quickly through the school. A few teachers looked at me disapprovingly as I walked back to my classroom at the end of lunch break. Mike McCartney said, "You have to step it up."

During my next class, Herb Hermanson came right up to me in the middle of my lesson, put his arm around my shoulder and turned us both so we were facing the chalkboard. "I have two years left, Sam. You are messing with my pension," he whispered. "I need a good settlement with this contract."

Later, as the students arrived for my eighth period class, a student named Kristen asked why all the teachers were mad at me. "I heard them talking last period," she said.

I didn't respond.

Normally my days ended with the quiet solitude of my empty classroom. Then, around 3:30, I huddled with other teachers in an English classroom or in the Teachers' Room telling quick stories, laughing, or complaining about the latest mandate thrust upon us. These were great ways to wind down the stressors as the day came to a close. Then, at 3:40 on the dot, we would walk out of the building as a unified body to head home.

On this day, I turned off my classroom lights, locked my door, and sat in the front corner, away from the window in the door so I couldn't be seen.

I saw the need to help a child and gave my own time to do it. This action brought me in conflict with my colleagues. I knew I could fix this easily by apologizing to Charlie and never again helping kids on "my" time until the contract was settled. I could agree to follow all the association's dictates.

I was conflicted. These were good people, my colleagues, and I considered many of them true friends. They worked hard and cared about kids. They also cared about their families. They felt the Board of Education was treating their requests in negotiations unfairly. There wasn't much we could do as an association except to begin to withhold services that were, at least contractually, voluntary. I understood my weak link would hurt all the staff because then they would be asked why they didn't give up *their* lunches or other personal time to help kids. I was undermining the only negotiating position they had.

If we lost the negotiation, our salary increases, if any, would be reduced. My actions could end up taking money away from each teacher and from their families. I knew of a few colleagues who were struggling to make ends meet, some of whom had second, and third, jobs just to pay the bills.

I also knew that Charlie Rizzuto drove a Mercedes. Jim Conway owned a beach house. Rich Horton often bragged about the 35-foot sailboat he kept on the Hudson River near Haverstraw. These men didn't seem to be hurting for cash. They had families and were able to support their children. They had been teachers their whole lives and were seemingly doing fine. Every September I learned of the travels my colleagues took over the summer. We had some world travelers on staff. And I know *I* felt like I had plenty of money. I wasn't rich, but I was comfortable. Then again, I lived in my parents' house and it was paid off. I never had to deal with a mortgage.

I also knew that what others did with their money, be they seemingly well-off or struggling, wasn't my business. It didn't change the fact that negotiations were apparently not going well.

On the other hand, I also knew that the people on the Board of Education were generally noble, hard-working, and caring individuals. On the occasions when I met them, they were kind, and they gave of their time freely as volunteers who were elected to serve the community as overseers of the school district. They had an obligation to carefully manage costs. No Board of Education could give every teachers' association everything they requested.

Over the years I had met and worked with the members of the Board in various capacities. I attended some meetings (as we were required to do), gave a few presentations, and even worked with a number of the members on curriculum committees. I knew these were good people. They frequently offered praise and were always supportive of the school and our programs.

From my darkened classroom, I saw the teachers leave en masse at precisely 3:40. I still did not understand how that helped their bargaining position. "We'll show you...we'll do less," they seemed to say. But it was also becoming apparent that I didn't understand a lot about what was taking place.

I resolved, on this day at least, to stay in my classroom doing what was right for kids—planning lessons, grading papers, and preparing for the weeks ahead. This would be my silent protest against all that was unfair.

"I will stay all night if I have to," I said out loud to myself.

But in the solitary and quiet room, I was distracted by these thoughts. I couldn't decide if I was being noble or a jerk, if I was a rebel or an idiot. I was afraid that this time I had finally severed ties with my colleagues and friends in the school, and I couldn't get my mind to focus on anything related to students or social studies. I left not fifteen minutes later.

This was a Failure Day.

I failed by staying at the school and I failed again by leaving.

–86–

The next day was Friday, but I needed time to think about my decisions regarding the contract and how I would get along with my colleagues—most of whom, I still believed, and still hoped, were my friends.

The only solution I could come up with was to avoid the entire situation altogether.

I called in sick.

When I was a kid growing up, my mother sometimes let me take "personal days" from school. This didn't happen often, maybe once or, if was very fortunate, twice in a school year. A personal day was a gift—a day I could spend doing whatever I wanted. Truth be told, my mother saw right through my lies when I pretended to be sick. This was her way of acknowledging that even a kid sometimes needs a break.

I remember the first day I stayed home from school, alone.

My parents had to go to work, so I, as a twelve or thirteen-year-old, had the house to myself for six long hours... to do whatever I wished.

I wasted the day doing stupid things. Pretty much every time I stayed home I wasted it.

One year I watched TV game shows for the entire day—The Match Game, Joker's Wild, Family Feud, and, of course, The Price is Right. The rare day off also gave me a chance to catch-up on the imaginary baseball leagues I played with my Strat-o-Matic cards. I remember one particular game: Yankees pitcher Catfish Hunter threw a no-hitter. I always wanted to meet the real Catfish Hunter after that and tell him how he threw a no-hitter on the day my mom permitted me to cut school. On another occasion, I took out my old action figures and tried, unsuccessfully, to recapture the joy I had as a younger child playing with toys.

I was one kid who never wanted to grow up.

Today I didn't feel like running or riding the exercise bike, and I had no interest in music or TV. I tried to read, but I couldn't find a book that interested me in the slightest. Instead, I spent most of the day sitting in an easy chair strumming my fingers on the arm and staring into the room, trying to find a person—or better, people—to be angry with. I couldn't. I felt sad for myself—and for everyone. I had hoped to find some inner rage at Charlie Rizzuto, Dr. Alexander, the Board of Education, or even guys like Herb Hermanson, but I couldn't. I liked and respected all these people.

I didn't eat and I didn't care.

I needed a true friend.

I finally decided to call Rachel and open up totally. I still didn't want to complain to her about work, given how awful I had acted in the past in these discussions, but if our relationship was going to develop to the next stages, I needed to be honest with her. More than that, I desperately wanted to hear her thoughts and perspectives. I took a risk by calling Rachel at work and quickly invited her to come over for dinner.

"I will make something good," I said, "Maybe pork chops. I'll even fry up some potatoes."

"That sounds nice," Rachel said. "But we could order out." She knew I was no chef.

About two hours later, Rachel arrived. I had been watching the window, and as her car pulled up, I quickly opened the front door and stood on the stoop in my socks. A cold wind was blowing, and dried leaves scuttled down the road. Rachel stayed in the car longer, it seemed, than was necessary. She finally popped open the door when I walked down the driveway toward her car, and hoping (I am sure) that I wasn't about to be a jerk. I know I was determined not to again drive away the one person I cared most about.

"Hey, Rachel!"

"Hi, Sam."

"I hope you're hungry. I bought a lot of food."

"We'll see. You have always cautioned me about your limited cooking skills," Rachel said. A small smile appeared on her face. "I have the name of that Chinese place in my purse."

"Well, come in. It's cold out here."

Rachel sat at the table in my kitchen while I started broiling the pork chops and cutting potatoes into wedges to be fried.

"Sam," she said, "the last time we talked like this, before the marathon, it didn't go so well."

"You are right, and you were right," I said quickly. "Sometimes I can't get out of my own way." Then I told her what had transpired the previous day and how, like a coward, I called in sick to avoid everybody and everything.

"No matter how someone looks at this, Sam, you'll look selfish," Rachel said. "If you follow the teachers, the parents and the kids might think that about you. If you help the kid, you'll upset your colleagues...at least some of them. Well, it sounds like you already did."

"So what do I do?" I asked.

"We had one rough negotiation at Walnut Valley. It was my second year. It never got to this point, though. I hated all of it. But I'll be honest, Sam. I don't know what I would have done."

"Rachel, am I too self-centered?"

"At times you might be," Rachel said, but then she smiled.

"But maybe we're all that way sometimes."

I walked to the table and sat next to Rachel. "What do I do?"

"The right thing to do is always found in your heart," she said. "You will know it. I trust you. I also won't judge you."

And with that statement the smoke alarm began blaring. I had burned the pork chops to a crisp. Dinner was ruined.

"Now what?" I asked as I scraped the hardened meat into the garbage.

"Forget the Chinese take-out," Rachel said. "I know a great place with French onion soup."

-87-

Things at work didn't get any better the next week, or the week after that. I did not have the courage to confront Charlie Rizzuto or any of my colleagues. They were all civil but certainly not warm towards me. I also didn't offer extra help to students or do any of the other extras I would have done a year ago. In short, I conformed totally with the job action. I tried to please everyone and failed everyone.

I smiled less in class and told fewer jokes. The students engaged me less. Classroom banter became nonexistent. When formerly my lessons were delivered with passion and exuberance, I now found it easier to write notes on the whiteboard and pass out worksheets. In between class periods, I found myself less in the halls and more often seated behind my desk.

I never saw the principal, Dr. Alexander. It seemed that he, too, was avoiding everyone.

I was glad when it came time for Rachel's marathon in Philadelphia. The last few weeks had been miserable, but the chance to get away and focus on something besides work brought me comfort. I also looked forward to the role reversal. Now I would be the one supporting the long-distance runner.

Rachel had made the reservations months before—long before we ever met. Not knowing what was in store for us bed-wise, I was a little nervous when we entered the hotel and checked in. Since Rachel made the reservation, I waited in the hotel lobby as she took care of the arrangements at the front desk.

I tried to remain nonchalant as we walked to our room at the Embassy Suites mere steps from the starting line. Rachel opened the door and revealed one king sized bed. She looked at me and smiled. "I have a race to run," she said. I put my things on the sofa bed in the "living room" of the suite. This wouldn't be the night to cross the threshold into Rachel's bedroom.

The expo for the Philadelphia Marathon was a few blocks away at the Philadelphia Convention Center. It was a different experience to attend an expo as an accomplished marathoner. I still thought of myself as a champion after my success in New York. I proudly wore my New York City Marathon shirt and was thrilled when some people looked at me and asked with envy, "You ran New York?"

Unfortunately, I was an easy mark for any seller. I listened as the dealers explained all the latest fads in clothing, shoes, nutrition bars, and gadgets. Still wanting to recapture my elation from finishing the New York City Marathon, I was ready to buy anything. My money and I were often separated, and my arms were soon weighed down with bags full of items designed to improve my running performance. While I was listening to a dealer explain the benefits of his performance socks, Rachel tugged at my arm. "Hey," she said firmly. "Time to go." She saved me from another purchase. That was too bad. The salesman said those socks would have helped me qualify for the Boston Marathon. I guess I will never know.

Rachel wanted to carbload, so, having been burned by the New York pasta dinner, we found an Olive Garden restaurant. Rachel ate penne with plain marinara sauce and a ton of breadsticks. Since I still considered myself in excellent shape (I hadn't run much since the marathon, but facts did not matter to me at this point), I overate on the endless pasta bowl.

When we returned to the room, Rachel went straight to sleep. I spent a long night one bed away longing for the day when I might join her, but knowing that on this night, her dreams were not about me. She had more important things on her mind.

Early the next morning, while Rachel was changing into her racing gear, I brought up a bagel and a banana from the buffet downstairs for her breakfast. I also gave her a special gift—a Power Bar and two energy gels for the course. It was still dark and cold when she left. Our room overlooked the start area, so I watched the slow progression of the runners as they silently moved forward by the thousands and prepared for their own challenges, hopes for glory, and opportunities to define or redefine themselves.

Once the race began, I watched closely from the balcony hoping to see Rachel go by, but the crowd was too dense. I knew I would see her twice on the course, so after the runners had passed, I went into the warmth of the hotel room, showered, and prepared for my first marathon... as a spectator.

I wore my New York City Marathon jacket proudly as I stood on Broad Street waiting for Rachel to pass. When I saw her, I did not jump into the course as she had done for me, but I held up a sign that said, "Rachel is my Super Hero." Rachel, who was making excellent time according to my Timex Ironman watch, stopped, hugged me and then continued on. I shouted encouraging words to her and then listened closely to see if she would ask *me* to marry *her*.

She didn't.

Later, when I saw Rachel at the half-way mark, she was under two hours, so far crushing my time. I gave her a quick kiss and said, "GO! You are doing great!" And off she went, heading toward Manayunk and the final thirteen miles.

Knowing I had at least two hours to kill, I stayed to watch other runners pass by. I shouted encouraging words to them and was thrilled when some participants thanked me. I knew from my own experience how valuable the words were and how much they helped when I ran. Eventually, I made my way to the Philadelphia Museum of Art near the finish. I wanted to run the "Rocky steps" and visit the Rocky statue, but the crowd was too thick. Rocky would have to wait.

Running is a singular sport. Even when we run with others, we are alone. The pains, discomforts, and even the good feelings are all kept inside. And each run feels different. For every struggle we surmount, there's another one waiting in the wings.

Even the good feelings are difficult to describe. Maybe this is why runners write so much. We keep looking, searching, for the right words that truly explain how we feel at our best and at our worst.

I pushed my way to a spot right in front of the twenty-six-mile marker, which allowed me to see thousands of runners as they approached the apex of the race and, for some, their lives. A marathon is not like other sporting events because spectators can get right up close to the action. The only thing separating me from the runners were the metal barricades.

Thousands passed me on their final push to the finish, but I found myself captivated by certain individuals. Each person's form, gait, and demeanor told a different story. I tried to imagine what each was experiencing as they passed:

A tall and thin young man sprinting with all of his efforts...

Another man, I assume in his thirties, balding, wearing a shirt proclaiming that he ran this race for the American Cancer Society, carefully measuring each step...

A young girl, she couldn't have been more than seventeen, darting between others making her way enthusiastically to the finish...

Another man with blood running down his shirt, seemingly oblivious to his pain as he glared straight ahead...

A person in a baggy clown suit—wig and all—who would stop at times and blow kisses to the spectators before continuing. I half expected the clown to start making balloon animals.

A woman, clearly overweight, but still having the fortitude and inner strength to push herself beyond all reasonable physical expectations... and she was well ahead of the rest of the pack!

A couple, man and woman together, holding hands, imploring each other to get to the finish...

A man crying, muttering to himself, "I did it, I did it, I did it, I did it..."

One runner who had to be at least in his mid-sixties kept yelling to the crowd, "I am younger than all of you!"

Then I saw a woman reach for the iPod clipped behind her waist and throw it with fury to the ground. She stopped and just stood there for a moment before shaking her head and shuffling off toward the finish.

And there was another runner who stopped. He quit. Right there. "I knew I could do it," he said. And he climbed over the barricade and into the crowd.

I saw smiles, frowns, looks of hopelessness, of hope, and of determination. It was inspiring to see each runner, slow and fast alike, strong and weak, joyful and sad. I tried to remember how I felt at that same point in my marathon.

I saw a blind runner being led by a guide. The blind runner, hearing the cheering, sensing the conclusion of his epic struggle, bellowed, "I can almost see the finish."

One woman ran three steps and then walked three steps, repeating this pattern endlessly to cover the final distance.

Some of the "runners" were now walking, but not all. Some were smiling. Some were in obvious pain. I was fascinated by the vast differences of their gaits—some running smoothly, others hobbling and barely lifting their feet. How all of these athletes ended up in this spot at the exact same time was amazing to me. Some had probably gone out too fast and struggled over the rest of the course to just hang on. Others may have injured themselves. The ones who looked strong had probably paced themselves well, or maybe they did their walking in the early miles.

Many runners talked to themselves as they ran, and over the roar of the crowd, I heard some of the same words over and over again. Many were expletives—there is no need to list them here. But more than those words, I heard others, better ones, runners uttering, between gasps, words of hope, redemption, and... God. People in the throes of their most difficult physical challenge, saw fit to give praise as the finish came into view. It was amazing to witness this utter faith and thanksgiving.

I was watching all of these people, trying to empathize with their accomplishments or pain, when I was distracted away from the nameless individuals by a runner with whom I felt an immediate connection—Rachel.

Rachel wasn't in pain, nor was she smiling. She had a determined focus in her eyes. I loved watching her brown ponytail bouncing along as she headed to the final steps of her race. I screamed for her, but I do not think she heard me among the other cheering spectators—that same wall of sound that so engulfed me in New York.

I knew that after her finish, Rachel had to proceed through throngs of runners, guides, race officials, first-aid workers, distributors of finishers' medals, and the others who make the finish area a congested mess. I wondered if Philadelphia's finish area was as frenetic and busy as New York's.

I pushed back through the crowd and headed toward the finish to find her. I glanced at the giant digital finishers' clock and saw that Rachel covered the marathon in just over four hours.

I was finally able to meet up with her as she exited the corral. She was now limping slightly. I embraced her sweaty form, and she buried her head into my shoulder. I could feel her softly crying, then she lifted her face, and I kissed her long and hard.

"Can we get a Pepsi?" Rachel said when our embrace ended, and I laughed. As I walked, and she shuffled, back to the hotel, I purchased a soda from a street vendor. I must have told her a hundred times how inspired I was by her performance.

I also told her that in my next race I would beat her time. She laughed.

Once inside, Rachel couldn't wait to get into the warm shower. I excused myself and went to watch more of the race that was off in the distance from the balcony. I enjoyed seeing the colors of humanity converging and moving in and around that one area of the city. It was one of the most beautiful sights I had ever seen.

About an hour later, Rachel stumbled outside with me and put her hand on my shoulder. "This is a dumb sport," she said.

I agreed, but then added, "I also think I am hooked on it."

"Me too," Rachel affirmed.

–88–

One of my favorite places to find peace is a little park near my house affectionately known as the Wildlife Center. A visitor can almost always find a quiet corner of the world on one of the many park benches scattered along the nature trail and around the small pond. I went there sometimes if I needed a peaceful location to ponder quietly or, sometimes, pray.

On this day I wasn't praying. Rather, I was sitting alone on a bench near an oak tree, gathering my thoughts. I remembered the evening in Cooperstown when I took stock of myself in Doubleday Field. At that time, the aspect of my life that most troubled me was my loneliness. I was constantly trying to convince myself that there were great reasons to live alone, but I also knew that I wasn't happy with that arrangement.

I had now found a woman who continually filled me with a gladness I had never before experienced. I knew that I wanted to spend the rest of my life with her. But I also faced the reality that I had only known Rachel for a few months. Although she gave no indications otherwise, I didn't know if she was ready to commit to me, and that thought scared me. I couldn't imagine a future without Rachel. When I was around her, I felt different. She radiated such warmth and compassion. I wanted to hold her, love her, and be with her in every way. I also knew that I couldn't rush it, that the day would come in time, if, or when, it was right.

I began to contemplate the word 'honor.' I tried to list synonyms in my head: integrity, dignity, virtue, goodness... I determined that there was no greater compliment than being called a person of honor and that I would try to live my life with that goal in mind.

My father was one of the most honorable men I knew. The trips I was taking for him were coming to an end, and I found myself unexpectedly melancholy. I would have never asked for this task, but because of it, I was able to forge a stronger relationship with my father. I opened up to him in silent prayers, and the words he shared through the letters became treasured bits of advice. Most of all, I knew that my father loved me. That mattered a great deal.

As I sat, the weather turned cold, and I put my hands in my pockets. I saw some joggers pass me and remembered the times I added this park to my runs. I always did this reluctantly. As much as I enjoyed the Wildlife Center, it made for a challenging run because it sat at the bottom of a steep hill. Running that hill out of the park was always a struggle no matter what physical shape I was in. The cold dusk of late November told me that it was time to head home.

I walked back to my car knowing that I was ready. When the time came, I was ready to ask Rachel to be my wife.

I hoped, beyond hope, that she would agree.

–89–

After focusing on my marathon and then Rachel's marathon, and our growing relationship, it was time, again, to give my father some attention.

I planned for our trip to Disney World to begin on the evening of the Wednesday immediately after the Philadelphia Marathon—the day before Thanksgiving. Melissa had actually invited me to spend the holiday with her family in Arizona, but I politely declined.

Rachel and I left for Disney that night, right after work. I felt a need to be someplace other than home for Thanksgiving. If my father's wishes were for him and me to travel to Disney World, I could think of no better time.

As a child, I had visited Disney World with my family many times. We had also visited Disneyland in California once, but our favorite family vacation spots were the epic Disney parks in Florida. During my childhood, that meant the Magic Kingdom and Epcot. The newer parks were not part of my childhood experience, because my parents liked to stay in the more traditional parts of the resort, and, as such, those locations would also not be part of our visit on this occasion.

My task in Disney was to find the perfect spot to scatter my father's ashes. Since most of our memories centered on the Magic Kingdom, I resolved that most of our time on this trip would be spent there. Rachel agreed.

We landed in Orlando and boarded the special Disney World

coach bus that served as a shuttle. I was overcome with excitement when I saw the pictures of Mickey Mouse on the sides of the bus. I couldn't wait to experience the park and wished, I imagine like the other adults on the bus, that I was a child again. I knew if there was one place in the world where I would always have the opportunity to be childlike, it would be at Disney World.

We had reservations at the Contemporary Resort Hotel. This was the hotel where I stayed as a child the first time we visited Disney. I loved the fact that the monorail drove right through the center of the building.

By the time we checked into our room it was getting late. I surprised Rachel by booking a suite. We were only going to be in Disney World for three days, and I decided we should travel in style. (I debated on whether or not my father would have approved of this luxury, but decided, in the end, that he would want me to enjoy myself.) Rachel turned in early. I was so overcome with excitement that I sat in front of the television watching Disney cartoons and travel tips well into the night.

The next morning would be Thanksgiving. Our plan was to explore the park, enjoy the rides, and then have a nice Thanksgiving meal in the Magic Kingdom. I had arranged reservations at the Crystal Palace. This was a character dinner, mostly for children, but I figured if we didn't have family around, at least we would get to dine with Mickey Mouse and Winnie the Pooh. In a way, they really were part of all our families.

–90–

What a magical feeling it is to wake up in Disney World. Rachel surprised me with custom-made shirts so we would match as we strolled through the "Happiest Place on Earth." Each shirt featured a graphic of Mickey Mouse running on the front and the words "Marathon Champion" on the back.

Until that day, I had never spent a major holiday away from family. Before my grandparents passed away, we'd spend Thanksgiving at one of their houses. Grandma Holmes made the greatest bread that I've ever tasted. Of course, as time went by and people died, and once Michael and Melissa moved away, "family" just meant my mom and dad. Neither of my siblings made coming home for the holidays a priority, especially once they started having kids of their own.

Walking into Disney World, I was surprised by the number of people who were celebrating Thanksgiving in the same manner as us. The park was extremely crowded, so much so that I half expected to see Melissa and Michael and their families there. In Disney it was just another magical day—or so they wanted us to feel. And they were succeeding.

Even though we only had a few days in the Magic Kingdom—and, if time allowed, Epcot—we decided to explore the park slowly and not rush. I wanted us to enjoy each experience. I thought again of the father and his young children at the Lincoln Memorial, and I told myself to savor the moment, to live in the present.

Of course, I also had a job to do. I needed to find a location for my dad's eternal resting place in Disney World.

This was the first time Rachel and I had planned to be away together for an extended time. In reality, we had only three days, but it seemed like we had forever. As I sat on a bench outside one of the brightly decorated buildings on Main Street USA while Rachel waited in line at a gift shop, I began to think about "forever." Or, at least "forever" on Earth as a living person.

I thought in pictures and images. Baseballs, marathon finishes, hand holding, blue skies. I thought of Walt Disney's *Robin Hood* movie, of shooting arrows at a target, and, of having a catch with my dad. My thoughts also turned to Mary Poppins and flying kites—images of childhood. I also contemplated adulthood and, specifically, my father's life. His was a modest life, nothing fancy, nothing special. He was raised during the years of post-World War II America; he grew up, worked as a school teacher, fell in love, married, bought a house, raised a family, retired, lost his wife, lived with his son, moved out to live in an assisted living facility, and died. I think he was mostly happy. I know he was happy when his family was with him. It was a good life, and I hoped for one just like it. I wondered what my father would think of my life at this point. I was certain that he'd like Rachel.

I think children sometimes spend their lives chasing approval from their parents. My father was proud I was a school teacher, and he always encouraged me to be my best—for the students. But I wished that he had been more honest about the realities of public employment, teacher contracts, and school principals. It was certainly true that the disillusionment I felt at work was souring me on my chosen profession. I shook my head and watched the happy families strolling by. I was determined not to think about the strife at work while we were away. Try as I might, though, I couldn't quite squash the angst.

As my dad's life was ending, he watched and encouraged my growth as a runner. He wished he had been able to run a marathon. Suddenly, there in the bright sun as I sat on the bench, I realized I had completely overlooked the most obvious of great ideas. I should have brought my father's ashes along with me in the race. I should have left some of his ashes at the finish. He, too, could have been a marathoner. He would have covered the distance with me. I wished I had had the foresight to include my father in my marathon quest.

Rachel came out of the store, and I immediately felt my cloud of anxiety dissipate. She was wearing Minnie Mouse ears and was holding a pair of Mickey ears for me. We wore the ears proudly around the park, and I was grateful that Rachel embraced the childishness of Disney World as much as I did.

It's cliché, but the Magic Kingdom is... a magical place. To begin, every person we encountered seemed full of joy. Smiles abounded and cheerful Disney tunes played at every corner. The smell of freshly popped popcorn filled the air. I tried to count how many people were wearing shirts with Mickey Mouse on them but quickly lost track. I felt exactly like I had when I was a kid, caught up in the excitement. At once, I wanted to eat sugary foods, visit every gift shop, and rush to the rides. On this particular day, every person seemed joyful. I think it's always that way at Disney.

I contrasted the feelings I was experiencing here with those of marathon day in Manhattan. Both places were seemingly full of happiness. New York was joyful because of the throngs of people celebrating individual accomplishments. Yet, I had had the sense that the city would soon put the race behind and get back to its furiously fast pace. Disney World, on the other hand, seemed to be eternally happy. The joy that is present at Disney World seems to be the same joy that makes childhood so special. It's a never-ending and wonderful joy.

Rachel and I enjoyed all the attractions and didn't mind waiting in the long lines, even for children's rides like Snow White's Adventure and Peter Pan's Flight. We rode It's a Small World three times in a row, smiling back at the animated dolls that represented children from around the world. The song and the displays filled me with nostalgia for my childhood. I wanted to look everywhere and see every scene. I tried to take it all in, but even after three rides, I felt that I must have missed something.

I did not enjoy the roller coasters as much as Rachel did, but we rode them all. Space Mountain was as terrifying as I remembered it from my childhood, flying (seemingly flying) fast through the dark. When we finished, Rachel rushed right back to the line to ride it again. Later, we sat side by side on the Great Thunder Mountain Railroad roller coaster, and, as our cart rolled over the tracks, Rachel stole a few quick kisses. It was no secret that I wanted to ride that coaster a few more times!

As we meandered around the Disney campus—eating hotdogs, ice cream, and popcorn, and buying souvenirs—I kept looking for just the right spot to spread my father's ashes, but as wonderful as Disney World is to visit, it was difficult to find the spot that would be appropriate for this specific task.

I did not think my father would wish to be laid to "rest" on any particular ride. As great as the rides are, that might be a horrible way to pass an eternity, moving over and over on the same path. I needed something different—something special.

In spite of the fun of the day and the joy of Rachel at my side, I started to feel anxious about completing this task correctly. Our entire first day passed quickly. It was almost perfect. The Thanksgiving dinner wasn't the most delicious, but I figured, Disney specializes in comfort food, not family meals.

After we turned in, I spent the early part of the night sleeplessly pacing our suite without even the shadow of an idea of what to do with Dad's ashes in Disney World. Soon I found myself walking the halls of the Contemporary Resort and ended up at a quiet lounge where, on the advice of the bar tender, I ordered a martini.

As I stewed in my thoughts, sipping, and not at all enjoying, the drink, Rachel sat down next to me.

"I heard the door close and wondered where you were going," she said.

"I'm frustrated," I replied. "This was supposed to be easy. If it was my ashes, I'd be happy to be put anywhere in Disney World, but nothing seems right for my dad."

"You're thinking too much."

"Maybe I am, but I want to do this right. I have to think it all through."

"Sam, that's a problem you have. You try to think everything through. You don't let things happen. You try to plan everything. Just let it happen. You'll figure it out."

"Maybe you're right." I picked up my fancy glass and frowned into it. "Want to stay and have a drink? I'll order whatever you want and buy myself something better than this awful concoction."

As Rachel and I enjoyed a quiet drink, my thoughts began to drift away from my dad and more to her. When we tired of the lounge, we took a monorail to Epcot where we walked the grounds hand-in-hand. I was amazed at how many children were awake and full of energy at an hour that seemed very late to me. Eventually, Rachel and I found a quiet bench, and she collapsed against my body. We both nodded off on the bench and were awoken by a man in a blue uniform. "You can't sleep in the park," he said. I blinked and wondered what time it was. That's when I noticed Jiminy Cricket standing next to the maintenance worker, nodding. He put his arms out, palms up, and shrugged.

Laughing at being scolded by a "Cast Member," we sat awake on the bench for a few more minutes. Rachel kissed my ear and whispered to me.

"Sam, I really love you. I need something from you, but not what you might think."

"Rachel, you have built me up and helped make me... me. I'd do anything for you."

"I want to spend tonight in your arms. I want to sleep with you, but not... you know, I'm not ready for... *that*. Not yet."

"You want to spend the night in my bed?"

"Yes, sort of. Well, yes. But I'm not ready for... The last time I was in a relationship with a man, I resolved that I wouldn't ever again be with a man until that man and I were married. I want that moment to be special. I want it to come only when I have committed myself to one man, forever, in front of God. You know, the right way."

"Ummm, I guess that's ok."

"Sam, I know it sounds silly, but it's who I am and how it has to be, but while I'm not ready for all of it, I need to spend the night in your arms. I need your strength. I need you. I want to wake up and have the first thing I see be you."

"I love you Rachel. I'd do anything for you. I think I understand. I don't necessarily... like it. No... I understand. I do. When it's the right time... it will be, the right time."

"You sound like that old baseball player who always talks funny on those commercials."

"Yogi Berra?"

"Yeah, him."

"As long as you don't think I look like him. People always said he wasn't the most attractive fellow."

"You don't have to worry about that."

A short while later, we made our way back to our suite where we enjoyed our first night together. Rachel fell asleep almost at once, her arm across my midsection and her head resting on my chest. My right arm was wrapped around her back and resting on her right shoulder. As I reclined in this position, I struggled mightily for a sleep that I was certain would never come as a million thoughts, some (actually many) that were not so pure, constantly raced and rushed through my head. It took every ounce of my being to not allow my hand to fall downward so I could finally touch Rachel in ways I never did before, but my love and respect for her outweighed and out lasted every desire I was having.

I actually thought I'd never fall asleep. It was a frustrating position to be in.

To come *this* close...

But, I learned, bit-by-bit that very night, as I finally, finally, fell asleep, that there is nothing more wonderful than having someone you love in your arms even if the only thing you're doing is thinking, wishing, wanting, and sleeping.

I simply wanted to hold Rachel forever.

–91–

Friday had arrived. In each of my previous Disney experiences, I couldn't wait to wake up early and explore the parks. But on this day, the only place I wanted to be was right there in that bed. I awoke first and watched Rachel breathing softly next to me, contemplating how wonderful my life had become. She was correct, I reasoned. I do have a tendency to try to control everything. I determined to try to change that aspect of my personality, although I knew it would be challenging. I turned on my side, put my arms around Rachel, and fell back asleep.

Later, as we were finishing breakfast at the hotel, we discussed the day—our last full one before we had to return home. Rachel suggested that we avoid the rides and just walk the grounds of Disney World. She suggested that we'd find the perfect place for my father's ashes if we stepped back and experienced the park in a different way.

As we walked, sometimes hand-in-hand, through the Magic Kingdom, we explored areas of the park that I had often rushed past or never noticed. We relaxed for a while by the small pond that sat at the base of Cinderella's Castle, rode on something called the People Mover, walked through the Swiss Family Robinson Tree House, and eventually found ourselves at a place known as Tom Sawyer Island.

Rachel suggested that this would be a perfect location to spread my father's ashes. "It would even be a special place you could come back to and visit. It's quiet..."

"No," I said quickly.

"No? Why not?"

"I don't know. This isn't it though."

"Ok. Then what is?" Rachel begged.

"I just don't know."

We wandered some more, but my nerves were tense, and I could sense Rachel getting frustrated with me.

Rachel suggested we go on a ride or two, but I wasn't in the mood, so we took a break from traipsing the park to have some ice cream. On a day when I should have been exuberant, I was feeling quite the opposite. What's wrong with me? I wondered. Did it really matter that much where in Disney World I left my dad's ashes? Rachel suggested that I take some time alone. She kissed my forehead. "We can meet back here, at the same spot, in three hours," she said.

And, suddenly, abruptly, I was alone.

I did not know what I was looking for.

If there is something lonely about running a marathon, it is even more lonely to be alone in Disney World. As I wandered through the park, I saw happy families, happy couples, and, most of all, happy children. I remembered when I had been an exuberant child at my parents' side. My mother loved Cinderella's Castle. If she had put me up to this task, I could have scattered her ashes there. She would have been thrilled. But it didn't seem right for Dad.

I kept returning to the idea of the It's a Small World ride. We loved that ride, and Dad always exited the ride quietly humming the song; he would continue humming it for hours, sometimes days after. "*It's a world of laughter, a world of tears. It's a world of hope and a world of fears...*" I realized that I had done the same thing with Rachel yesterday. For whatever reason, though, and

I couldn't quite explain why, I didn't think that was the place to leave my father's ashes.

I ventured out to Tom Sawyer Island to reconsider Rachel's idea. This quaint little corner of the Magic Kingdom was a perfect location in many ways. The island is tranquil and it's a great place for reflection. Most people don't even know it exists. But I didn't recall if my father had even been on that island, and I thought it was too far removed from the excitement of the park.

I again walked the length of the entire park. Nothing seemed right. After grabbing a hotdog at a food stand called Casey's Corner, I started to think that this small open air restaurant was the right place. Dad loved baseball, of course, and we always ate at this exact location whenever we visited Disney. Plus, it was in the shadow of Cinderella's Castle. I had almost convinced myself that this would be the best spot, but then I reconsidered. Laying forever among hot dogs, french-fries, and ketchup? No.

When I was a kid, I rushed through everything at Disney World. I had to. I wanted to be everywhere and do everything all at the same time. Further, I always knew that no matter how much fun we were having, that we would eventually have to leave to return home. I always left Disney World asking the same question, "When will we be back?"

I stood by the carousal and watched the horses, children, and parents happily circling. More, I watched the smiles. Smile after smile after smile.

"There you are." It was Rachel. This wasn't our meeting spot.

"Hey," I said. She had broken my daydreaming.

"You didn't find a place, did you?"

"No."

"I did. It's perfect. Do you trust me?'

"Of course."

"You're not going to be mad because this is my idea?"

"No...."

"Really?"

I smiled. "No, show me what you found. I can't come up with anything. I've wasted the entire day."

Rachel led me to the nearest stop for the Walt Disney World

Railroad that circled the park. We sat down on the train moments before it began another of its endless circles. I recalled this train. The only times I would get frustrated at Disney World as a child were when my father (or mother) would get tired. When they needed a rest from all the walking, my dad would announce, "Let's take the train." We probably rode that train more than any other visitors. Since they were older than most parents, Mom and Dad tended to get tired a lot.

As we rode, Rachel didn't say a word. After about thirty minutes, now on our second loop of the park, I finally asked, "When are we getting off?"

Rachel replied, "Sometimes you are so oblivious."

The train rattled over the rails. I saw the Jungle Cruise ride off in the distance.

"Rachel, what are we doing?"

"Sam, open your eyes..."

"The train? Leave my dad on the train?"

I reached into my pocket to feel the small plastic bag with my father's ashes. The train had now stopped at Frontierland Station.

"Your father loved trains. He even had a model of this very train in your basement. Don't you recall telling me how many loops you made on this track, over and over , while your parents rested?"

I told Rachel that she was the smartest girl I had ever met. "You're right," I said. The Walt Disney World Railroad was the place where my parents found the most peace in this chaotic amusement park. As the engine whistled and we slowly pulled away, I took the ashes in my hand and let them fall off the back of the train car.

I took Rachel's hands into my own and said aloud,

"Dear God, and Dad,

Dad, as I release your ashes into the air over this small railroad, I remember all you did and all you gave to bring us joy. We always shared great times in Disney World together. I hope your soul can enjoy the happiness and love and spirit of family that is the heart of this place...forever.

I love you Dad.
Amen."

And with that, my father became part of the fabric of Disney World.

I looked into Rachel's eyes and knew that soon the request I shouted to her during the marathon would be asked from me in total sincerity.

But not yet. It wasn't quite time.

–92–

The spirit of our school was a far cry from the Magic Kingdom. Our first Faculty Meeting after Thanksgiving break was extremely short. Dr. Alexander had no enthusiasm. He basically stated, "Just do a good job." He didn't offer any motivation. There were no quotes from Theodore Roosevelt. He didn't initiate a new program. He didn't even share the coming events on the school calendar.

After the meeting Charlie Rizzuto and a few other teachers commented, "We are wearing them down."

In truth, Dr. Alexander, as the principal, had nothing to do with negotiations. He wasn't on the Board of Education and he wasn't in our association. As a principal, he was caught between two warring parties. Nonetheless, the teachers felt that if the principals got worn down, they might pressure the Superintendent and the Board of Education to settle with us. We all felt that meant they would acquiesce to our requests. We would win.

Being a confused mess, I continued to put up walls between the students and myself. When a student came to me one Friday with tears in her eyes, upset over a poor test grade, I replied, "I can see you after school next Tuesday. We don't offer extra help on Fridays." The student didn't come after school that next Tuesday, or any day.

I felt caught in a trap with no solution. My needs, the students' needs, and the needs of my colleagues all seemed to conflict. I wanted to help everyone, but at that point, I felt the most loyalty to my colleagues. I didn't know if this was right or not. But it's what I believed was right.

For the first time in my life, I hated my job. It had finally come to that. I actually hated my job.

That evening, as I arrived at Rachel's apartment for dinner, she greeted me with a smile. "I have a surprise for you!" she said. She brought me over to her computer and showed me her updated resume.

"I don't understand," I said.

"I decided that I don't want to work in some office. I want to be a teacher again."

"A teacher?" I responded. "Why would you want that?"

"It's what I went to school for. I hate working in an office. I want to teach kids. I want to help them. It's what I've always wanted."

I sighed and shook my head. I stated, "The job isn't what it seems to be."

"You're wrong," Rachel said. "So wrong."

"No, on this I am right. One-hundred percent right." I was parroting Charlie Rizzuto. "You won't be happy. You'll work hard, but the Board of Education, or the parents, or the principal will fight you. No one will help. You'll just be another number they consider when making a budget. That's what happened to you in Walnut Valley. Why would you want to go back to this?"

Rachel took a deep breath and said, "Because it matters what teachers do."

"Haven't you seen what I have been through this year? My worst days come from work," I said.

We had been standing near her computer desk during this discussion. Rachel took my hand and guided me to her small sofa. Before she spoke, she ran her hand through my hair and then kissed me long and tender. "Look at me."

I stared into the eyes I had come to love and appreciate.

"I love you," she said. "I don't want to argue. But you're wrong. You are so wrong about this. You love teaching and from what I have heard, you are a remarkable teacher. Just the other day I met someone who knew you. It was a woman, Mrs. O'Carroll, or something like that. She said that you were the most re-markable teacher her children ever had."

"That's only because I try to be funny."

"No," Rachel said. "You really teach kids. I know that. They learn from you. But that's not the point. That's… not the point."

"Then, what is the point?"

"Focus," Rachel said. "Focus. Your focus right now is wrong. You are focusing on contracts and money and benefits. That's not why we teach. We teach to help kids."

"But…" I began.

Rachel interrupted me. "The negotiations, the job action, the supposed anger… it's all part of a process. I'm not saying that everything is good or that your district isn't trying to rein in costs. I'm sure they are. But all this talk… it will go away. The contract will be settled—and then everyone goes on. It's the way business is done in schools. The Board and the teachers always settle…eventually. They always do."

I reached for Rachel's hand and sat silently for a moment. Then I got up from the seat and paced across her small room. Outside the window I noticed for the first time a place called Quackenbush Lumber. I laughed. "When I was a kid," I said, "I used to joke around with my dad about a pretend Doctor. His name was Quackenbush. My dad would pretend to be him and he'd chase me around the house. My dad… always made me laugh."

I returned to Rachel on the couch and sighed. "You're right," I said. "I have been feeling the same thing in my heart, but I haven't been able to admit it. Of course they will settle. Even in the tough old days Charlie Rizzuto talks about…they always settled."

"Yes, they did. And they will. You just need to bring some perspective and not make every little thing a crisis."

"What would I do without you?" I asked.

"I hope we never have to find out."

–93–

December traffic on Route 4 can test anyone's patience. My thoughts of "forever" were forefront in my mind as I sat in the interminable gridlock, late to my appointment with Mr. Stevens.

When I finally arrived, he greeted me kindly. "Tell me," he began, "about your latest excursion."

Mr. Stevens, of course, was easy to talk to. He was also someone who remembered my dad as I had—not as a ruthless negotiator for teacher benefits, but as a kind man who was adored by his students. I wanted to let him know, finally, that I was in love.

"Well...," I began, "I have a lot to share. "Believe it or not, my father sent me to Disney World."

"Disney World? That is unique."

"I have always loved Disney World. I logged my expenses, but I am afraid I broke one of my father's expectations."

"What was that? Too many souvenirs?"

"No. I think I went a little overboard on the room."

"I recall," Mr. Stevens said slowly, "That your dad asked you to be reasonable. Didn't you suggest Denny's as a standard? I'd think a budget motel would have been more appropriate."

"Yeah, that's not what I did."

"Where did you stay?" Mr. Stevens asked, his voice rising with intrigue. I was not sure if he was playing the role of an inquisitive parent or if he was actually concerned over the expenses.

"Mr. Stevens," I replied with a huge smile, "I'm not bringing this up because I want to be reimbursed. I'm bringing this up because, well, without my father around, I wanted to share my good news with you."

And from there I began telling about some of my experiences with Rachel. Mr. Stevens's first reaction to hearing I had a serious girlfriend was to laugh loudly and clap his hands. "That," he said grinning, "was not what I was expecting!"

Once again Mr. Stevens seemed not at all concerned about how much time our meeting was taking. He seemed genuinely interested in Rachel and asked questions about her career, her family, and what she looked like.

"Mr. Stevens," I said proudly, "she is beautiful in every way."

As I finished explaining how I finally found the perfect place to leave my dad's ashes in Disney World, Mr. Stevens leaned back in his chair and briefly closed his eyes, and I suddenly noticed how tired he looked. I apologized for talking so much time.

"Not at all," he insisted.

Although I imagined he would allow me to stay as long as I wished, I decided it was probably time to leave. Mr. Stevens took out the next letter from my father.

As he handed it to me he said, "There aren't many left."

−94−

Dear Sam,

I have given you some task. At times I sit here and wish I hadn't done it. If I had just let you settle my estate, you would be able to live your own life now. I fear these trips to remember things... this quest to live forever, and have you never forget me, is probably just a burden for you.

I guess I just didn't want to go. I wish we were together as I write this... even more, as you read this.

In case you are wondering, I do not have any international trips or cruises or major adventures planned for "us." There are just a couple of final stops.

When you visited me yesterday (I have no idea what your situation will actually be when you read this), you were upset about the tone of many of your colleagues as you faced the potential of a difficult negotiation period. You saw some teachers taking a hard line. You told me, "That's not me, Dad. I just want to teach the kids, make connections with them, and put them on the path for a successful life."

You had the right idea.

In my day I was a tough union leader in my district. It was different then; we had to fight for every cent. Your mother and I struggled to make ends meet. In addition to working at Carnegie's Men's Store (oh how it upset me when that darned McGregor would come in and treat me with such disdain) I worked many odd jobs in the summers and at Christmas. Those weren't easy days for our profession, but we held tough and we made it work. In those battles though, I lost focus on what our profession is all about. I lost the enjoyment, often times. Sure, I loved the kids. They say I was a good teacher. I hope so. But I also saw everything as a battle with the administration and the Board. I know now they weren't my enemies.

Work isn't a battle. It isn't. This is why I admire you. You see teaching as something beyond compensation—something beyond salary increases and health care. Good for you. Go, be true to yourself. Don't ever change. It is always, and must be, about the kids you are fortunate to teach.

Now, though, let's go together, for one of our last trips. (I am having a hard time writing things like "last").

I have sent you to many places, but I've ignored the big city near us. I have always loved New York City. I love all of it. I can't decide where I would like to rest there. Maybe that is the point; there is nowhere to rest there.

When you were little, I took you to the Guggenheim Museum. I didn't understand the art work, to be honest, but maybe the culture would do me well as a final resting place. Or there is always the Empire State Building, or Times Square. I always loved the ferry. John's Pizza on Bleeker Street? Head into the city, you will find a good spot. I know you will.

But, do me a big favor—not Yankee Stadium. And nothing in the Bronx please—or any of the outer boroughs. Please leave me in Manhattan, son.

Hey, how did you do in the marathon? I hope I lived long enough to ask you in person.

Be strong. Have fun. I love you.

I miss you.

Love,

Dad

–95–

New York City in December is a wonderful place to be. Unlike my previous adventures with my father, this time I knew exactly where I wanted to go, but Rachel and I had some exploring to do in the city first.

There was more than a chill in the air when Rachel and I arrived in Manhattan on the New York Waterway Ferry from Weehawken, New Jersey. We had already decided to explore the big city on foot. Being marathoners has its advantages, walking the city didn't intimidate us in the least bit.

Our first stop was the Empire State Building. I bought us each hot chocolates at a coffee shop before we ventured to the line for the observation deck. We held hands and smiled a lot at each other as we stood eagerly awaiting our turn to the top. The forty-five minute wait passed quickly, and we soon found ourselves eighty-six stories up, looking out over Manhattan and across the Hudson River to New Jersey.

"Is this the spot?" Rachel asked me.

"No, we'll get there. Trust me."

"I do."

I didn't rush our time at the top of the Empire State Building. It was quite chilly, especially when the wind blew, but the breathtaking view of Manhattan was worth the discomfort. I held Rachel in my arms and pointed out toward Central Park. "One of the greatest experiences of my life ended there," I said. "I can't wait to run that race again."

In spite of my plan for my father's ashes, I thought about leaving them there at the top of this majestic building. They would get to blow across the sky and float over the entire city. Remembering, though, that my dad was afraid of heights, this did not seem quite right. And I had a better plan anyway. It was nice to have a plan.

On Fifth Avenue, we stopped at the New York Yankees Clubhouse store. I bought Rachel a Yankees ski hat to keep her head warm as we continued to explore the city on foot.

Times Square was bustling with excitement. The frenetic pace of the city seemed to radiate from this exact location. Was this the heartbeat of America? As we walked past Lindy's, Rachel expressed interest in a slice of cheesecake, so we went inside, enjoyed a light lunch, and warmed ourselves before heading further uptown.

My brilliant idea of ice skating at Rockefeller Center was dashed by the long line. Rachel's hopes for a piece of jewelry from Tiffany's were dashed when we saw the asking price for what seemed to be a simple pair of earrings. I asked the saleswoman, "Will these be on sale soon?" The reply: "Nothing is ever on sale at Tiffany's."

I purchased a stuffed bear for Rachel at FAO Schwarz. It was great to hold her hand, and, at times, just watch her walk holding the bear as we strolled further uptown through Central Park. I kept remembering places I had passed as I was struggling to finish the marathon. I seemed to think about that race constantly. "Let's run it together next year," Rachel said.

We arrived a while later at the Guggenheim Museum. I couldn't believe it, but there was a long line there as well. We decided to wait it out.

Most of the art inside made no sense to me. A plain white canvas? A black canvas? A canvas with nothing more than a small red dot? There was a movie screen with a strange looking person talking. This was art? Not wanting Rachel to think me an ignoramus, I pretended to appreciate all the works. As I stood looking at one particular sculpture (was it an abstract nude or just twisted shapes?), Rachel said, "What do you like about this work?" I didn't know how to respond and had to admit that I did not understand it at all.

"Neither do I," said Rachel with a smile. It may have been immature of us, it might have showed our lack of culture, but the rest of the time Rachel and I enjoyed silent (and not so silent) laughs at the artwork—at times earning stern looks from other Guggenheim visitors.

Next, we meandered back into the park. Rather than strolling on the main roads, we ventured off into the center of Central Park.

I brought Rachel to the giant statue of King Jagiello who sat mightily on a horse, wielding a sword in each hand. I told her how King Jagiello had united Poland and Lithuania in 1386. The statue depicted the king with the two swords crossed above his head to symbolize these twin enemies as he reined victorious at the Battle of Grunwald. Most people are unaware of this majestic statue sitting in Central Park, but it is one of my favorite sites.

Next, we "discovered" Belvedere Castle. Although I knew this building was there, I had never ventured inside. We climbed to the top of the castle and enjoyed the greatest secret view of Central Park imaginable. We were certain that no one had ever seen Central Park in quite this way before. If I had a ring, I would have proposed at that instant. The touching of our cold lips brought me the greatest delight.

Coming from the castle, we began walking through an area of Central Park known, simply, as the Ramble. This was the location where I had decided to leave my dad. The Ramble is a series of quiet paths, some seemingly going in circles, that make the walker forget he is even in a city. We stumbled over small hills, climbed some rocks, found secret passages, tunnels, and archways. There were a few mounds of snow, but the cold winter that sometimes visited our area hadn't really arrived yet. I asked a Park Ranger who happened to be walking through the Ramble if he had a map of the paths. "No," he replied. "The

Ramble is a place for reflection and thought. There are no maps of the Ramble."

Rachel and I found a bench and sat down, and I pulled the plastic bag of ashes from my pocket. "You know," I said, "I haven't once given him a proper burial." With that, I wandered a bit and found two small sticks, just the right size.

"I learned this in Summer Bible Camp a long time ago," I said as I sat back down.

I fashioned the sticks into a small cross using some string and bits of yarn I had in my pocket to support the cross beam and make it sturdy. Next, I grabbed a stone that was about the size of my hand and started digging into the near-frozen ground. It wasn't easy work, but I eventually created a small hole and asked Rachel to bend down with me. I poured my father's ashes into the hole, covered them with dirt, and said a very brief, quiet prayer. If this had been spring or summer, the Ramble would have had many more visitors and someone might have stopped us or asked what we were doing. Not today. I took the cross that I made and placed it gently on the ground over the small burial site. This final resting place in the idyllic wilderness in the middle of Manhattan couldn't have been more appropriate. I secretly hoped that maybe one day I'd be buried there too.

Our task complete, we found our way out of the Ramble, pausing for another long kiss on Bow Bridge. People claim that Bow Bridge is one of the most romantic bridges in the world. I didn't care about that. I just enjoyed kissing Rachel.

I was very happy with my selection for my father's resting place in Manhattan. And I was certain, absolutely certain, that I was madly in love.

–96–

Within a week of our return from New York City, I was back in Mr. Stevens's office.

When I arrived, Mr. Stevens seemed a different man. He sat less erect, and there were bags under his eyes. His normally

styled hair was uncombed. His suit, which usually compliment-
ed his powerful figure now just seemed to lay on him. He seemed
older. Much older.

"I'm not myself, today," he said apologized.

"Are you feeling well?" I asked. "Is everything alright?"

"Don't get old, kid."

"I don't plan to… any time soon, but it happens to the best
of us… right?"

Mr. Stevens nodded. "Sit down and listen close," he said
gravely.

With that Mr. Stevens told me that he was sick, very sick. He
had been diagnosed with a type of lymphoma and he was not
yet sure what the long, or short term, prognosis was. "My doctor
saw some shadows on an MRI that he didn't like. The pictures
concerned him…it was just a few weeks ago. He said we'd keep
an eye on it. Last week I fell a few times. I went to see him again.
They ran tests. Invasive stuff. That's when he said they were sure
it was cancer. I have to fight this thing aggressively. I might be
able to beat it…but I am not sure."

"Is there anything I can do?" I asked.

"Yeah, don't get old."

"Seriously…"

Two thoughts went racing through my head. First, I had
grown to cherish my visits with Mr. Stevens. He was the last father figure in my life. I wasn't ready to lose him. I also worried
about the letters…what if Mr. Stevens died? How would I get
them? Would my father's final wishes get lost and unfulfilled?

Mr. Stevens interrupted my selfish thoughts. "I know you're
worried about the letters," he said. "There are only two more.
In case I don't make it…back to work, any time soon, I will give
them both to you now."

"No, I don't want them both," I said quickly.

"You will take them. There is no arguing that fact. I can't
have this unusual request of your dad's hanging over my head
as I try to get well."

"Yes sir."

"Secondly, it is nothing major, but you are mentioned in

my will. This is something your dad and I also worked out. No, you're not getting any of this wealth," Mr. Stevens waved his arms around the room, smiling. "And the furniture is too ornate for a classroom, or, God forbid, a principal's office should you ever decide to go that route. It's just a little something. Nothing really. But it's important. I want you to know I've grown to really admire you. I admire your spirit—and understanding. I see the love you had for your father."

"You'll beat this," I stated with conviction.

"Yes, I plan to, but I had to tell you these thoughts anyway."

"You haven't met Rachel," I said. "I was hoping to introduce her to you."

"Well, you might want to be quick about that."

"Don't talk like that, Mr. Stevens."

"Just being a realist. When the clock strikes, it strikes. Neither you nor I can control that." Mr. Stevens handed me the last two letters from my father. He pointed at me and looked sharply into my eyes. "Don't open the last one until it is time. Make me that promise. Now that it is in your hands, it will be tempting."

"Of course."

"I know. I trust you, kid. Now get on. Bring that special girl to see me soon. A pretty face could really lift my spirits."

"See you soon."

"I admire you, kid."

–97–

Dear Son,

(I am crying as I write this. This is much too difficult.)

(I'm sorry.)

It is time for our last trip together. When we're done, don't forget to put my urn at the Hackensack Cemetery. I hope you realized that. I need the rest of me to remain with your mother.

You've been a great son to me—and your mom. We were always

proud of you. You have heart and spirit and energy. You work hard. You care.

I don't think I have many more days. My heart hasn't been right. I never told you about this. I didn't want to burden you with that. I'm not afraid of death. I can't wait to see your mom again. And Jesus. But, I'm also not ready to say a final goodbye.

I wish I could be with you until the end of time. I wish I had the strength and the energy to travel and do things with you.

Let me give you some last advice. Always know that the most important thing in life is finding happiness and bringing happiness to others. Always look to the good. You'll make mistakes. Bury your regrets and move forward. Do what's right in your heart, and you'll always make the right decision.

Also, pick a kind wife. Pick a girl with character. Make your wife your best friend.

Ok, son...this is where our adventures end. Most times when you were growing up I chose the destinations for our family vacations. In doing so, though, I tried to find places that we would all enjoy. I focused on locations that would be fun for you and your brother (when he was around) and sister (a little bit more). I wish I had been able to give Michael and Melissa the experiences I gave to you. Anyway, life can be full of regrets. I always tried to make the places we visited as interesting as they could be. I should have sent you to Gettysburg as part of this. We learned a lot there, but, now that I think about it, there are enough memories buried on that field.

I would like to remind you that a father will always go anywhere for his child. But I never got us to one place I knew you wanted to see. This might not be my favorite place, or remind me of my favorite movie, but since it's yours, I'd like to spend part of my eternity sharing that joy with you. Head to Philadelphia and leave me by the

Rocky statue. I know how those movies inspired you. This is where our travels together will end.

It will also be, I guess, where my life will finally end (much too soon) and yours really begins.

I love you, son.

Always and Forever,

Dad

P.S. - Don't forget to see Mr. Stevens after you visit Philadelphia.

P.P.S. - I miss you!

–98–

I decided that Rachel and I would fulfill my father's request in Philadelphia as part of a day trip. All we needed was a weekend day and good weather. It was not to be. The weekends leading up to the Christmas break were each cold, bitter, and rainy. Our trip to Philadelphia would have to wait until the New Year.

In the meantime I had to make a decision at work. After much reflection, I resolved to do the right thing for the kids. I met with Charlie Rizzuto and told him that I couldn't do the job I needed to do within the constraints and the parameters of the job action. I explained that it was too constricting and that I knew this would make me an outcast, but I had to do what was right. If a child needed my help, if a parent wanted to meet with me, if I needed more time in my room to prepare a lesson, or any of it, I would make myself available.

"You'll walk alone," Charlie told me.

"I am aware."

"You'll hurt our cause."

"I doubt that," I said. "I'll only hurt your cause if others follow my lead, but if they don't, I'll just be an outcast for a while. I'm okay with that. I'd rather that than to be untrue to myself and not available for my students."

"I admire your principles, but you're a fool, kid," Rizzuto said. He sat behind his desk in his classroom, and I couldn't help but think that he looked a little more tired than usual. "You'll lose the respect of so many."

"Listen, I think the kind of job action we're engaging in really hurts our cause. I may be wrong, but I think doing the minimum sends the wrong message to the kids, the parents, and the school board. Contracts are always settled, job actions or not. And they're usually settled for close to what all the other districts settle for. In the end, we're going to get a contract. I respect what you're doing. I really do. But I can't do it. To me, teaching is a calling. I need to be there for my students. I need their respect. I need the parents' respect. And I'd like to earn back Dr. Alexander's respect."

"Respect, again?" Rizzuto scoffed. He then stood and faced me directly. "I'm trying to explain, you will lose the respect of your colleagues."

"Maybe," I argued, "they'll respect me more."

"I doubt it."

"The kids and the parents will..." I began.

Charlie interrupted, "Don't count on that either. Many of the parents are members of unions. To them they'll see you for what you are—a scab."

"A scab that wants to help kids."

Charlie shook his head. "Your dad would never approve of your decision."

"I think he would," I said.

Charlie Rizzuto just stood there, with his hands folded across his chest looking at me. It was then that I said, remarkably, "In fact, I know he would. He told me."

"He told you? How?"

"Let's just say, he did. I know what he'd want me to do." And with that, I walked up to Charlie Rizzuto and gave him a hug.

"What the hell is that for?" he exclaimed.

"I appreciate what you're trying to do—protect me and fight for the rights of the teachers." I knew what he was doing was noble in its own way—even though I didn't agree with it.

"You're an excellent teacher, kid," he said as I left his room. "A great teacher, but a confused kid."

I turned around. "Thanks."

"I'll do my best to make sure they don't harass you too much," Charlie called.

–99–

I again turned down an invitation to travel to Arizona for a holiday. Rachel also sent her regrets to friends in Chicago who asked her to come out. Instead, Rachel and I decided to enjoy a very modest Christmas together. I knew the vacation from work would do me well. I was proud of my decision to put the students first, but I was tired and needed some time to get my mind straight. Rachel was proud of me too. "I always knew you would do the right thing," she said.

On Christmas morning, I woke up early and could barely wait to pick Rachel up at her apartment. When I finally pulled up to her building with Christmas songs playing softly on WQXR, New York's Classical Radio Station, and a few snow flurries drifting down from the heavens, Rachel ran outside. Wearing a bright red Santa hat with Mickey Mouse ears, she rushed over to the driver's side. She was wearing bright red lipstick, and when I rolled down the window, she gave me the most wonderful Christmas kiss I ever received.

We drove, holding hands, to the Old Paramus Reformed Church for their Christmas morning service. The minister gave a beautiful short sermon about the power of giving, not receiving. There was an elderly man in the back pew who, with his red blazer and a long white beard, looked exactly like Santa Claus.

As we drove home after the service, we passed a lot where the VFW had staged their Christmas tree sale. A few trees were still left, and a sign next to them read, "Trees left after Christmas Eve are free." I realized that with all that had been going on, I had not taken the time to decorate my home for Christmas. Rachel and I chose a small tree, stuffed it as best as we could into the trunk of my car, and struggled to set it up in the living room. I had the most difficult time getting the tree to stay upright the correct way in the tree stand. Even though it was Christmas, the local Walgreens was open, so we walked there and purchased a bundle of their remaining stock of decorations. These were not the prettiest ornaments, but they would serve our purpose.

Our tree stood somewhat crooked in the corner, with an eclectic assortment of mismatched decorations, but we admired it. Our first Christmas tree. Why can't every day be as perfect as this? I thought.

Rachel decided that we should bake Christmas cookies, so we did—sugar cookie cutouts with vanilla frosting. I didn't have any cookie cutters—my mom had long ago donated our old cutters to a school for the students to use with Play-Doh—so we used the tops of mugs to make circles. I decorated some of mine to look like baseballs. Rachel made hearts.

Eventually we sat down by the tree and exchanged Christmas gifts. We laughed when we discovered that we had each bought each other new running shoes. Rachel also gave me a watch and tickets to a Yankees game the next spring. In Rachel's stocking, I left Gatorade and some Power Bars.

The best gift, though, was something I put in an envelope that I told Rachel she would have to open later.

After exchanging the gifts, we put on our coats and went for another walk. I wanted to show Rachel the annual decorative display on the Ridgewood Water Company property. Every year at Christmas time, they decorated this area with likenesses from Disney movies along with Santa Claus and his helpers.

"I used to love to come here as a child and look at all these characters," I said to Rachel.

"They are cute."

"So are you," I paused. "I hope we are always this happy together."

Rachel kissed me tenderly. I held her in my arms for a long while, enjoying her warmth and the smell of her hair.

As we ended our embrace, Rachel said, "We will be. Always."

We returned home and fell asleep on the couch in the late

afternoon watching old Christmas specials on the television. It was the best Christmas I ever had.

–100–

Dear Rachel,

You are the love of my life. You once commented that you wished someone would send you a letter like the ones I received from my father. Here is your letter.

Don't worry, the good news is that I am not dead, nor am I dying. I plan on a long and healthy life.

First, I think you know this already... I am madly in love with you. I think of you as I wake up in the morning. You are my last thought before I fall asleep. My dreams, both when I am asleep and when I am awake are about you. You bring me peace and happiness. The first time you kissed me, and every time since, brings a tear to my eye because I cannot imagine anything better than that sensation. I love you.

My favorite runs are the ones I share with you. I hope we can run together forever.

I love to hold hands with you. I love to look into your eyes. Your eyes have always told me that everything will be alright, no matter how I am feeling.

You tell me frequently, "I trust you." You told me that the first day we met. I have always tried my hardest to live up to that trust, and I always will. Please know, I trust you too.

I am so glad and fortunate that you have been able to accompany me on my final travels with my father. Your strength and support has helped me through this sad period of my life. Because of you, I haven't been as sad...

in fact—and I know my father would be happy to know this—being with you has brought me untold joy.

I am in love with you. I am in love with you.

For a special Christmas gift, I would like to take you to a unique place not far from here. I think you'll like it. I will leave a little bit to mystery, and just give you the address. (203 Ridgedale Avenue, Florham Park, NJ.) We can travel there together and enjoy a special day. Want to go tomorrow?

I love you. I love you. I love you.

XXX OOO

Sam

–101–

Ridgedale Avenue in Florham Park was easy enough to find. Rachel drove to the site on the morning after Christmas, with me as the silent passenger. I kept quiet mostly. I did not want to give away my secret.

After we got out of her car, Rachel looked around and said, "A big red schoolhouse?"

I looked at her and smiled. "Yes."

"You didn't buy this big old building, did you?" Rachel asked.

"No, I don't think it's for sale. It's a museum. They call it, appropriately, the Little Red Schoolhouse. It's from the 1800s. I wanted to take you someplace special..."

"Here?" Rachel asked.

I walked over to her and took her hand. "Let's walk..." The grasses, cut short, were now December brown. Small rocks, gravel, and dirt surrounded the exterior of the building. I noticed that the white trim around many of the wavy glass windows was peeling. I put my hand against the red siding. "This old school," I said, "represents your dreams—and mine. I know you want to be a teacher again. You radiate such joy and happiness when you talk about it. The students will be lucky to have you."

"You are so sweet," Rachel interrupted.

"Rachel..."

"Yes?"

Then, in front of the old schoolhouse, I knelt and took Rachel's hand. "Rachel, I want you to be with me, forever. Forever and ever. Today, tomorrow, and for all eternity..."

I took a small box out from my pocket and opened it, exposing an antique ring with a small diamond on a gold band. The ring had once been my grandmother's.

"Rachel, dear Rachel... I love you... will you marry me?"

Rachel's eyes filled with tears. She stood in silence for a moment and then smiled. "Yes. Yes. YES! Of course, you are the love of my life!"

I stood up, pulled the glove off her hand, and placed the ring on Rachel's finger. It fit perfectly, like it was meant to be. Because it was.

We embraced, kissed, hugged, and kissed some more. I grabbed Rachel around the waist and spun us around, lifting her feet off the ground. I just kept saying, "I love you, I love you, I love you!"

–102–

I don't think as a society we take enough time to grieve. The typical wake, the viewing for someone who has died, if people even have one, is an afternoon and evening followed by a burial—usually the next day. Then we rush right back into our "normal" lives. How is that possible? A loved one is no longer with us. There is nothing normal about that.

I admire the Jewish practice of sitting Shiva for up to a week. This allows more time to mourn. It allows for more quiet reflection and time to be invested in close friends and family.

My father's final wishes, the quest for these journeys, brought the two of us closer together—even after he passed. He gave me the gift of a long grieving process. I had plenty of time in cars, hotel rooms, and at home to remember him and appreciate him. I had myriad opportunities to say goodbye.

Rachel and I prepared to head to Philadelphia for my last journey with my dad, but I, in spite of all the preparation, I still wasn't ready for this final parting.

After coming home from Mr. Stevens's office and reading my father's final destination letter, I had felt paralyzed. I found it difficult to breathe. I was numb. I had no emotions left to give. I sat in a stupor in my living room for quite a while. Then I read the letter again. And again. I thought of my father writing this letter—and all the others he sent to me from the grave through Mr. Stevens. I tried to imagine how difficult it must have been for him, how hard it was to say goodbye. I knew he didn't want to leave, but I appreciated this crazy scheme he had invented.

The location for our last trip was kind of ironic since Rachel and I had recently been to Philadelphia for her marathon. But this time the occasion was more somber. A long process was ending. My last journey with my father would soon be over.

I also couldn't stop thinking about Mr. Stevens, my last close link to my father besides my siblings, and my new knowledge of his illness. It was a lot to absorb.

As I drove with Rachel down the dreaded New Jersey Turnpike, I succumbed to the grief. I didn't care about the rest stops and who they were named after; I began crying and could not stop. I finally had to pull over and ask Rachel to drive. She took us right to the parking lot across the busy street from the Philadelphia Museum of Art.

When we got out of the car, the crisp air helped me pull my thoughts together. I dried my eyes with a tissue, and Rachel took my hand. My thoughts were pulled back and forth between the lost childhood behind me and the future before me. I thought of my parents. I imagined what my life might be like when I would be facing death. Would I have the courage my father demonstrated?

We crossed the busy street at a traffic light and came almost face-to-face with the Rocky statue. I looked up at the (fictional) former Heavyweight Champion of the World and thought of my dad laughingly telling me, "You're wasting your time watching those movies over and over. You already know all the lines, what more is there to see?"

"Rocky inspires me, Dad," I would say time and again.

Together, Rachel and I sprinkled his ashes on the ground around the statue. It was another cold day. There were no people around to infringe on our private ceremony.

"I miss him," I said to Rachel.

She nodded and squeezed my hand. "You were lucky to have these last experiences with your father."

"And because of his wishes, I met you."

"I'm glad," Rachel said.

"Me too."

As we stood there holding hands, I whispered the final prayer in my quest to scatter the ashes.

"*Dear God,*

Thank you for watching over me as I fulfill my father's final wishes. In this, I think I have learned some of life's most important lessons. I learned that a father's love never dies. I found new experiences and made new memories that I will always treasure and always remember.

I will always honor you, God.

Thank you for bringing Rachel into my life. I promise to be a great husband. I hope to someday be a wonderful father. Like mine was to me.

Thank you for all my blessings, and, in advance, our future blessings.

Dad...I don't really know what to say. I'm sad. Real sad. I am sad I don't have a father to visit. I am sad I no longer have trips to take to remember you by. I will treasure these memories.

Because of you, Dad, I have met the girl I love. I plan to love her forever. I will work hard to be a great husband, like you were to Mom...and I hope to be a great father, like you were, to me.

Thank you, again Lord, for all my blessings. Please watch over my dad and my mom and my whole family. Please too, here on Earth, watch over Mr. Stevens and give him the strength and cour-

age to fight his terrible disease.
I wish this all wasn't over.
God bless you Dad.
Amen"

Rachel put her arms around me and began the Lord's Prayer. I joined in.

We cried. And I cried some more. It was difficult to say goodbye.

It's always difficult to say goodbye.

–103–

We were back in New York City once again, walking through Central Park, only this time we had a different destination. We approached Mt. Sinai Medical Center with trepidation. At the front desk, I asked for Mr. Donald Stevens's room number.

The receptionist found his information on the computer but stated, "You cannot see him. Only family is permitted."

"There must be some mistake," I responded, hoping that they would allow an exception even though I had not arranged for this. "Please check." And after what seemed to me a rather long delay, the receptionist called the floor above. She asked for my name and an ID, and then, seemingly with reluctance, granted us permission to visit.

I knocked on the door we had been directed to on the eighth floor. "Mr. Stevens, sir?" I called. "You probably weren't expecting us, but we happened to be in the area."

"Sam? Sam Holmes?"

"Yeah. Can we come in?"

Inside the hospital room, we found Mr. Stevens propped up in his bed wearing a faded green hospital gown. He looked pale, and his eyelids drooped, obscuring his once strong gaze. He was alone in the room. The nurse informed us that his wife and son had recently left to get lunch.

"Mr. Stevens, I have somebody for you to meet." I held Rachel's hand as we approached his bedside.

Mr. Stevens looked up and smiled. "She is beautiful," he said, coughing.

"I've heard a lot about you," Rachel said.

"Don't believe it. That guy you are with is too sentimental. He makes even stupid things have meaning. One day he asked about an old stapler on my desk. He wondered if it was an heirloom. It was an old frickin' stapler."

"He is that way..." Rachel laughed.

"Mr. Stevens. In my journeys for my father, I met my future wife. Rachel has agreed to marry me."

"Well, you'd be a fool to let her get away, but I am sure she might get a better offer," Mr. Stevens laughed. "Oh that hurts," he said. "But it's good. I haven't laughed like that in quite a while."

We were not allowed to visit long, but immediately before we left, Mr. Stevens took our hands and looked at us. He said, "Rachel, seriously, you found one of the good ones." Then he looked at me and said, "Son, I'm going to beat this thing and see you back at my office. Remember, also, I have something for you."

"I know, sir. I have to thank you. You've been so good to me. You helped me through a very sad period in my life—losing my father."

"I wouldn't have done it for just anyone, but your dad was good. A good man. I see he raised you right." After a long pause he added, "You didn't read the last letter yet, did you?"

"No, I kept my word. I couldn't read it until I saw you again."

"Don't rush to read it. Save it for a special day. There are no more travels. Your dad's urn can be put in the niche with your mother at Hackensack Cemetery. May he rest in peace."

"Thank you, Mr. Stevens."

"Thank you, Sam. And, Rachel, good luck. Make sure you invite me to the wedding. I'll make sure to be there."

–104–

I was back at my home, alone.

The pizza I had ordered sat half-eaten and pushed to a corner of the kitchen table. I had a large glass of iced tea and a slight stomach-ache from eating too much. Before me sat two piles of Strat-o-Matic cards: the 1946 Red Sox and the 1977 Yankees. The Yankees had been winning 4-0; Reggie Jackson and Graig Nettles had each belted a homerun. But now, the Red Sox had jumped to the lead following a two-run double by Dominic DiMaggio. I was making a pitching change for the Yankees because Ted Williams was due to bat...

I rose to stretch my back. Sometimes if I sit too long on those hard kitchen chairs, my back tightens. I drank the remainder of the iced tea and went to the refrigerator to refill my glass. Since I was up, I decided to put the game on hold and walk down the hall to the room with my dad's old dresser where the urn with his ashes sat.

I picked up the urn and looked carefully at it. So much had changed since my father had passed. I knew I wasn't the same man who had first driven to Cooperstown, New York, all the way back in August. My feelings about work had come full circle. I was in it for the students, even though my decision strained some relationships. (Not all though. A number of teachers had quietly come to my room to say they admired my principles. Charlie Rizzuto even called me at home one night to let me know that a new contract was said to be forthcoming. "Once it is settled, they will all forget," he promised me. "You'll be fine, kid. You're too well liked for people to be mad for long.")

I ran a whole marathon—26.2 miles. It was a day I will never forget. If a race defines a person, that struggle proved to me that I have the strength, courage, and ability to persevere through any physical or mental challenge.

Of course, I had also fallen in love. I met the woman of my dreams. We were now planning our wedding and our future life together.

I said to the urn, "Dad, tomorrow, I will bring you to rest, finally, alongside Mom. You deserve peace. You lived your life for others. Now rest. I will remember you in my heart forever."

-105-

One problem with goals is that once you accomplish them it is sometimes difficult to find new goals to set. I found this to be true in regard to the marathon. Since that glorious day in November, I had not run much. But after putting my father's urn back on his dresser, I decided it was time to change that. I realized that I didn't run only to finish a marathon but because I enjoyed the challenge and I liked pushing myself.

I would continue to run, I told myself, to find out who I am each day—and every day.

I have always been more of a warm weather runner. I find it much more difficult to head outside in the cold to log miles. I think, to a certain extent, I am afraid of the cold. I am afraid that I might not make it back home and that I'll die out on the lonely streets. I never have those types of fears when I run in the warmth. I don't think of dying when it's warm.

Cold or not, I determined that this was a good day to begin running again. I pulled out my cold weather running gear, layered up, found my running gloves and a knit hat, opened the door, and braced for the cold winter chill.

I was running much slower than I would have liked, but I was pleased to be outside pushing forward. I did not have a specific route or distance in mind; I just set out and began running.

In the weeks since the marathon, my plantar fasciitis had healed, I assumed. In any case, my heel didn't hurt any longer.

I was enjoying the cool air and the quiet solitude of winter as I ran through neighborhoods. On cool days like this, it is often rare to come across even one other person. I saw no one. Months before, when I ran alone for the first time after the marathon, I was shocked and disappointed by the stillness and the quiet. On this day, I embraced it all.

The phrase, "Quiet solitude," entered my mind. I repeated it in my head over and over in rhythm with my stride.

I kept pushing myself, amazed at my ability to run as far as I had after taking so much time off. As I ran through what might be called "downtown Midland Park," I realized that I had covered close to seven miles. This was certainly not a failure day. Even if I had to walk the rest of the way home, I covered more miles and was stronger than I thought possible. I knew that I had found a pastime that would always serve me.

There is a certain magic in the long run, I said to myself. It may not be the Disney kind of magic, but it is miraculous nonetheless.

–106–

I drove slowly on Hackensack Avenue after exiting Route 4 and then made a careful right turn under the ornamental wrought iron gates of Hackensack Cemetery. My father's urn sat comfortably on Rachel's lap. We crept slowly toward the mausoleum and parked behind a black Chevy Camaro with a 26.2 bumper sticker on the back. There were two other cars there—both with Avis Rental stickers.

Rachel waited in her seat until I came around and opened the door for her. She handed me the urn which I took carefully. Rachel climbed out, and when she smiled at me, I saw a tear form and slowly make its way down her cheek.

I bent forward and softly kissed her cheek, catching the tear before its journey ended. We held hands as we walked into the mausoleum to lay the remains of my father's ashes to rest. First to greet us were Michael and Melissa. I hugged them both.

"I am so glad you came," I said.

Mr. Stevens was also there. His car followed mine into the small parking area. I introduced him to my siblings, and he gave them each the strong handshake that had become very familiar to me. Smiling, he reached into his pocket and handed them each an envelope. "These are from your father," he said. Michael clenched the paper in his hand, tighter than I would have guessed. He nodded and started weeping. Melissa held hers to her chest and then gave Mr. Stevens a hug.

Inside, Reverend Ed was already waiting for us. Ed held in

his hand three books and some notes. I recognized the books as a hymnal, a Bible, and the Book of Common Prayer.

"Thanks for coming here to be with us, Ed," I said. "This means a lot to me."

"It is my pleasure," Ed replied. "And I am so glad to finally meet Rachel." Ed extended his hand, which Rachel took. "I have heard a lot about you," he said to my fiancée.

"And I have heard a lot about you, Ed," Rachel said with a smile. "Sam thinks the world of you."

My father and mother's niche had been left open by a worker at the cemetery. Ed carefully took the urn from me and placed it in the wall. "Let's begin," he said.

I do not remember the entire service, but I do recall some of my thoughts because I still think about them quite often, even today.

I think, once we realize that we are all mortal, we slowly begin to prepare our hearts for the eventual passing of our parents. But I don't think we really know what that will be like— and I don't think we're ever really prepared for it. I thought I was ready to say goodbye to my father when he died over the summer. Now, after the months of journeys with my father and all that entailed, including meeting and falling in love with Rachel, I wasn't ready for this.

Ed was reading from the Gospel of John, *"Jesus said to her, 'I am the resurrection and the life. He who believes in Me, though he may die, he shall live. And whoever lives and believes in Me shall never die.'"*

I looked past Ed and saw the flowers and plants left on the floor in front of various niches, and tears filled in my eyes. Rachel took my hand in hers and held tight.

Ed paused and held out the hymnal to share. The book was already opened to the appropriate page. Rachel took it and held it in front of us as Ed began singing. We soon followed along.

"Come thou long expected Jesus, born to set thy people free; from our fears and sins release us, let us find our rest in thee..."

I had never heard Ed sing before and was amazed by the richness of his voice. We didn't need an organ or guitar as we followed his melodious lead. Rachel, too, sang with beauty. I was honored to be part of this little service.

I realized, again, how little I knew about the other people in my life. Sure, I had run with Ed, and we had pushed each other over many miles. We even swore (under our breath or otherwise) at each other on long, difficult runs. We shared our innermost thoughts and hopes and dreams. He was a dear friend. But I never knew he could sing. Rachel either.

Why did it take sad occasions, like death, to force us to make the time to really know and be with one another? Why did it take my father's death to get me to begin to find myself?

As I listened to Reverend Ed's words, I felt great emptiness. I missed my father. I missed my mother too. I knew this would be the place where I could always be with them, but of course, they were gone—at least from this life. Our relationship now would exist only through prayers and memories.

"Dust thou art, and unto dust shalt thou return..."

I thought of the dust my father had become, of his ashes scattered across some of our favorite locations in the United States: Cooperstown, Washington, D.C., Newport, and Disney World. I thought of the ashes spread near a cannon in Princeton and buried in a tiny grave in Central Park and of the ashes sprinkled in Philadelphia, not because he wanted to be there, but because he wanted to be with me when I was there. And I thought of him and my mom, resting together here in Hackensack and, of course, in Heaven.

I knew that I would carry my father's love for me through the remainder of my days.

"Yet he will hereafter have life. Even if he dies, he shall hereafter live..."

My father's life had continued past his death through his letters and our travels. I felt his presence with all of us in that room. I felt his happiness because of the experiences we shared together.

The service was now over. Ed hugged Rachel and then me. He offered to stay with us, but I said it wouldn't be necessary. Now, with our travels finally behind us, I wanted one last moment to be alone with Rachel and my parents and my siblings.

As I closed the door to their niche, I said, "God bless you, Mom and Dad. I miss you terribly. Thank you for everything. I will love you forever. Amen."

Rachel and I got in my car and slowly drove to a highway restaurant for a family repast. As we left the cemetery, I had one thought:

A father's love can last forever.

–107–

Mr. Stevens welcomed me into his office, and I had a flashback of the first time we met. Mr. Stevens looked pretty good. His eyes had regained some of the sparkle that had been present when we first talked about my father.

For this meeting, I brought lunch.

"Mr. Stevens, it's not much, but I think you'll agree there aren't many things in life as tasty as burgers from White Manna."

"I haven't had these in years. God, my office smells of onions already. Thank goodness it is getting warm out. Put those bags on the table over there and open a window or two."

"It is good to be talking to you," I said. "You look great."

"I feel the same, young man. I feel the same. When you called offering to bring lunch today, I was thrilled. I don't have any appointments until two o'clock. I was actually getting bored."

"I am glad we arranged this—especially on short notice."

"What can I do for you, kid?"

I told Mr. Stevens that I had one small fear I needed to talk through with him. I explained how my life had been recently comprised of a series of adventures. I didn't know where the next adventure would take me. But now that I had finished all the tasks my father set for me, I wondered if I would get complacent.

Mr. Stevens sat back after listening to me talk for quite some time. He looked into my eyes and asked me a direct question. "Do you love Rachel?"

At that moment Mr. Stevens's secretary walked into the

office. "My goodness!" she exclaimed, "It smells like a cheap restaurant in here."

"It does," stated Mr. Stevens. "And it's great!"

"Mr. Stevens," the secretary continued, "your two o'clock appointment just cancelled. Do you want me to see if we can move up your three-thirty?"

"No, I think I have plenty to keep me busy right here."

As the secretary left his office, Mr. Stevens laughed uproariously. "A cheap restaurant. That's what she said! Oh, how funny is that!" And, then, just as suddenly, he looked me squarely in the eyes again. Mr. Stevens could still control a situation. There was no doubt about that. "Do you love her?" he asked again.

"Yes," I replied. "Yes. Yes, yes, yes. Of that I am certain."

"Then, son, you have no concerns. You are coming off a roller coaster of emotions. You are going to make an excellent husband, and although you will not have adventures that your father sends you on, you will make new adventures with your wife and someday your new family."

Mr. Stevens smiled. "It's all about love," he said.

Then Mr. Stevens got up slowly. He grabbed the old stapler off his desk. "Here," he said. "I want you to have this, but I have something else I need to you to hold for me." And with that Mr. Stevens handed me eight envelopes, addressed in his handwriting to a certain Donnie Stevens.

"These are for my own son," he said, "for after I pass, although I don't plan on that happening any time soon. I feel too good now. When my son gets these, he might be upset with the stipulations I placed in my will. I trust you will help him understand."

–108–

The next day Rachel and I laced up our sneakers and embarked on a leisurely run together. Our plan was to run a few miles from her apartment before stopping at a somewhat secret Park Ridge location known as Atkins Glen. We planned to sit in the quiet solitude of the glen and enjoy the first warm air of the coming spring.

Rachel, spry and in better shape than I, led the pace. She kept saying, "I'll be in shape for the wedding. What about you?"

Panting and struggling to keep up, I replied, "When the time comes, I'll be ready."

Our time at the glen was intoxicating. Like kids we held hands, took our shoes off and splashed in the cold water, and kissed. We kissed a lot. It was wonderful. As we sat on some flat rocks I said, "After the wedding and the honeymoon, I have a great idea for something for us to do together."

"What is it?" Rachel asked.

"I think," I began, "that we should run the Marine Corps Marathon in Washington, D.C. this fall. We can train together. We can help each other through the tough patches. I can't think of anything I'd rather do than hold your hand for twenty-six miles."

"If you hold my hand the whole way," Rachel said, "you will slow me down."

–109–

It took a while for me to gather the courage to open the final letter from my father and close, once and for all, that chapter of my life.

I had come home from work, feeling pleased that I had given my best efforts. The letter had been on my mind a great deal over the last month, and I had wanted to open it ever since I had it in my possession, but I needed to find the right time. This seemed like just that moment.

I took off my dress shirt and tie and changed from pressed slacks to shorts.

Rachel was out making the final wedding arrangements— things she said that she needed to do without me.

There is something good about being home alone, but I knew I much preferred the idea of sharing my life with the woman I loved.

I did not know what to expect when I took the letter out of my dresser. Feeling the need for fresh air, I walked outside and sat behind my house on a stone wall, which in the imagination of my youth, was a baseball dugout. This was where my imaginary Wiffle Ball players sat during the games. It was a perfect spot to read the letter. I was surrounded by bushes open only to my backyard. I took a deep breath, gently broke the seal of the envelope, and began reading my father's final words to me.

I read the letter once, paused, and then read it again.

I read the letter a third time and began to cry.

I cried for a good long while.

THE FINAL LETTER

Dear Sam,

First, 1 must say that there is nothing a man wants more in life than to raise a son who becomes someone he is proud of. 1 am proud of you for so many reasons. You are good and kind and have what we used to call "character." You have always been honest and true. 1 am proud to be your father.

Know that 1 miss you. 1 can't imagine being gone. But, at the same time, 1 have the faith that 1 will be with you as you are reading this note. 1 absolutely believe in Heaven and 1 know that 1 will be watching you from there.

1 never wanted to stop living. 1 felt there was so much more to do—so many places to see. 1 loved creating memories. 1 loved being with you. 1 hoped my life would go on and on—and in a sense, through our final travels together, it did. At least for a bit. Thank you for allowing and fulfilling my final dreams.

1 hope that in those final travels with me you had a chance to figure out what will matter the most in your life.

As 1 sat here reflecting on my life and taking those final travels with you in my mind, 1 found what matters most. I'm not profound enough to claim 1 found the meaning of life, but at least 1 found, 1 believe, what is most important. As 1 sent you to spread my ashes, 1 found myself. 1 found...peace. It is okay that my travels are now over.

And it is so simple. What matters most is one simple word: LOVE.

My final wish for you is that you will be able to take the time to love and cherish everything about life—including the struggles. Love your family. Love your siblings. Love your wife. Cherish your wife. Love your job. Love the people you are with. Love the hard work you will do. It's easy to remember the good times and to appreciate them. But love all that life has to give. Trust me—it passes too quickly.

Notice how love is everywhere.

If you look, you can find it. You can find love in small rural towns, in cities, and in big amusement parks. Love is there. Love is present near statues, it is in museums, on college campuses, and on remarkable paths near water. It's there. Love is there. Notice it. Appreciate it all.

The Bible talks about faith, hope, and love and says, "The greatest of these is love." It is. Absolutely.

Know, my dear son, as I now say goodbye to you for the last time on this Earth, that I love you—and that I will love you forever. And ever.

Always and forever,

Dad

Author's Note

A writer often writes from his heart and bears his soul. I do this a lot in all my writings whether they be works of fiction or not. A writer writes what he knows. In spite of what some people think, this was not a story about me, or my dad, but it is a story about much that is close to my heart - baseball, running, education, family, faith, God, and love.

The inspiration for this story came from my own experiences with my wife and three sons, the true joys and the most special people in my life. I wouldn't be who I am without them. If ever a person loved being the dad of little kids, it was me. Each day was a blessing and a treasure. As an educator myself, I always relished in those down times, especially the days I'd have off in the summer, when I could relax, play, and travel with my family. We spent a lot of time going to a lot of places all across this wonderful country, some of which were featured in this novel. While this story is fiction, people who know me well will be able to quickly determine the aspects of the novel that relate closest to my life. When I am with my family, I want the special moments to last forever. I don't want those moments to ever end. That, in essence, is where this story came from - a desire to stop time and never let the good days pass; a wish to never grow up or grow old or any of that. I would like to spend my eternity with my wife and kids at home, in Yankee Stadium, at Cooperstown, by the beach, and in Disney World. Like the father in the book, when it comes time for me to go, whenever that is, I won't be ready.

A book like this couldn't happen without the love and support of so many. Of course, this means, most of all, my true love, the sunshine of my life, my wonderful wife Laurie. She's always been the rock - the one who takes care of everything while I'm trying to live my dreams and trying to capture something that continually alludes me. She always understands when so many other things like work, my school, writing, running, and playing ball distract and consume me. She has always supported all of my dreams. She is the love of my life and my best friend. I love you Laurie.

My sons, Ryan, Alex, and Ethan are the most special people in my life. They inspire me each and every day. I love them with all my heart and soul. I am continually proud of all of their accomplishments, but am most proud that they are good people and honest men. I love the memories we made together as they grew up and look forward to creating many more with them as they now build their own lives as adults. I hope each lives out his dreams, as I have lived out mine. Guys, always remember to go for it. You can always achieve more than you think! I love you more than words can ever say.

I'm blessed to have two wonderful parents who have always supported and encouraged my dreams and who have taught me so much. My loving parents have helped me to become my best self in every way. Mom and Dad also served as early editors of this book's original manuscript. It wasn't easy to ask and say "Hey Dad, I wrote a book about a guy whose father dies...wanna read it?" The fact that they loved the story helped me to believe that I was on the right path. My parents have given me so very much. I love you, Mom and Dad.

I am also blessed to have great In-Laws. If the only thing my Mother-in-Law and Father-in-Law did was give me the person who became my wife, that would surely have been enough, but their kindness, generosity, motivation, friendship, and understanding have added to my life, and all of our lives, significantly. They are special people who helped me become the man I am. I love them a great deal.

Special thanks also go to my dear friends Dan Diljak, Ed Hasse, Bob Dietz, and Dave Wiley. They read early versions of this story and, in spite of the fact that they knew I put my heart into it, were still able to point out its many flaws and make some great suggestions while convincing me that the story had potential. Never once did any of them give me anything other than their support, encouragement, and friendship. These are very special people. I love each of you.

My editor, Britta Eastburg Friesen has been wonderful. She

pushed and pushed me to make this novel better. She has a great way of helping me find my writer's voice and become the writer I wish to be. Thank you also to Rob Skead for his support in this journey we call writing and publishing.

Thanks of course go to Geoff Habiger, my publisher. I owe a lot to you. I have been often told that this story is a good one, but you are the one who believed in it enough to risk publishing it. It has been, and is, a great pleasure working with you. In spite of all the other work you do and all the authors you support, you always made me feel like I was your highest priority. I can't thank you enough for that. I hope this is just the first of many collaborations we have together. Thanks for believing in me. (I'll get you my next manuscript soon. I have a few more great novels to share with you... and the world.)

Finally, a special thank you to God. We have spent many hours together talking through prayer about this book and my efforts to have this story told and it published. Through all the trials and travails, and failure, I never stopped knowing that God was there with me making sure that when the time came for this to be published, that I would be humble and appreciative, and that I would use this book, and all my writings, to help make the world, His world, a better place. I try to live my life each day the way God wants, but I fail a lot. I am so fortunate that He loves me anyway. It is my hope that as I share and discuss this book, and as people read the story, that many are brought closer to God. I hope we can all live our lives with compassion, love, and understanding. God is love and love is what I hope to share with the world. If we all just took the time to love each other, our lives, would be infinitely better. In the story, Sam's father noted that love is really all around us. It certainly is. If that's the only thing that anyone remembers from this story, I'll be more than pleased.